A Double Deception

A DOUBLE
DECEPTION

Clive Egleton

St. Martin's Press
New York

Library of Congress Cataloging-in-Publication Data

Egleton, Clive.
    A double deception / Clive Egleton.
      p.   cm.
    ISBN 0-312-07736-X
    I. Title.
    PR6055.G55D68   1992
    823'.914—dc20   92-2753
                                              CIP

First published in Great Britain by Hodder & Stoughton.

First U.S. Edition: July 1992
10 9 8 7 6 5 4 3 2 1

For his patience and forbearance this book is dedicated to
Anthony Goff

Although this book is a work of fiction, the events which took place in Warsaw on Thursday, 21 September 1939 when foreign nationals from neutral countries were evacuated from the beleaguered city are completely factual. Likewise, certain of the American consular officers and Polish officials depicted in the story are drawn from real life.

A DOUBLE DECEPTION

1939

Tuesday, 12 September
TO
Friday, 28 September

CHAPTER I

ANDREW KORWIN had found the horse and droshky tethered to a lamp post in Marszalkowska Street. The mare was mostly skin and bone which was why the Veterinary Corps hadn't bothered to impress the animal when they had been looking for remounts. Korwin reckoned there was a good chance the mare would drop dead between the shafts before they reached the Eastern Station in Praga across the Vistula but the buggy was the only means of transportation he had been able to procure for his sister and young brother. The army had commandeered every taxi in Warsaw before hostilities had started, the trams had stopped running two days ago and his father had taken the family limousine with him when he had set off for Modlin on the thirtieth of August. If the mare looked sickly, she was at least alive which was more than could be said for her former owner; he had been gunned down by a low-flying Heinkel 111 before he could reach the air-raid shelter.

No one had questioned the right of a captain attached to the General Staff as aide-de-camp to the Garrison Commander to appropriate the horse and buggy. Korwin was also banking on his army uniform to get him through the street barricades when the dusk to dawn curfew came into force. He turned into Ujazdowskie, the tree-lined boulevard his cousins from New York had nicknamed the Fifth Avenue of Warsaw, and went on past the American Embassy which, except for a few shattered windows, was still in pristine condition.

Although this was the twelfth day of the war, many of the luxury stores were still open, their wares displayed behind plate glass windows crisscrossed with brown sticky paper to reduce the effects of blast. But who wanted jewellery, expensive French lingerie or Meissen porcelain when there was a food shortage? And who in his right mind would contemplate buying the Polish edition of *Mein Kampf*?

Korwin led the horse and buggy through the wrought-iron gates fronting the family residence and tethered the mare to one of the chestnut trees in the grounds, then let himself into the house. No one came to meet him in the hall. Of the seven indoor and two outdoor staff, the chauffeur, footman and gardener had departed on the twenty-eighth of August to join their reserve army units on general mobilisation, while the cook, scullery maid, general handyman, and the two upstairs maids were working in an emergency hospital which had been established on Senatorska Avenue near the Opera House. Despite being over age for military service, the butler had insisted on accompanying General Korwin to the front when the latter had been appointed to command the 20th Infantry Division in the Modlin Army which guarded the northern approaches to Warsaw.

"Is that you, Andrew?" his sister, Christina, called from the landing above.

"Yes. Are you ready?"

"Are we walking to the station or what?" she asked, evading the question.

"I've managed to borrow a droshky."

"Didn't the owner mind?"

"He had no further use for it," Korwin said dryly.

"Oh. Well, I'm almost ready."

"Almost? What have you been doing all day?"

"Jan is being difficult about leaving."

No further explanation was necessary. Their fourteen-year-old brother had been born with a rebellious streak but for once it was hard not to sympathise with him. Jan had made it clear often enough that as the son of a soldier and the brother of another, he thought it cowardly to leave Warsaw at such a time, especially when other boys of his age were risking their lives carrying messages between the Red Cross Headquarters and the emergency hospitals.

"I'll have a word with him," Korwin said and started up the staircase.

Christina was in her room at the back of the house overlooking the rose garden. Few strangers would take them for brother and sister; while he was dark and cast in the Junker mould so that he was frequently mistaken for a Prussian, Christina had ash-blonde hair, grey eyes and a slender figure. Although only twenty-one and five years younger than himself, she was the one who had held the family together after diphtheria had claimed their mother in the

4

autumn of 1936. Beautiful was a much-abused adjective; it was however something of an understatement when applied to Christina. Korwin had lost count of the number of proposals his sister had received, but she had decided long ago that marriage wasn't on her agenda until Jan either went to university or joined the army.

"Where is our young brother?" he asked.

"In his room; he's locked himself in."

"The little wretch, I'll box his ears when I get hold of him." Korwin slipped off the web haversack he was carrying bandolier-fashion across his left shoulder, undid the buckles and placed reel after reel of film on the bed. "I hope you can find room for all these in your travelling bag."

"How many have you got there, Andrew?"

"Twenty." He took out a money belt and handed it to Christina. "Wear this next to your skin, there are seven hundred and fifty US dollars in the pouches."

He wasn't just concerned for the money. Christina was far too attractive to be travelling unprotected in these dangerous times and the sweater and tailored slacks she was wearing did nothing to hide her figure. The money belt would add an inch or so to her waistline but that was hardly likely to put anyone off. He could, however, provide her with a much more formidable deterrent, a 1915 model 7.65mm Beretta semi-automatic pistol.

"Why do I need that?" Christina asked.

"For self-protection," Korwin told her. "It's not only the Germans you have to worry about; some of our own people are getting pretty lawless." He turned away from Christina, pointed the Beretta at the window and pulled the slide back to chamber a round, then gently eased the hammer forward under pressure and applied the safety catch. "The magazine is loaded with eight rounds," he continued. "If you have to use the pistol, thumb the hammer back like so, push the safety catch forward towards the letter F stamped on the left side below the slide and then squeeze the trigger. The mechanism will automatically eject the empty case, recock the hammer and feed another round into the breech. When you've finished shooting, apply the safety catch." He looked at his sister, then said, "Do you think you can remember all that?"

"I think so."

"All right, suppose you tell me how to fire it."

Christina repeated everything he had told her more or less word for word. Despite this, he took her through the elementary safety precautions twice more to make absolutely certain she would be able to handle the weapon with the minimum danger to herself.

"Where are you going to carry it?"

Christina frowned. "How about my handbag?" she suggested.

"Someone could snatch it from you."

"In my coat pocket then?"

"That would seem the best place for it."

Korwin left her to pack the reels of film while he went to see Jan. His young brother wasn't open to reason and it wasn't until he threatened to break the door down that he reluctantly allowed him into his room.

"I hear you don't want to leave Warsaw?" Korwin said.

"I don't want to run away, if that's what you mean."

"You won't be running away."

"Says you." Jan raised his chin pugnaciously. He was a tall, gangling boy, all arms and legs, who had outgrown his strength. He had inherited the heart-shaped face of their mother but there was nothing effeminate about him. "Anyway, I don't want my friends calling me names."

"You want to be a soldier, don't you?"

"Yes, but what has that got to do with it?"

"The first thing you have to learn as a soldier, Jan, is to obey orders. And they won't always be agreeable; take it from me, sometimes you have to do things you don't want to."

"Like running away from the enemy," Jan said acidly.

"We all have a job to do. As for Christina, she has to deliver twenty rolls of film to Uncle Zygmunt in New York. He is a very influential man and will ensure the pictures are printed in every newspaper so that the Americans can see what the Nazis are doing to Poland and know it will be their turn next if they don't help us."

"Isn't that what the British and the French are supposed to be doing?"

"You can't have too many allies," Korwin told him.

The newspapers were full of wildly optimistic reports – the RAF were sending six hundred bombers, the French had captured Cologne and Karlsruhe. The truth was very different. The RAF had very few bombers and what they did have were incapable of reaching Poland. As for the French, General Gamelin had made it very clear during talks with the Polish Minister of War back in

May that they would not be able to launch a major offensive earlier than the fifteenth day after mobilisation.

"Anyway, I want you to go with Christina and look after her."

"Are the Germans going to capture Warsaw?" Jan asked.

"Not if I have anything to do with it."

A vain boast if ever there was one. The 3rd German Army advancing south from East Prussia and the 4th striking east from Pomerania had all but annihilated the Polish forces in the Corridor and north of the Vistula. Now, all that stood between them and Warsaw were a few thousand battered survivors from nine infantry divisions and four cavalry brigades. And if that wasn't enough, the capital was also being threatened by the armies, the 8th, 10th and 14th advancing east and north-east out of Silesia and Slovakia. It could only be a question of time before the city was encircled. The sudden realisation that this development was inevitable was all the spur Korwin needed.

"Get your things together," he said curtly. "We don't have a moment to lose."

Leaving Jan, he told Christina that he would wait for them in the drive, then went downstairs. The sunset was more vivid than usual thanks to several large fires which were still burning out of control in the Kolo district near the Jewish quarter. Farther to the west, he could just hear a distant rumble like thunder as the Germans shelled the outer suburbs with light artillery.

A reluctant Jan appeared carrying a large carpetbag, a jokey souvenir that Uncle Zygmunt had given them when he had visited Warsaw two years ago. Dumping the bag in the back, he climbed into the open droshky and sat down. Christina locked the front door behind her and handed the key to Korwin, then looked back at the house with a wistful expression on her face as though she didn't expect to see it again.

"Cheer up," said Korwin, "it will still be here when you return."

Korwin untethered the mare, led her out into the road and climbed up on to the driver's bench seat, then headed north on Ujazdowskie. Halfway to the Poniatowski Bridge, a horse-drawn battery of 75mm field guns passed them going at a gallop in the opposite direction towards Lazienki Park. The curfew was over an hour away but there were no civilians on the street. Every morning, air raid or no air raid, the housewives of Warsaw queued for bread at their local bakeries with scant regard for their own safety, but it was a different story at dusk. From experience, they knew that

7

nightfall was when the shooting started and there was something particularly unnerving about being shot at. Bombing was indiscriminate and survival a matter of chance but when a sniper opened fire, he was aiming at a specific target. Most of the population believed those involved were Fifth Columnists but there were far too many incidents for all of them to be attributed to German agents. It was more likely that there were a lot of nervous sentries about who preferred to be safe rather than sorry and didn't hesitate to fire at shadows.

At the top of Ujazdowskie, Korwin turned right on Jerusalem Avenue for the Poniatowski Bridge and crossed the Vistula into Praga. The workers' suburb on the east bank had been turned into a fortress; trenches had been dug in all the public parks and every main thoroughfare had been barricaded with trams, cars, trucks and farm carts. Challenged at every roadblock, it took them well over an hour to cover two kilometres so that it was dark by the time they reached the Eastern Station.

The Luftwaffe had been hammering the rail network from day one and the station had been attacked on several occasions but although the bombers had made a mess of the surrounding area, very little structural damage had been done to the target itself. According to the transportation branch at Garrison Headquarters, a train was scheduled to leave for Lwow at 2000 hours; considering it was also likely to be the last one out of Warsaw, surprisingly few people were waiting for it in the concourse.

"Where is everybody?" Christina asked.

"All those who were ordered to leave departed a week ago," Korwin reminded her.

The President, members of the government, senior civil servants, the High Command and most of the General Staff had left Warsaw for Lublin on the fifth of September, so had all the foreign ambassadors together with their diplomatic staffs. Car owners who had managed to fill up before all the pumps were closed and existing stocks impounded by the military had also fled the city on the same day.

"Are you sure there is a train, Andrew?"

There was no sign of one on the track in either direction but Korwin wasn't going to admit that he too was beginning to have doubts.

"Of course I am," he said. "You wait here while I have a word with the station master."

There were no lights in the concourse and he hadn't thought to bring a torch with him. He groped his way past the ticket hall, buffet and waiting rooms, shards of glass from the roof crunching under his feet. The station master's office was just up from the luggage department; finding it wasn't difficult, running the official to ground was however a very different story. From a porter, Korwin learned that he had last been seen over on Platform 2 talking to an officer in the military police. When he got there, a ticket collector directed him to the marshalling yards on the north side of the station. After setting out on what proved to be a wildgoose chase, Korwin eventually found him half an hour later back in his office. Although the original departure time had long since come and gone, the station master confirmed that a train was leaving for Lwow that night and was able to provide other reassuring news which Korwin passed on to Christina and Jan.

"There's nothing to worry about," he told them. "The train is on the south-eastern loop, tucked away in the forest. It's been delayed because the track was blocked with fallen trees after the Luftwaffe tried to bomb it this afternoon and the gang workers have only just cleared the line."

"When is it due to arrive?" Christina asked.

"Soon." Korwin peered at the luminous face of his wristwatch. "Unfortunately, I can't stay to see you off. I was only given leave of absence until 2100 hours and I'm fifteen minutes overdue already."

"It's all right, Andrew, we understand."

"You may have to change at Lwow and catch a stopping train to Cernauti in Romania."

"Yes, I know, we've been over all this."

So they had, but there were other possible contingencies that hadn't been aired before which they needed to discuss now.

"If the train doesn't get through to Lwow, don't try to make it on foot. Get back to Warsaw if you can and go to the American Embassy . . ."

"You think Warsaw is going to fall?" Christina said, interrupting him.

"I know the ambassador and all the diplomatic staff have gone to Lublin with our President and the government but all the officers from the consulate are still there looking after those Americans who have been stranded in Warsaw . . ."

"You haven't answered my question."

"Ask to see Frank Ayres, he thinks a lot of you."

9

Christina stared at him. "Those films aren't important at all, are they?" she said in a hollow voice. "You just want to get Jan and me out of Poland."

"You're wrong," Korwin lied. "Of course I'd be a lot happier if I knew you were both safe but believe me, those films are important and we have to get them to America one way or another." He looked at his wristwatch again. "Now I really do have to go."

Korwin kissed her on the forehead, rumpled Jan's hair and said he was relying on him to look after their sister, then hurried out into the yard. The horse and buggy which he had tethered to the railings had disappeared. Although there were two soldiers on duty outside the entrance, both sentries claimed they hadn't seen the thief. The officer in charge of the military police had a spare bicycle but he wasn't prepared to lend it to him, and although he tried to phone Garrison Headquarters to let them know he was on his way, there was a fault on the line and he couldn't get through.

Garrison Headquarters was situated in Pilsudski Square in the town centre and the quickest way there was via Kierbedzia Bridge to the north. To save time, he decided to avoid the roadblocks on the main thoroughfares by cutting through the back streets to the river promenade.

He had been walking for approximately twenty minutes when he became aware that someone was following him. It started with a shiver down the spine which prompted him to look over his shoulder and developed from there. On the way down to the river, he stopped a couple of times and turned about. Although he didn't see anything, the notion persisted that someone was watching him from the shadows. He unbuttoned the leather pistol holster on his belt, raised the flap and took out the 9mm Radom automatic. Korwin shouted to the man to come out, then squeezed off two shots in rapid succession when he failed to show himself. The only scream came from a ricochet which cannoned off an apartment house. He waited, straining his ears to catch the slightest sound of movement, but heard nothing.

"It's just your imagination," he told himself aloud. "There's no one there."

Korwin turned about and continued on down the street towards the Vistula. He had taken exactly eight paces when something with a kick like a mule struck him below the right shoulder blade. He stumbled forward, lost his balance, and went down on all fours; as the pistol slipped from his numbed fingers, he heard a loud crack and knew he had been shot. He scrabbled after the automatic, grabbed it with his left hand and rolled over into a sitting position to face the sniper. The whole of his right side was on fire and he could feel the blood seeping down his arm. He aimed the Radom pistol in the general direction of the unknown marksman and squeezed off the remaining six rounds in the magazine before he blacked out.

The crater was one of eight from a stick of a hundred and ten kilogram bombs which some navigator/bombardier in the Luft-waffe had planted in the potato field. Kurt Bender assumed he had been aiming for the railway track some four hundred metres to his left and was profoundly thankful that his fellow countryman had missed the target. Neatly spaced apart in a straight line, the craters stretched almost as far as the cemetery wall directly to his front; more importantly, they provided a series of funk holes for his three-man reconnaissance patrol as they worked their way towards the superintendent's office inside the gates.

Bender came from Chemnitz, was twenty-four years old, and had joined the army as a regular soldier in 1934. Thus far, he had marched into the demilitarised zone of the Rhineland in March '36, had taken part in the annexation of Austria two years later and had helped to liberate the Sudetenland on the first of October 1938. In five years, he had risen from Soldat to Obergefreiter; if promotion in the peacetime army had been slow, at least he hadn't had to fire a shot in anger and no one had done their level best to kill him either. But now things had changed and in the last few days he had learned what it was like to know fear and when to keep his head down.

The reconnaissance patrol had been the Feldwebel's bright idea. Their platoon had been tasked to clear the cemetery when the attack jumped off at 0830 hours tomorrow morning and he had wanted to know if the superintendent's office had been turned into a strongpoint. "Take two men with you and have a look-see. The password for tonight is KNIGHT, answer TEUTONIC." That had been the sum total of the Feldwebel's orders and while Bender was all for keeping it simple, the dunderhead had carried it to extremes. The password alone wouldn't save them from a nervous sentry on night duty; if he didn't know which way they would be coming back and when to expect them, there was a good chance he would shoot first and challenge afterwards. In the absence of guidance from above, Bender had taken it upon himself to warn the NCO in charge of the right forward section to keep an eye out for them as they approached the company position.

The company had been advancing in a north-easterly direction and had reached the outskirts of the Mokotow district which meant they were about ten kilometres from the centre of Warsaw. For a whole week, things had gone pretty much their way and apart from a lot of sore feet from trying to keep up with the Panzers, they had suffered few casualties. But for the last five days they had encountered stiff resistance and a number of familiar faces were no longer with them. They weren't the only ones who had taken a few punches; from what Bender had heard, the Poles had given the 30th Infantry Division a bloody nose in the battle for the Bzura River and 4 Panzer Division on their right flank were said to have lost over fifty tanks when they had tried to bounce their way into the capital on the eighth of September.

Mindful of these reverses, Bender had been determined to exercise the utmost caution. Before setting out, he and the other two members of his patrol had smeared their hands and faces with a compound of axle grease and mud to remove the sheen, and had tied down the sling swivels on their rifles to ensure nothing rattled. They moved forward in bounds, the two riflemen covering him as he advanced from crater to crater. Away to the north, there was an unnatural red glow where some fire was burning out of control, but that was the only tangible sign of the war. Counter-battery fire by the artillery had ceased an hour ago and a kind of fragile peace had descended on their sector.

Bender dropped into the last crater and slowly raised his head above the far lip. The entrance to the cemetery was roughly a hundred metres to his right and all he could see of the superintendent's office was the sloping roof which rose above the boundary wall. There was, in short, no way he could obtain the information the Feldwebel wanted without getting a damn sight closer. Ordering the two riflemen to cover him, he left the crater and crawled forward on his belly. Twenty-five metres became fifty, then seventy-five and the sweat ran into his eyes, partially blinding him. He crossed a narrow dirt road that paralleled the cemetery wall and got to his feet, chest heaving from the exertion. It was his intention to move sideways towards the entrance with his back to the wall but he never got a chance to put it into practice.

The hand grenade came over the top and landed almost within

touching distance, a wisp of black smoke escaping from the four-second delay fuse. Bender swore, turned his back on the grenade and broke into a run, then threw himself flat after a few paces, a split second before it went off. Metal fragments lacerated him from neck to ankles and all but sliced the calf from his left leg. Unable to move, he lay there slipping in and out of consciousness while a fire fight raged about him. When the shooting finally stopped some considerable time later, he came to again and saw a figure crouching over him. At first, he thought it was one of his soldiers but then he realised the shape of the steel helmet was all wrong.

"Nicht schiessen," he muttered feebly. "Nicht schiessen."

The Poles had no intention of shooting him; he was the first prisoner they had taken and they were determined to bring him back alive. One of the soldiers picked up Bender in a fireman's lift and carried him through the gates on the double and then on to the company command post beyond the cemetery. From there, he was eventually taken to hospital on a horse and cart belonging to a coal merchant.

CHAPTER 2

THE SUN playing on her face eventually roused Christina from a troubled sleep. Her right arm was numb from the elbow down because Jan was leaning against her, pillowing his head on her shoulder. Her neck was also uncomfortably stiff as though she had been sitting in a draught. The eight-car train to Lwow had finally arrived at the Eastern Station a few minutes after midnight and had departed an hour and a half later. The booking office had closed at sunset never to reopen so that, like the vast majority of the other passengers, she had boarded the train without a ticket. There had been no last minute rush of would-be refugees and there had been seats to spare in her through coach when the train had got under way.

They had crawled through Praga at little more than a fast walking pace, frequently stopping for no apparent reason, sometimes for as long as twenty minutes. They had cleared the outskirts of Warsaw shortly before dawn and thereafter the train had picked up speed to maintain a steady forty kilometres an hour. The rhythmic click-clack of the bogies had had a soporific effect and she had gradually dozed off, her head lolling backwards and forwards. Whenever she had surfaced momentarily, the train had been in motion; now wide awake, she suddenly realised it had stopped. There were no landmarks Christina recognised, only an unending vista of flat, open fields, isolated farmhouses and the occasional hedgerow.

"Do you know where we are?" Christina asked the middle-aged man sitting opposite her. He was an Italian civil engineer from Naples, their common language was his rusty and her schoolgirl French which she had rarely spoken since leaving finishing school in Geneva following the death of her mother.

"We passed through a station called Deblin at seven thirty this morning but now I am lost." He smiled apologetically. "This is only my second visit to your country, mademoiselle."

"Well, I must have done this journey a dozen times and even I don't recognise the countryside."

Jan stirred beside her and slumped forward, his head dipping towards her lap. The sudden movement woke him and he sat up and looked around. "We've stopped," he said, yawning. "What time is it?"

Christina glanced at her wristwatch. "It's five minutes past nine," she told him.

At seven thirty they had passed through Deblin which was roughly ninety kilometres from Warsaw. In the hour and a half since then they would have travelled a further sixty kilometres which meant the train should be close to the outskirts of Lublin. Christina went over her calculations again, forehead wrinkling in a frown.

"I fear we have been waiting here for over an hour," the Italian engineer informed her, as though reading her thoughts.

The distant throb of aero engines killed any further conversation and she instinctively looked up at the roof. Beside her, Jan pressed his face against the window and searched the sky. For several moments all forty-eight passengers in the coach were frozen in different attitudes like waxwork figures in a museum, then an anonymous voice shouted for everyone to get down. The Italian grabbed Christina by the wrists, pulled her on to the floor and fell on top of her. There were two attacking aircraft and they came in low, raking the train from end to end with cannon and machine-gun fire. The metal skin of the carriage was punctured from above, each strike of shot making a hollow clang as though someone was using a dustbin for a bass drum and was beating it with a hammer. The windows blew out, raining shards of glass on to the track, and splinters gouged from the wooden seats became lethal darts. Presented with a defenceless and stationary target, the pilots continued to make pass after pass until finally their ammunition was exhausted.

There was an unnatural silence after the aircraft had departed as if the survivors could not believe they were still alive and were afraid to open their mouths in case the Germans heard them and returned to finish the job. But the lull did not last; suddenly it was shattered by agonised screams, curses and the despairing cries of those who found their loved ones had been killed. Christina waited for the Italian engineer to get up, then tried to do so herself but only succeeded in banging her head against a solid, immovable object. To her surprise she discovered that like an ostrich burying its head in the sand at the scent of danger, she had ended up with her head under the bench seat. She wriggled clear and saw Jan lying face down across the seat and there was blood on the floor and on her hands after she touched him.

"Don't look," the Italian advised her.

But Christina did, and there was this hole in his chest bigger than her clenched fist. Her legs suddenly felt weak and she started to tremble, then the realisation that Jan would never tease, never smile, never argue, never talk to her again, sank in and she began to cry. She neither saw nor heard the conductor come through the coach and order everybody off the train. And later when she was standing by the track, Christina could not recall the Italian helping her to climb down from the coach, but he had his arm round her shoulders and was trying to console her so she assumed he must have done. When eventually she stopped crying, he left her in order to help the other men bring the dead and wounded out of the train.

Every coach had been systematically hit with cannon and machine-gun fire and there wasn't a single window intact. But it was the locomotive which had suffered the most damage; holed repeatedly in the boiler, it was gently expiring in a cloud of steam. As she stood there numbed with shock, the dead were laid out in a neat, straight line by the track – five men, nine women and four children. A priest had appeared from a nearby village and was moving amongst them offering sympathy to the bereaved and prayers for the dead and those who were about to die. If the number of handcarts and farm wagons which had also appeared on the scene were anything to go by, it looked as though he had brought half the population with him.

"I think this is yours, mademoiselle?" the Italian engineer said in his hesitant French.

Christina looked down at the carpetbag which he had placed at her feet. "Yes, it is, you are very kind . . ."

"Please, it is nothing." He shifted his weight from one foot to the other and looked everywhere but at her. "There is something else," he said awkwardly. "The priest is asking what you wish to do about your brother."

"Do?" Christina frowned. "I'm sorry, I don't understand."

"The funeral. Perhaps you wish to make your own arrangements?"

"Oh, I see."

"If not, he will be buried with the other victims in the village
churchyard."

"Yes." She found it hard to concentrate on what he was saying
and her thoughts wandered off at a tangent. The one thing that
really haunted her was the conviction that Jan would still be alive
if they hadn't been sitting there in the open. "Why did we have to
stop?" she said aloud.

"What?"

"The train. Why did it stop?"

"I don't know. If I understood the priest correctly, we couldn't
go on because the Germans have captured Lublin. But he also told
me the conductor said a railwayman had flagged the locomotive
down to warn the engineer that saboteurs had blown up the track
about a kilometre from here." He paused, hesitating to return to
what was obviously a very painful subject for her. "What shall I
tell the priest?" he asked eventually.

"I can't take Jan back to Warsaw. Perhaps after the war . . . ?"

"Yes, that would be a wise decision. If you would like, I will
attend to it?"

"Would you?"

"But of course."

Left alone again while he sought out the priest, Christina went
through the contents of the carpetbag, discarding everything but
the most essential items. There was no point in attempting to get
through to Romania now; instead, she would make her way back
to Warsaw and see if Frank Ayres could help her. Out therefore
went all the tinned food she had packed for the journey, the change
of clothing for Jan – his socks, vests, shirts and underpants, as well
as her own underclothes. She kept only the twenty rolls of film and
the bars of chocolate for sustenance. By the time she had finished,
the Italian was back again.

"It is done," he said simply. "They are taking your brother to
the village."

A lump rose in her throat and it was difficult to hold back the
tears. "Thank you," she said huskily.

"You will have to see the priest. As you know, I have very little
Polish and his knowledge of French is very basic, so we had to talk
a lot with our hands. However, there are things I could not tell

17

him – your brother's name, his date of birth. You know how it is."

"Yes." Christina picked up the carpetbag. "I will go and find him."

"He is on the way back to the village with some of the injured. I will go with you."

"Oh, I couldn't put you to all that trouble."

"It is no trouble. I am going to look for somewhere to stay until the trains are running again. What will you do?"

"I am going to find someone who will sell me a bicycle," Christina told him.

Kurt Bender stared at the rubber tree plant on the table. The leaves should have been green, but they were white, and he wondered if it had been snowing. There was certainly a definite nip in the air even though it was only mid-September. Or was it? Maybe it was later than he thought and weeks, if not months, had slipped by without him being aware of it? He remembered the grenade exploding just behind him, the agony of being carried through the cemetery and the Polish officer who had questioned him in halting German. And some time after that, they had laid him face down in the coal dust on a horse-drawn wagon. He recalled little of the journey through the war-torn streets and couldn't think where he was now.

The Poles had tried to murder him, that was one thing he wasn't going to forget in a hurry. Four of them had held him down on a table while an evil figure in a mask and white bedsheet had tried to smother him with a pad soaked with some foul-smelling liquid. Ether: yes, that was the stuff, and the man in the white gown must have been the anaesthetist. But what kind of hospital were these people running, for God's sake? Although there was a thunderstorm on the way, they were quite happy to leave their patients out in the open. Why the hell didn't they bring him inside before it started raining? Except that what he could hear was artillery not thunder and plaster from the ceiling had turned the rubber tree plant white, and he was cold because all the windows in the ward had been shattered.

So who else was in the ward? He was lying face down on the bed, his head over to the right, and all he could see was this stupid plant. Gritting his teeth, Bender raised himself up, turned his head the other way and collapsed back on the pillow exhausted. When he opened his eyes again, he found himself face to face with another German soldier.

"My name's Bender," he croaked, "Kurt Bender. What's yours?"

"Korwin."

"You got a first name?"

"Yes, it's Andrew."

Andrew Korwin. That didn't sound very German but maybe he came from the Sudetenland and there was some Czech in there. That would account for his funny accent. "Where did you get hit?"

"In the shoulder."

Wherever he came from, this Korwin was as thick as two short planks. "No, I meant where did it happen?"

"Oh. Down by the river near the Kierbedzia Bridge."

"Really? I didn't know we had got that far."

"You haven't," Korwin told him. "I'm a Polish officer."

There was, Bender thought, no answer to that.

"And before you think of starting something, I should warn you there is an armed sentry sitting at the foot of your bed."

There was no answer to that one either.

Shortly before 1400 hours, Frank Ayres climbed up on to the roof of the embassy and took over the duties of air observer from Ed Symans of the Commercial Attaché's office. With Warsaw under almost continuous bombardment from the air, the all clear had no sooner been sounded than the sirens were wailing the alert for another raid. In the early days of the siege, they had all dutifully trooped down to the cellar whenever the alarm went, but it was impossible to get any work done when you were spending nineteen hours out of every twenty-four huddled together in the dark. So they had rigged up a one-to-one field telephone system and now everyone carried on as usual until the spotter on the roof gave three short rings to signify that aircraft were actually overhead. But, for once, there were no bombers in the skies above Warsaw.

Ayres leaned against the parapet and looked down into Ujaz-dowskie Boulevard. A couple of days ago, a homeless peasant from Lowicz had been selling fresh milk from his cow right outside the gates to the embassy, while every morning and evening soldiers of the garrison commuted from their homes to the front line. The milk had been for babies only and the soldiers returned to their families at night because the army got better rations than the civilians and they wished to share them with their parents, wives and children. It was that kind of war.

He wondered how Christina Korwin was managing. He had met her just over two years ago when she had accompanied her father to the reception at the embassy which the ambassador gave every July Fourth. Although only a lowly member of the consulate, Ayres and the other vice consuls had been roped in to help act as joint hosts with the embassy staff. The moment she had walked into the room, he had known that Christina was the nicest thing that had happened to him since he had been posted to Warsaw on his first foreign assignment. No other guests had been so assiduously looked after as the Korwins had been. Indeed, Ambassador Biddle had made that very point the following day when he had gently reprimanded him for neglecting the Swiss Chargé d'Affaires and his wife, the First Secretary Commerce at the French Embassy and several other diplomats whose names and appointments he had long since forgotten.

Getting rapped over the knuckles hadn't bothered him; what had been worrying was how he was going to find an excuse to see Christina again. The Korwins were wealthy landowners and numbered among the most important families in Poland, whereas his father was a bank teller with First National and he was on the bottom rung of the Foreign Service with little prospect of advancing a whole lot farther. It had seemed an insoluble problem; the hard courts at the Resursa Kupiecka Club and Andrew Korwin's enthusiasm for tennis had provided the solution. Ayres had taken up one of the honorary memberships extended to the American diplomatic staff and had bided his time until an opportunity arose to offer Korwin a game. That first tennis match had led to a friendship which had enabled him to see Christina between thirty and forty times over the next two years.

They had been to the opera, dined at the Bristol, played tennis, gone riding in the park, danced to the band playing in the Saxon Gardens on a summer's evening, and he had been invited to the Korwin house on several occasions. But he had always been part of a group and they had never once been alone together. He was infatuated with Christina and more than a little in love with her but he didn't and probably never would know if his feelings towards her were reciprocated. Christina was unobtainable, but it didn't stop him thinking about her, sometimes to the exclusion of all else.

The distant uneven berroom-berroom-room finally penetrated

his thoughts and he looked up and instinctively swept the sky with his binoculars. Dornier Do 17s, the twin-engined bombers with a bulbous nose and pencil-slim fuselage; he recognised the aircraft from the description Major Colbern, the military attaché, had given him. He counted forty of them flying in a series of loose V formations. There was, of course, no sign of the Polish Air Force; their planes had been shot out of the skies or destroyed on the ground in the first few days of the war. Their basic combat aircraft was the P11c, a high-wing monoplane with a fixed undercarriage and a large radial engine that looked like an all-metal version of a First World War fighter plane. Pitting these slow, poorly armed machines against the Messerschmitt Bf 109 had been like the massacre of the innocents.

Although the bombers were making for Praga across the river, they were a little too close for comfort; moving to the field telephone, he cranked it three times and got a plaintive ring back, signifying the alert had been received. A little belatedly, the sirens began to wail.

The bombers came on, seemingly invulnerable at ten thousand feet. Black, cottonwool puffs of smoke appeared amongst the raiders as the three-inch anti-aircraft battery in Lazienki Park opened fire. And suddenly, just as the bombs began to fall, one of the Dorniers staggered out of formation and started to break up in midair. Ayres threw his steel helmet in the air and danced a victory jig while yelling himself hoarse. It was hardly the act of a neutral, but his feelings were biased in favour of the Poles.

The bicycle had been fit only for the scrapheap when Christina had bought it from the village blacksmith. The predominant colour was rust, the tyres were paper thin and the brakes nonexistent. The blacksmith, however, had pretended he didn't want to sell it and had only been persuaded to do so by the priest and then only for the outrageous price of two hundred zlotys. She had covered approximately thirty bone-shaking kilometres on back roads when the inevitable puncture had occurred. The purchase price hadn't included a repair outfit, nor was the bike equipped with a pump which at least would have enabled her to keep inflating the inner tube until it finally gave out. So she had continued to ride the bike on the rear flat tyre and then on the rim itself after the outer cover had come off the wheel. Not long after that, the spokes began to buckle and spring loose as the circumference became more and more distorted. If this wasn't enough, the slack and overextended chain kept slipping off the cog so that she was for ever dismounting to put it back on again. By late afternoon, the bicycle had become more of a hindrance than a help and in the end she was reduced to wheeling it.

The farm in the distance was the only reason why Christina hadn't abandoned the machine. Even if the owner couldn't repair the bike, he could probably give her a bed for the night because there was no way she was going to reach Warsaw before last light. Head down, she walked on, her calf muscles rock hard, her whole body a mass of aches and pains. It had been the worst day of her life since her mother had died and she was never going to forget the awful moment when Jan had been laid to rest in the communal grave the villagers had dug for the victims of the air raid. One day, she would come back for him and see to it that he was given a proper burial in the family vault and they would hold a memorial service for him.

She heard the drone of aero engines and looked up to see three twin-engine monoplanes low down on the horizon and heading due west into the sunset. Although unable to distinguish friend from foe, there was not the slightest doubt in her mind that they were German simply because, to all intents and purposes, the Polish Air Force had disappeared from the skies days ago. A few hours back, Christina would have flung herself into the nearest ditch, but this was the third time she had encountered the Luftwaffe since the train had been attacked and she had learned a thing or two in the meantime. Those planes were too far away to spot her and in any case they appeared to be heading towards the German lines.

The farmhouse was approximately four hundred metres back from the road up a grassy track. Left and forward of the white-washed house, there was a small orchard of gnarled apple trees which were now too old to bear fruit. No one was working in the fields and the house appeared to be deserted but as she entered the yard, a farmhand emerged from the dilapidated cowshed on the right. He was in his mid-twenties, had short dark hair and had obviously outgrown the clothes he was wearing. The collarless shirt was far too tight across the chest and the black trousers barely reached his shins. Christina didn't care for his surly expression, nor did she like the way he stared at her as though he had never seen a woman before. The last thing she wanted from him was a bed for the night.

"You've lost a tyre," he said.

"Yes." Christina nodded. "I don't suppose you know where I can get another one?"

"I might be able to fix you up." There was a note of antagonism in his voice rather than the respect she was used to.

"Could you?" she asked nervously.

"Yeah, we've got a spare wheel in the shed. You want to bring the bike with you?"

Christina hesitated. There was something very wrong about him. His face was pale and didn't have the weatherbeaten look of a man who worked on the land.

"What are you waiting for? Do you want it or not?"

"I've changed my mind," Christina told him.

She turned about and started to wheel her bicycle towards the road. She heard his footsteps behind her and before she had a chance to reach for the Beretta pistol in her jacket pocket, he had pinioned her arms and wrestled her to the ground.

"Look what I've got, Pawal," he shouted. "A very tasty looking arystokrata."

There were two of them, deserters from the Polish Army who had taken refuge on the farm. Christina screamed, twisted and squirmed and kicked out but the second man grabbed hold of her legs and between them, they carried her into the shed. Somewhere along the way, the pistol slipped out of her pocket but neither man noticed it.

"We've got ourselves a regular spitfire," Pawal said.

"Beggars can't be choosers."

"Who said I was complaining, Jakob? I like a woman with spirit."

They dumped her on the ground, Pawal holding her down while his friend, Jakob, stretched both arms above her head and tied them behind a post. Then Jakob ripped her blouse apart, raised the brassière above her breasts and began to tweak both nipples between thumb and index finger. While he enjoyed himself, Pawal undid the side buttons on her slacks and started to remove them. Christina never stopped fighting; even when the slacks were down around her ankles, she lashed out and managed to kick him in the crotch. The satisfaction that came from knowing she had hurt him was short-lived; bellowing with rage, Pawal repeatedly punched her in the stomach. The pain was excruciating, she couldn't move, couldn't breathe and was half-unconscious, so that he was able to strip her from the waist down without further resistance.

"What the hell is this, a chastity belt?" Pawal said and laughed.

"It's a money belt," Christina gasped. "Take it and let me go."

Jakob stopped mauling her, grabbed the belt from his companion and undid one of the pouches. "What kind of money do you call this?" he said and threw the notes in her face.

"American dollars." Christina swallowed. "They are very valuable."

"How many dollars?"

"Seven hundred and fifty."

"Maybe we should count them to make sure," Pawal suggested.

"I'll count them," Jakob told him. "You can have first go with our arystokrata."

Pawal forced her thighs apart and knelt between them. He took out his thing, as her friends at finishing school had called it, and tried to ram it up her. The assault was brutal, savage, painful and humiliating.

"I think we've got ourselves a virgin here," Pawal said. "Her twat is as tight as a drum."

He shoved again, hard enough to make her cry out in pain, then he started to move up and down, pumping away like a piston engine. He grunted, screwed up his eyes, bared his teeth and worked himself into a frenzy while Christina lay supine beneath him, crying silently. He climaxed with a loud shriek as if he had just lifted a huge weight that had taxed his strength to the limit, then collapsed on top of her and shuddered.

"Have you finished?" Jakob asked.

"For the time being."

"Well, move your arse, it's my turn now."

"What's your hurry, she isn't going anywhere." Pawal pushed himself up and withdrew, then chuckled. "You jammy old bugger," he said, "you're going to have an easier ride than I did. Seems I've broken her in for you."

"That's what friends are for," Jakob told him.

They changed places and the multiple rape continued unabated. Her vagina felt as if it was being torn and ripped apart and she hated them for the way they were dehumanising her, using her body as a mere receptacle for their semen. In her worst nightmare, Christina could not have imagined a more terrifying or degrading experience and she wished she had died with Jan on the train. But the worst thing of all was knowing that when Jakob had done with her, Pawal would start all over again.

"I don't think much of that," Jakob said and rolled off her. "I could have had a better time fucking a dummy in a shop window."

"Yeah, well perhaps she will show a little more enthusiasm next time around."

"I don't know about that. What I fancy right now is a drink. You think they've got anything up at the house?"

"There's only one way to find out," Pawal said and got to his feet.

Christina watched them leave and wondered how long it would be before they returned. As soon as they were out of earshot, she began to work on her hands, flexing her wrists in an effort to loosen the bonds. It was a long, slow and painful business but eventually she managed to get enough leverage on the rope to work it part of the way over the back of her left hand. She took a deep breath, then gritted her teeth while she rubbed the cord over the knuckles. After that, the rest was easy, even though she did skin herself in the process.

Time was something she couldn't afford to squander when every second counted. The dollar bills on the floor didn't matter, nor did the carpetbag she had carried on the handlebars of the bicycle. What mattered was escaping from the two rapists. Christina stepped into her slacks and pulled them up quickly, readjusted her brassière and tucked the torn blouse into the waistband. She opened the door of the shed and resisting the temptation to run, started to tiptoe across the yard.

"Where the hell do you think you're going?" Pawal roared.

Christina sprinted towards the orchard, realised he would cut her off before she reached the grass track leading to the road and turned back. As she did so, Jakob stormed out of the farmhouse and moved to his left to intercept her.

"Are you going to get it now," he snarled.

They had her cornered and there was absolutely nothing she could do; then she stubbed her toes on something in the grass and there was the Beretta pistol. Christina bent down, picked up the automatic and pointed it at Jakob who was the nearest.

"Don't come any closer," she screamed. But her hands were shaking so much, she couldn't hold the weapon in the aim.

"I don't think you know how to use that," Jakob said.

He was just ten metres away when she squeezed the trigger, but nothing happened. Jesus, God, what was it Andrew had told her? "If you have to use the pistol, thumb the hammer back like so, push the safety catch forward towards the letter F on the left side below the slide . . ." She could hear his voice and did exactly what he had told her before squeezing the trigger again.

The bullet struck Jakob close to his nose below the left eye and exited behind his right ear, taking a piece of his skull and a lot of brain tissue with it. Nothing in life had surprised him half as much as the manner of his death and it showed in the astonished expression on his face before he went down. Whirling round to face Pawal, Christina emptied the rest of the magazine into him at point-blank range, then sank down on to her knees and hugged herself. It was a long time before she felt strong enough to get up and prepare to move on.

CHAPTER 3

THE FOOD storage depot was on the eastern outskirts of Praga some four hundred metres beyond the Polish front line and roughly equidistant from the foremost German unit. Ayres took one look at the depot and decided it was the least desirable piece of real estate he had seen since the war had begun. The Garrison Commander had given him written authority to take whatever supplies he needed to feed the American expatriates who had taken refuge around the embassy. What he had been unable to tell him was the layout of the depot and where the nonperishable items were warehoused and the location of the cold stores. The company commander whose platoons were dug in opposite the depot couldn't enlighten him either, but he knew where the Germans were and could predict how they would react should Ayres take the Ford truck into the depot.

"You seem to understand Polish well enough," the captain said.

"I like to think so," Ayres told him modestly.

"Good. Then you will know what I mean when I say all hell will break loose. The Germans have several observation posts in this sector and they will call for an artillery concentration before you reach the front gates."

"You think they will fire on the American flag?" Ayres had borrowed the largest one the embassy had but the flagpole wasn't big enough and even though he had lashed it to the canopy bar behind the cab, Old Glory still hung limply from the truck like a strip of tired bunting.

"Who knows?" The Pole shrugged his shoulders. "They will have to see it first."

"Thanks a lot."

"Excuse me please?"

"Nothing," Ayres said. "I was talking to myself."

Ayres left the command post and walked back down the road

towards the solitary block of workers' flats where Viktor Wiktorzak, the embassy's boilerman, was waiting for him. Right now, the truck was parked behind the tenement where it was relatively safe, but according to the captain, that happy state of affairs wouldn't last. If the Germans really had established an observation post somewhere in the depot, they would spot the Ford truck the moment he drove it out on to the road and headed towards them. Ayres doubted if they would take much notice of the flag, even supposing they happened to notice it. Chances were that any vehicle coming from the general direction of Praga would be regarded as hostile, which meant the Polish Army could scratch one more Ford truck. Not that they would miss this particular vehicle with its flat battery, nonexistent brakes and balding tyres.

Wiktorzak saw him coming and jumped down from the cab with the starting handle. When they had collected the truck from the vehicle pool earlier that morning, it had taken them fifteen back-breaking, palm-blistering minutes to coax the damned thing into life; now, however, the engine was still fairly warm and the Pole managed to get it firing on all eight cylinders at the first attempt.

"What do you think of that?" Wiktorzak asked him in Polish. "Pretty good, huh?"

"You are one hell of a fine mechanic, Viktor."

Ayres got in behind the wheel, waited for the boilerman to join him, then shifted into gear, released the handbrake and pulled out on to the road. The concrete ribbon stretched in front of them, deserted and menacing. A forest of metal stakes cut from tram rails had been planted in the ground to make an anti-tank obstacle in front of the slit trenches that had been dug on either side of the road. There were no obstacles on the road itself. Instead, combat engineers had laid charges under all the culverts and wired them to a battery-powered initiator in the command post. All the company commander had to do was push a button and several tons of concrete would disappear along with any Panzers that happened to be in the immediate vicinity at the time. Ayres just hoped he wouldn't develop an itchy finger while they were busy looting the food depot.

The depot seemed a million miles away across open, flat country without so much as a blade of grass for cover. In all his life, Ayres had never felt so lonely, exposed or nervous. Eyes fixed on the entrance and whistling tunelessly to himself, he drove on, expecting at any moment to see the landscape erupt under a salvo from a German artillery battery. Then, miraculously, they were through the gates without a shot being fired at them and he began to feel a little more sanguine about their chances.

The cold stores were locked and damn nearly burglar proof. Unwilling to waste valuable time trying to force the steel doors with a tyre lever, Ayres took what he could from where he could. Many of the warehouses had already been cleaned out, but one shed yielded precious sacks of flour, while in another he found three large cases of butter and some cans of fruit. They had just backed the Ford up to a third shed and were about to help themselves to several fifty-kilogram bags of sugar when the Wehrmacht arrived.

There were four of them, intimidating figures in coal-scuttle helmets, leather equipment, jackboots and field grey-green uniforms. Three were armed with bolt action Mauser rifles; the NCO in charge of the patrol carried a machine pistol and made their presence known with a warning burst of three to four rounds into the roof. Although he had never been shot at in anger before, Ayres was convinced that if the German had aimed only a fraction lower, his head would have been reduced to a bloody pulp. Scared witless one moment, shaking with anger the next, he rounded on the NCO.

"You goddamn stupid idiot," he shouted, "you could have killed me. What the hell do you think you're playing at? That's the American flag on that vehicle over there."

He wasn't sure whether he was getting through to the German; the NCO looked angry enough but it could be that he simply didn't like his tone of voice. Ayres watched his finger tighten on the trigger and decided it was high time he emulated Viktor Wiktorzak and raised his hands.

"Verstehen Sie englisch?" he asked in stilted German.

"Nein."

"Terrific." Ayres closed his eyes and tried to recall some of the vocabulary he had learned in high school. "Amerikanisch. Ich bin ein Amerikaner, nicht polnisch. Verstehen?"

"Nein."

The NCO smiled at him as though secretly amused by something he had said. It was however a little hard to share the joke when the machine pistol was pointed straight at his chest and the NCO had the steeliest blue eyes he had ever seen.

"Mein deutsch ist nicht gut aber Ich habe ein Reispass hier." Ayres lowered one arm to pat the inside pocket of his jacket, then quickly raised it again.

"Bitte, geben sie mir." The NCO snapped his fingers, then

stretched out his left hand, palm open, to make his meaning clear.

Ayres reached inside his jacket, took out the passport and handed it to him. The eagle on the front cover should have put him wise but the German acted as though it didn't ring any bells for him. He turned the pages, compared the photograph with the man standing in front of him and frowned. Ayres tried to tell him that it wasn't a good likeness but his German really wasn't up to it and he couldn't find the right words.

"That's okay, Mr Ayres," the NCO finally told him. "I never met a guy yet who resembled his passport photo."

Ayres stared at him, a glazed expression on his face. For the better part of ten minutes, this son of a bitch had pretended not to know a word of English and had made him sweat it out trying to explain who he was in lousy deutsch.

"How long were you in the States?" he asked.

"I spent two years in Milwaukee making beer, came home in '35." The NCO returned his passport. "You can put your hands down now."

"Thanks."

"What are you doing here, Mr Ayres?"

"Getting what food I can for my hundred or so fellow Americans who have taken refuge in the embassy. I've got written permission from the Garrison Commander." Ayres realised the full import of what he had just said and smiled ruefully. "But I guess that won't cut much ice with you?" he added.

"I'm sure our High Command would not like to see your Americans starve."

"Does that mean I am free to go?"

"It surely does. Of course, your Polish friend will have to stay here with us."

"Viktor is our boilerman."

"So?"

"So he enjoys diplomatic immunity."

There wasn't a grain of truth in the assertion but when said loudly and forcibly enough, Ayres hoped that someone like the noncom who wasn't familiar with the Convention would be taken in.

"I don't think so."

"It doesn't matter what you think, Viktor is coming with me."

"The Pole isn't going anywhere."

Although he had played a lot of poker and had yet to lose his shirt, Ayres couldn't tell whether or not the German was bluffing. He was also inhibited by the knowledge that if he got it wrong, it would be Viktor Wiktorzak who paid the price.

"I want you to understand something," he said carefully. "This man is under my protection and he is leaving with me. The only way you can stop us is to point that Tommy gun in our direction and squeeze the trigger. Now, you may think killing two more people isn't going to make a jot of difference in the middle of a war, but you're wrong, Fritz . . ."

"My name is Heinz Peter," the German said, correcting him.

"Right, Heinz Peter it is. But for how long? A lot of people at the embassy know I'm here and they also know that the Poles have pulled out of the depot. So if I am killed, it will be down to you and I know your Führer isn't going to like that because it will make Mr Roosevelt madder than hell, and right now, Germany has enough enemies as it is without poking a stick in Uncle Sam's eye." Ayres stepped down from the loading platform, smiled winningly at Heinz Peter and clapped him on the shoulder. "So we are going before anyone does something they'll have cause to regret. Okay?"

He beckoned Viktor Wiktorzak to follow him and walked on through the knot of German soldiers and got into the cab, an itchy feeling between his shoulder blades. He prayed there was enough juice in the battery to turn the motor over because there was no telling what would happen if one of them had to get out and use the starting handle. He switched on the ignition, pressed the button and got a very laboured response from the starter motor. The battery faded rapidly, then, just when it seemed it was going to die on him, the engine suddenly caught and he managed to coax it into life. Shifting into gear, he waved goodbye to Heinz Peter and took off.

A machine gun opened up on them while they were still two hundred metres from the Polish outposts. Seconds later, the first ranging shell from a battery of field artillery landed uncomfortably close. As they approached the command post, the company commander decided it was time to fire the ring main demolition, and the road erupted behind them. Ayres drove on to the first block of flats, then stopped for a breather. It was some considerable time before his hands were steady enough to light a cigarette.

Bender furtively made another scratchmark on the iron frame of the hospital bed with his spoon to signify this was his third day in captivity. He wondered how long it would be before the Poles transferred him to the old Pawiak Prison where he had been told all the other German POWs were being held. But of even greater concern to him was how much longer Warsaw could hold out. If patients at this military hospital counted themselves fortunate to get one bowl of watery soup a day, how was the rest of the population faring? The whole system of food distribution appeared to have broken down which meant the inhabitants were probably on the verge of starvation.

Hunger, shellfire and bombing; those were the principal weapons the Wehrmacht were now employing to subdue the Polish garrison. To minimise casualties, house to house clearing by the infantry was out and the Panzers were holding back for fear of being ambushed in the streets. Instead, it looked as if the army intended to tighten its grip on the capital while leaving the Luftwaffe and the artillery to administer the coup de grâce. The longer the siege continued, the more dangerous it would become for him; not only would he be on the receiving end of everything that was being dished out, but if the Luftwaffe failed to kill him, there was a good chance that one of the Polish guards would. He represented the enemy and in view of what Goering's lot were doing to Warsaw, they could hardly be blamed for wanting to get their own back.

That no one as yet had raised a hand against him Bender attributed to the Polish officer in the adjoining bed. As the aide-de-camp to the Garrison Commander, Korwin was regarded with awe by the soldiers; as long as he continued to enjoy his protection, Bender believed he would come to no harm. Unfortunately, Korwin was anxious to return to duty and was for ever pleading with the chief medical officer to discharge him from hospital.

Bender heard the distant throb of aero engines a few moments before the air-raid sirens started wailing and raised himself up on both elbows. Through the shattered window behind his bed, he could see several trimotor planes heading due east across the city at an altitude of roughly three thousand metres. The unusual configuration identified them as Ju 52 transports and he wondered if the High Command had decided to throw in the paratroopers in an all-out bid to capture Warsaw. There were hundreds of planes in the sky and a large percentage of them sounded as though they were directly overhead.

Their visiting cards smashed through the roof, a couple penetrating the ceiling at the other end of the ward. The searing white light from the magnesium-filled incendiary bomb completely dazzled Bender so that even after he had turned away from the glare, his vision still remained impaired. One of the patients was already on fire and his demented screams of agony were the most horrifying sounds Bender had ever heard. As the fire in the loft space took hold, acrid smoke filled the ward and like everyone else, he was racked by a paroxysm of coughing.

They were on the top floor and were cut off by the conflagration from the fire escape and staircase beyond the swing doors at the far end of the ward. He heard the armed sentry sitting at the foot of his bed yelling at him and glanced over his shoulder to find himself staring at a Mauser rifle. Fear galvanised Bender into action and he forgot that most of the calf was missing from his left leg, forgot too that grenade fragments had lacerated his body from neck to ankle. Rolling over in bed, he threw himself on to the floor a split second before the Pole squeezed the trigger and put a 7.92mm bullet into the feather pillow. The sentry opened the bolt to eject the empty cartridge case, then closed it to feed another round into the breech. Had it not been for Korwin, he would have been a dead man. Without a thought for his own safety, the Polish officer pushed the Mauser aside and slapped the half-crazed soldier across the face. Even though he had used his good arm, the physical effort made him groan and the blood started to seep through the first-aid dressing on his right shoulder. Somehow, Bender managed to get to his feet, somehow he managed to stand on his one good leg, grab the rifle from the sentry and toss it out of the open window.

There was only one way they were going to get out of the ward alive. Hopping from bed to bed, Bender stripped off the sheets and started knotting them together. Korwin tried to help, realised he couldn't do much with one hand and ordered the sentry to assist him. There were only four other patients in their half of the ward, none of whom could be called walking wounded. Lashing one end of the rope sheet to his bed, Bender and the sentry began to lower the seriously wounded to the ground where some members of the nursing staff had foregathered. Bits of the blazing ceiling fell around Bender and the intense heat singed his hair. Almost overcome by the smoke, he had no recollection of tying Korwin on to the rope before pushing him out of the window. But everything became crystal clear when the sheets suddenly parted as he started to climb down hand over hand from the fourth floor.

*   *   *

Ayres was dog tired and it seemed to him that he had scarcely got his head down before some inconsiderate son of a bitch was doing his level best to wake him up. He made a determined effort to ignore the hand on his shoulder in the hope that the intruder would eventually give up and leave him in peace. In what became a clash of wills, he found himself pitted against someone who was equally determined to rouse him. Very reluctantly and very slowly, Ayres finally opened his eyes and found himself looking up at Viktor Wiktorzak.

"A young lady to see you, Mr Ayres," he said.

"Me?"

"Yes, upstairs in the hall."

Ayres got to his feet and followed Wiktorzak out of the cellar. He went through all the American expatriates he had met in the course of his duties and couldn't think of one who could be described as young with any accuracy. Christina Korwin was therefore the very last person he expected to encounter. He was about to say what a pleasure it was to see her but then, as he drew nearer, he noticed the distraught expression on her face and the bedraggled state of the clothes she was wearing and knew that something was terribly wrong.

"What's happened, Miss Korwin?" he asked.

"Is there somewhere private where we can talk?"

"Yes, of course."

The Consular officers had taken over most of the rooms on the ground floor of the embassy with the exception of the one belonging to Ambassador Biddle. Since the ambassador was in Lublin with the Polish Government, Ayres didn't see why he shouldn't make use of it.

"Can I get you a cup of coffee?" he asked. "We've got a pot on the boil all the time. Coffee is the one thing we are not short of."

"My younger brother, Jan, is dead," Christina told him in a chilling monotone.

And then, in the same dead tone of voice, she told him how their train had been machine-gunned and why she had had to have Jan buried in a mass communal grave and of the two army deserters she had killed after they had raped her.

"I was lucky," she said. "They had already murdered the farmer, his wife and their two children before I arrived. They had stabbed them to death with their bayonets."

Christina had found their bodies and the discarded uniforms of the killers when she had entered the farmhouse hoping to beg, borrow or steal a bicycle. Although she had half-expected it, the discovery had so unnerved her that she had turned about and stumbled out of the house without bothering to look any farther.

"They had stolen the money belt Andrew gave me but I didn't stop to look for it. I just picked up this carpetbag and started walking."

It had taken her nearly three days to do so but she had trudged all the way back to Warsaw, sleeping rough in the fields at night. She had avoided the main roads for fear of running into the Germans and had given the more sizable villages a wide berth for much the same reason. The only food she had had to eat in all that time was two small bars of chocolate. Finding something to drink had not however been a problem and Christina had slaked her thirst whenever she had come across a horse trough, water butt or fast-flowing stream. The Wehrmacht had practically encircled Warsaw but she had managed to slip through the jaws of the pincers.

"I don't know how you did it, Miss Korwin," Ayres told her when she had finished. "You've got more courage than a dozen men put together."

"I had a job to do."

"A job?"

"Yes." Christina lifted the carpetbag on to her lap and took out roll after roll of film which she placed on the desk in front of him. "I was supposed to deliver these to my Uncle Zygmunt in New York. They show what the Nazis are doing to Poland. Andrew said it was very important that the American people should know what is happening to our country. He also said that if our train couldn't get through to Lwow, I was to return to Warsaw and give the films to you, Mr Ayres."

He thought theirs was a curious relationship. For all they had known one another for over two years, they had never addressed each other by their first names. At dinner parties and other social functions, it had always been the impersonal "you"; on more formal occasions, it had been "Miss Korwin" and "Mr Ayres".

"He implied you would know what to do with the films."

"Sure. I'll put them in the diplomatic bag."

He didn't have the authority to do that and it was by no means certain that Roy Rizzi, the Administrative Consul, would agree to any such thing, but his father had always said he could talk the hind leg off a donkey.

"Thank you." Christina stood up. "I'm sorry to have taken up so much of your time."

"Where are you going?"

"To Garrison Headquarters. I have to let Andrew know I am back in Warsaw."

She had crossed the Vistula some distance below Warsaw and had come north through the suburb of Mokotow to Lazienki Park and thence to Ujazdowskie Boulevard. She had stopped by the American Embassy first simply because it happened to be on the way to the military headquarters in Pilsudski Square.

"You can't go on," Ayres told her. "It's almost curfew time."

"I know." She smiled wearily. "Perhaps if I hurry I may get there before dark."

"I can't let you do it, there are a lot of jumpy sentries out there. Only the other evening, Colonel Lysinski, the chief aide to the mayor of Warsaw, gave a talk on the radio suggesting it might make his work a lot easier if Polish sentries did not shoot at his car when he was driving through the streets late at night. Of course he made a joke of it but you could tell he didn't think it was a laughing matter."

"You don't understand. I can't get into our house because I gave my key to Andrew."

She was exhausted and wasn't thinking straight. It was only natural that Christina should want to get in touch with her brother. After the disaster that had happened to the Modlin Army, who could say whether her father was still alive? Andrew might well be the only family she had left, but he had to make Christina see that she owed it to her brother not to take any unnecessary risks.

"The key isn't a problem," Ayres said soothingly. "I'll get you into the house and then I will contact Andrew and let him know that you are safe. We have a direct line to the mayor's office and I will ask Colonel Lysinski to get a message to him. Then we'll go and see your brother first thing tomorrow morning. At least you won't have to worry about being shot at by your own side in broad daylight. Okay?"

"Yes." The wan smile made another brief appearance. "I am most grateful to you."

"It's nothing. I wish I could invite you to stay in the embassy but we've got seventy-three refugees in the cellar and the air-raid shelter we dug in the garden is filled to overflowing too. Matter of

36

fact, most of the vice consuls have had to open up their flats and houses to people who have come in from Eastern Poland."

"You don't owe me an explanation, Mr Ayres."

"Would you do me a favour?" he asked. "Would you call me Frank?"

"Only if you will call me Christina," she said.

"I'll be only too happy to do that." Ayres took the carpetbag from her. "Shall we go?" he said.

For the past forty-eight hours, the Luftwaffe had paid particular attention to Ujazdowskie and Nowy Swiat Boulevards, the main supply route to the Polish forces in Mokotow. Despite the presence of an anti-aircraft battery in Lazienki Park, low-flying Messerschmitt Me 110s and Stuka dive bombers had tried to interdict this vital artery. They had not succeeded, although they had inflicted considerable damage in neighbouring areas. One near miss had fallen in the street behind the Korwin residence and the blast from this two hundred and fifty kilogram bomb had shattered every window at the back of the house. Effecting an entry was therefore even less of a problem than Ayres had thought it would be.

There was no power, but the gas was functioning again although the pressure was reduced. There was some tinned food in the larder and there was no shortage of water. Like every other citizen in Warsaw, Christina had obeyed the mayor's instruction at the beginning of the siege to fill every bath, washbasin and bucket, none of which she had bothered to empty before leaving the house. Satisfied that she could manage and advising her to sleep in the cellar, Ayres returned to the embassy, rang Colonel Lysinski and asked him as a special favour to inform Captain Andrew Korwin that his sister had returned to the city. He said nothing about Jan's death, believing Christina would prefer to break the news herself.

Two hours later, Lysinski rang back to say that Korwin was missing presumed killed after the Knights of Malta emergency hospital on Marcelego Nowotki had been fire-bombed that morning. There was no question of mistaken identity; Korwin had been hit in the shoulder by a sniper some three days ago and had been fully documented on admission to the hospital. In the space of seventy-two hours, Christina had lost her two brothers and was, in all probability, the only surviving member of the Korwin family in Poland. Ayres didn't know whether they were the sort of influential people the Gestapo would have on their books but he believed this was a case for playing it safe. Senior Vice Consul Roy Rizzi was the man American expatriates went to see when they needed to renew their passports or obtain a new one. Ayres figured he had better obtain a blank from him before orders came through to destroy them.

CHAPTER 4

THE EMBASSY roof had almost become a second home for Ayres who had lost count of the number of hours he had spent up there on watch. Time had ceased to have a great deal of meaning in Warsaw where one day was pretty much like any other with continuous air raids supplemented by frequent and often prolonged shellfire from medium and heavy artillery. According to his diary, this was Thursday, September the twenty-first but apart from noting when he was supposed to be on duty, he hadn't written it up since last Sunday. That had been the day when the Russians had invaded Eastern Poland and Roy Rizzi had shovelled the embassy's stock of blank passports into the incinerator.

By now, the Red Army would have shaken hands with the Wehrmacht at Brest Litovsk on the River Bug and all of Poland with the exception of the capital had probably been overrun. He did not understand what made the citizens of Warsaw fight on when the situation was so clearly hopeless. The capital was surrounded by the 3rd, 4th, 8th and 10th German Armies and there was no prospect of the siege being lifted. The Poles were on their own; apart from some patrol activity in the Saarland, the bulk of the French Army was still sitting behind the Maginot Line and the RAF seemed curiously reluctant to bomb the Third Reich with anything heavier than propaganda leaflets.

Meanwhile, the Luftwaffe enjoyed complete air supremacy over Warsaw, so much so that they were able to use Junker Ju 52 transports as bombers. He had seen the trimotor planes dodging the flak as they lumbered across the city, their crews tipping basket loads of incendiaries out of the side doors. The Garrison and civilian population had every reason to surrender, but the Poles had not been nicknamed the Madmen of Europe for nothing. Somehow, despite everything the Luftwaffe could do, life went on, the telephone continued to work, water still occasionally came out of the tap when it was turned on and the local bakery hadn't yet stopped baking bread.

Ayres heard a low buzzing noise and eyed the field telephone with some suspicion. It was an alarm system, not a means of communication, and he lifted the handset in the confident expectation that a faulty connection was causing it to short. Instead, he found he had Roy Rizzi on the line.

"Come on down, Frank."

"Why, what's up?"

"I need your help."

"Okay. Who is going to stand watch in my place?"

"No one," Rizzi said. "There isn't going to be an air raid."

"How do you know? You got a private line to Goering?"

"I can do without the wisecracks, Frank. All I want is your body down here."

"You're the boss."

Ayres swept the cloudless sky with his binoculars one more time and still failed to spot a single plane. He also became aware that the artillery had ceased firing and an unnatural kind of peace had descended on the city. Indeed, the only sign of war was a soldier in the street below cycling towards Lazienki Park, a rifle slung diagonally across his back. Puzzled to know what was going on, he came down from the roof and sought out Roy Rizzi. The senior vice consul in charge of administrative affairs was equally eager to see him.

"Let's go in here, Frank," he said and ushered Ayres into the ambassador's office, then closed the door.

"Why all the secrecy, Roy?"

"We're getting out."

"What?"

"All the neutrals. The Germans have proposed that hostilities should cease from 1400 to 1700 hours this afternoon while all foreigners with passports from neutral countries are evacuated."

"Have the Poles agreed to this?"

"Yes. The news will be given out on the radio at 1330. We are going to assemble at the Bristol Hotel; transport from there will be provided by the Polish Army."

The Bristol Hotel was at the top end of Nowy Swiat Boulevard where it merged with and became Krakowskie Avenue. Roughly one and a half miles from the American Embassy at 29 Ujazdowskie, the hotel was reasonably near the Kierbedzia Bridge, the centre one of three road bridges spanning the Vistula.

40

"There are a hundred and seventy-eight American expatriates in Warsaw," Rizzi continued. "I don't want to discover we've got a hundred and seventy-nine when we are counting heads at the Bristol Hotel."

"What are you implying?"

"Aw, come on, Frank, don't give me that horseshit. You know damn well who I am talking about. Six days ago, you persuaded me to part with a blank passport for Christina Korwin. Now, I don't mind her using it after we have gone but she is not coming with us."

"You've got to be joking. If we leave Miss Korwin behind, the Gestapo will stick her into a goddamn concentration camp."

"I can't help that."

"What do you mean, you can't help that?" Ayres said angrily. "You must know what the Nazis will do to her."

"I'm sorry, Frank, my first concern has to be the wellbeing of our own people. I don't want the Germans making life difficult for them should they catch us trying to smuggle a Polish citizen out of Warsaw. Besides, what do you suppose the 'Generals' will think if we show favouritism? The evacuation plan isn't going to work without their help, but there is no safe conduct pass for them and they know it."

The 'Generals' were five Polish girl secretaries who had worked for the embassy and consular staffs before the war. They were the coolest people under fire Ayres had seen and they had earned their nickname by refusing to leave their desks every time there was an air-raid alert. It had been their determination to carry on as usual that had led to the embassy organising their own plane spotters.

"You hear what I am saying, Frank?"

"Yeah, sure. What can I do to help?"

"I'll want you to call on those people the 'Generals' can't raise on the phone. Okay?"

"You bet."

"Then let's get with it."

Ayres felt like a high school student who had just been given a pep talk by the principal. The ground rules which Rizzi had laid down had however gone in one ear and out the other and he had absolutely no intention of observing them. When he had obtained the blank passport from Rizzi, he had never envisaged that the Germans would offer safe conduct to the citizens of

41

neutral states. At best, he had hoped the passport would afford Christina some degree of protection after Warsaw had surrendered until such time as he could come up with a better solution. Now that one had been handed to him on a plate, he didn't propose to pass it up.

By eleven fifty-five, the embassy staff had succeeded in raising all but a handful of expatriates. Of those individuals and families they had failed to contact, Ayres volunteered to get in touch with two households in the Central district, both of which happened to be near City Hall. His reason for choosing those two particular addresses was very simple. After spending two fruitless days looking for her brother, Christina Korwin had joined the Citizens Defence Force and was now working in the mayor's office.

The message from the fire chief had been the one piece of good news Christina Korwin had recorded in the log since she had reported for duty in the Incident Room that morning. The conflagration in the narrow streets of the old Jewish quarter near the Pawiak Prison had started yesterday morning after ten Heinkel bombers had dumped thousands of incendiaries on the area. Now, twenty-four hours later, the blaze had at last been extinguished. But for how long, she wondered? The Nazis had proposed that there should be a ceasefire for three hours, starting at two o'clock that afternoon, to enable the foreigners to leave the city. Once they had departed, the systematic destruction of Warsaw would continue, probably with even greater ferocity, since the Luftwaffe wouldn't have to worry about killing civilians from neutral countries.

She supposed that Frank Ayres would be leaving with all the other officials from the American Embassy and was saddened by the thought that she was unlikely ever to see him again. She had always liked Frank and now she would never be able to repay him for all the many kindnesses he had done for her. The false passport was only one example. Christina did not know what good it would do her but she was deeply touched that he should have gone to so much trouble to obtain one for her. Trouble was an understatement; Frank had jeopardised his career to get it.

Christina felt a hand on her shoulder and looked round. "You are wanted in the mayor's private office," Colonel Lysinski told her.

"Now?" she asked.

"So his secretary informed me."

Christina left the Incident Room in the basement and went upstairs to the mayor's private office on the third floor directly above the entrance to City Hall. Frank Ayres was waiting for her at the top of the staircase.

"I know what you are thinking," he said. "You're wondering what I am doing here. Right?"

"I had asked myself that question," she admitted.

"The answer is that I have come to collect you. You're getting out of Warsaw this afternoon."

"That's quite impossible, the mayor wants me."

Ayres shook his head. "That's what Colonel Lysinski was instructed to tell you. The fact is you are going to America with me."

"No, no, I can't . . ."

"You've got a job to do over there. Remember those rolls of film you gave me which I hoped to send to Washington in the diplomatic bag? Well, there hasn't been a diplomatic bag and I am taking them with me, but they will make ten times the impact if you are there to tell the American people how it really was."

"I can't run away, Frank, I can't desert my brother and all my friends . . ."

"Listen to me," he said fiercely. "You won't be running away, nor will you be deserting anyone. I hate to remind you but Andrew is dead, and you will be doing what he wanted you to do, taking those films to the States. Poland is finished and you know it . . ."

"How dare you say that . . ."

"The Germans and the Russians have swallowed the whole country; all you've got left is this island of resistance called Warsaw and that won't last much above another week. You won't help Poland by staying on to the end. The mayor wants you to go where you will do the most good; if you don't believe me, ask him yourself. Only don't be too long about it because we don't have much time."

Christina didn't think Frank would lie to her, but she wanted someone to tell her it was her duty to go and Mayor Stefan Starzynski was the very man to do that. In the absence of the central government which had fled to Lublin in the first days of the war, he more than anyone else was the embodiment of Poland. A heavyset man of immense energy, Stefan Starzynski was everywhere, cajoling, encouraging and inspiring the population. It was therefore something of a shock to discover that he had suddenly aged and grown tired as though the weight on his shoulders had become too great a burden. If a slightly tetchy Starzynski was unable to give her the unequivocal instructions she had hoped for, at least he intimated she could do valuable propaganda work for Poland in America.

Frank however did not give her time to brood on it. As soon as she emerged from the mayor's office, he grabbed an arm and led her downstairs and out into the courtyard where he had parked one of the Buicks from the embassy.

"Where are we going?" she asked.

"My place," he told her. "There are a couple of things I need to collect."

Frank had a small apartment in the Prudential skyscraper near Napoleon Square which of course she had never seen before. Despite all that had happened to her, she had the odd feeling that somehow it was wrong of her to go there without a chaperone. She needn't have worried; the flat was on the eighth floor and the lifts were out of action because there was no power, and there was nothing like climbing sixteen flights of stairs to cool anyone's ardour.

"I hope you are good with a needle," he said breathlessly.

"I can sew."

"Good." Frank beckoned her to follow him into the bedroom, then went through the wardrobe and chest of drawers selecting various items of clothing which he then dumped on the bed. "We need some labels for your clothes," he said. "Gimbel's, Sak's, Macy; you'll find a pair of nail scissors in the bathroom."

"Yes, Frank."

"It's in case the Germans decide to check the contents of your suitcase."

She thought it was yet another example of his thoroughness in all things. Before taking her passport photograph, he had decided she should change her appearance as a precaution lest the Gestapo had a picture of her that had appeared in a society magazine. He had advised her to darken her ash-blonde hair and cut it short; he had also created a whole new identity for her based on what she had been able to tell him about her cousins in New York.

"I'd like to get out of here as soon as we can," Frank said quietly. "The ceasefire doesn't start until 1400 hours and this building is a little conspicuous."

Christina knew what he meant. The Prudential was sixteen storeys high, the only skyscraper in Warsaw and a seemingly irresistible target for every artillery battery within range. Every window at the front of the building had been shattered and huge lumps of masonry had been gouged from the façade. She had thought his apartment was one of the few that hadn't been damaged but knew different when she walked into the bathroom and found the ceiling on the floor.

"Our people have been told to report to the Bristol Hotel at two p.m.," he continued when she returned to the bedroom. "However, Rizzi doesn't anticipate the convoy will be ready to move off much before three thirty, so I want you to stay out of sight and avoid the American contingent until I tell you to board the transport."

"You don't want your colleagues to see me."

"Don't be silly. It's for your own protection in case one of my fellow countrymen inadvertently betrays you."

Christina wanted to believe him because her resilience was at a low ebb, but she instinctively knew he was lying.

Roy Rizzi was thirty-eight and next to the Consul General was the senior consular official in Warsaw. He had been fourteen years in the Diplomatic and had previously served in China and Abyssinia before being posted to Poland. War was not a new experience for him, he had fought in the Argonne with the 77th (New York National Army) Division in 1918 and had been in Addis Ababa when the Italians had bombed the capital. People who had known him in those days could testify to his coolness under fire but organising the evacuation of a hundred and seventy-eight refugees from a city under siege was something else.

A tidy man with a tidy mind, it offended Rizzi's sense of orderliness when his arrangements were loused up at the last minute by a third party. He had prepared a nominal roll of the American evacuees for the German authorities in triplicate. All one hundred and seventy-eight names on the list had been carefully arranged in alphabetical order and now, just when he had finished counting heads to make sure they were all present and correct, Marta Tarnowska, one of the five 'Generals' had taken the manifest from him to add another name in ink.

"Just who the hell is this Renate Ozelski?" he demanded angrily. "Where did she come from and why haven't we heard of her before?"

"She is an American citizen from New York, Mr Rizzi, and she

45

has been staying with a Swiss couple for the past few days – or so Mr Ericson told me."

The name rang a bell with Rizzi. Looking him up on the list, he saw that Lars Ericson was a sanitation engineer under contract to the Polish Government who had arrived in Warsaw in January 1939.

"I must be getting dense in my old age, Marta. Would you mind explaining to me what Mr Ericson has to do with Miss Ozelski? Are they related by any chance?"

"No. The Swiss couple happen to live in the same apartment building as Mr Ericson. When they heard they were to be evacuated, they suggested to Miss Ozelski that she should go and see Mr Ericson and ask if he knew what was happening to the American expatriates. Mr Ericson then telephoned the embassy and gave us Miss Ozelski's details."

"But not the number of her passport."

"She didn't have the passport with her and couldn't remember it."

"I bet I can," Rizzi said darkly. "I bet Renate Ozelski is a slender twenty-one-year-old with ash-blonde hair and grey eyes."

"You know of her?" Marta asked, frowning.

"In a manner of speaking." Rizzi looked for a familiar face in the crowded hotel lobby. "You see Mr Ayres anywhere?" he asked.

"He was here only a few minutes ago. Perhaps he has gone outside to check on the transport?"

"Maybe. Where's Mr Ericson?"

Marta stood on tiptoe in an effort to spot him amongst the milling crowd, but it was like looking for a needle in a haystack. "I'm afraid I can't see him."

"He's probably hiding his face in the men's room."

"Hiding? Why would he want to do that, Mr Rizzi?"

"It's just a figure of speech, Marta. You stay here and keep an eye on things while I take a look outside."

Frank Ayres had taken him for a ride. Renate Ozelski was Christina Korwin and despite the warning he had given him, Ayres intended to smuggle her out of Poland. The young asshole was so enamoured with his Polish girlfriend that he was prepared to hazard the safety of his fellow countrymen. Well, the son of a bitch wasn't going to get away with it, or his name wasn't Roy Rizzi.

The scene outside the Bristol Hotel was even more chaotic than it was in the lobby. The Poles had assembled fifty army trucks to

46

transport some twelve hundred refugees of thirty different nationalities and the vehicles were double-banked along Krakowskie Avenue, around the Saxon Gardens and outside the Europa Hotel opposite the Bristol. And if that wasn't bad enough, the more senior diplomats had brought their official cars with them, so adding to the traffic jam. He scoured the area looking for Ayres and finally ran him to ground near the Saxon Gardens apparently practising his Polish on one of the truck drivers.

"I'd like a word with you," Rizzi said menacingly and drew him aside.

"Sure. What can I do for you, Roy?"

"Passport number W26154 – does that mean anything to you?"

"Is it the blank you gave me for Christina Korwin?"

"You know goddamn well it is, only the name inside the cover is now Renate Ozelski."

"I don't think I know the lady."

"Don't come the innocent with me, you son of a bitch. I told you this morning that I wouldn't allow you to use an American passport to smuggle Christina Korwin out of Warsaw but you went behind my back and involved this guy Ericson in the deception. I don't know what sob story you pitched him and I don't care. I'm just ordering you to find that Renate Ozelski and tell her to go back home."

"You got any idea what she looks like?" Ayres asked him.

Rizzi grabbed the younger man by the lapels of his jacket, then froze, his whole attention suddenly captured by the sound of aero engines. He craned his neck, looked up at the sky and saw four Heinkel 111s in a diamond formation. Their altitude was low enough for him to see the bomb bays open to release a cloud of confetti which floated gently to earth. One piece, measuring some five inches by seven, landed on the sidewalk behind Rizzi. Brushing him aside, Ayres bent down and picked it up.

"It's a propaganda leaflet. You want to know what it says, Roy?"

"You're the linguist," Rizzi told him.

"Yeah, well, the guy who wrote this knows about as much Polish as I do, but it says, quote: 'Poles give up. Your government has deserted you. Surrender your arms. If you do not do this at once, we will be obliged to bomb you from the air and shell you with artillery.' Unquote." Ayres laughed derisively. "Some joke, huh? I mean, what the hell else have they been doing for the last three weeks?"

Half a dozen black puffs appeared in the sky to herald the crump, crump, crump from a battery of anti-aircraft guns. Shell splinters rained down, some breaking the tiles on nearby houses, others ricocheting off the road. One large fragment punctured the roof of the Consul General's Buick and was still hot enough to set the back seat on fire.

Rizzi looked up at the sky and shook his fist. "For Chrissakes," he yelled, "what are you bastards trying to do? Break the cease-fire?"

"I don't know about that, Roy." Ayres tapped him on the shoulder and pointed to the greyish plume rising from the Buick like an Indian smoke signal. "But there's something else for you to worry about."

Rizzi followed the line of his outstretched arm and saw the fire in the back of the sedan was rapidly taking hold. "Just don't stand there," he snapped. "Do something, get a fire extinguisher."

"Yeah? Where from?"

"Try the hotel, try using some initiative."

It was unlike Ayres to be so dense and helpless and he wondered what had got into him. In the heat of the moment, Christina Korwin was only a minor irritant, one that rapidly slipped from Rizzi's mind.

Christina thought she was going to be sick. No water was getting through to the Bristol Hotel and the stench in the ladies' room was both nauseating and overpowering. Frank had told her to hide in one of the cubicles until he fetched her but she didn't know how much longer she could bear it. She glanced at her wristwatch and sighed with relief when she saw it was twenty minutes past four because it meant that in another forty minutes the truce would be over and so would the uncertainty. The ladies' room was silent; no one had come in or out for some time now and she wondered if the convoy had moved off without her. Frank wouldn't have forgotten her but he could have been injured and now be lying in a hospital somewhere. A nightmare thought that he might even be dead became a conviction and was only dispelled when she heard him calling for Renate Ozelski and remembered with a jolt that that had now become her name.

"I'm here," Christina said loudly, then unlocked the door, picked up her small suitcase and left the cubicle without regret.

"Good girl." Frank gave her an encouraging smile and a quick hug. "You've nothing to worry about, we're travelling together in the back of the eighth truck."

She nodded dumbly and clung to his arm as he walked her out of the deserted hotel lobby and on round the corner into Krakowskie Avenue. Although it was a fine sunny afternoon she felt cold, as if bleak midwinter had laid its icy fingers on her. She would never see Jan again, or Andrew, or her father and apart from memories, the only thing she had to remind her of the family she had loved was the gold locket that had belonged to her mother. She had retrieved it from the jewellery casket which Jan, on Andrew's instructions, had buried in the garden that first day of the war. It was the last thing she had done before leaving the house on Ujazdowskie Boulevard for ever, and she carried it now concealed under her slip attached to a piece of string she had tied around her waist.

"This is our vehicle," Frank said quietly.

Several willing hands reached down and helped her into the back of the eighth lorry; then Frank handed up her suitcase and climbed in after her. One of the soldiers raised the tailgate and secured it in place with two cotter pins; a few moments later, the convoy moved off and went on up Krakowskie Avenue to the palace square. The roof of the old Zamek Castle had gone but the Sigismund the Third column was still intact, which seemed to be a good omen because according to legend, Warsaw would be in danger if the sword ever slipped from his grasp.

They crossed the Vistula by the Kierbedzia Bridge and headed north through Praga. Some five and a half kilometres from the city centre, they reached the Polish outpost line and stopped.

"This is where we get out and walk," Frank told her. "The diplomats get to ride across no-man's-land in their official cars."

Even to her untutored eyes, the defence works looked slender – a few slit trenches, the odd field gun concealed in a partially demolished house, and an ineffective barbed-wire barricade across the road. Less than four hundred metres from the front line, a group of schoolchildren were kicking a football around.

The evacuees walked across the flat, open countryside and on past the wreckage of a Karas bomber reconnaissance plane of the Polish Air Force that had crashed by the roadside. As they neared the German lines, smiling soldiers in clean, field grey uniforms came forward to assist them with their baggage. A small army of press photographers and movie cameramen just happened to be on hand to record the scene for posterity as they boarded the factory-new Opel trucks. Within minutes, the convoy was heading north again into the gathering dusk.

All the bridges over the River Bug had been blown by the Poles and they crossed the obstacle by a floating pontoon. And all the time, a steady stream of ammunition trucks, troop-carrying vehicles and heavy artillery pieces were moving purposefully in the opposite direction towards Warsaw. At Nasielsk, the evacuees were driven to a bomb-damaged railway station where a long train of first- and second-class coaches was waiting for them. On the dot of 9.25 p.m., the train pulled out for Königsberg in East Prussia. Half an hour later, the conductor and escorting soldiers issued each compartment with a huge sausage, a loaf of black bread and a plate of butter.

The train stopped only once at a place called Deutsch Eylau near the East Prussian border. Although it was three o'clock in the morning, there was no blackout and the station was ablaze with lights. To everyone's astonishment, vast quantities of meat, cheese and ham had been laid on wooden trestle tables which took up the entire platform. There were also urns of steaming hot coffee but none of it went to the Polish POWs locked in the twenty freight cars on the opposite platform.

At nine a.m., one hour ahead of schedule, the train pulled into Königsberg where the evacuees were then marshalled into nationality groups and taken to various hotels in town. It was the first time Frank and Christina had had to surrender their passports and both were on tenterhooks the whole time in case the phoney disembarkation stamp which showed that Renate Ozelski had entered Poland through the port of Gydnia on the twenty-first of June 1939 was detected by the Gestapo.

On learning that a group of Swedish nationals were leaving for Riga in Latvia by train on Saturday, September the twenty-third, Ayres managed to persuade the German authorities to return their passports so that they could accompany the contingent. By a stroke of luck, he then managed to get two seats on a plane to Stockholm less than twenty-four hours after arriving in Riga. From the US Embassy in Stockholm, Ayres learned that a Norwegian boat was leaving Bergen bound for New York two days later. On Friday the twenty-eighth of September, one month after the war had begun, he and Christina sailed on the *Bergensfjord*.

* * *

Frank Ayres and Christina Korwin were married on Thursday, the eighteenth of January 1940 at the Church of Holy Cross on West 42nd Street at two thirty in the afternoon. The bride was given away by her uncle, Zygmunt Ozelski with the Misses Renate and Katerina Ozelski in attendance. On the eleventh of October the following year, Christina gave birth to a baby girl weighing six pounds five ounces whom they christened Stefanie Korwin Ayres.

1967

Tuesday, 16 May
TO
Wednesday, 31 May

CHAPTER 5

THE HOUSE in Matthew Dalton Street was known as Number 4 Central Buildings and looked as though it belonged in a Dickens' novel. Tall, narrow and hemmed in on either side by identical neighbours, it was situated at the bottom end of the cul-de-sac and was fronted by an impressive wrought-iron gate and railings that would not have disgraced Buckingham Palace. Behind the solid front door with its brass knocker lay the outer hall which had been subdivided by a hardboard partition to form the facing wall of a reception booth.

The inner hall was a much bigger and far more impressive affair with its crystal chandelier and wide spiral staircase to the fourth floor. Apart from the somewhat worn Axminster carpet which hid some of the black and white tiles on the floor, the only other item of furniture in the hall was a mahogany pedestal table. No one could explain what it was doing there, but if nothing else, it provided a suitable resting place for out-of-date copies of *Field*, *Country Life*, *Tatler* and the *Illustrated London News*. Not that any visitor was allowed to browse through the magazines; as soon as any outsider had been issued with a pass by the duty receptionist, he or she was escorted to the solitary, ancient lift and was then met at the appropriate floor by the officer they had been directed to see.

Number 4 Central Buildings was part of the Foreign Office and was occupied by the FO security department whose responsibilities included the positive vetting of all members of Her Majesty's Diplomatic Service. One office on the second floor was however set aside for use by officers from other and far more sensitive agencies to enable them to interview members of the public with a degree of anonymity. Campbell Parker was one of the interlopers who used Room 24 from time to time.

Campbell Parker owed his Scottish Christian name to his mother, Moira Campbell, a native of Edinburgh who had met his

55

father while reading Politics, Philosophy and Economics at Lady Margaret Hall, Oxford. He was thirty-four and a widower; in 1963, his wife, Sheila, had booked herself into a small hotel in Bayswater and had methodically swallowed ninety phenobarbitone tablets after her third successive miscarriage. In addition to that mental scar, he carried a physical one inflicted by a hand grenade which had shredded his back during the third battle of The Hook in Korea when he had been a National Service officer in the Duke of Wellington's Regiment. His research assistant, who knew him as well as anyone, thought he was a very nice, ordinary-looking man whose strong suits were his patience, dry sense of humour and unfailing good temper.

Ten minutes after Parker had walked into Room 24, the duty receptionist rang him to say that his visitor had arrived and was on her way up to the second floor. He went to meet her at the lift, a preconceived but confused image in his mind which had been put there by Harry Freeland, the Assistant Director who ran the Rest of the World Department and who, in turn, had also got his description second-hand from the Conservative Member of Parliament for Kensington North. Confident, articulate, intelligent and mature beyond her years were some of the adjectives the MP had used when giving a thumbnail sketch of her character. But, according to Harry Freeland, he had been less forthcoming about her physical appearance and had limited himself to tall, dark and slender. The girl who stepped out of the lift was all of these and a lot more.

"Miss Stefanie Ayres?" he said.

"Yes, and you must be Mr Parker."

She had a firm handshake and a cool way of appraising him with her eyes. As he walked her back to Room 24, it occurred to him that the American girl was also very poised and sure of herself, so much so that he was left wondering who was going to do the interviewing. Parker supposed that her manner wasn't altogether unexpected; Stefanie Ayres was a management consultant and was used to dealing with people. It was perhaps one of the reasons why her head office in New York had sent her over to their London subsidiary to do some talent spotting.

"Do please sit down," he said, and waved her to a fireside chair.

"Thank you."

"I gather you have been endeavouring to trace the whereabouts of your uncle, a Mr Andrew Korwin?"

"That's right." Stefanie Ayres opened the briefcase on her lap and took out a folder. "He was supposed to have been killed during an air raid on Warsaw in September 1939." She paused, then said, "I've made some notes which you may find useful," and placed the file on his desk.

The notes told him little more than he had already heard from Harry Freeland. Andrew Korwin had been admitted to the Knights of Malta emergency hospital on Marcelego Nowotki on the thirteenth of September, 1939 after being shot and wounded by a Fifth Columnist. Three days later, the hospital had been set on fire by incendiary bombs and he had been one of the twenty-eight victims who had died in the conflagration. But, in June 1948, her mother, Christina Ayres, had received a letter from a Herr Kurt Bender, a former NCO in the German Army, who claimed that Andrew Korwin had survived the raid and had subsequently been taken prisoner. His letter, written in a poor, semi-educated hand, and the neat translation were both on the file.

"What made Kurt Bender get in touch with your mother when he did?"

Stefanie frowned. "I thought he explained all that in his letter. Herr Bender believed his Polish captors were determined to kill him and were only prevented from doing so by my uncle. In return, he was able to save the man who had protected him when the hospital was set on fire. Herr Bender was taken prisoner himself and had to wait until the Russians released him from a forced labour camp before he could write to my mother."

It was a lucid answer but not the one he was after. "I think I may have put the question badly," he said. "What interests me is how he was able to get in touch with your mother? I accept that your uncle may have told him a great deal about the Korwin family, but how did he know your mother's married name and where she was living?"

"He didn't, he simply wrote two letters asking for information, one to the Polish Minister for the Armed Forces, the other to the US Ambassador in Warsaw. It so happened that the Counsellor for Consular Affairs was a man called Roy Rizzi who had returned on promotion to Warsaw in 1947 and he put Herr Bender in touch with my parents through the State Department."

All Bender had been able to tell them was that both he and Andrew Korwin had sustained further injuries when escaping from the fourth floor of the emergency hospital and in the ensuing confusion, they had been evacuated to different casualty reception stations. On September the twenty-eighth, some twelve days after the hospital had been reduced to a fire-blackened shell, Warsaw had surrendered and Bender had been liberated. Repatriated to Germany, he had spent four months in an army convalescent depot at Potsdam before appearing at a medical board to be permanently downgraded to rear echelon duties only. According to his account, Bender had then submitted a report to the Oberkommando des Heeres through his commanding officer respectfully drawing the attention of the Army High Command to the gallant and correct behaviour of Captain Andrew Korwin of the 9th (Carpathian) Lancers and inquiring after his wellbeing. As a result of his initiative, he subsequently learned that the Pole had been sent to Oflag IVc at Colditz in January 1940 following an unsuccessful attempt to escape from Stalag XXa at Thorn on the banks of the Vistula.

"Do you believe your uncle was alive in 1940?" he asked.

"There are records in the Bundeswehr archives to prove it, Mr Parker. They also show that my uncle was admitted to Leipzig General Hospital with pneumonia in November 1941 from where he made a successful escape six weeks later. He was never recaptured."

It was hard to believe that Korwin could have been so well-treated at that stage of the war. Although Colditz was not run by the SS, it was still a punishment camp for persistent escapers and the Poles were considered as subhuman and were treated as such. Even had the commandant wished to send Korwin to a civilian hospital, the authorities would surely have rejected his request. Maybe Bender had put in a good word for him but who was going to take any notice of a lowly Obergefreiter? And how could a mere corporal have secured such preferential treatment for a prisoner of war?

There were other questions which begged an answer. How had a Polish officer managed to escape from a hospital in a city like Leipzig which had been stiff with troops, SS, police and Gestapo agents, not to mention a hostile population? Who had helped him to make a getaway? Where had this girl's uncle gone to? Had he really made his way across the frontier of the General Government of Poland, that area of Polish territory which, before the Soviet Union was invaded, had acted as a buffer state between the Russians and the western lands restored to German nationals? Had he in fact joined the Home Army, the Armja Krajowa? Neither Frank

Ayres nor Roy Rizzi had got much joy out of Warsaw on that score.

"I see the Polish Government maintains there are no records to show that your uncle was ever a member of the Resistance."

"Well, they would say that, wouldn't they, Mr Parker? It's a Communist state; unless you were in the People's Guard or the People's Army, you were a reactionary Fascist. As far as those people in Warsaw are concerned, the Home Army was a bunch of power-hungry collaborators who would just as soon have fought the Red Army as they would the Nazis." Stefanie Ayres leaned forward, both forearms resting on her thighs, jaw set in a determined line, her eyes a steely blue. "Let's be very clear about one thing. My uncle was no traitor to his country; he took part in the Warsaw uprising in 1944 and only stopped fighting when General 'Bor' Komorowski ordered his men to lay down their arms."

"How do you know that?"

"There's a letter from one of his comrades at the back of the file."

The comrade was a Mr Tomas Rojek of 11 Cathedral Road, Lincoln who had written to Stefanie Ayres care of 'The Editor, *The Sentinel*, 6 Varley Mall, Upper Holloway'.

"What's *The Sentinel*?"

"A newspaper for Polish exiles living in Britain. It used to be a daily but now it's a weekly with a circulation well under two thousand. The proprietor is Mrs Irena Puzak. If you want to know who amongst the Polish community fought in the Home Army, she's the fountainhead of all knowledge."

Parker went back to the letter, read it through, then looked up frowning. "But Mr Rojek only refers to someone called 'Talmunt'."

"That was my uncle's codename – everybody in the Resistance had one. You read the letter again and you will see he says 'Talmunt' had been a regular officer in the 9th (Carpathian) Lancers and had been the ADC to the Garrison Commander in the first siege of Warsaw. He also writes that 'Talmunt' told him he had put his sister, Christina, and younger brother, Jan, on the last train to leave Warsaw for Lwow before the city was encircled."

It was difficult to understand why Korwin had bothered with a codename when he had been so forthcoming about himself. If Rojek had been picked up and questioned by the Gestapo, his interrogators would have had little difficulty in identifying who "Talmunt" really was. But that was beside the point. What mattered was the fact that after years of silence, Bender had written to the family again in September 1966, barely two months before Christina Ayres, née Korwin, had been knocked down and killed by a drunken driver.

"I imagine that last letter from Herr Bender must have meant a great deal to your mother?" Parker said quietly.

"It did. Right from the day my father rang Colonel Lysinski and learned that her brother was missing presumed killed after the Knights of Malta hospital had been firebombed, she had been reluctant to accept that he was dead. It almost became a bone of contention between them. I don't think my father was jealous, it was just that he hated the idea of my mother spending the rest of her life living on false hopes."

Parker suspected she was presenting the relationship between her parents in the best possible light for his benefit. Before the outbreak of war, the Korwins had had money, position and influence whereas Frank Ayres had been the only son of a bank clerk and a mere junior officer in the Consular Service. And, according to what Harry Freeland had told him, he still wasn't exactly a rising star in the State Department. Marrying Christina Korwin was the best thing that had happened to him and any suspicion that his wife sometimes hankered after her former way of life would probably make him feel insecure. It didn't matter that the war had beggared the family; he would regard the possibility that Andrew Korwin might still be alive as a potential threat to his marriage. It was, of course, a pretty big assumption but Parker didn't have to wait long for confirmation.

"My father takes a lot of convincing," she continued. "Until we received Herr Bender's letter in September last year, the most he was prepared to concede was that his brother-in-law might have been still alive in November 1941. Thereafter, he required proof."

Bender claimed that he had seen a photograph of Korwin in the *Frankfurter Allgemeine* that had been taken at a trade fair in the city. Although he hadn't been named in the caption, and his profile had only appeared in the background, Bender had recognised him immediately. The following morning, he had absented himself from the A. G. Mann (Frankfurt am Main) Gesellschaft showrooms where he was employed as a car salesman, and had gone to the trade fair to seek out Korwin, only to discover that Korwin was now calling himself Arthur Kershaw and much to Bender's surprise, he had vehemently denied they'd ever met. Roughly a fortnight later, Bender had thrown up his job and gone to England.

"Have you seen this photograph which appeared in the *Frankfurter Allgemeine?*" Parker asked.

"No."

"What about your father?"

"He was trying to obtain a print but he sort of lost heart after the accident."

Or interest, Parker thought. "But even without the picture, you still believed Herr Bender?"

"Sure. Why would he lie about it? What could he hope to gain?"

"I can't think. Do you have any idea why he came to this country?"

"I am hoping Mr Eastham will give me the answer to that question if ever I should get to see him again. He has been rather elusive of late."

Dennis Eastham was the private inquiry agent that Stefanie Ayres had hired to trace the German. Freeland hadn't been able to tell him much about the investigator other than that he was listed in the Yellow Pages under Sphinx Inquiry Agency, a two-man operation with an office in the Caledonian Road.

"Is he also looking for the mysterious Arthur Kershaw?"

A slight, mocking smile made a fleeting appearance. "I thought you people already knew that," she said. "The last time I heard from Mr Eastham, he told me that things were getting pretty hairy and there was talk of Bender being deported."

"When was this?"

"Almost three weeks ago. He rang me at home. Since then, I have neither heard from Mr Eastham nor have I been able to get in touch with him."

"Have you been to his office?"

"Yes, I went there before I saw Sir William Larborough. His partner said he was away on business and didn't know when he would be back. He was very evasive and I got the impression someone had been leaning on him."

Larborough was the Conservative Member of Parliament for Kensington North and a leading light of the Commons Select Committee on Defence. Stefanie Ayres had gone to his surgery in Kensington High Street a week ago last Saturday to ask why Mr Eastham and his partner were being harassed by the police and if there was any truth in the rumour that Kurt Bender was going to be deported. Larborough had a Grace and Favour apartment in Dolphin Square, as did Harry Freeland with whom the MP was acquainted. He was also aware that Freeland was a member of MI6, the Secret Intelligence Service, and was therefore well placed to look into a matter which appeared to have security implications. Although not a member of the Rest of the World team, Parker had been lumbered with the task because of the Polish connection and the fact that he was the most junior desk officer in the Warsaw Pact Department.

"What's this Mr Eastham like, Miss Ayres? Is he any good? I mean, do you trust him?"

"I thought he was honest. He was quite open with me, said what he could do and what he couldn't. I reckon he's in his early fifties, a cheerful little man with a kind of leathery complexion, looks as though he's spent most of his life outdoors in all sorts of weather. I would say he is pretty fit even though he does have a bad limp. He's got a steel foot."

"He what?" Parker looked up from the notes he was making.

"It seems he was involved in some awful automobile accident and they had to amputate his left foot above the ankle before they could free him from the wreckage. I really don't know if he is any good at his job, Mr Parker, but I felt sorry for him." She smiled ruefully. "I guess that's why I hired him."

"It's as good a reason as any." Parker stole a surreptitious glance at his wristwatch, saw that it was five minutes past three and realised that almost an hour had passed since he had met Stefanie Ayres at the lift without him offering her so much as a cigarette. "Can I get you a cup of tea, or coffee, or something?" he asked belatedly.

"Thank you, but I'm not thirsty."

"Right. Well then, first of all, let me assure you that wherever he is now, Kurt Bender is not under arrest. Nor, as far as I am aware, has he committed an offence that would justify his deportation. What I am going to do now is make a few inquiries concerning the whereabouts of Mr Eastham and the mysterious Arthur Kershaw. As soon as I have anything, I'll let you know."

"Thank you, Mr Parker. It's very good of you to spare me so much of your time when you obviously have more important matters to attend to."

He doubted if she meant it but it was nice of her to say so. "Do I have your phone number?" he asked.

"It's in the file," she told him, "along with my home and business addresses."

All visitors to 4 Central Buildings had to be escorted from the moment they stepped across the threshhold until they left. Such were the obvious attractions of Stefanie Ayres that for once Parker did not regard this as an irksome chore.

"Tell me something," she said as they parted company in the hall below, "why is the Foreign Office handling this inquiry?"

"Bender is a German national," Parker said blandly, "and your uncle wasn't born in this country."

"Uh huh." Her eyebrows met in what seemed to him a contrived frown. "But in this country, isn't the Home Office responsible for the police?"

"Generally speaking."

"And your Home Secretary would be the man who would sign the deportation order if it was decided to expel Kurt Bender?"

"Yes."

"Good. I just wanted to be sure of my facts," she said brightly.

Something in her voice led Parker to suspect that Stefanie Ayres didn't believe she had been dealing with a Foreign Office official. Larborough had told Harry Freeland that she was intelligent but that appeared to be something of an understatement. Parker stood there watching her retreating figure until she turned the corner at the bottom of Matthew Dalton Street, then returned to the office on the second floor and rang Freeland to ask when he would be free to see him.

The Warsaw Pact, Western Europe, Northern Ireland, the Middle East, African and Far East Desks were all self-explanatory. The Rest of the World Desk looked after the leftovers which, in practice, meant the Falkland Islands, the West Indies and South America. Since accommodation at the combined premises of 54 Broadway and 21 Queen Anne's Gate was at a premium, the Rest of the World Desk was colocated with Personnel, Training and Administration at Benbow House in Southwark, south of the river, which was an indication of its relative importance in the scheme of things.

The Assistant Director in charge was Harry Freeland, a man of vast experience who had joined the SIS from the wartime Special Operations Executive. He was forty-eight, a fraction under six feet and at thirteen stone three had gained a mere five pounds since January 1941 when he had been a raw gunner subaltern serving with a heavy anti-aircraft battery near Dundee. The passing years had however left a number of grey streaks in his dark hair.

There were other more noticeable physical characteristics; the little finger of his left hand was missing, leaving only a mutilated stump, and the sight of his right eye was impaired so that he was obliged to wear glasses at all times. The little finger had been amputated in 1944 without the benefit of an anaesthetic by an SS butcher, and he had practically lost the sight of one eye eight years later to a splinter. The splinter had been gouged out of a door frame when ex-Sturmbannführer Joachim Hausser had tried to blow him away with a Walther 7.65mm PPK automatic and had ended up under a Pacific Class locomotive for his pains.

Harry Freeland had done more time at the sharp end than anyone else in the Service. During the war, he had been sent into Occupied France on two occasions, had been tortured after capture and had then survived nine months in Flossenburg concentration camp. In May 1949 he had been ordered into Shanghai to recover an agent and had only just got out of the city himself before it fell to the People's Liberation Army. Five years later, he had been heavily involved in the defection of a Soviet agent in New York which had culminated in a minor blood bath. To the agent in the field, there was no better man to have at your side than Harry Freeland when you were in trouble; among the top strata at Broadway, informed opinion maintained it was probably Harry Freeland who had got you into trouble in the first place.

Parker had heard rumours that in the past a number of question marks had been raised against Freeland's name. Just how much credence could be given to latrine gossip was problematical, but it was a fact that throughout his career Harry had been dogged by bad luck. Too many operations had gone sour on him and because of this, there was not the slightest chance that he would ever make Deputy Director, let alone Director General of the Service. But the knowledge that he had reached his ceiling long before his fiftieth birthday didn't seem to bother him one bit. His more ambitious colleagues couldn't understand why he wasn't embittered; those who had met his wife and had got to know Jenny could see why he was a contented man.

Although not in the same department, Parker was one of his many admirers. What he particularly liked about Harry was the fact that he was a good listener.

"So what do you recommend we should do, Campbell?" Freeland asked after he had finished telling him about his interview with Stefanie Ayres.

"I'd like to run a check on Kurt Bender with the West German authorities. To be specific, I want to know if he has a criminal record."

"Why?"

"Because I am wondering if the reason he came to England was to try his hand at a little blackmail. Of course, this mysterious Arthur Kershaw could simply be a look-alike, but what if he really is Andrew Korwin? Wouldn't that mean he had something to hide, that he might even be prepared to pay a lot of money to preserve his anonymity?"

"It's a possibility, but why would he write to Ayres and tell him that he had seen his wife's long lost brother?"

"I don't know." Parker shrugged. "Maybe he was hedging his bets."

"Perhaps he was. What are you going to do about Kershaw?"

"The trade fair in Frankfurt was held in September '66. I thought I would ask our people in Bonn to obtain a list of exhibitors from this country and take it from there."

"Good."

"The thing is, I need your help, Harry, and your advice. You know my background, I've never been a field agent. I'm a desk man, always have been, from my very first overseas posting to the embassy in Warsaw."

"All right, Campbell, what sort of help do you want from me?"

"The name of a police officer with the sort of connections in the Federal Republic who can get me a rundown on Kurt Bender without having to explain why we want the information."

"That's easy." Freeland wrote something on his scratchpad, ripped off the top sheet and handed it to Parker. "Detective Chief Superintendent Iain Wirral, Metropolitan Police Special Branch. I'll give you a ring as soon as I've prepared the ground, otherwise all you will get is a very cold shoulder."

"Thanks, Harry."

"Anything else?"

"Not at the moment."

"A word of advice then. Any time you run into something that seems like an official brick wall, either back off or come to me before you go barging on. Okay?"

"You bet." Parker got up and moved towards the door, then stopped and turned about as if struck by some last minute thought.

"This fellow Eastham," he said. "Miss Ayres got the impression that someone was leaning on him and his partner."

"Really?"

"We're not trying to warn them off, are we, Harry?"

"Not as far as I know," Freeland told him. "You got any other questions, Campbell?"

"Well, I assume you've taken a good hard look at Stefanie Ayres?"

"I've talked to the State Department, our friends at Langley and her employers. They all gave her a clean bill of health."

"Does that mean she is legit?"

"She is not an impostor," Freeland said.

The naked body was thought to have been in the water for at least six weeks before it was netted ten miles offshore by a fishing smack from Whitby. A preliminary medical examination indicated that the dead man was aged between forty-five and sixty, was approximately five feet seven and weighed under eleven stone. The cause of death was not readily apparent due to the advanced state of decomposition especially to the face, hands and feet. The fact that the body had been shackled to a concrete block before it was dumped in the sea indicated that the deceased might have been murdered.

CHAPTER 6

IF IT was difficult to understand what had drawn Stefanie Ayres to the Sphinx Inquiry Agency, it was even harder to fathom why she had employed them to find Kurt Bender. The offices of the management consultancy she worked for were in Throgmorton Street, behind the Bank of England, which was hardly convenient for the Caledonian Road in King's Cross. Nor was the Sphinx Inquiry Agency anywhere near the top of the listings under Detective Agencies in the Yellow Pages, and she would have had to have gone through most of the alphabet before she came to them. Furthermore, Parker thought that one look at their office would have been enough to put most people off. Situated near the junction with Northdown Street, it was sandwiched between a shop selling girlie magazines and a newsagent displaying window cards from the likes of Miss Lash, who was seeking a position as a governess, and Mademoiselle Claudette who was available for French lessons, while farther up the road there was a bookshop run by The New Left-Wing Cooperative.

The interior of Sphinx Inquiries had been subdivided with hardboard partitions to form two interview rooms for the partners and a front office cum reception and waiting area. The latter was furnished with two armchairs of the sort usually found in a dentist's waiting room and a round coffee table with a chipped veneer and a lot of cigarette burns. To the right of the entrance, a receptionist sat behind a kneehole desk on which there was a telephone and an Underwood typewriter. The desk that morning was occupied by a blonde in her early twenties who used a lot of make-up and was busy doing her nails when Parker walked in.

"'Morning," he said. "If Mr Eastham is around, I'd like to see him please."

The blonde admired her varnished fingernails, then looked up, still holding the brush between the thumb and index finger of her right hand. "So would we," she said. "He's supposed to be up north working on a case, but you can never tell with him – comes and goes as he pleases."

"What about his partner?"

"Mr Zanti? Who shall I say wants to see him?"

"My name's Parker, I'm here on family business."

The blonde gave him a knowing smile, buzzed Zanti and repeated what he had said word for word, then invited him to go on in.

Stefanie Ayres had said that Eastham was a small man in his fifties. His partner was about fifteen years younger than that, was an inch or so taller than Parker and a lot heavier. Zanti had black curly hair which all but concealed his ears, a swarthy, pockmarked face and a moustache à la Clark Gable. He had broad shoulders, a thickening waist, large meaty hands and a smile which though it showed off his capped teeth to maximum advantage contained little warmth. He looked the sort of man who would be very successful at repossessing goods from debtors who had defaulted on their hire purchase agreements.

"Melanie tells me you have a family problem, Mr Parker," Zanti said after they had shaken hands. "Do we mean a runaway child, or what?"

"Actually, I'm here about a missing relative, a Polish national called Andrew Korwin."

"The name sounds familiar."

"It should do," Parker said, then added, "Perhaps I should explain that I represent Miss Stefanie Ayres."

The fixed smile on Zanti's face rapidly disappeared. "What are you?" he demanded truculently. "Her lawyer or something?"

"Miss Ayres came to see me yesterday afternoon because the last time your partner called her was about three weeks ago and she hasn't been able to contact him . . ."

"Listen, if Miss Ayres is dissatisfied with the service we're providing, she has only to phone me and I will do my best to answer any complaints she may have. But I'm not dealing with some busybody of a neighbour."

"Mr Eastham told her things were getting a bit hairy and talked about police harassment."

"Yeah? Well, that's the first I've heard about it. Are you sure you're not making this up?"

"Now you're being evasive," Parker said coldly, "like you were

68

with Miss Ayres when she tried to find out what was going on."

"That's it; I don't have to explain anything to you." Zanti pushed his chair back and stood up, flexing his shoulders like a prizefighter. "Now you've got just one minute to leave this office before I throw you out."

"Why don't you call Miss Ayres? It could save us both a lot of trouble. Her office number is 248–5797."

"Are you deaf or something? I just told you to get out of my office."

"If you throw me out, I'll only come back again with a solicitor or a writ or whatever it takes to put you out of business."

Zanti stood there glaring at him for some moments, apparently uncertain what to do, then suddenly coming to a decision, he sat down again, picked up the phone and dialled a seven figure number. The subscriber answered his call within a matter of seconds.

"Miss Ayres?" he grated. "This is Max Zanti. I have a man here, name of Parker, who claims he's a friend of yours."

His whole tone was that of a man who was looking for a quarrel. He didn't want to listen to what Stefanie Ayres had to say, nor did he give her much opportunity to get a word in.

"I've got no time for a client who goes behind my back," he snarled. "If you don't like the way we are handling this inquiry, you should have come to me and we could have sorted it out between us. But no, you have to involve your heavy-handed friend here who's threatening to put the law on me. Well, I don't need any aggro and we're not exactly short of work, so you had better find some other agency to look for your missing uncle. Tell you what I am going to do, I'm going to refund half the two hundred pound retainer you paid my partner and we'll call it quits."

Parker watched him slam the phone down, wondered how much of his anger was genuine and whether he was supposed to be impressed or even intimidated by the display.

"On your way, Buster. You heard what I said to the lady."

Parker decided there was nothing to be gained from provoking him any further. His whole purpose for going to the agency was to see for himself what kind of a firm Stefanie Ayres had been dealing with, and now he knew. Zanti, however, was not prepared to let it go at that. As Parker got up and moved towards the door, he came round the desk and tried to hustle him out of the room, one hand grabbing his jacket collar, the other reaching for the seat of his pants. The last person who had tried to do that to Parker had been his head of house at Dover College who had collected a broken nose for his trouble. Zanti didn't fare much better. Before he could get a firm grip, Parker backed into him, stamped on the toes of his right foot, then swung round and put the whole of his weight behind a short arm jab which caught Zanti in the pit of the stomach under the ribcage. All the breath went out of his body in a strangled gasp, then he buckled at the knees and started retching. Parker opened the door, walked out of the office and ran into Melanie on her way in.

"What's going on?" she asked.

"Your boss could do with a couple of aspirins," Parker told her. "I think he's got a pain in his stomach."

He walked out into the street, crossed over to the other pavement and went on up the Caledonian Road towards the Ace Café.

The Ace Café was not the kind of place to be mentioned in *The Good Food Guide*; the menu, which was chalked on a blackboard outside the entrance, listed meat pie and chips, egg and chips, sausage and chips, tea or coffee. With an hour and a half to go before lunch, the only customers were three old men sitting at separate tables with only their newspapers for company.

Parker asked for a cup of coffee and took it over to one of the tables by the window from where he could see the shop front of the inquiry agency. Ten minutes went by, then another ten. He toyed with his coffee which tasted like nothing on earth and chain-smoked his way through two cigarettes. He told himself he would give it another five minutes and was on the point of abandoning the vigil when Zanti suddenly left the office and walked off in the direction of the Euston Road. Parker gave him a head start before leaving the Ace Café to follow him.

Zanti turned right and limped on towards St Pancras Station. Tailing him was a bit of a nightmare; there were no shop doorways to linger in and few pedestrians about, which meant that he was obliged to hang well back to minimise the risk of being spotted. His task was made even more difficult by Zanti's erratic behaviour. After joining a bus queue, he subsequently crossed the road to spend several minutes hobbling up and down the opposite pavement before retracing his steps.

A Number 30 bus to Hackney Wick came and went, so did a Number 73 to Stoke Newington. Zanti glanced at his wristwatch, checked the timetable at the bus stop, then walked into the station yard at St Pancras and flagged down a cab. Parker watched the vehicle make a U-turn in Euston Road to head towards Marylebone and assumed from the reversal of direction that the private investigator had spotted him. Annoyed that he had come unstuck at the first hurdle, he returned to the offices of the Sphinx Inquiry Agency in the Caledonian Road.

Melanie, the blonde receptionist, was in the middle of a long conversation with a girlfriend called Ella when he walked into the office and was in no hurry to get off the phone. The weekend was still two days away but they were busy making plans; by the time she condescended to hang up, they had decided on a day out in Brighton provided the weather was fine. Money however was going to be a problem.

"Maybe I can help there," Parker said and placed five one pound notes on her desk.

"What do I have to do to earn that?" She looked up at him, lips parted and moist. "Something naughty, I bet."

"How long have you worked for Mr Zanti?"

"Old Maxi the Malteser?"

"Is that what you call him?"

"Yeah, well, he comes from Malta, don't he?"

"I wouldn't know. How long did you say you'd worked for him?"

"I didn't." Melanie picked up the five one pound notes to put them away in her handbag and suddenly found her wrist clamped in a grip of steel.

"You haven't earned it yet," Parker told her quietly.

"I've been here nine months. That do you?"

"It's a start. What's his line. I mean, what sort of cases does he usually handle?"

"Debt collecting, repossession of goods; it's our bread and butter and Maxi is mustard at it."

"What else?"

"Sometimes we get a bloke anxious to trace his runaway wife or vice versa."

"Or someone like Miss Ayres, the American girl who is trying to locate one of her Polish relatives?"

"Yeah. Can I have my wrist back now?"

"By all means." Parker released her hand. "What made her go to Mr Eastham?" he asked.

"Search me." Melanie shrugged her shoulders. "Maybe Maxi wasn't in when she called?"

"Is Eastham any good?"

"Sometimes, but he's fond of the bottle and you can't rely on him. He'll go off on a binge and you won't see him for days."

Parker moved round her desk to the window. Only the lower half of the frame was screened by a net curtain and he stood there looking out at the street.

"So why doesn't Mr Zanti get rid of him if he doesn't pull his weight?"

"Well, he's got friends, hasn't he? Contacts who will do him a favour for old times' sake. He used to be a detective sergeant or something like that."

"Do you have his home address?"

"You want a lot for your money, don't you?"

He thought about giving Melanie another couple of pounds and decided against it. Like the five pounds he had already parted with, the money would probably have to come out of his own pocket. Maurice Orde, the head of the Warsaw Pact Department and his superior officer, hadn't said anything about expenses when he had briefed him, neither had Harry Freeland to whose empire he had been temporarily attached.

"There's no harm in asking," he said. "If it's a problem, there are other ways of getting his address. I just wanted to save myself a lot of time and effort."

"He lives out at Sudbury at 23 Beechwood Avenue. It's near the tube station."

"Thanks."

"Anything else?"

"Yes. Do you have a boyfriend who owns a white Ford Cortina?"

Melanie joined him at the window. Although not fat, she was over endowed in certain areas and her forty inch bust looked ready to pop out of the white blouse she was wearing. The mini skirt was also on the tight side and hugged her plump thighs and well-developed buttocks. She had also been pretty heavy-handed with a bottle of scent that was more powerful than subtle.

"Where?" she asked.

"Across the street."

"That's not Cliff." She bumped him with her hip. "'Tisn't my husband either," she added with a throaty chuckle.

"Somehow I didn't think it was."

It was a set-up. As soon as he had left the office, Zanti had got on the phone and somebody had told him what to do. All that dithering about in the Euston Road had been a ruse to put him in the frame.

"You're not going, are you?" Melanie asked, smiling.

"Got to."

"Want me to tell Maxi you came back?"

"I think he already knows."

Parker left the office, pretended to look at the girlie magazines in the window of the shop next door while he read the reflected number plate of the Cortina and committed it to memory. Then he walked round the corner into King's Cross Station and rang Harry Freeland from a pay phone.

"You're a difficult man to get hold of, Campbell," Freeland said by way of greeting.

"I haven't been into the office this morning."

"So I gathered." Freeland paused, then said, "I've warned Wirral to expect a call from you."

"Thanks."

"Is something bothering you?"

"Whatever gave you that idea?"

"You sound a bit uptight to me, Campbell."

"It's probably the connection. You know what the GPO telephone system is like."

"Yes. See you then."

"Sure, Harry."

Parker replaced the phone and backed out of the kiosk. Freeland would probably have thought he was cursed with a hyperactive imagination had he confided in him and maybe that was the trouble. But it did seem to him that he had suddenly become popular and he was curious to know the reason why.

Eastham drove across the bridge over the Piccadilly Line at Sudbury Hill, went on past the Underground station, then dropped into third gear, tripped the indicator and turned off the Greenford Road into Beechwood Avenue. Although his Morris Minor 1000 had been fitted with a remote clutch control so that he didn't have to use his foot when changing gear, the whole of his left leg was just one big ache. Six and a half hours behind the wheel was no joke when you had a steel foot. Ordinarily, he would have broken the journey from Scarborough, but he was running short of the readies and gullible people like Stefanie Ayres didn't grow on trees. When she had come to him seven weeks ago, he had managed to squeeze two hundred out of her as a retainer; now, with a little bit of luck, he could persuade her to part with that much again and perhaps a bit more.

Eastham ran the Morris up on to the garage front of 23 Beechwood Avenue and switched off the engine. The semi-detached house was a typical example of the ribbon development that had taken place in the mid-twenties. For nine hundred pounds in those days, a builder gave you separate dining and sitting rooms, a narrow hall, kitchen scullery, pantry and adjacent garage, while upstairs there was a bathroom and lavatory plus three bedrooms, although the one over the porch was no bigger than a boxroom. The rooms at the front had bay windows, and there were mock Tudor beams set in the plaster façade of the pyramid-style roof over the porch. There was a small front garden and a ninety by forty plot of grass at the back which Eastham had been known to mow on those rare occasions when he was feeling energetic.

Alighting from the car, he flexed his left leg to ease the cramp, then retrieved his suitcase from the boot and let himself into the house. Eight days' worth of mail was lying on the doormat along with the newspapers which he had forgotten to cancel before going away. The only letter amongst the circulars and the brown envelopes from the Inland Revenue, Gas and Electricity Boards was an airmail letter from his daughter in Australia. Leaving the mail on the hall table, he carried his suitcase upstairs and went into the bedroom overlooking the back garden.

The room looked as if it had been hit by a bomb. The contents of every drawer in the wardrobe had been emptied on to the floor to form one untidy heap of vests, socks, underpants, shirts, pyjamas and ties. The burglar had also been through the only two suits he possessed, turning all the pockets inside out. When he went downstairs, he found the sitting room was in an even bigger shambles. The drop-leaf writing desk had been tipped over and was lying on its side. The pigeon holes had been crammed with old letters, receipted bills, family snapshots and bank statements but these were now scattered all over the carpet. The bookcase had also been upended and the spines of every abridged novel which the *Reader's Digest* had been sending him for the last five years had been ripped off.

Eastham didn't have to look very far to discover how the intruder had effected an entry. As a former police officer, he knew that most break-ins lacked finesse and were usually committed by young

74

tearaways who used a sledgehammer or tyre lever to force the back door. This particular villain however had merely removed a pane from the French window with a glass cutter and then reached through to unlock the door. There were other anomalies. The TV and the silver cigarette box that had been a wedding present were the only things in the house which were worth stealing but the thief had apparently ignored them. Many thieves who realised they were going to come away empty-handed would vandalise the place before they left, but this one had been comparatively restrained.

Eastham went out into the hall to phone the police but acting on an impulse, decided to call the office first. Melanie answered after several rings.

"Is Max in?" he asked.

"No, you're safe enough," Melanie told him. "I haven't seen him since he left the office just before lunch. Where have you been all this time?"

"Never you mind. Has anyone been asking for me?"

"Yes, a man called Parker. Said he was representing Miss Ayres and gave Maxi a hard time."

"What with? His mouth?"

"Something a lot more solid. He gave Max a real thumping."

"Jesus." Eastham felt his stomach lurch.

"Are you coming into the office this afternoon?" Melanie asked.

"No, I'm about to ring the police. I've been burgled."

"You've been what?"

"You heard me," Eastham said and put the phone down.

Two or three weeks ago he had told Stefanie Ayres that things were getting a bit hairy, but that had been something he had made up on the spur of the moment to hide the fact that he hadn't done anything to earn her retainer. Now it looked as though his words were going to come true and he didn't like the way the situation was developing. Feeling in need of a drink, he went into the dining room, opened the cupboard and poured himself a large double whisky from a bottle of White Horse.

Detective Chief Superintendent Iain Wirral was a big man in the true sense of the word. Born on the ninth of January, 1919 at Wednesbury in Staffordshire, he had known what it was like to be poor and deprived. When he was only six, his father had been killed in a colliery accident, four years later his mother had succumbed to diphtheria and he had ended up in an orphanage. With such a start in life, it would have been understandable if he had gone off the rails. Instead, he had left school at fourteen to become an errand boy and then a bricklayer's labourer until he was old enough to join the police. Still only a probationary constable on the outbreak of war, he had immediately volunteered for the RAF and had been accepted for aircrew training.

Sent overseas to Canada in March 1940, he had learned to fly in Ontario and had been awarded his wings some eleven months later. Considered too tall and too heavy to be a fighter pilot, he had been trained on Wellingtons at 11 Operational Training Unit and had then been posted to Linton-on-Ouse. At that stage of the war, there had been no set number of missions to an operational tour; once they had been assigned to a front line squadron, a pilot and crew went on one raid after another until they either became casualties or were posted to various training establishments to pass on their skills.

On his forty-second raid, Sergeant Pilot Wirral had been awarded the Distinguished Flying Medal for pressing home an attack on the railway marshalling yards at Hamm when his plane had been severely damaged and the starboard engine set on fire by flak. Back on operations again in 1944 after being commissioned, he was subsequently awarded the Distinguished Flying Cross for a similar exploit over Nuremberg while piloting a Lancaster.

The war over, Wirral had rejoined the police as an ordinary constable and had transferred to the Met largely because his wife was a Londoner. For two years he had pounded the beat in Shoreditch, one of the poorest and toughest areas of the city. During that time, he had qualified for promotion to sergeant and had got to know every villain and potential villain on his patch which had stood him in good stead when he had joined the CID. The successful detective was the one who had reliable sources; Wirral had a small army of informers. It was this ability to build an intelligence network which had led his superiors to suggest he was a natural for Special Branch. From then on his career had really taken off and it was generally agreed by his contemporaries that he would make Commander or even Assistant Commissioner before he retired.

But Wirral himself was modest about his achievements and never forgot who he was or where he had come from. He had a reputation for being firm but fair and it wasn't only his subordinates who shared that opinion. In his philosophy, loyalty extended in both directions and whoever had earned his retained it for keeps. He considered Harry Freeland had earned his loyalty several times over and was the reason why he had agreed to meet Parker in the bar of the Ariel Hotel way out at Heathrow.

Although a good forty minute drive from his office in Victoria, the airport hotel had a lot going for it. For one thing, the chances of encountering one of his colleagues were fairly remote to put it conservatively. For another, what airline passenger in transit would remember two men enjoying a quiet drink in the bar? Furthermore, at two thirty in the afternoon the hotel was at its quietest, which was a bonus because despite Parker's vague description of himself, he had no difficulty in recognising the younger man.

"What can I get you to drink?" Parker asked.

Wirral said he would like a pint of bitter, then sat down at a table and waited for him to return with the beer.

"I ordered a couple of ham sandwiches," Parker said. "I hope that's all right with you?"

"It'll do me very nicely." Wirral raised his glass. "Cheers," he said.

"Mud in your eye."

"Harry tells me you're after some information about a German called Kurt Bender?"

"Yes, he used to be a salesman for A. G. Mann Gesellschaft of Frankfurt." Parker reached inside his jacket, took out an envelope and passed it across the table. "I'm afraid this is all I know about him."

Wirral turned the envelope over and saw that written on the back were details of Bender's date and place of birth. "Chemnitz?"

"They call it Karl-Marx-Stadt nowadays."

"I can't get anything from the East Germans."

"I appreciate that. I just wondered if he had committed any offences in the Federal Republic."

"And? I mean, you must want more than that, otherwise why drag me all the way out here?"

Parker smiled. "You're right, I do want more. I'd like to know what his last employer thought of him, where he lived in Frankfurt, who his friends were, whether there is a wife, mother, girlfriend or anyone else who would miss him enough to make a few inquiries about his whereabouts. He came over here last September and now it's the middle of May. What's he been doing with himself for the last eight months?"

"I'll see what I can find out from the Ministry of Labour. He would certainly need a work permit and he would need to register with the National Health."

"If he's legitimate," Parker said quietly.

"Right."

"Then there is the matter of his Record of Service during World War Two . . ."

"That's something else I can't get you," Wirral said, cutting him short, then looked at the envelope again. "I see you made a note about the Sphinx Inquiry Agency. Who are they?"

"A seedy-looking private detective agency in King's Cross."

"And Dennis Eastham?"

"He is one of the partners, the other is Max Zanti. Eastham is said to be in his mid-fifties and is supposed to have been a detective sergeant. Seems he still has a number of friends in the Met who are prepared to do him the odd favour. It would be helpful to know a bit more about him."

"This is getting to be quite a shopping list."

"Sorry."

"No, it's okay. If Eastham was in the Force, his personal file will be on my desk before today's over; getting the German stuff will take a little longer."

"Thanks." Parker caught his warning glance and remained silent until the waiter who brought the ham sandwiches to their table had moved away. "You mind if I ask you a personal question?"

"Depends what it is," Wirral told him.

"How did you come to meet Harry Freeland when you're not in the same line of business?"

Special Branch had been formed in 1884 to combat the wave of terrorist bombings by the Fenians. In those days it had been known as the Special Irish Branch, but after all the dynamiters had been rounded up, the word "Irish" had been dropped from the title. Nowadays, the Branch was responsible for dissidents, subversives, anarchists, close protection and the surveillance of foreign communities. It also did a lot of legwork for MI5, the Security Service. It had nothing whatever to do with MI6, the Secret Intelligence Service.

"Our wives served together in the Women's Auxiliary Air Force during the war," Wirral said. "Afterwards, Jenny Freeland kept in touch with Kate, and Harry became a good friend."

How good was something Wirral preferred to keep to himself.

Shortly after the Freelands had returned from Quebec in 1958, Kate had become a victim of multiple sclerosis and he was never going to forget the support they had given them. But it was after Kate had died four years later that Harry had really pulled out all the stops for him. A tumour on the brain coming on top of the multiple sclerosis had pushed him to the edge and he had started drinking heavily. Fortunately, Harry had got to hear about it before his superiors did and he had whisked him up to Jenny's house in Lichfield for a long weekend and while there, he had gone down with flu which had turned to double pneumonia, which was the story Harry had given the Yard. He did not know how Harry had persuaded his own doctor to sign the necessary sick notes or how he had arranged for him to spend three weeks convalescing in the South of France at a villa owned by some friends he'd made in the French Resistance, and most remarkable of all, how he had convinced the Commander (Administration) Special Branch that the sick leave was vital if he was to regain his health, but by the time he had eventually returned to duty, he had managed to get a grip on himself.

"You know," Parker said thoughtfully, "I'm beginning to feel that I could do with a friend like Harry Freeland."

Wirral swallowed a mouthful of the ham sandwich he had started eating. "What prompted that observation?" he asked.

"A white Cortina GT, licence number EGY 996C – any chance you can tell me who it belongs to?"

"You can get it yourself. All you have to do is go to the vehicle registration department at County Hall, Westminster, give them the number and say you bumped it in a car park. They'll tell you who the car belongs to."

"I don't think so," Parker said evenly. "I believe EGY 996C is a very special number."

Chapter 7

Parker barely had time to open the combination safe and put the In and Pending trays on his desk before Maurice Orde, Head of the Warsaw Pact Department, was on the phone to ask if he could possibly spare him five minutes. It was almost as if he was asking Parker to do him an enormous favour, but that was typical of the man who was modest, unassuming and unfailingly polite. Before joining the SIS in 1940, Orde had been a Fellow of Queen's College, Oxford, where he had taught Modern French and Russian History. Even twenty-seven years later, he still gave the impression that he would be far more at home amongst the "dreaming spires" than in the somewhat gloomy offices of Broadway and Queen Anne's Gate. A high forehead, receding light brown hair and a perpetually thoughtful expression contributed towards this notion, as did the briar pipe which rarely left his mouth.

"Kind of you to drop by, Campbell," he said and waved him to a chair. "I was just wondering how things were going and what you make of this Korwin business. Do you think he is still alive?"

"I've got an open mind."

"Which is another way of saying you're not sure."

Parker smiled. "That would be an accurate summation. At the moment, I've got more questions than I have answers."

"For instance?"

"Well, if Arthur Kershaw really is Andrew Korwin, why did he pretend not to know Kurt Bender? Was it because he is unwilling to forgive the Germans for what they did to Poland and refuses to have anything to do with them? Or has he got something to hide?"

Orde inspected the bowl of his pipe to see if it had gone out, decided there was still a spark of life there and put it back into his mouth, then drew on it as if sucking through a straw. Spittle bubbled in the stem and a thin plume of blue grey smoke rose languidly into the air.

"If he hates the Germans that much," he said in a puzzled voice, "what was he doing at the Frankfurt Trade Fair?"

"Quite. Personally, I'm inclined to think Mr Kershaw has the odd skeleton he wants to keep hidden in the cupboard. It might explain why Bender followed him to this country and how he has managed to support himself for the past eight months without getting a job."

"You don't know he hasn't found employment."

"He hasn't applied for a work permit – I've checked. Of course, if he has been moonlighting on the black economy, nothing is going to show up anyway. That's why I'm more hopeful of tracing Arthur Kershaw than I am of finding Bender."

"But I assume you haven't lost interest in him, otherwise why ask our people in Bonn to obtain his military record of service?"

It was Maurice Orde's practice to be in the office a good half-hour before anyone else so that he could read the flimsy copies of all outgoing signals despatched the previous day and any incoming ones that had been received during silent hours. Although the department ran a float file, this often gave an incomplete picture because every desk officer had his own idea of what constituted "a need to know". By coming in early, Orde was able to keep a finger on the pulse of his department and had seen a copy of the signal Parker had sent just before the close of business the previous day.

"Bender is an important piece of the jigsaw," Parker said. "I'd like to know why this ex-German soldier was so concerned about one of his former enemies that three years after the war had ended, he went to enormous trouble to get in touch with the next of kin. They met in '39 and only knew each other for a few days. How come he could still remember Korwin's name in 1948? I would have forgotten it long before then."

"What else puzzles you?"

"Stefanie Ayres. I can understand her wanting to trace this long lost uncle, but why employ a deadbeat private detective to find him? In her place, I would have gone to the Home Office first and asked for their assistance. If they were unwilling or unable to help, then I might go to an inquiry agency, but it would have to be a highly reputable one."

"How long has Miss Ayres been in London?"

"A couple of months," Parker told him.

"Well, there you are, she's hardly had time to find her way around yet."

"One look at the Sphinx Inquiry Agency would be enough to deter the average person."

For some moments, Orde didn't say anything. He merely sat there mentally digesting everything he had been told, his face so passive that it was impossible to guess what he was thinking.

"How long do you see this business lasting?" he asked eventually.

"That's hard to say, it depends on how deep you and Harry Freeland want me to dig. What will it take to get the Honourable Member for Kensington North off our backs?"

"Quite a lot," Orde said dryly. "Sir William Larborough is the kind of MP who sees a Red under every bed. I'm afraid our assurances that Eastham and his partner are not being harassed by the police will carry little weight with him; he'll think it's a cover-up."

"He seems to have taken everything Miss Ayres told him on trust."

"Is she pretty?"

"Very."

"There's your answer then. Larborough has always had an eye for an attractive woman." Orde allowed something akin to a sigh to express his feelings. "I just wish I had fought my corner a little better when the Deputy Director was looking for a desk officer to assist Harry Freeland. I may have to ask the DD to release you. Things are hotting up in the Middle East; Nasser is getting more bellicose and will probably demand that the UN should withdraw its peace-keeping force in the Sinai. If Secretary General U Thant agrees to that, the Israelis will undoubtedly launch a pre-emptive strike. The Mid-East Department will be working day and night when the fighting starts. But I suspect it won't be long before we find ourselves in the same boat. The Egyptian Army has been equipped by the Eastern Bloc and who knows how the USSR will react should the war go badly for the Arabs with Brezhnev in charge."

It was one of the longest dissertations Parker had heard him utter and he was left wondering exactly what it was Orde wanted of him. He did not have to wait long to find out.

"I'd like you to wrap this Korwin affair up as soon as you can, Campbell."

"Right."

"Meantime, perhaps you would keep me informed on how things are progressing?"

Parker said he would do that and returned to his office to find that Sarah Yendell, his research assistant, had left a message for him on his desk. It said: "Someone called Iain rang but wouldn't leave a message. He said you would know where to reach him." The heavy indentations on the scratchpad were an accurate barometer of her feelings towards a man who would not give his surname and declined to leave either a message or his phone number. Lifting the receiver, he rang Wirral's office.

"It's me, Campbell Parker," he said when the Detective Chief Superintendent answered. "I got your message."

"I hope you've got a pencil handy because I don't intend to repeat this."

"I'm ready when you are," Parker told him.

"Okay. Eastham was a detective sergeant; if he hadn't been invalided out of the Force six years ago, he would have been forced to resign. His chief super wanted to send him down for a ten stretch but the Director of Public Prosecutions didn't think the evidence would stand up in court."

"What exactly had he been up to?"

"Bribery – corruption – he was on everybody's payroll. There was talk that at least one of the villains he put away was fitted up as a favour to some Baron. Anyway, as luck would have it, Eastham got smashed up in a car crash while on duty and the rescue services had to amputate his left foot before they could free him from the wreckage. He had been on the sauce and should have been done for DIC . . ."

"What's that?"

"Drunk in Charge," Wirral explained. "He got away with that one too because some people took the view he had suffered enough already. However, after a few quiet words in his ear, Eastham decided a medical discharge with a disability pension and retention of superannuation rights was infinitely preferable to what his chief super had in mind for him should he think of returning to duty."

"What did his peers think of him?"

"He wasn't without friends," Wirral admitted reluctantly.

"Would those friends still be prepared to lend him a helping hand?"

"They might, for old times' sake."

Parker thought he sounded uncomfortable, which was understandable. Evidently, Detective Sergeant Eastham was not the only police officer who had been on the take, and six years on, some of those bent coppers had moved several rungs up the ladder. East-ham had only to remind them he knew where the skeletons were buried to secure their cooperation.

"One last thing," Wirral continued. "I'm afraid I haven't had time to check out the car number you gave me."

"There's no immediate hurry."

"Well, don't worry, I'll be in touch as soon as I have the answer."

Parker thanked him for getting in touch, reiterated how grateful he was and put the phone down. He had all the proof he needed that Eastham was a liar, a thief and a cheat. He could go to Stefanie Ayres and tell her in so many words that Eastham's allegations of police harassment were pure fiction and that the best thing she could do was find herself another investigator. After what Zanti had said to her, she would have to do that anyway. Maurice Orde had asked him to finish the Korwin business as soon as possible and Wirral had given him the perfect let out. But it was the white Cortina that continued to bother him and he decided to stay with it a while longer.

The man who had changed his name to Kershaw and made a new life for himself in England was only fifty-five, but the years had not been kind to him. His face had been disfigured below the mouth when his lower jaw had been shot off and although the plastic surgeons had rebuilt it as best they could to resemble the original features, the reconstruction was not pleasing to the eye on seeing him face to face. There was no depth between the unnaturally white bottom lip and the pointed chin and like many skin grafts, the tissue looked dead. His physical disability was however more than adequately compensated for. To friends, neighbours and acquaintances, Arthur Kershaw was a cheerful and generous host as well as a highly successful businessman.

Born in Poland, he had arrived in England in 1950 by way of a displaced persons camp outside Hanover. All he had had in those days were the clothes he stood up in and a certain amount of jewellery which he had managed to smuggle out of Poland before Stalin ceased to be good old Uncle Joe and before anyone had ever heard of the Iron Curtain. He had settled in Middlesbrough, bought a run-down garage from a man who was teetering on the verge of bankruptcy and in partnership with another refugee, had gone into the second-hand car market. The secret of his success was founded on his knack of recruiting and holding on to a skilled workforce and his willingness to plough most of the profits back into the business.

The rearmament programme occasioned by the Cold War had made him prosperous. Before the new range of combat vehicles started to roll off the assembly lines at Cowley, Luton and Longbridge, a greatly expanded army, navy and air force had had to live off the fat left over from World War Two. A significant percentage of the staff cars and trucks, which had been mothballed in 1946, had needed to be reconditioned and overhauled before they could be issued to field force units. It had been Kershaw's good fortune to land one of the lucrative contracts which the Ministry of Supply were awarding to small companies willing to undertake this kind of work so that Austin, Leyland, Vauxhall and Morris were free to concentrate on the new range of vehicles. From this starting point, he had never looked back.

By 1956 Kershaw had felt confident enough to go public and branch out into electronics. With the extra capital engendered by the share issue, he had also gobbled up several other small manufacturing firms in the Northeast. Good entrepreneur though he was, Kershaw was the first to admit that the reason why he was able to stay ahead of his competitors was largely due to Victor Stevens, his partner and head of research and development.

Victor Stevens had been born Viktor Stashinsky at Zhitomir in the Ukraine in 1915. A graduate of Kiev University, he had been doing research work on the industrial and military application of lasers when the Germans had invaded the Soviet Union on the twenty-second of June 1941. A reserve lieutenant in the Signal Corps, he had been ordered to report to the communications battalion supporting General A. A. Vlasov's Corps in Lwow. It had taken him three days to reach his war station and he had arrived just in time to go straight into the bag.

Of the five million seven hundred thousand Red Army soldiers captured by the Wehrmacht between 1941 and 1945, three million three hundred thousand died in captivity, mostly of starvation. Tens of thousands had not simply died as a result of neglect; certain categories amongst whom were Jews and political commissars had been singled out for special treatment, which meant they had been executed before they reached a prisoner of war camp. As a Jewish lieutenant, Stashinsky had been doubly fortunate to survive. After being screened and segregated from the other prisoners, he had been sent to Treblinka Concentration Camp roughly sixty miles from Warsaw. That he should have escaped the gas chambers was nothing short of miraculous, but his luck hadn't ended there. At the Yalta Conference in February 1945, Churchill and Roosevelt had agreed that all Soviet citizens, civilian and military, who were in German hands would be repatriated to the USSR even if this was against their wishes. Thanks to a humane American infantry officer, Stashinsky had managed to avoid this fate.

Like Arthur Kershaw, he had married a local English girl; like his partner, he too now lived in a large detached house in Redcar on the coast some nine miles from Middlesbrough. For the last three years, he had been working on a laser rangefinder and target acquisition sight in association with Elta Industrielle of Boulogne-Billancourt. The system had passed the trial and development stage and was ready to go into production, but all they had so far was one potential buyer. Stevens wanted to go ahead but Kershaw had definite reservations.

"I don't know, Victor." Kershaw pursed his lips. "The Ministry of Defence has been evaluating the sight and have expressed an interest. They've slapped a Top Secret classification on our data so we could find ourselves in serious trouble if we supplied the system to a country which is not a member of NATO."

"The MOD isn't going to buy it while Harold Wilson is Prime Minister. He has already scrapped the TSR2 and sunk the Fleet Air Arm and now he's talking about reducing the army."

"Even so . . ."

"And the French aren't really in NATO."

"You're splitting hairs," Kershaw told him.

"An initial order for six hundred lasers at fifty thousand pounds each. Think about it, Arthur."

"I am."

"Where is the harm in talking to Hassan al Jaifi?"

"Where are you thinking of meeting him and when?"

"Seville, next Monday. Marcel Verlhac of Elta Industrielle has made all the necessary arrangements. I'll fly out on Saturday with Jean, leave her to sunbathe on the beach at Malaga while we negotiate with Hassan al Jaifi, then return to England the following Saturday. You can tell everyone at work that I felt in need of a short holiday."

Kershaw thought about it, then nodded. "You're right," he said, "there's no harm in talking to him."

It was, Stevens told him, the best afternoon's work he had done in a long, long time.

Freeland turned off Maida Vale into Hall Road and went on up the hill to Cleveland House where, some years ago, Wirral had taken a long lease on one of the prewar four-bedroom luxury flats. Even when Kate had been alive, the apartment had been a trifle large for three but once his only daughter had married at the age of nineteen, there had been plenty of busybodies ready to tell him that he was silly to go on living there alone. But Cleveland House was handy for the office and lay within easy walking distance of Lord's Cricket Ground where he continued to spend many a happy hour during the season. However, the most attractive feature of the flat was the fact that the low rent had been fixed at the end of the war and had hardly been allowed to keep pace with inflation since then. Wirral knew that if he did move out before he retired from the Metropolitan Police, he would end up paying a king's ransom for a shoebox.

Freeland parked the Rover in a vacant slot on the forecourt and took the lift up to the fourth floor. While individual tenants were responsible for the upkeep of their own apartments, the landlord was charged with the maintenance and redecoration of the communal areas. Perhaps not surprisingly in view of the uneconomic rents, the lobby, the lift and the corridor on the fourth floor hadn't received a lick of paint in years. Furthermore, one of the fluorescent ceiling lights in the passageway was defective and it wasn't easy to find the small bell button in the prevailing gloom. Inside the apartment it was a different story; shortly before she had died, Kate Wirral had had the whole place redecorated and five years later, the paintwork and wallpaper were still in pristine condition.

"What can I get you to drink?" Wirral asked.

"A whisky?"

"With ice, soda, ginger ale, water or neat?"

"I'll take it with a splash of soda."

"Me too." Wirral poured two doubles from the bottle of Haig on the sideboard and added a squirt from the siphon. "Here's to you, Harry."

"And you, old friend," Freeland said and raised his glass.

"How are Jenny and the children?"

"They're fine. You want to come home with me this weekend and see for yourself?"

"Ask me another time and I'll probably take you up on it."
Wirral paused, then said, "I met your protégé yesterday
afternoon."

"Parker isn't one of my chicks, Iain, he's merely a supernumer-
ary on loan."

"But you know him?"

"Only by reputation. His head of department thinks he could
make it to the top but there is a long haul ahead of him and there's
many a slip between the cup and the lip."

"And maybe he is about to take a fall."

"I knew there was some reason why you asked me here this
evening," Freeland said.

"He asked me to run a check on a white Ford Cortina. As soon
as he told me the licence number was EGY 996C I knew who it
belonged to."

"MI5, Five, Box, the Security Service or whatever it is they are
calling themselves this week."

"Plumb right."

Freeland wasn't surprised. The idea that the Security Service
was somehow involved had been germinating before Parker had
seen the white Cortina. What was it he had said to him the day
before yesterday when they had been talking about Eastham and
his partner? – "We're not trying to warn them off, are we, Harry?"

"So what have you told him, Iain?" he asked.

"Nothing. I gave Parker some of the other information he had
asked for and said I hadn't had time to check the vehicle number
with County Hall. Now, I don't want to know what's going on,
Harry, but as an old friend, I think you should watch your step."

"I'll try to bear that in mind. What blanket cover are they using
for the Cortina?"

"The Medway Trading Group."

"Are they listed?"

Wirral nodded. "The company appears in Kelly's Trade Directory, but that won't fool Parker; he already suspects the vehicle is
one of a fleet run by the Security Service."

"Interesting. I wonder how he twigged it?"

"I didn't ask him." Wirral frowned. "Why would they want to
keep an eye on your legman?"

"Damned if I know."

But maybe if he really put his mind to it, he could think of a
reason. Parker had fought in Korea with the Duke of Wellington's

Regiment at the Third Battle of The Hook. Had he been among the missing, some of whom had later turned up in a POW camp after that desperate hand-to-hand encounter? No, the Dukes hadn't been overrun, they had stood their ground and the number who had actually been captured hadn't run into double figures. Besides, after George Blake had been arrested in April '61, anyone who had been a prisoner in Communist hands had been put under the microscope. It had happened to him, for God's sake, even though that guerrilla unit of the People's Liberation Army in Shanghai had only held him for a little over twenty-four hours. If Parker had been captured by the Chinese, MI5 would have put him through the mangle years ago.

Some other reason perhaps? Something to do with his late wife, Sheila, who had committed suicide four years ago? Who knows what sort of character defects might have surfaced after that traumatic event? Had the KGB got wind of some aberration which they were now trying to exploit? Freeland took a good nip from the tumbler of whisky and mulled it over. Hell, if he had come to the notice of MI5, they would have lost no time in advising the Director General of the SIS. And if Parker wasn't kosher, why would the Deputy Director attach him to his department? When a man was suspect, he was kept in isolation and denied all access to classified information. The last thing you did was give him an opportunity to do further mischief. No, what they had here was a typical cock-up. The Security Service wasn't interested in Parker; they had their eyes on the private detective agency. Parker had gone there with this preconceived idea that Eastham had been targeted and had then spotted the Ford Cortina.

"A penny for them."

"What?" Freeland looked up.

"A penny for your thoughts."

"They're not worth it."

"If you say so, Harry. Can I get you another drink?"

"Provided it's very weak. This time it had better be a splash of whisky with a lot of soda."

Wirral removed the empty glass from his hand, took it over to the sideboard and added half a tot from the bottle of Haig, then drowned it with the siphon. "You're very preoccupied for someone who claims his thoughts aren't worth a penny."

Freeland smiled. "I'm just trying to remember who I know in 'A' Branch," he said.

"A" Branch of MI5 provided technical and physical surveillance. Before he went home to Lichfield for the weekend, he was going to find out just what it was they found so interesting about Eastham and his partner.

A postmortem carried out on the corpse forty-eight hours after it had been recovered from the sea off Whitby had still failed to establish the cause of death. All the pathologist had been able to establish was that the widespread destruction of the face and hands had been caused by sulphuric acid administered after death. It was also evident that at some time in the distant past, the deceased had suffered injuries to the back and legs, perhaps resulting from an industrial accident. Hazarding a guess, the pathologist thought the damage was not inconsistent with the effects of a firedamp explosion.

CHAPTER 8

BONN WAS one hour ahead of British Summer Time which meant that the list of exhibitors at the Frankfurt Trade Fair would have started to come through at 0800 hours. By the time Parker arrived at Broadway and Queen Anne's Gate half an hour later, details of the one hundred and seventeenth and last exhibitor were already on record. The information had been transmitted over the BRUIN link, the codename for a secure facsimile network which had been developed by the Royal Signals Research Establishment at Malvern and had just come into service with the SIS. Collecting the print-out from the fax room, he returned to his office to study it at length. In fact, a casual glance at the amount of information under each listing was enough to indicate that someone would have to do a lot of spadework to identify which company had been represented by Mr Arthur Kershaw. That someone was, of course, going to be his research assistant, Sarah Yendell. Stepping next door, Parker asked her to come into his office.

Sarah Yendell was an "army brat" and the eldest of three sisters. Born in Cairo towards the end of the war, she had spent her childhood in such diverse places as the Canal Zone, Cyprus, Singapore and Malaya. At the age of ten, she had been packed off to prep school and then on to Cheltenham Ladies College, and had only seen her parents on two occasions during the whole three years they had been stationed in Washington. Boarding school had given her poise and confidence as well as all the social graces. Not that her family background had exactly been a handicap. Daddy had been the last General Officer Commanding British Troops Austria and had retired from the army in 1960, three years after being promoted to Lieutenant General with the customary knighthood. Mummy of course was an Abercrombie and a Lady in her own right, though naturally Sarah was too well-bred to mention this. She merely assumed it was known to everyone who mattered.

91

And it had been known to the right people at the right time. Where academic standards were concerned, entrants to the SIS from the universities were required to have at least an upper second. Sarah Yendell had left Cheltenham with three very indifferent 'A' Levels and had gone to secretarial college where she had mastered shorthand and typing up to the minimum standard demanded by the Civil Service. However, an uncle on her mother's side of the family had secured a position for her in a merchant bank, the first of a number of similar appointments. Eventually, one of the General's friends had mentioned her name to the Deputy Director of the SIS at a time when there were insufficient applicants to fill all the purely administrative appointments. A research assistant was a somewhat over-inflated title for a secretary, but Sarah Yendell had a lot more aptitude for beavering after information than she had for typing.

"I've got a job for you," Parker said and gave her the print-out. "I'm looking for a Mr Arthur Kershaw who attended the Frankfurt Trade Fair last September. I don't know which company he represented but it has to be one on that list."

"How many are we talking about, Campbell?"

"One hundred and seventeen."

Her eyebrows rose in disbelief. "My God, checking that little lot is going to take for ever."

"You can forget all the German companies."

"Thank heavens for that . . ."

"Have you got a Biro handy?" Parker asked her.

He wondered why he bothered to ask because it never occurred to Sarah to bring a notepad and pen with her unless she knew he wanted to dictate a memo.

Quite unperturbed, she gave him a warm smile and with a polite "May I?" helped herself to one of the pens in the holder on his desk, then reversed the print-out to write on the back.

"All right," he said, "after you have whittled down the companies, look up those that are left in *Kelly's Trade Directory* and note where they are located. Next step is to go to the Registry of Business Names which comes under the Board of Trade and ask them to look out the Memorandum and Articles of Association pertaining to each limited liability company. That should give you the names of the directors. There are separate registrars for Scotland and Northern Ireland but they operate from the same address in City Road." Parker broke off, opened the bottom drawer of his desk and took out a copy of *Whitaker's Almanac* of 1966 which he had flagged up. "You'll find all the details you need in here under the section dealing with Government and Public Offices."

"I could have found out all that myself, Campbell," Sarah chided him.

Ignoring the interruption, he went on, "Should you manage to identify Kershaw, get out the telephone directories covering the area where his company is based and see if you can find his home address. If it appears he is ex-directory, ring Enquiries, give the supervisor the Merlin codeword for the week and ask her for it."

"That had occurred to me, Campbell," Sarah said with a deep sigh.

"Sorry."

"You're forgiven," she told him with another warm smile.

Sarah frequently gave the impression that her mind was predominantly occupied with the next forthcoming event on her social calendar, with the result that he was inclined to treat her like a vacuous debutante lacking brains and initiative. For the umpteenth time he made a mental note to remind himself that, given an interesting job to do, she was quite capable and had far more common sense than a lot of the university graduates who had joined the SIS at the same time.

"Is there anything else I should know?" Sarah asked.

"Well, if what I have been told is correct, Kershaw is a former Polish national who changed his name by deed poll when he applied for British citizenship. The Home Office claims there is no such animal; you're going to help me prove otherwise."

"Does this take priority over everything else?"

"Yes. Maurice wants me to wrap this thing up as soon as possible."

"Good. If there's one thing I hate, it's typing the monthly Intelligence digest on the war potential of the Polish economy."

"I have news for you," Parker told her, "If there is one thing I hate doing, it's compiling the damned report."

Sarah laughed, a little dutifully, he thought. It was one of the many tricks she used to flatter the male ego, though he couldn't understand why she thought it necessary. She was a remarkably attractive twenty-four-year-old brunette who looked elegant no matter what she was wearing. She had only to crook a finger to have any young man she fancied dancing attendance on her.

Parker opened the combination safe, removed the overflowing In and Pending trays and placed them on his desk, then started to tackle the backlog he should have cleared the day before. Twenty minutes into the chore, Detective Chief Superintendent Iain Wirral rang him to say that according to his source, Kurt Bender was as clean as a whistle except for two convictions for speeding. That was the official line; off the record, it seemed his employers, A. G. Mann of Frankfurt were none too happy about him. From what Wirral could gather, Bender, in common with several other sales-men, was believed to have been working a neat little racket on the trade-in value of the Mercedes, Opels, Volkswagens or Audis which he accepted in part exchange for new models. If the buyer appeared gullible, the salesman would find something wrong with the car and offer the lowest possible trade-in price, then sweeten the client's disappointment with the promise that whatever A. G. Mann got above his offer when the vehicle was sold to a second-hand dealer, would be passed on after deduction of the usual expenses. The usual expenses covered a multitude of sins and the dealer the sales-man used was not recognised by A. G. Mann. After the victim of the confidence trick had been paid just enough to placate him, the mark-up on the real trade-in value was split between the salesman and the used car dealer. That was the theory, but A. G. Mann had never been able to prove that Bender was involved.

Not a lot more was known about him. His first wife had been killed in an air raid on Kassel in October 1943, his second, whom he had married less than a year after being released from a Russian prisoner of war camp, had divorced him on the grounds of adultery in 1962. In September 1966, Bender had been living in an expensive rented apartment near the city centre with the latest in a long line of live-in girlfriends. He had given his employer one week's notice and had left Frankfurt after collecting his severance pay and draw-ing every pfennig from his current account with the Dresden Bank. He had not left a forwarding address and none of his neighbours had heard from him. The only person to have missed Bender was his landlord to whom he now owed six months' rent.

"What about the girlfriend?" Parker asked.

"She packed her bags and walked out of the apartment a week after Bender departed." There was a faint rustling noise as Wirral flipped through some papers on his desk. "I thought I had seen her name somewhere in this cable," he explained. "Anyway, I'll drop it into the post together with the translation and perhaps you can find it."

"Thanks."

"Don't mention it," Wirral said and hung up.

Parker replaced the phone and went back to the files, satisfied that if Bender wasn't a crook, he was certainly a man who was prepared to sail close to the wind. The phone barely gave him time to move a couple of files from the In to the Out tray before it started ringing again. Lifting the receiver, he found he had Harry Freeland on the line wanting to know if he was planning to pop round to Benbow House before the weekend was upon them.

"I wasn't thinking of doing so," Parker told him. "Is it important?"

"Not particularly. Have you got a secure phone in your office?"

"Yes, but the system is only good for Confidential and below. If it's Secret and above, I'll have to go to another phone and call you back."

"It's not that earth-shattering," Freeland said and asked him to switch to secure means.

Parker depressed the button on the cradle, checked the black box on the floor by the desk to make sure it was showing a green light, then confirmed that his end of the line was guarded.

"Remember the Cortina you were asking about?" Freeland continued. "Well, you were right, it does belong to our friends, but you are not in the frame. They are interested in that little bookshop up the road from the agency. You know the place I mean?"

"Yes." The bookshop was painted a deep red in keeping with the political leanings of the cooperative who ran it. The window was crowded with photographs of Ernesto 'Che' Guevara, Chairman Mao and Ho Chi Minh. Parker could not remember seeing too many books on display, but there were a large number of pamphlets, all of which looked as though they had been processed on an office duplicator. "What's their interest, Harry, or is it a state secret?"

"Only so far as Joe Public is concerned. For your ears, they are watching the shop to see who goes in and out. Student agitators, left-wing activists, anarchists, Trotskyists – it's a hotbed of subversion."

"Where have I heard that one before?"

"Hey, come on, we've had sit-ins, peace rallies and antiwar demos at every university. Back in March, the London School of Economics was closed more times than it was open. You've got students protesting against the syllabus because it is designed to perpetuate the capitalist system and in the next breath they're howling that the grants aren't big enough to live on and they are being victimised. Who do you suppose is organising all this unrest?"

"I had Wirral on the phone earlier this morning, he didn't even mention the Cortina. Why do you suppose that was?"

"Because he told me about it last night, because he is my friend, not yours, Campbell, and he wasn't about to go out on a limb for a man he only met for the first time yesterday. This morning I rang our friends to find out what was going on, and now you know."

"This was another close friend you spoke to, was it, Harry?"

"He's an acquaintance, but I've known him a long time."

His tone was cool and Parker frowned, wondering how he was going to put the next question without seeming offensive. "Forgive me for asking this," he said hesitantly, "but do you believe this acquaintance?"

"I've no reason not to – yet."

Parker thought the pause was significant and the nearest thing to an admission from Freeland that he had his doubts. "Thanks, Harry," he said.

"That's all right; stay in touch, okay?"

Parker said he would be sure to do that and replaced the phone. He pulled another file from the tray and found himself reading a report from the Military Attaché in Warsaw who had been interviewed in London during his mid-tour leave. The MA and his staff assistant, a warrant officer in the Intelligence Corps, had suffered the usual kind of harassment when they had visited Gdansk and Poznan. Their car had been deliberately forced off the road a couple of times, someone had slashed the offside front tyre the first night they were away from Warsaw and the hotel manager in Gdansk had claimed that he did not have a room for them even though he had confirmed their booking in advance.

The KGB narks had also tried to intimidate the MA's wife. They had broken into the apartment while she was out, emptied the chest of drawers on to the floor and urinated all over her underwear. She had also received obscene telephone calls whenever her husband was away. The aim of these tactics was so to demoralise her that she asked to be sent home, and if she had gone back, her husband would have had to be relieved because the SIS didn't like the idea of a married man remaining in post after his wife had left him. The army had very few Polish linguists and in all probability the appointment would have gone unmanned for some months before a replacement could be found. Had that happened, the KGB would have won a victory. The lady, however, had been made of steel. She had stopped the obscene telephone calls by telling her tormentor that he wasn't a big enough man to satisfy her and had then put an ear-splitting whistle to her lips and blasted him off the line.

Parker initialled the report and tossed it into the Out tray. Although this did not make much of an impression on the pile which still awaited his attention, he persuaded himself that it was more important to deal with the Korwin inquiry. He picked up the phone, rang the Sphinx Inquiry Agency and learned from Melanie that she had no idea where Eastham was or when they were likely to see him. After telling her that he would call back later, Parker unlocked the centre drawer of his desk, took out the folder Stefanie Ayres had given him and looked up the telephone number of *The Sentinel*. Unlike the recalcitrant private detective, Mrs Irena Puzak, the proprietor, was in the office and indicated she would be happy to meet him.

The registered offices of *The Sentinel* were in Varley Mall off Junction Road, which was a five-minute walk from Archway Underground station on the Northern Line. It was as far removed from Fleet Street as it was possible to get. Instead of a modern office block, *The Sentinel* made do with two rooms on the ground floor of a terraced house across the hall from Appleton, Crabtree and Forsythe, Solicitors and Commissioners for Oaths. There was no sign of any reporters when Parker arrived and the staff in the front office appeared to consist of a very elderly clerk and an audiotypist. The proprietor and editor occupied the room at the back of the house overlooking a very neglected garden.

Mrs Irena Puzak was a tall, well-groomed woman whom Parker assumed was in her mid-sixties until he discovered later with something of a shock that she was in fact almost ten years older than he had thought. What was immediately apparent was that she spoke English as though it had been her native tongue from birth.

"It's very good of you to see me at such short notice," Parker told her.

"Not at all. Do sit down."

The only spare chair in the room was an old ladderback with loose joints that creaked alarmingly when he sat on it.

"I'm from the Home Office," he began.

97

"So you said on the phone, Mr Parker."

Something in her voice told him that she was not altogether convinced. For all her twinkling eyes and friendly smile, Irena Puzak had a cutting edge and was ready to whittle him down to size.

"I actually work in the Immigration and Nationality Department," he continued. "A couple of days ago, a young American woman called Stefanie Ayres came to see me about her Polish uncle, Andrew Korwin. I believe she came to you first?" Parker waited expectantly but it seemed Mrs Puzak was keeping her own counsel. Mildly disappointed, he picked up the official briefcase which he had brought with him and balancing it on his knees, dug out the key and unlocked it, then undid the straps. He took out the file, extracted a letter and passed it to Irena Puzak. "That's a photocopy of the one Mr Tomas Rojek of 11 Cathedral Close in Lincoln wrote to Stefanie Ayres. It was addressed to her care of The Editor, *The Sentinel*, 6 Varley Mall, Upper Holloway."

"I remember her now, Mr Parker," she said with a smile.

"I'm glad you do because I find myself in an awkward position. You see, Mr Korwin is living in this country but he has changed his name by deed poll to Arthur Kershaw and I don't know why he doesn't wish to meet his niece. Now, although it's my job to protect his privacy, I can't help wondering why he should want to avoid his only kith and kin," Parker allowed a few moments for the implication to sink in, then said, "unless of course he isn't who he claims to be."

He had no reason to say that. In fact, it was by no means certain that Arthur Kershaw and Andrew Korwin were the same man but now he had Mrs Puzak's undivided attention.

"What is it you want to know, Mr Parker?" she asked.

"I'd like to know what story Miss Ayres gave you when she asked for your help. I'd also like to know how she found you?"

Irena Puzak found it easier to answer the second question first. Stefanie Ayres had joined a Polish Circle in Ealing soon after arriving in England in order to improve her second language and in the hope that she might meet someone who could put her in touch with her uncle. It was at the Circle that she first heard of *The Sentinel* and what the newspaper did to help Polish exiles living in the UK.

"How good is her Polish?" Parker asked.

"Miss Ayres has a fairly good vocabulary and can hold a conversation, but she is hardly fluent. Her mother taught her the language when she was a child but she has rarely spoken it since then or had any need to."

Irena Puzak had obviously tested the American girl's story to satisfy herself that Stefanie Ayres was genuine before she had agreed to help her through the columns of *The Sentinel*. To do that, she had had to know where Andrew Korwin had been during the war and what he had done.

"So Miss Ayres told you her uncle had been the ADC to the Garrison Commander of Warsaw when the city was besieged in 1939, had escaped from Colditz after being taken prisoner, and fought in the '44 uprising?"

"She was a good deal more informative than that, Mr Parker, otherwise we would not have been able to use our card index link system."

"How does that work?"

"You had better talk to my husband; he can explain it better than I can."

Mr Puzak, it transpired, was the very elderly clerk Parker had seen in the outer office, except that he described himself as the advertising manager. There were, however, precious few retailers who used *The Sentinel* and most of the income was derived from the announcements of births, marriages and deaths. The card index was more of a service to the community than a profit-making enterprise. Every Polish serviceman known to Puzak was allocated a card which recorded his name, date and place of birth, military history and any pseudonyms used in the Resistance. The card was also cross-referenced to show the names of men who had served in the same sub-unit. The one for Andrew Korwin looked as though it had only recently been added to the index.

"When did you make his card out, Mr Puzak?"

"When Miss Ayres came to see us – that would be about a month ago."

"She knew that 'Talmunt' was the codename her uncle used when he was in the Home Army?"

"Not immediately. We sat down and went through the index together until she saw a name she recognised."

"That would be Tomas Rojek, the man who subsequently wrote to her from Lincoln?"

"I don't remember, let's have a look."

Puzak went through the Rs until he found the card he wanted, then showed it to Parker. "Talmunt" was just one of several codenames which appeared on Rojek's card. It was different only in that the letters NT had appeared alongside it together with a question mark, both of which had now been struck out and replaced with a reference to Andrew Korwin.

"Does NT mean what I think it does?" he asked.

Puzak nodded. "We used the English abbreviation for 'No Trace' because it is shorter than the Polish equivalent."

There was no need to ask what the question mark had stood for. At some stage, the codename itself had been in doubt until Stefanie Ayres had linked it to her uncle.

"Is there anything else you would like to know, Mr Parker?"

"I don't think so, you've both been very helpful."

"What are you going to tell Mr Kershaw when you find him?"

In the little time Parker had known her, he had learned that Irena Puzak could be relied upon to ask the awkward question.

"I am going to let Miss Ayres have his address. I shall tell him that if he doesn't want to see his niece, he will have to ring her up himself and explain why. Of course I shan't mention *The Sentinel* but if there is a happy family reunion, I will make sure he is aware of the debt he owes you both."

Parker wondered if he should offer to make a donation to the newspaper but on reflection, decided they might be offended. Instead, he thanked them again, said his Minister would undoubtedly be writing to say how much the Home Office appreciated their cooperation, and managed to leave before Mrs Puzak could think of any more difficult questions.

Stefanie Ayres had led him to believe it had been Tomas Rojek who had made the connection between "Talmunt" and her uncle; now it was beginning to look as if it had been the other way round. It was the sort of stroke you could only pull once with people like the Puzaks and he couldn't think what she had hoped to gain from it, but it did call into question again just why she had hired Dennis Eastham.

Parker turned into Junction Road, found a pay phone near the Underground station that was still in working order and called the Sphinx Inquiry Agency in time to catch Melanie before she went to lunch. Eastham, she told him, had rung up to say he was feeling off colour and would not be coming into the office until Monday. She assumed he was calling from home but wasn't prepared to bet on it and offered to find out, which was the last thing he wanted. Melanie said she quite understood and wished him the best of luck.

Replacing the phone, he fed two coppers into the coin box and called Sarah Yendell to let her know where he was going. Then he walked into Archway station, caught a train to Leicester Square and changed on to the Piccadilly Line. If Eastham was at home, he really would be feeling off colour by the time he was finished with him.

CHAPTER 9

PARKER SPENT ten minutes looking for an off-licence after leaving Sudbury Hill Station, then made his way to Beechwood Avenue clutching a bottle of whisky in a brown paper bag. There was a beat-up Morris Minor 1000 on the garage front of Number 23, a bottle of milk on the doorstep and the curtains were drawn in the bay window upstairs. Mr Eastham, it seemed, was enjoying a long lie-in. Parker tried the doorbell, found to his surprise that it was still in working order, and kept his finger on the button until Eastham finally answered it.

The private investigator was unshaven, had bloodshot eyes and looked like death warmed over. He was wearing a food-stained dressing gown over striped pyjamas and a pair of carpet slippers with rubber soles and felt uppers. The big toe on his one good foot peeped through a hole that was frayed at the edges.

"I'm not interested," he said, "whatever it is you're selling."

"I'm doing a survey on behalf of Distillers," Parker said and showed him the bottle of malt whisky. "We'd like to know what you think of this blend?"

Eastham blinked several times, stepped backwards involuntarily and almost fell over. Before he had a chance to object, Parker stepped into the hall and closed the door with his heel. "Watch yourself," he said and reached out to steady the older man.

"Who said you could come in?"

"Didn't you?" Parker smiled. "Where do you keep the glasses?"

Eastham hesitated, eyed the malt whisky, then shrugged. "The sideboard in the dining room."

He opened a door on his left, lurched into what was the front room and crouched in front of an ornate, machine-carved reproduction of a nineteenth-century dresser complete with brass fittings. Mumbling under his breath, he opened the nearer of the two cupboards and took out a couple of dusty tumblers.

"Better give them a quick wipe over," he muttered, and went through to the kitchen.

Yesterday's dirty plates were still in the sink awaiting his attention, and the tea towel he used to wipe the glasses looked as though it had doubled for a floor cloth at some time or other. Parker grabbed one of the tumblers from him before he had a chance to contaminate it further and poured himself a single tot. When it came to Eastham, he was much more heavy-handed.

"You want some water?" he asked.

"As long as you don't drown it," Eastham told him and gave a phlegmy laugh.

"Maybe you had better do it yourself."

Eastham was happy to oblige and passed the glass under the tap just long enough to catch a few drips. "Cheers," he said. "The first today."

"Me too."

"This is good stuff, Mr . . . ? What did you say your name was?"

"How does Ayres grab you?"

Slowly, comprehension dawned and his eyes glittered. "You're a relative of Stefanie Ayres?" Eastham pulled out a chair and sat down heavily at the kitchen table. "I've just about had a bellyful of that young woman."

"Been giving you a hard time, has she?"

"I wish I'd never heard of her. She's got a lot of bad enemies, that one."

Parker joined him at the kitchen table and topped up his glass. "Like who for instance?" he asked.

"Like the toerags who did their best to fit me up. But you already know about that, don't you?"

"We've had a number of complaints from Miss Ayres alleging that you were being harassed by the police, but she was unable to give any examples. That's why I am here."

"Yeah?" Eastham stared at him with bloodshot eyes. "Who's we?"

"The Home Office. Actually, my name is Parker."

"Sounds familiar." It was some moments before the penny dropped but Eastham finally made the connection. "Melanie told me about you," he spluttered. "You're the bloke who gave Max a real thumping."

"And now I'm giving you a bottle of whisky. It must be your lucky day."

"What other surprises have you got up your sleeve? Another packet of 'C'?"

"What?"

"You know what I'm talking about," Eastham said irritably. "'C', Charlie, Coke, Cocaine. Day before yesterday, I come home from Scarborough to find the house has been burgled. You've never seen such a mess; the bedroom upstairs looked as if it had been hit by a bomb, but that was nothing compared to what had been done to the sitting room. The writing desk had been upended, so had the bookcase, and there's sixty novels lying on the floor with their spines ripped off. It didn't look right, I mean the guy did a neat job on the French window with a glass-cutter and then he doesn't bother with the TV and the silver cigarette box which are the only things worth taking. Wouldn't you be suspicious?"

"I don't know, I've never been burgled. I haven't been a policeman either."

"Yeah, well, you get to know what to look for if you've been on the Force. At first I was going to ring the local nick but then I had second thoughts. See, it suddenly occurred to me that maybe I was being warned off."

Eastham looked hung over and his speech was still slurred but he seemed more in control of himself than he had been earlier on even though he had put away the equivalent of three doubles.

"You got a cigarette on you?"

Parker took out a packet of Embassy. "Help yourself," he said, then lit it for him.

"Thanks." Eastham leaned back in his chair, blew a smoke ring towards the ceiling. "Where was I?"

"You suspected you were being warned off."

"Too bloody right. I went through the house with a fine toothcomb and found this waterproof packet hidden in the lavatory cistern upstairs. Soon as I tasted it, I knew it was coke."

"So what are you going to do about it?"

"Not a lot. Stefanie Ayres can have her money back and find herself another investigator. I know when I'm beat; next time they'll plant more than one packet and the Drug Squad will be knocking on the door before I can flush the stuff down the pan."

Parker looked round the room, noted the cracks in the ceiling and the poor state of the paintwork and could see how it would look to the police. Hard up, ex-detective sergeant with underworld contacts becomes drug trafficker; he doubted if a jury would have much difficulty in believing the allegation.

"It's a pity Stefanie Ayres chose your agency to help her."

"I bloody well regret it, I'll tell you that."

Parker remembered what Stefanie Ayres had said of Eastham. According to her, he was a cheerful little man with a leathery complexion who looked as though he had spent most of his life outdoors. She had thought he was honest and he was supposed to have been very open with her regarding what he could and could not do. She had also said Eastham had appeared to be pretty fit which indicated that either Stefanie Ayres didn't know what she was talking about or he had rapidly gone downhill since she had hired him.

"Do you have any idea why Miss Ayres chose your agency?" he asked.

Eastham took his time about answering the question. Leaving the table, he collected a saucer from the rack on the draining board and used it as an ashtray to stub out his cigarette. "She tried two other agencies before she came to us. They didn't want to have anything to do with her after she told them what a hard time the Home Office was giving her. Anyway, she talks to this lawyer, Kevin Mullinder, who lives in the same block of flats in Chelsea and he put her on to us."

"Why?"

"Mullinder's not your usual lawyer. He's a very trendy left-winger, represents the sort of political activists who are always having a go at the police. I've done the odd job for him, like finding out whether Special Branch has got a phone tap on one of his clients. I've still got a few friends in the right places."

Parker believed him if only because Wirral had said much the same thing.

"When did Miss Ayres first get in touch with you?"

"Six, perhaps seven weeks ago." Eastham shrugged. "Who's counting?"

"She is. The last time Miss Ayres heard from you, she was led to believe that things were getting a bit hairy. That was towards the end of April and now we're well into May."

"That was just an excuse. I mean, I hadn't done a stroke and I had to say something to get her off my back."

"So you told her you were being harassed by the police and

that the Home Office was thinking of deporting Kurt Bender?"

"Right." Eastham grinned. "Of course I was stretching it a bit but she put the idea in my head in the first place."

Parker nodded. In a slightly different context, she had done the same thing with Tomas Rojek by suggesting that the Resistance leader known as "Talmunt" was her uncle. Was she simply being over eager in her anxiety to enlist all the help she could get, or was she devious enough to have some ulterior purpose in mind? Then he reminded himself that Stefanie Ayres was only twenty-five going on twenty-six and thought he ought to give her the benefit of the doubt.

"But now it's no longer an excuse and you really are being harassed?"

"Yeah." The smile rapidly disappeared from Eastham's face.

"What were you doing up in Scarborough?"

"Looking for Kurt Bender. I heard he'd got a job up there."

One of Eastham's friends had a friend in the Immigration Service who was seconded to the head office at Lunar House in Croydon. Told that Bender had arrived at Heathrow sometime between September and October '66 on a flight from Frankfurt, the friend of a friend had gone through all the landing cards completed by aliens during that period and had found Bender's. Asked to state the reason for his visit, the German had written, "Extended holiday, staying with friends in Scarborough" and had given a fictitious address.

"Of course, Immigration didn't know it was a fictitious address until another of my mates rang the local police."

"And then what happened?"

"We didn't tell Immigration, if that's what you're on about." Eastham helped himself to another cigarette from the packet on the table. "But I went up there and nosed around a bit. I discovered that Bender had got himself a job as a barman at Bay View Hotel on the North Parade. It's one of those places that caters for old age pensioners and is open all year round. He'd also found himself a divorcée who was happy to give him free board and lodging."

"You saw Bender?"

"No, he left Scarborough at the beginning of April, packed his gear and cleared out. Told his girlfriend he'd had enough of England and was going home."

"What's the name of this girlfriend?"

"Linda something or other. North? Northover? Norris?" East-ham snapped his fingers. "Yeah, that's her. Linda Norris has a semi up by the station."

"Well, I guess that's it," Parker said and pushed his chair back.

"You leaving?"

"Yes, I've got what I came for."

"What about the whisky?"

"What's left is yours, keep it for services rendered." Parker retrieved the packet of Embassy cigarettes and moved towards the door. "Don't bother to see me out," he said.

"I wasn't planning to," Eastham told him.

Harry Freeland had spent his formative years in Lichfield, and so had Jenny, but it had taken a war to bring them together. They had met at Ringway near Manchester when SOE, the Special Operations Executive, had sent him on a parachute course and Jenny had been the WAAF sergeant in charge of the girls who packed the 'chutes. It had been the hint of a Staffordshire accent that had prompted Free-land to ask her where she came from and had learned to his amaze-ment that they had grown up in the same town. His parents had owned Warley Farm Preparatory School while Jenny's father, Sid-ney Vail, had been the biggest estate agent in town with other offices in nearby Tamworth, Cannock and Walsall.

The firm was still known as Vail and Son, but the son had died twenty-six years ago, killed in a flying accident during the war when he had ploughed the Airspeed Oxford he had been piloting into the Brecon Beacons. And Sidney Vail was now living out his days in a nursing home, a senile old man who was for ever confusing his daughter with the matron.

The business continued in being because Jenny was determined to hand it on to their children one day. Fifteen-year-old Veronica had already made up her mind that she wanted to be a vet and so far, neither Mark, who was approaching seventeen, nor James, who was just thirteen, had shown much interest. Between them, they provided three very good reasons why the business should be sold to the highest bidder, yet whenever Freeland raised the question, Jenny always maintained it was early days yet and they might change their minds. So one stayed in Lichfield while the other worked in London, both of them counting the hours to the next weekend from the moment he left the house early on Monday morning till he stepped off the train the following Friday.

The only difference between this Friday and the previous one was that he had managed to slip away from the office immediately after lunch. Grabbing his bag from the overhead rack as the train began to slow down, Freeland moved out into the corridor and closed the sliding door behind him. As always, he was the first passenger on to the platform when it stopped, the first across the footbridge, and the first to pass through the booking hall into the station yard where Jenny was waiting for him with the Ford Zephyr. By the time the next passenger arrived, they had already embraced warmly.

Dumping his bag in the boot, Freeland walked round the near-side of the car and got in. "What sort of week have you had?" he said, and found himself asking the question in unison with Jenny.

"You first, Harry."

"I'd sooner hear your news."

"Well, I've had a good week. Things have been a little slack in Cannock but the Tamworth and Walsall offices have each sold two houses, and I've moved three."

"Terrific."

"So tell me what you've been doing."

"I've got a new man working for me, at least I think he is."

"Do I know him?"

"His name is Campbell Parker. I think you met him once at a drinks party when you were up in London."

"I can't say I remember him. What's the matter, don't you two see eye to eye?"

"It isn't Parker who's the problem." In the time it took Jenny to drive from the Trent Valley station to their house in Whittington Village three miles away, Freeland told her about Scarborough, Stefanie Ayres, Andrew Korwin and why he had a feeling that Parker could find himself in trouble. "I was hoping he would phone before I left the office."

"But he didn't?"

"No. Maybe I had better ring him from home."

"How old is he, Harry?"

"Campbell is thirty-four," he told her.

"Then he's old enough to look out for himself," Jenny said firmly.

Parker left the Underground station at St James's Park and dodging the traffic, hared across the street to 54 Broadway. The threatening clouds which had started gathering while he was waiting for a train at Sudbury Hill had culminated in a violent thunderstorm accompanied by torrential rain. His only protection against the weather was a copy of the *Evening News* which was next to useless as an umbrella and practically disintegrated before he'd gone twenty yards. Hair dripping water, his suit looking as though it had just come out of the washtub, he flashed his ID card at the War Department policeman on duty inside the door and went on up to his office.

He took off his jacket, draped it around a coat hanger and hooked it on to the hatstand, then removed his tie and stripped off his shirt.

"Is that the end of the show, Campbell?" Sarah asked him from the adjoining doorway. "Or is there more to come?"

"Don't want to frighten the children," he said with a laugh.

"You're absolutely soaked. Have you got a towel?"

"But of course, I never leave home without one."

"You can borrow mine." Sarah disappeared into the adjoining room only to return a few moments later with a pink face towel hardly bigger than a pocket handkerchief. "I'm afraid it's a bit on the small side," she said, stating the obvious.

"Never mind, it's the thought that counts."

"I've just had another one. How about a cup of coffee?"

"You're a life-saver."

Parker wiped his face and hair and found the diminutive towel was then wetter than the rest of him. Giving it up as a bad job, he retrieved the crumpled packet of Embassy cigarettes from his jacket pocket, selected a dry one and lit it. He walked over to the window and stood there looking down at the street and the first of the office workers, umbrellas raised as they scurried towards the station, homeward bound for the weekend. Forked lightning cleaved the dark sky with a loud crackle and was followed two, perhaps three seconds later by a deafening roll of thunder.

"Sounds as if the storm is right overhead," Sarah said behind him.

"Does it frighten you?" he asked.

"I once saw a man killed by lightning. It was about six years ago and I was following Pa round this golf course outside Münster. The storm broke when we were at the farthest point from the clubhouse and this man who was struck was on the same fairway as us and had just reached the green. I've been scared of thunderstorms ever since."

"No wonder."

"Yes, well, you had better get this down you while it's still hot."
Sarah placed a mug of coffee on the desk and held a bottle of whisky
aloft with her free hand. "Left over from the office Christmas
party," she said. "How do you want it? In your Nescafé or straight
from the bottle?"

"In the coffee I think."

Parker remembered the "gunfire" brews Brigade had authorised
in Korea when the temperature dropped to ten below zero and the
tea had been laced with so much treacle-thick rum that you could
have stood a spoon up in it. The Nescafé didn't quite measure up
to that standard but it was strong enough to put some fire in his
belly.

"Give yourself a medal," he told her, "you really have saved my
bacon."

"Actually, I think I may deserve one. I've found your Mr
Kershaw."

"That was bloody quick."

"I took a few short cuts."

There had been twenty-one British exhibitors at the Frankfurt
Trade Fair. Major companies like Ferranti, Plessy, Leyland and
the Rootes Group had accounted for four-fifths of this total and she
had simply telephoned each one in turn and asked for the names
of the salesmen who had represented them at the Fair. After
whittling the list down to single figures, she had backed a hunch
and ignored companies based in Scotland and Northern Ireland.
Then, instead of phoning the Registrar of Business Names, she had
gone there in person and persuaded the appropriate department
head to drop everything and dig out the Memorandum and Articles
of Association for the remaining firms.

"He was very helpful, Campbell."

"I bet he was."

When Sarah Yendell chose to turn it on, even the most hide-
bound of civil servants would have to be made of ice not to want
to please her. And the staff of the London Search Room in City
Road had certainly gone out of their way to help her by working
through their lunch hour.

"Kershaw is chairman and managing director of Ward Tandy
Engineering PLC. Their head office is in Middlesbrough." Sarah
picked up a slip of paper she had previously tucked under the
blotter on his desk and waved it at him. "This is the works number
and his home address. You were right, Kershaw is ex-directory."

Parker stubbed out his cigarette. "Did you have any trouble with Directory Enquiries?"

"The duty supervisor didn't recognise the codeword and I had to tell her where to find 'Larkspur'. After that, we got along famously."

"Congratulations, you did a terrific job."

"Thanks. What size collar do you take, Campbell?"

"What?"

"Your shirt is never going to dry off before you leave and you ought to change out of those trousers. If I hurry, I can get to Marks and Spencer before they close."

"It's still raining," he protested.

"I've got an umbrella and I can take a cab." Sarah reached for the millboard on his desk, folded the top sheet and tore it in half to use as a shopping list, then helped herself to one of the Biros in the pen holder. "Now, come on, stop protesting and give me your measurements."

"I take a fifteen and a half collar, a thirty-three inside leg and a thirty-four waist."

"Good. Don't go away, I shan't be long."

Parker turned to fetch his wallet from the inside pocket of his jacket but she had disappeared into her office to collect an umbrella before he could extract some money. He heard Sarah call out to say he could pay her back later.

He looked at the slip of paper she had left on the desk and saw that Kershaw's address was Seaview, 9 Beach Road, Redcar. Whether he was Andrew Korwin or not didn't matter; he was the man who had represented his company at the Frankfurt Fair, the man whom Kurt Bender had claimed he'd recognised. If, after she had met him, Stefanie Ayres subsequently maintained that he was a stranger and not the long lost uncle she had been looking for, then that would be her tough luck. At the end of the day, there was a rational explanation for everything. So far as Bender was concerned, he had either been mistaken or else he had made up the story, hoping the family would pay through the nose for the bogus information he proposed to give them. Eastham was a crook, a drunk and such a proven liar that his allegations of police harassment needed to be taken with a very large pinch of salt. That only left the white Cortina and he could understand why MI5 would want to keep an eye on the New Left-Wing Bookshop in the Caledonian Road.

If they gave Kershaw's address to Stefanie Ayres, Harry could assure Sir William Larborough that there was no cover-up and the MP could start looking for another stick to beat the Security Service with. Lifting the phone, Parker rang Benbow House only to be told that Freeland had left the office shortly after lunch to spend the weekend in Lichfield. Did he leave it until Monday or did he use his initiative and wrap the whole thing up before calling it a day? In another ten minutes, offices around Whitehall would begin to empty and if he left it any longer, the only person on duty would be the resident clerk who would be reluctant to give him a decision. Lifting the phone again, Parker rang the Home Office, which was responsible for all internal affairs ranging from the administration of justice to the granting of licences for scientific experiments on animals. He started with an inspector in the Immigration Service, was referred to an assistant secretary in the Police Department and then ended up with an unfortunate principal in the Nationality Branch in Croydon whose name was Harold Nash.

"I'm calling from extension 0028 at Broadway," Parker said, then put the phone down and waited for him to ring back. When he did so five minutes later, he did not sound best pleased.

"I don't know why you people have to be so damned secretive," Nash complained. "Why can't you give your name like anyone else?"

"Because we're shy," Parker said. "Like Mr Arthur Kershaw."

"Who's he?"

"A former Polish national called Andrew Korwin who changed his name by deed poll when he applied for British citizenship. His home address is Seaview, 9 Beach Road, Redcar."

"Why are you telling me all this?"

"Mr Kershaw has a niece who is anxious to get in touch with him and I propose to give her his phone number and home address. The time is now seventeen minutes past five, Mr Nash. If I don't hear from you by seven o'clock, I'm going to assume the Home Office has no objection."

"Do we know when Kershaw applied for naturalisation?"

"I believe it was shortly after the war. Start in '45 and you won't go wrong."

"What you are asking for can't be done in five minutes. Can't this wait until Monday?"

"No, I'm afraid it can't," Parker said and hung up.

Sarah Yendell returned at five minutes to six with a pair of dark grey trousers and a blue and white striped shirt which she had bought at Marks and Spencer in Oxford Street. In a hurry to bath and change before the latest boyfriend arrived at the flat in Lancaster Gate to take her out to dinner, she told Parker to pay her on Monday and left the office. At a quarter to seven, Nash rang back to say the Home Office knew of no reason why Mr Kershaw's home address should be withheld from his next of kin.

Parker made two more phone calls, the first to Arthur Kershaw in Redcar, using the cover name of Humphries. Most people in his position would have been incredulous, then astounded, but Kershaw took the news calmly and had obviously been forewarned. Parker was inclined to believe him when he said he had been led to believe that his sister had died in a concentration camp and didn't know he had a niece, let alone that she was working in London. He also believed Kershaw was overjoyed at the prospect of meeting Stefanie Ayres and couldn't wait to get in touch with his niece, provided the ground was prepared and she knew what to expect.

Stefanie Ayres sounded equally thrilled with the news when he rang her at home, but it didn't stop her asking the odd pertinent question, particularly with regard to Kurt Bender.

"Your uncle met him at the Trade Fair all right," Parker told her. "He just didn't want to have anything to do with him. He may do business with the Germans but as he said himself, that doesn't mean he has to socialise with them. Besides, he was convinced that he was the only surviving member of the family and he believed Bender was looking for a hand-out and would lie his head off to get it."

"I guess that explains a lot."

"There's something else you should be aware of. I don't know if you have a photograph of your uncle, but if you have, you'll find he's changed a good deal. It seems he was very badly wounded in the '44 uprising and the surgeons had to rebuild the lower half of his face as best they could."

There was a long silence from her. Had he not been able to hear her breathing, Parker would have assumed they had been cut off.

"Your uncle asked me to break the news," he continued. "I'm sorry if I put it badly."

"You mustn't blame yourself, Mr Parker. I'm just a little shook up, that's all."

"I can imagine."

"Look, I should really have said this before but I can't thank you enough for all you've done for me."

"It's nothing – but you could do me a small favour."

"Name it."

"Let me know how you get on with your uncle."

Parker was ninety-nine point nine per cent certain that Arthur Kershaw was genuine but there was nothing like being totally sure.

CHAPTER 10

THE POLICE report on Kurt Bender which Wirral had promised to send on, was waiting for Parker when he arrived at the office on Monday morning. So was a copy of Bender's record of service in the army. It had been transmitted over the BRUIN facsimile link from the SIS cell in the British Embassy, Bonn. Although both documents had been overtaken by events, Parker skimmed through the stuff from the Bundeswehr archives purely out of interest. Bender had started the war as an Obergefreiter and had finished it as a Feldwebel, the equivalent of being promoted from corporal to sergeant in six years which was hardly a meteoric career.

It wasn't that he had lacked the necessary qualities to go any higher; medically downgraded after being wounded in the first few days of the war, he had been declared unfit for combat duties and the opportunities for advancement had therefore been denied him. By January 1944, however, the Wehrmacht had been reduced to scraping the bottom of the barrel to make good the losses incurred on the Eastern Front. Consequently, Bender had been plucked out of the Infantry School at Potsdam where he had spent almost four years training potential NCOs. But instead of being sent to a regular formation, he had been assigned to a partisan unit of Ukrainian separatists who were fighting both the Red Army and the Polish Underground to establish control over the Pripet Marshes and borderlands. Six months later, the Wehrmacht had been forced to withdraw behind the Vistula and the partisan unit had ceased to exist.

In common with survivors from other shattered units, Bender had been scooped up and fed into the replacement system to be drafted to the 184th Infantry Division. Ultimately, he had finished the war in the so-called Fortress Breslau and had marched into captivity with the rest of the garrison when the city had surrendered to the Red Army on the 6th of May 1945.

The final enclosure in his personal dossier was the transcript of a statement he had made to investigators from the Allied War Crimes Commission following his release from a Soviet POW camp in 1948. The statement concerned the activities of SS Standartenführer Gerhardt Terboven whose death squads had murdered thousands of Russian Jews in the Ukraine. Bender had been a witness for the prosecution but as far as Parker could make out, he couldn't have been particularly important as an informant because he had not been called to give evidence at the trial. Someone with a small hand had written a lengthy postscript which the fax transmission had rendered practically illegible. Any inclination to decipher it vanished when Stefanie Ayres phoned.

"I'm not interrupting anything, am I?" she asked.

"Absolutely not," Parker assured her, then asked how she had got on with the Kershaws.

"I had a swell time, they couldn't have been nicer to me. I caught a train to Middlesbrough on Saturday morning because Uncle Andrew said it was quicker than going direct to Redcar and he met me at the station. Like you warned me, his face had been pretty badly smashed up but I could see the family likeness as soon as he introduced himself. I had planned to return the same day but Aunt Nancy insisted I stay the night."

It wasn't Mr and Mrs Arthur Kershaw but Uncle Andrew and Aunt Nancy. Stefanie Ayres had met the missing branch of her family and had unhesitatingly accepted them.

"I'm glad everything worked out the way you hoped it would," he said.

"It's only thanks to you, Campbell." She paused, then said, "You don't mind me calling you Campbell, do you?"

"Not in the least."

"Well, now that we've established that, are you free to have dinner with me tonight?"

"Well . . ."

"Tell you what, if you've made other plans for this evening, choose whatever day suits you."

"I'm not doing anything this evening," he said, "and I would be delighted to have dinner with you."

"Great. See you my place, seven thirty. Okay?"

"It's a date," Parker said and waited for Stefanie to hang up before he put the phone down.

The Korwin Inquiry was over – finished. Stefanie Ayres had dispelled the last percentage point of a lingering doubt about Mr Arthur Kershaw. Lifting the phone again, he rang Benbow House to give Harry Freeland the news, only to be informed that he wasn't in yet. Thwarted, he picked up the facsimile record of Bender's army service together with the police report and went next door. Sarah Yendell was engaged in her least favourite occupation and was hitting the old-fashioned Underwood at a lethargic rate of under fifteen words a minute.

"I'm typing the monthly Intelligence Digest on the war potential of the Polish economy," she said without looking up. "Fascinating stuff."

"I can tell you're enthralled."

Sarah stopped typing long enough to open her handbag and extract five one pound notes. "By the way," she said, "this is what I owe you. The cheque you put on my desk before I arrived this morning was over the top. The shirt and trousers came to just over fifteen pounds."

"How much over?"

"Four and six."

Parker tucked the documents under one arm while he went through his pockets and found the requisite amount in loose change. "Now we're all square," he said, then placed the fax transmission on her desk. "These papers refer to Herr Kurt Bender, a former NCO in the Wehrmacht. They are largely irrelevant now but I think we'll hang on to them for a bit."

"You want me to open a temporary branch memorandum for them?"

"Yes. Put a 'bring forward' date on the cover and we'll look at them again in three months' time with a view to putting it through the shredder."

"Right."

"But finish the Intelligence Digest first."

Her sigh was eloquent and said it all. Returning to his office, he called Benbow House once more and this time had better luck. In a few brief sentences he told Freeland what had happened.

"And the Home Office didn't object when you informed them you proposed to give Kershaw's address to Stefanie Ayres?"

"No. In fact, Nash said they knew of no reason why it should be withheld from the next of kin."

"Who's Nash?"

"A principal in the Nationality Branch of the Immigration Service."

"A principal?" Freeland clucked his tongue. "I hope you gave him time to contact his superiors, Campbell?"

"Two hours all but seventeen minutes."

"That should have been long enough."

There was another brief pause, then Freeland thanked him for all he had done and said it ought to make Larborough happy. It certainly made Maurice Orde happy when Parker informed him a few minutes later that the Korwin/Kershaw affair had been satisfactorily resolved.

Malaga to Seville was a hundred and thirty-four miles by road. In a Fiat 600, which was the only self-drive vehicle Victor Stevens had been able to hire in the resort, it seemed almost twice as far. By the time he had taken several wrong turnings in Seville and got himself thoroughly lost in the narrow streets of the old Jewish quarter of the Barrio de Santa Cruz, he was in a foul temper. His ill humour evaporated, however, the moment he found the luxurious Hotel Alfonso XII near the Alcazar Gardens. From the desk clerk, he learned that Marcel Verlhac of Elta Industrielle, Boulogne Billancourt, had arrived on Sunday and was in Room 525. Ten minutes after checking in, Stevens called his room number and arranged to meet him in the bar.

Marcel Verlhac was forty-four, resembled Olivier Todd and like the handsome French political journalist, looked as though he belonged in front of a TV camera. He was sauve, urbane, amusing, and with some justification liked to claim that he never forgot a face or a name. He spoke fluent English and had a brain quicker than an IBM computer when it came to calculating the finer points of a deal. He was a tough negotiator but one who also knew how to attract business. It was he who had interested Hassan al Jaifi in the laser tank sight developed jointly by Elta Industrielle and Ward Tandy Engineering PLC which had a thirty-seven per cent stake in the French company.

Stevens ordered a Campari and soda for Verlhac and a gin and tonic for himself, then made small talk while the waiter fetched their drinks from the bar. Although the Frenchman had travelled alone, Stevens had brought his wife, Jean, with him to Spain but had left her behind in Malaga.

"I thought we would combine business with pleasure."

"Very sensible," Verlhac murmured.

"Well, at least in Malaga you can be sure of the weather. We've been having a very indifferent summer at home." Stevens broke off to pay for their drinks and tip the waiter, then resumed on a different tack. "How long do you think our business with Hassan al Jaifi will take?" he asked.

"It's hard to say, but I doubt if it will be concluded this evening."

"Damn."

"Hassan will send a chauffeur-driven car to run us out to his villa near the Hacienda de la Soledad . . ."

"Whereabouts is that?" Stevens interrupted him.

"About twelve kilometres from here on the road to Mairena del Alcar. He bought the villa as a present for his latest girlfriend, Ingrid something or other. Comes from Stockholm."

Hassan al Jaifi was one of the international playboys whose exploits were monotonously reported in the tabloids. Born in Manama, Bahrain, he was said to be distantly related to the ruling family, but Stevens suspected that this was one of those unattributable reports put about for the benefit of gossip columnists. The only certain thing was that his father had probably been the most successful merchant in the Persian Gulf. From America and Europe, he imported and sold Buicks, Cadillacs, Bentleys, Rolls Royces, Mercedes, television sets, deepfreezes, dishwashers, bone china, in fact every luxury item known to man and woman. His emporiums were to be found wherever there was oil and money in Shajar, Dubai, Qatar, Abu Dhabi and Kuwait.

Rumour had it that on Hassan al Jaifi's twenty-first birthday, the old man had given him one million pounds sterling. Whatever the truth of the matter, he had certainly provided his son with the necessary financial backing to start him on his way to becoming the biggest independent arms broker in the world. Unlike his father who continued to live in a modest house midway between the British Bank of the Middle East and the souk, Hassan al Jaifi flitted between his house near Kusnachi on the shores of the Zürichsee, the villa at Cap d'Antibes, the mews house in London's Belgravia and the apartment he maintained on Park Avenue in New York.

"Will this Ingrid woman be present tonight?" Stevens asked.

"Undoubtedly. Hassan enjoys a party and it's possible a girl will be provided for you and me. We will get down to business after dinner when the ladies are no longer with us."

"I'm glad to hear it."

"Initially, he may only wish to place an order for ten lasers."

"Ten?" Stevens echoed, then raised his voice in anger. "We were led to believe he wanted six hundred."

"That's correct," Verlhac said, unperturbed. "The initial order is for trial and evaluation purposes. We are, after all, talking about thirty million pounds or four hundred and five million francs. It's only natural therefore that Hassan should wish to assure himself that our laser sight is everything we claim it is."

"Hasn't he seen the data we produced?"

"But of course. Unfortunately he is aware that certain unscrupulous arms manufacturers are not above doctoring the performance evaluation tables in order to impress a potential buyer. Now, if we could show him a visual record of the laser sight in use under battle conditions, it might be a different story."

The laser sight had been evaluated by the Trials and Development Wing at the Royal Armoured Corps Depot at Bovington where it had been fitted to the 105mm main armament of a Centurion tank. In live firing tests carried out at Lulworth Cove, it had totally eclipsed the standard coaxially mounted .50 calibre spotting rifle even at ranges under a thousand yards. The laser-equipped gunner had obtained a first round hit as soon as he had aligned the sight with the target. Forced to rely on a spotting rifle, his opposite number had frequently had to fire at least three rounds before seeing the white splash made by a .50 calibre bullet as it struck the target. To make the kill, he then had to switch to the main armament. In simple terms, the laser-aided gun could engage and knock out two, possibly three enemy tanks in the time it took the current weapons system to neutralise one. All this was recorded on film; unfortunately it had been classified Top Secret and had been retained by the Ministry of Defence, as had the scientific papers and technical drawings produced by Ward Tandy Engineering. The French Government had imposed no such restrictions on Elta Industrielle, which was why Marcel Verlhac had been able to give Hassan a photocopy of the data. What he had not been able to give him was a copy of the film.

"I don't like it," Stevens complained. "Why can't we get your army interested in the project?"

"Oh, I think they would like to see it on their AMX 30 main battle tank and they would probably get it too if the laser was a hundred per cent French designed and manufactured. But it isn't, and your country, my friend, is not a member of the Common Market."

And never would be while de Gaulle was President of France. Not that Stevens believed it would have made a jot of difference if the UK had been inside the Common Market. The French liked to go their own way while pretending they were good Europeans. They were more out of NATO than in it because de Gaulle believed the organisation was dominated by the Americans. Whatever policy was proposed by the US State Department was automatically opposed by the Quai d'Orsay. That was the kind of intractability that passed for foreign policy in France in the fond delusion that the half-baked Force de Frappe provided them with an adequate nuclear deterrent.

"How long is Hassan's evaluation likely to take, Marcel?"

Verlhac shrugged his shoulders. "Who knows? A month? Two months? It is not only the user country we have to convince; those holding the purse strings will want to be satisfied that they are getting value for money."

"Who are we talking about? Saudi Arabia?"

"Kuwait is putting up half the money," Verlhac told him.

"So what tanks are they using for the trial?"

"Russian-built T54 and T55."

"Then the user is Egypt. I know the Syrians have also been equipped by the USSR but they earn a handsome revenue from the oil pipeline and they can afford to pay for their own lasers."

"Does it bother you?"

Stevens shook his head. He knew it ought to because Nasser would use the lasers against Israel and he had been born a Russian Jew in Zhitomir. But that was all in the past; he had turned his back on his origins when he had changed his name to Stevens and married Jean in a Baptist church.

"If it doesn't bother you," Verlhac said, "why are you looking so worried?"

"Because I have a feeling the evaluation tests on the first batch of lasers will be carried out in Moscow."

Parker had no idea what a management consultant would be paid in America but judging by the flat in Cheyne Walk, it was a lot more than what he was getting. He had seen photographs of similar luxury apartments in *Homes and Gardens* which Sheila, his wife, had subscribed to when she was alive but this was the first time he had been inside one. The Adam fireplace was the focal point of the sitting room and the three-piece suite had been arranged to show it off to maximum advantage. The watercolour on the chimney breast was a Turner landscape and it wasn't a reproduction. The other work of art was an elegant moulded ceiling. On a more contemporary note, the plain, cream-coloured fitted carpet looked as though it had only been laid the day before yesterday.

"It's a company apartment," Stefanie said, guessing from his expression what he was thinking. "Doesn't cost me a cent."

He didn't know whether the company also stocked her drinks cupboard but she was able to offer him a choice of three brands of whisky. It subsequently transpired that she had inherited two bottles from her predecessor who had left them behind as a sort of house-warming present for the next incumbent when he had returned to head office in New York. Parker wondered who had paid for the expensive velvet pants suit she was wearing, wondered too why on earth he should feel vaguely jealous.

"Dinner won't be long," Stefanie informed him, then sat down on the sofa, one leg tucked under her rump. "Cheers," she said and raised her glass.

"To Andrew Korwin," Parker said. "He who was lost and is found."

"Thanks to you."

"What did your father think of the news?"

"He was as thrilled as I was when I phoned him in Washington yesterday evening."

"So, is he coming over?"

"I don't rightly know. Much as Dad would like to, he can't drop everything and get on a plane. Right now, things are kind of hectic in Washington."

It sounded like a well-rehearsed excuse; reading between the lines, he got the impression Ayres wasn't all that keen to meet his brother-in-law.

"We're pretty busy too," Parker said. "All eyes are on the Middle East wondering which way U Thant is going to jump and what Nasser has in mind."

"Yeah, well, Dad knows he has an open invitation to visit him any time he can get away."

"Will he take it up?" Parker saw her eyes narrow and realised he had hit a tender spot. "I'm sorry," he said, "I shouldn't have asked. It's none of my business . . ."

"No, you are right in thinking my father is reluctant to meet him. You see, Dad feels he let him down and in a way I guess he did. It goes all the way back to 1939 and is about twenty rolls of film which he was supposed to smuggle out of Poland. They showed what the Nazis were doing to Warsaw and Uncle Andrew wanted to see them published in America because he thought the pictures would have a profound effect on public opinion. He entrusted the rolls of film to my mother and put her on the train to Lwow in the hope it would link up with a connection to Romania. But the train didn't get through, so she made her way back to Warsaw and handed the films over to my father."

By that time, any hope of getting them out in the diplomatic bag had long since vanished. Had he been inclined to do so, Ayres could have taken advantage of the temporary ceasefire which had been observed by both sides while citizens from neutral countries were evacuated from Warsaw. He had rejected the idea at the last moment because he had not been prepared to put twelve hundred innocent people at risk.

"I guess he lied to Mom about the films. If she had known that Dad had already thrown them away, she would never have agreed to leave the city with him." Stefanie looked down at the glass in her hand. "At least, that's the accusation she sometimes threw in his face when they had a fight. And then, when they made it up again, which they always did, Mom would tell him she hadn't meant it."

Parker could guess the rest. No matter how she tried to reassure her husband, Ayres had still been left with a guilty conscience. It would explain a lot of things including why he had been so tardy about obtaining a copy of the photograph that had appeared in the *Frankfurt Allgemeine* after Bender had written to him.

"What did your uncle have to say about it?"

"He didn't even mention the subject until I brought it up. What he did say was that he would have done the same in my father's shoes. Matter of fact, I think he had forgotten all about the wretched films."

"But he remembered everything else?" Parker asked idly.

"Oh yes. I showed him the gold locket which had belonged to my grandmother and he recognised her picture immediately. Andrew said he thought the locket had been buried in the garden of the house on Ujazdowskie Boulevard with the other jewellery and I told him that Mom had dug the casket up and removed it before she left Warsaw."

It was Andrew now without the "uncle". Parker wondered what, if anything, he should read into that. Maybe Stefanie felt it was kind of silly for a twenty-six-year-old woman to refer to someone as uncle whom she had only met for the first time on Saturday.

"What about Kurt Bender? Did he have anything to say about him?"

"Only that Bender had accosted him at the Trade Fair and he had given him the brush-off."

The way Andrew Korwin saw it, just who had saved whose life in Warsaw was open to question. He could not forget what the Germans had done to his family, nor could he forgive them. He hated it every time he had to set foot in their country, but the Federal Republic was Europe's economic miracle and no one who was in manufacturing could afford to be choosy.

"The Luftwaffe killed Jan, his fourteen-year-old brother when they machine-gunned the train, and then the SS executed his father. Andrew said he had been a major general commanding one of the infantry divisions in the Modlin Army and had been captured when his formation had been surrounded north of the Vistula. The SS claimed he was shot while trying to escape but that was after they had removed him from the POW camp on the pretext that he was being transferred to Berlin under escort."

"I can see why he wouldn't like them," Parker said.

Stefanie removed his glass and went over to the sideboard to fix him another whisky and soda. "Something else you should know," she said over her shoulder. "Andrew was picked up by the Gestapo forty-eight hours before the Warsaw uprising began in August '44. First thing they did was to inform him that my mother had been hanged in Auschwitz concentration camp after spitting on one of the guards. Then they started to rough him up and when, after two days of rigorous interrogation, he still refused to tell them anything, one of the bastards held a pistol to his jaw and shot it off."

Parker groped for the right words to express his horror. "You hear about these things," he said slowly, "and you find them hard to believe until you come face to face with one of the victims. When I was on the staff of the British Embassy in Warsaw, I visited the concentration camp at Auschwitz Birkenau with a coachload of people. When we came away from there four hours later, the party consisted of forty-six very subdued men and women."

"Maybe we should change the subject, huh, Campbell?" Stefanie returned with his drink and set it down on the low table beside his armchair. "Whenever I think of what they did to Andrew, a cold shiver runs down my spine."

"Right. Let's talk about you instead."

"After I've checked on our dinner, okay?"

"What are we having?" he asked.

"Something to eat and a fun time I hope," she said and vanished into the kitchen.

Hassan al Jaifi was also planning a fun time for his guests that evening but on a far more lavish scale. Besides flying in the former chief chef at Maxim's in Paris, he had hired a troupe of flamenco dancers from Madrid. There were four of them, two lithe young men and two raven-haired voluptuous beauties. The throbbing guitars were on tape and their interpretation of a cante chico and the more dramatic cante jondo songs of love, death, jealousy and betrayal did not begin to compare with the top Andalusian standards; on the other hand, no flamenco troupe within a hundred miles of Seville provided their sort of entertainment. Before the evening was over, Stevens and Verlhac would discover that the handsome young men were girls and the voluptuous beauties were men.

There was another surprise in store for his guests. Before the evening was over, they would learn that his commission on the arms deal would be a cool twenty per cent of the sales price. In the anticipation that the sum of six million pounds would shortly find its way into his Swiss bank account in Zürich, Hassan al Jaifi could afford to be a generous host.

At seven thirty p.m., his chauffeur collected Verlhac and Stevens from the Alfonso Hotel in Seville and drove them out to the villa. Throughout the twelve-kilometre journey, neither the chauffeur nor his passengers were aware that they were being followed. But of course the moon was in the last quarter and had yet to rise. Furthermore, the driver of the Citroën 2CV behind them was only using his sidelights.

Chapter 11

Stevens felt decidedly queasy. They had dined too well on avocado and prawns, lobster, crab, game pie, cold roast turkey, beef, ham, Russian salad, profiteroles, strawberries and cream, Stilton flown in from England for the occasion and Irish coffee. They had also drunk too well, brandy sours before supper, champagne with it, liqueurs afterwards. The Havana cigar had not improved matters and the skinny dip in the olympic-size pool had been an act of crass stupidity in the circumstances. His body in a clammy sweat, he stumbled into the villa and just made it to the bathroom before he threw up.

The vomit rose in his throat again and he knelt in front of the lavatory pan as if in prayer, his stomach heaving. A long way off, he could just hear the sound of music, then someone on the patio turned the volume up on the record player and The Tremeloes hit him full blast with "Silence is Golden". A dozen little men with hammers began to attack his skull and in desperation, he clapped both hands over his ears to deaden the noise. He leaned forward and rested his forehead on the rim of the lavatory pan. The porcelain was cool to the touch and almost as soothing as an ice pack.

After a while, he felt a little better and gradually the room stopped revolving. Still in a kneeling position, he reached out and flushed the toilet. Lowering the seat, he then pushed himself up from the floor and sat down, forearms resting on his naked thighs, head between his hands. Outside, The Tremeloes gave way to Frank and Nancy Sinatra and "Something Stupid".

He wondered what time it was and managed to focus long enough on his Omega to see that it was five minutes past two. Six hours spent in the company of Hassan al Jaifi and Ingrid, his six foot vacuous blonde Amazon from Sweden was enough to turn the strongest stomach. Vain, conceited, arrogant, obese, ostentatious, self-important, narcissistic: there weren't enough adjectives in the dictionary to describe the arms broker. Hassan was a short, gluttonous man with an overwhelming greed for money, material possessions and beautiful but docile women like the Swede. "Fetch me this, fetch me that." "Do this, do that." All through supper he had ordered Ingrid about like a servant, except that no self-respecting servant would have tolerated the way he had treated her.

And the way she had buttered up to al Jaifi was sickening, hanging on his every word as though he was the fountainhead of all knowledge. So was the simpering way she had referred to him as Hassy as though he was some cuddly teddy bear. What was it she had said after Hassan indicated the sort of commission he expected to receive on the deal? – "I don't think Hassy is being unreasonable to ask for thirty per cent." Thirty per cent of thirty million; it didn't bear thinking about. Stevens swore aloud, exhausted every Anglo-Saxon four-letter word in his vocabulary, then fell back on some choice Russian epithets. So far, the only good thing about the evening had occurred when Hassan had ordered Ingrid to join the flamenco dancers and show them what she could do. The Swedish girl was shapely enough on a Junoesque scale but she was too heavy to be graceful, apart from which she had no idea how to dance a cante chico. In her ignorance, she had simply stamped her feet and clapped her hands in time to the music while displaying a fixed smile on her face as if determined to show how much she was enjoying herself. The mask had slipped briefly when the flamenco dancers had suddenly grabbed Ingrid by the arms and legs and tossed her into the swimming pool. She had surfaced, blonde bouffant hairstyle looking like a wet mop, the lamé dress plastered to her body like an extra skin. Her face had been a picture which mirrored her uncertainty whether to cry or scream. Hassan had laughed uproariously and presently Ingrid had joined in, endeavouring to sound even more hilarious to prove she could take a joke no matter how cruel it was.

If the bad joke had ended there, maybe he wouldn't have been feeling the way he did now, but it hadn't. Some kind of signal had passed between Hassan and the flamenco dancers and Ingrid had been drawn into another wild routine that had left all five of them naked. And at what stage of the proceedings had he been persuaded to take off his clothes and plunge into the swimming pool? Before or after the flamenco dancers had left? It must have been after the taxi had arrived to take the troupe back to Seville. The husband

and wife team who looked after the villa had certainly retired to their living quarters before the fun and games had started, but of course they wouldn't have gone to bed yet. In his capacity as butler, general handyman and chauffeur, the husband would have to drive Marcel Verlhac and himself back to their hotel. Stevens wondered how much longer that would be. His head drooped, his eyes closed; the last thing he heard before drifting off to sleep was The Supremes and "The Happening".

The three intruders had hidden the Citroën 2CV in a deep gully about fifty yards back from the road and had then kept the villa under observation for more than six hours before making a move. They were part of a team that had been watching Hassan al Jaifi since the beginning of the year and what they didn't know about the arms broker wasn't worth knowing. They had bugged his residence outside Zürich, the mews house in London, and the villa at Cap d'Antibes. They had his voice on tape and enough of him on film to make *Gone with the Wind* seem like a cartoon-length feature. They had known about the villa on the road to Mairena del Alcar before he had given the title deeds to Ingrid and could calculate almost to the day when he would dispense with her services.

Among the dossiers the team had compiled on Hassan's associates was one devoted to Marcel Verlhac. They had become interested in him when he had been no more than a voice on the telephone to Hassan al Jaifi; once they had identified him and discovered he was the sales director of Elta Industrielle, he had become a priority target for further investigation. Although his file was a good deal slimmer than the arms broker's, it had recently been allocated the same black star.

They weren't quite so well-informed about the isolated villa but they had a pretty good idea of the layout. The elderly couple who looked after the place had their own modest quarters the other side of the double garage. The villa itself was a sprawling ranch house wrapped around a swimming pool that owed more to the Hollywood school of architecture than either the Spanish or Moorish. The high wall which surrounded the property was intended to safeguard the privacy of the occupants; quite unintentionally, it also concealed an eyesore from the public.

The wrought-iron gates had not been closed after the taxi had driven off with the entertainers. Keeping in the shadow by the wall, the intruders silently made their way past the double garage towards the servants' quarters. They wore sneakers, black denims, singlets and hoods covering their heads and shoulders. All three were armed with the 1951 model of the 9mm Beretta automatic pistol which had been specially adapted so that it could be fitted with a noise suppressor. In a small holdall, the leader carried four sets of handcuffs, a roll of sticking plaster, surgical scissors, a hank of clothesline, a pair of bolt shears and a glass cutter. He did not however need any of these tools to effect a break-in. Like any burglar, he looked for an open window first, then tried all the doors and was lucky enough to find the one at the back was unlocked. When he walked in, the chauffeur was slumped over the kitchen table, his head resting on his forearms and breathing heavily. Moving closer, he tapped him lightly on the shoulder.

The Spaniard grunted, raised his head slowly and opening his bleary eyes, found himself looking at the bulbous silencer on the automatic. His eyes grew even wider when it also gradually dawned on him that, in addition to the man with the pistol, there were two other intruders in the kitchen.

"Don't do anything silly," the leader told him in Spanish.

The chauffeur nodded vigorously to show that he had got the message, then invited them to take whatever they wanted. Even after his hands had been manacled behind him, he was still assuring the intruders of his earnest desire to be cooperative. He only stopped talking after the leader had shoved a wadded handkerchief into his mouth and wound the sticking plaster round and round his head to seal it in place.

His wife, the cook-housekeeper, gave a loud shriek as they burst into the bedroom and was abruptly silenced by the youngest member of the team who clapped a hand over her mouth. Convinced they intended to rape her, she fought them all the way, thrashing about on the bed, kicking, biting and clawing at her assailants. It took all three of them a good five minutes to get the handcuffs on and truss her up, wrists to ankles, like a chicken. The noise they made in the process did not reach the poolside where the record player was still grinding out the latest singles from the hit parade.

The record player was making so much noise that Marcel Verlhac found it hard to think straight. Hassan al Jaifi had demanded an outrageous thirty per cent of the sales price as his commission and getting him to drop a lousy five per cent had taken a lot of haggling.

It had then taken hours of patient negotiation to persuade him to reconsider his position; now that he had, Verlhac wanted to make absolutely sure that no misunderstanding arose over his latest proposition. Without bothering to ask anyone's permission, he got up, walked over to the Grundig record player and switched it off.

"Let's hear that again," he said.

"Ten per cent on the lasers ordered for evaluation purposes, twenty per cent on the bulk order." Hassan waved a dismissive hand. "That's my final offer, take it or leave it."

Each laser would cost the buyer fifty thousand pounds or six hundred and sixty-five thousand francs. A twenty per cent cut of the sales price was still an awful lot of money but Verlhac doubted if the arms broker would take less.

"It's a deal," he said and retraced his steps, one arm hugging the towel around his waist to keep it in place, the other extended to shake hands with Hassan al Jaifi.

Ingrid clapped her hands and squealed in delight, then bounced up and down on the low springboard at the deep end of the pool in celebration of what she clearly regarded as a victory for her lover. Her unbridled joy lasted for just a few seconds before it was terminated by a scream of pure terror. Hassan rose from his chair, eyes bulging, his mouth open and suddenly gushing blood as he was hit in the stomach, chest and head. For someone with a needle-sharp brain, Verlhac was slow to react; hearing a series of faint plops, he turned slowly about and found himself face to face with three hooded men. Nothing in life had prepared him for such an encounter and he was still trying to come to terms with the situation when he was struck by a hail of bullets. The combined impact lifted him off his feet and dumped his lifeless body in the pool. The bath towel came adrift and floated away until, gradually becoming more sodden, it eventually sank beneath the surface.

Stevens woke up with a start, convinced he must have heard a dog howling in agony, then slowly realising that what he was hearing now was a terrified human being. It sounded like Ingrid and he wondered what the hell Hassan and those third-rate flamenco dancers were doing to her. A joke was a joke he told himself but this was getting out of hand. Calling on reserves of strength he didn't know he still possessed, Stevens stood up, lurched over to the washbasin and sluiced his face with cold water. Then he left the bathroom and moved down the hallway to the sitting room where there was a floor to ceiling picture window which looked out on to the patio and swimming pool. Through it, he saw Ingrid at the deep end of the pool aimlessly running to and fro like a headless chicken as two hooded men closed in on her from both flanks.

Hassan al Jaifi was sprawled in an upright canvas chair, head tilted back, legs out straight, arms hanging loosely over the sides. Verlhac was lying face down in the water, arms and legs spread like a starfish. In a blind panic, Ingrid ran towards the smaller of the two men and grappled with him, pummelling his head ineffectually with her clenched fists. As if anxious to use no more force than was necessary, he merely attempted to fend her off and in the process somehow managed to lose his grip on the automatic. Ingrid was as surprised as he was to find that she had snatched it from him. Stevens could tell that by the way she stood there staring at the pistol in her hand.

The other gunman behind her shouted something but Stevens was too far away to hear what he said. Either the hood distorted his voice, reducing it to an unintelligible grunt, or else Ingrid was too petrified to understand what he wanted. Like a nude statue in marble, she just stood there completely immobile, the palm of her left hand open as if she was offering to return the pistol to its rightful owner. Then she was hit in the back and in the split second before she went down, Stevens saw the exit wound erupt between her breasts.

"Niet." His voice rose to an anguished scream. "Niet."

Attracted by the noise, a third gunman who hitherto had been out of sight, suddenly appeared within his field of vision. For what seemed an eternity, they stared at one another through the window, then Stevens recovered his wits and fled from the room. He ran out into the hall, opened the front door and raced across the asphalt drive to the road beyond.

The villa was at least five miles from the nearest habitation in either direction. Commonsense told him that although there was no sign of a car, the killers undoubtedly had one which they had hidden somewhere nearby off the road. If he stayed on the highway in the hope of encountering a patrol car, they would run him down in no time. Furthermore, it was a known fact that the police were never around when you needed them. His only hope of losing the killers was to do the unexpected and double back on his tracks.

Stevens left the road and ran across the sun-baked earth on bare feet. In a matter of yards, both soles were bleeding from a dozen nicks and he had bruised several toes on projecting stones. He tripped and fell over, picked himself up and ran on down the side of the villa, a frightened, naked man fleeing for his life. Lungs bursting, he tumbled into a shallow depression and lay there exhausted, physically incapable of taking another step. The sound of voices reached him faintly, then some time later he thought he heard a car drive away from somewhere in the vicinity of the house.

The loud, insistent twittering of the dawn chorus woke Parker. Everything looked different in the grey light peeping between the drawn curtains and for some moments he wondered why someone had rearranged the furniture during the night. Then a hand pulled the bedclothes off his shoulder and the mystery was solved. It wasn't every day of the week that he was invited out to dinner and ended up in bed with his hostess but it had seemed, and still did seem, the most natural thing in the world. And in a way, that was the most puzzling thing about it. Last night was only the second time he had met Stefanie Ayres and yet he had felt he had known her for years. It was why he had been able to tell her things about Sheila he had withheld from his own family.

Everyone had been sorry for him when Sheila had committed suicide. Colleagues, friends, even her own parents had thought she was brittle, inadequate and immature, which in plain language meant that she had been ill-equipped to deal with an emotional crisis of the magnitude she had had to face. They had met early on in his first year up at Oxford. Sheila had just completed a secretarial course after dropping out of Nottingham University a bare six weeks before taking her finals, and had found temporary employment at his college. She was attractive, had good taste and had been sought after. Born in Derby and the youngest of four children, her father had been a bus driver, her mother a part-time office cleaner. Sheila though had given the impression that she came from a very different social background. She had never actually said that she had been to Badminton but the inference had been there. She had taken riding lessons while at secretarial college but people who didn't know her assumed she had been around horses all her life. The only blatant lie Sheila had ever told was to pretend her parents were dead.

It had all come out at the inquest and a lot of people had concluded that Sheila had duped him into marriage. But they had been wrong; he had known who she was and what she was before he had asked her to marry him. It was only halfway through his tour of duty with the British Embassy in Warsaw that he had begun to realise what a terrible mistake he had made. Sheila had wanted to make one last attempt to have a child because she had thought it would hold their marriage together; the tragedy was that even if she hadn't miscarried, they would still have been two unhappy people with nothing in common who happened to live under the same roof. All this and a lot more he had told this girl who lay beside him.

"How long have you been awake?" Stefanie asked him softly.

"Fifteen, perhaps twenty minutes," he told her.

"And the rest."

"Maybe."

"So why couldn't you go back to sleep?"

"I was thinking back on what I told you about Sheila and feeling guilty as though I had betrayed her memory."

"That's silly." Stefanie raised herself up on one elbow and leaned over him. "You've got nothing to reproach yourself with, Campbell."

"Then why do I feel that I have?"

"I'm going to make you stop thinking it." She fastened her lips over his and kissed him, her tongue darting in and out of his mouth. When he didn't respond, she said, "You were right to talk about Sheila."

"You think so?"

"I know so," Stefanie said and gently straddled him. "You've kept it bottled up long enough."

"Yes, I suppose so. I just wish I felt better for it."

"Look, you don't have to worry, I've never broken a confidence. What you told me last night is just between the two of us and always will be."

Stefanie was wrong there. Every word that had passed between them had been captured by an ultra-sensitive microphone planted inside the twenty-one-inch TV set in the sitting room and relayed to the watchmen across the street.

Stevens got to his feet and gingerly made his way back to the road. He had no idea of the time because his Omega had been smashed after a rocky outcrop had sent him sprawling. But with the sun well above the horizon and the temperature already in the seventies, he calculated it had to be somewhere between nine and ten o'clock.

He limped on to the road, looked both ways more in hope than expectation and saw nothing – not a bus, not a car, not a truck, not even a pedestrian. Although he didn't want to return to the villa, he could hardly walk back to Seville stark naked. Apart from that consideration, it was likely his feet would give out before he had covered half the distance.

The Mercedes was where the chauffeur had left it yesterday evening, and the up-and-over door of the double garage was still in the raised position. Stevens tried the front door but the killers had closed the place up before they left and the lock had been tripped. He hobbled over to the servants' quarters and rang the bell. He hadn't expected anyone to answer the door and wasn't disappointed. Slowly and painfully, he went on round to the swimming pool at the back of the villa.

It was still the same slaughterhouse but now he saw it with a different eye. The killers hadn't wanted to shoot Ingrid; if she hadn't grabbed the pistol, they would probably have tied her up so that she couldn't raise the alarm before they had got clean away. They had come to the villa with the express intention of killing Hassan al Jaifi, Marcel Verlhac and himself. He was alive now because things hadn't gone according to plan and they hadn't dared to spend too much time looking for him after he had given them the slip. The realisation of how close he had been to death sent a shiver down his spine and his only aim in life was to get the hell out of it in the shortest possible time. Collecting his clothes from one of the cubicles by the pool, Stevens opened the patio door and let himself into the house.

He went into the bathroom and stood under the shower, flinching as the water unerringly found every scratch on his body. He stuck the pain for three or four minutes before getting out to pat himself dry with a bath towel. Gritting his teeth, he then dabbed some witch hazel which he found in the medicine cabinet on the deeper cuts and used the best part of an unopened packet of Band-Aid to patch his feet. Although there was a bottle of aftershave on the glass shelf above the washbasin, Stevens couldn't bring himself to waste precious time looking for the rest of Hassan's shaving tackle. He dressed quickly, ran a comb through his hair and checked his appearance in the mirror.

Despite the beard, he looked fairly presentable and hopefully the desk clerks at the Alfonso wouldn't realise that he had been out all night. That, however, was the least of his problems. If ever the

British Government learned how close he had been to selling six hundred laser-guided sights to Hassan al Jaifi, he really would find himself in serious trouble. Apart from the fact that the equipment had attracted a Top Secret security classification, both he and Arthur Kershaw had been required to sign the Official Secrets Acts, which meant they were liable to be prosecuted if word of his involvement got out.

So who could connect him with Marcel Verlhac? The desk clerk who had given him the Frenchman's room number when he had checked into the hotel, the waiter who'd served them in the bar, and the goddamned chauffeur, assuming he was still alive. Stevens found himself hoping the chauffeur had not survived because he was the one man who could place him at the villa which was the most damning piece of evidence. There was, he decided, no point in resorting to wishful thinking. It wouldn't get him out of this mess and it was only sensible to assume the worst and plan accordingly. He would have to convince the British Government that he had gone to Seville in order to block any deal Marcel Verlhac and Elta Industrielle might be tempted to make with Hassan al Jaifi. It was a lie but a sustainable one provided Arthur Kershaw knew about it in time.

Stevens went into the sitting room and picked up the phone to call the office in Middlesbrough. He got as far as dialling the code for the international operator before it dawned on him that the line was dead. Venting his anger and frustration on the phone, he slammed it down and stormed out of the villa.

The only thing he could do now was ring Arthur from a public call box in Seville and the sooner he did that, the better it would be for both of them. He went into the garage to look for some flex which he could use to hot-wire the Mercedes, then decided to borrow the bicycle which was propped against the wall next to a Volkswagen. He wheeled the bike outside and was about to mount it when the Guardia Civil arrived. A few hours ago, Stevens would have welcomed them with open arms; now however, they were the very last people on earth he wanted to see.

CHAPTER 12

THERE WERE three separate law enforcement agencies in Spain: the Policia Municipal who were attached to the town hall, the Policia Nacional, a nationwide anticrime organisation, and the Guardia Civil who operated in both rural and urban areas. Victor Stevens had already met the Guardia Civil who had brought him into Seville, now he was about to become acquainted with officers of the anticrime force. Although an English-speaking member of the Guardia Civil had already taken a detailed statement from him at the villa, he had a shrewd idea he would be making another to the Policia Nacional, this time through an interpreter. What he had to do as soon as possible was to get in touch with Arthur and let him know what had happened. At the moment, however, he was not having much luck with the interpreter.

"I want to make a telephone call," Stevens told him for the umpteenth time. "It's important."

"You wish to see a lawyer?"

"No."

"The British Consul perhaps?"

The British Consul was one person he didn't want to see. If the Foreign Office learned what had happened at the villa before he had spoken to Arthur and rehearsed their story, there would be all hell to pay.

"I have to phone England," he told the interpreter.

"From here?"

"Yes. Is that a problem?"

"This is the police headquarters."

"I'm aware of that, but this is very important. I must speak to the chairman of my company."

"Company?" The interpreter frowned. "What is company?"

"My firm, my business . . ." Confronted with a blank expression, Stevens groped for a phrase which the Spaniard would understand, then had a flash of inspiration. "The place where I work," he said and was rewarded with a smile.

"Now I am knowing."

"Good."

"To make a telephone call you must go to the post office in the Plaza Del Cabildo."

Stevens closed his eyes, tried not to sound exasperated. "Well, can I go there now?" he asked.

"Later, after you have answered questions."

Stevens sighed. He couldn't think what information the Policia Nacional hoped to get from him that he hadn't already told the Guardia Civil. He couldn't describe the killers because he had never seen their faces. As for the rest, well, two were roughly his height but slimmer and one was shorter by several inches. It was all such a futile waste of time. Seville was only eighty miles from the border and the men who had killed Marcel Verlhac, Hassan al Jaifi and Ingrid had long since gone to ground in Portugal. That wasn't just conjecture on his part. The Guardia Civil had only gone to the villa because they had received an anonymous telephone call from the killers.

"So how much longer have I got to wait here?"

"Please?"

"The policeman who wants to question me," Stevens said slowly and distinctly, "when is he coming?"

"Soon, he is very busy man."

"He isn't the only one. I must speak to my friend in England."

"Perhaps you should talk to Señor James Anoveros, British Consul here in Seville."

"Mr Anoveros?"

The interpreter nodded. "His father is Spanish but he has an English mother. He is what you call Honorary Consul."

Stevens knew precious little about the workings of the Foreign Office but he very much doubted if an honorary consul in Seville would communicate direct with London. His most likely channel of communication would be via the embassy in Madrid which was bound to delay things a bit.

"Suppose my friend in England was to phone here," he said, thinking aloud, "would that be all right? I mean, would the police object?"

"I think not."

"Would you like to make sure?"

"Please?"

The interpreter's knowledge of colloquial English was decidedly limited. Stevens tried again and by confining himself to simple words managed to get the message across. Ten minutes later, the Spaniard returned to say that the Commandante would allow him to receive a telephone call from England.

"Is good news, yes?" he asked.

"Very good," said Stevens. "Now I'd like to see Señor Anoveros please."

The deputation arrived as Parker was going through the sequence of numbers to open the Manufoil combination lock on the safe. They were led by Maurice Orde and he recognised Roger Dent from the vetting section, but had never met the third member of the troika.

"We haven't caught you at a bad time, have we, Campbell?" Orde asked in his usual polite and diffident manner.

Parker shook his head. "There's nothing in the safe that can't wait."

"Good." Orde pointed to Dent with his pipe. "I believe you already know Roger," he said, and then aimed the stem at the stranger. "And this is John Garvey from Box 500."

Parker said hello and shook hands. Garvey was roughly the same height and was, he thought, about a couple of years older than himself. He had dark curly hair and a face that tapered to a fairly narrow chin. It could either be described as patrician or foxy, depending on your point of view. Box 500 was of course MI5, also known as Five, the Security Service and occasionally The Friends. Maurice was the only person Parker knew who used the full post office box number whenever he alluded to them by that particular synonym.

"John is hoping you can help him clear up one or two small points," Orde continued. "It's in all our interests to sort out the situation as soon as possible, so I hope you will be frank with him."

"That sounds ominous," Parker said breezily and drew a slightly disapproving frown from the head of the Warsaw Pact Department.

Dent managed a chuckle, then nipped into the adjoining office and returned with a chair which he had pinched from Sarah Yendell. Garvey made himself as comfortable as he could on the ladderback which in the room inventory was described as "chairs visitors quantity one". A quizzical look from the Five man reminded Orde that he had things to do and he shuffled out of the office, closing the door to the corridor behind him.

"No point distracting your secretary," Dent said and shut the communicating door.

"You mean my research assistant."

"What?"

"Sarah Yendell is not a secretary."

"If you say so, old boy."

"Can we get on?" Garvey said a touch impatiently.

"I'm not stopping you," Parker told him quietly.

"I understand you are acquainted with a Miss Stefanie Ayres?"

"I've seen her twice, the first time at the request of Harry Freeland."

"The Assistant Director in charge of the Rest of the World Department," Dent said helpfully.

"And the second time?"

"Last night. Miss Ayres invited me to dinner. It was her way of thanking me for helping to trace the uncle she had never met."

"So what did you talk about?"

Parker felt himself colouring. "You want to tell me what business it is of yours?" he asked coldly.

"We have reason to believe Miss Ayres is a security risk."

"You've got to be joking."

"I was never more serious." Garvey pressed his fingertips together. "Did she tell you that she had been to Warsaw?"

"When was this?"

"She was there for a fortnight in June 1961 . . ."

"For God's sake, she was only nineteen years old. Don't tell me she went to Poland on her own?"

"No, she travelled with a group of students sponsored by the Young People's International Friendship Society, a left-wing organisation based in Paris which is known to be funded by Moscow, the money having first been laundered by one of your discreet but oh so very helpful Swiss banks."

"And I suppose that makes her a Soviet agent, does it?"

Garvey ignored him. "Her second trip to Warsaw was in August 1965," he continued remorselessly. "She arrived on the fourth, departed on the twenty-ninth and was accompanied by two of her second cousins, Martina and Gregory Ozelski. They only stayed ten days, the rest of the time she was there on her own and never went anywhere near the US Embassy or the Consulate."

"Any reason why she should?"

"It would have been a sensible thing to do considering she was alone in the city from August the fifteenth onwards. She did a couple of Polorbis tours to Cracow, Zakopane and Lublin before returning to Warsaw again." Garvey offered a packet of Churchmans around, then lit one for himself. "You remember the Bristol Hotel from your days in Warsaw, Mr Parker?" he asked.

"Yes, we dined there a few times."

"That's where Stefanie Ayres stayed except for the couple of days she spent with her official guide and his family."

"How do you know all this?"

"We have our sources," Garvey told him smugly.

It didn't look good. Two holidays behind the Iron Curtain, one of them sponsored by a Communist Front organisation. And then there was the little matter of the official guide, many of whom were talent spotters for the Polish Intelligence Service. But the most disturbing thing of all was the fact that Stefanie had never mentioned the vacations she had spent in Poland.

"Did you tell her that you had served in Warsaw, Campbell?" Dent asked.

"I happened to mention it."

"Why?" Garvey asked.

"We were talking about what the Gestapo had done to her uncle and I said that having been to Auschwitz, I had some idea of what he must have been through."

First Garvey, then Dent, now Garvey again; they were beginning to sound like Mutt and Jeff. They had had plenty of time to work out their tactics before confronting him. Stefanie had given him breakfast but her razor was only good for shaving her legs and he had had to dash back to his flat in Ravenscourt Park to grab a clean shirt and make himself look presentable. Consequently, he had been late getting to the office.

"Does she know about Sheila?" Dent asked.

"Stefanie knows I was married."

"It's Stefanie, is it?" Garvey said with heavy emphasis. "I hadn't realised you were that well acquainted with the lady."

"I'm not," Parker lied.

"I think you deliberately misunderstood me, Campbell," Dent observed silkily. "I was referring to the wing-ding Sheila threw towards the end of your tour."

"Don't be stupid, what do you take me for?"

Sheila had hated Warsaw from the day she had arrived. She had tried to make friends with the other embassy wives but had always been prickly with her own sex and had seen slights where none had been intended. Hoping to further his career, Sheila had set out to cultivate the wife of the head of Chancery, the number two man in Warsaw, and had been so blatant about it that she had made herself the laughing stock of the diplomatic community. Retreating into herself, she had started counting the days to the end of his tour. When it had been extended for another six months, she had thrown a fit. "There was," she had told him, "one sure way of getting his extension revoked." A fortnight later, Sheila had claimed she had been sexually assaulted by one of the Polish drivers employed by the embassy who had taken her shopping. There had been no substance to the allegation, a fact known to the ambassador and the resident SIS officer, but Sheila had succeeded in getting his extension reduced from six to three months. She had also set his career back several years.

"You still haven't answered Roger's question," Garvey told him.

"I'm not in the habit of discussing my late wife with strangers."

"Is that a yes or a no?"

"It's a bloody no." Parker stubbed out his cigarette. "How many more times do you need telling?" he said angrily.

"Steady on, Campbell." Dent was playing the part that suited him best, the honest broker who was all sweetness and light. "John is only doing his job."

"And I'd like to help him if I knew what he wanted from me."

"What we would like from you is a little more discretion." Garvey half rose from his chair and used the ashtray on Parker's desk to stub out his cigarette. "At the risk of repeating myself, we regard Miss Stefanie Ayres as a security risk – to you."

"Me?"

"Yes. We believe she has identified you as an SIS officer. Is she trying to cultivate you? That's the question you have to ask yourself."

Although Parker was reluctant to admit it, the fact was Stefanie had made most of the running, and not only last night. It had started when she had insisted on inviting him to dinner. "Tell you what," she had said, "if you've made other plans for this evening, choose whatever day suits you."

"Who are you trying to kid?" Parker asked without much conviction.

"No one. We're just trying to open your eyes to what is going on around you. All this nonsense about how difficult it was to trace her long lost uncle. If Miss Ayres had been frank with the Home Office and had given them the information they needed, they would have found him in no time. But no, she had to make a big production out of it so that she could go to Larborough and persuade the MP that the Security Service was putting obstacles in her way."

"Why Larborough?" Parker asked.

"Because she reads the quality newspapers and knows he fancies himself as the world's greatest living authority on counter-espionage. For pity's sake, there's no avoiding him; he's either pontificating on the small screen or filling God knows how many column inches in the Sundays. Larborough may be on the Opposition benches, but he's got more connections than all the Labour Cabinet put together."

"So now Stefanie Ayres reads the social chit-chat in *Tatler*, does she?" Parker said derisively. "I mean, how else is she going to know that?"

"Oh, come on, Campbell, she works in the City and those people in Throgmorton Street have their ears to the ground."

"What are you suggesting – that she is on a fishing trip?"

"Why are you so sceptical?" Garvey asked. "She knows that if she can hook Larborough, he will either go to MI5 or the SIS. All Miss Ayres has to do is sit back and wait for someone to invite her round for a quiet chat about her uncle. If the bait is taken, she then tries to land her fish, which is when she will discover whether she has caught a sprat or a mackerel. Remember this, the Polish Intelligence Service isn't looking for results overnight; they have been trained by the KGB and have learned to be patient."

"This girl we are talking about is only twenty-five years old."

"What has her age got to do with it? She's been well-trained. Besides, she'll have a case officer to advise and direct her. The first thing Miss Ayres did when she arrived in this country was to join a Polish Circle in Ealing whose members have absolutely no love for the Russians or Communists – with perhaps one exception."

Parker had heard the same thing from Mrs Irena Puzak, owner and editor-in-chief of *The Sentinel*. But she hadn't said anything which would have led him to suspect that the Circle had been infiltrated.

"If Stefanie Ayres is such a risk," he said slowly, "why didn't you warn us?"

"There, I'm afraid, we cocked it up." Garvey smiled disarmingly and raised both hands shoulder high. "The Old Boy network defeated us; we overlooked the fact that Larborough and your Harry Freeland live next door to one another in Dolphin Square."

"So what happens now?"

"Nothing. Roger and I just thought you ought to know the score." Another smile appeared on Garvey's face as he stood up to leave. "Forewarned is forearmed. Right, Campbell?"

"Oh, absolutely," Dent said before he could answer for himself. "I'm sure neither of us would knowingly do anything which might prejudice our vetting status."

Garvey shook hands again, thanked Parker for being so helpful and apologised for taking up so much of his time. Dent said much the same thing in an equally hearty manner, then hastily backed out of the room as if anxious to have one last quick word with Garvey before he disappeared. Parker walked round the desk, picked up the chair he had vacated and returned it to the adjoining office.

"What was that all about?" Sarah Yendell asked him.

"A subject interview," he told her. "To do with my positive vetting."

It didn't make sense. If Stefanie Ayres really had been recruited by the Polish Intelligence Service, why hadn't Garvey briefed him to get close to her with a view to exploiting the situation? That would have been the normal procedure, but he had simply chosen to warn him off.

"You know the old saying, Campbell, a problem shared is a problem halved . . ."

"Thanks for the offer, Sarah," he said, "but I don't have a problem."

He left her office and went looking for a room with a telephone that was unoccupied. Maybe he was being a little jumpy but he didn't want anyone listening in when he rang Harry Freeland and arranged to meet him for lunch.

Señor James Anoveros, Honorary British Consul in Seville, was the last person Kershaw had expected to hear from. Even at the best of times, a phone call from a total stranger was not something he welcomed and this one had certainly been no exception. Although he had always felt they would be courting danger if they did business with Hassan al Jaifi, he had never in his worst nightmare imagined that it would result in bloodshed. After listening to the garbled account of the shooting which Anoveros had given him, it was evident the consul had been equally devastated by what had happened at the villa. The only consolation was that Victor was all right, the worrying thing was the news that the police were holding him for questioning.

Kershaw was not a man who kept a bottle in the office but at that particular moment, he would have given almost anything for a large brandy while he waited for his secretary to obtain the number in Seville which Anoveros had given him. The consul hadn't said whether the Foreign Office had been informed of the incident and he hadn't dared ask. To have done so would only have aroused his suspicion and provoked a lot of awkward questions which would have been difficult, as well as time-consuming, to answer. And time was something he couldn't afford to waste, especially when it was vital to discover what story Victor intended to give the authorities in Spain before London did.

The phone pinged and set his jangled nerves on edge; a few seconds later, it rang normally and he snatched at the receiver. There was a brief three-way conversation between his secretary, the operator on the international exchange and a Spanish police officer, then Victor came on the line.

"Are you all right?" Kershaw asked him. "I mean, is there anything I can do for you from this end?"

"You could phone Jean at the Emperador Hotel in Malaga and let her know there is nothing to worry about. With any luck, I should be with her in time for dinner."

"That's good news." Kershaw chewed his lip, wondered how he was going to discuss what line they should take with the Ministry of Defence when Victor's whole demeanour suggested that someone was listening to their conversation.

"I didn't know Hassan al Jaifi was going to be present," he said tentatively.

"Neither did I. What exactly did Marcel Verlhac say to you when he asked to see me?"

They had the basis of a common story, now all he had to do was flesh it out. Keep it simple, Kershaw told himself, then said, "He led me to believe his government was interested in the project, subject to certain modifications to the system. Of course, he couldn't say what these were over the telephone for obvious reasons. Naturally, Marcel promised to confirm all this in writing in due course, but I don't know what is going to happen now."

"I doubt if we will hear anything from Elta Industrielle; they've always been reluctant to commit themselves in writing."

There was a good deal of truth in what Victor said. The agenda and the minutes of every meeting were on record, so were all the major administrative decisions, but many of the day to day telephone conversations were not. Given this, Kershaw was confident he could persuade the Ministry of Defence there was nothing sinister about the fact that there was no documentary evidence to show that Marcel Verlhac had asked for this particular meeting.

"You're right," he said. "In fact, knowing Marcel, I wouldn't be surprised if he had neglected to inform his fellow directors about the meeting."

"Well, it was all arranged pretty much in a hurry."

Kershaw agreed, said it could hardly have come at a more inconvenient time for Victor and apologised for mucking up his holiday in Malaga, then put the phone down. After carefully rehearsing what he was going to say, he rang the number Garvey, the liaison officer from MI5, had given him when he had become his Guardian Angel in September 1966.

The Duke of Buckingham in Villiers Street off the Strand was roughly halfway between Benbow House and Broadway. One of several pubs near the offices of the Ministry of Defence in Northumberland Avenue, it was invariably crowded with civil servants during the lunch hour.

"There's such a thing as safety in numbers, Campbell," Freeland said and edged his way towards the bar. "Soon as you said you'd rather not discuss whatever it is that's bothering you over the phone, I knew it had to be a mite sensitive. Worst thing you and I could do is meet in a park or some place like that; it would look damned suspicious. Here we are just two colleagues meeting for a lunchtime drink. Right?"

"Yes."

"And you came straight here, no farting about like doubling back on your tracks to make sure you weren't being followed?"

"I got on a District Line train at St James's Park, got off at the Embankment and walked up Villiers Street," Parker told him. "You can't be more direct than that."

"So what'll you have?"

Parker settled for a lager, took a beef sandwich with English mustard from the food counter, and left Freeland to get the rest of the order while he looked for a niche well away from the crush at the bar. Eventually, he found a spot to the left of the entrance where they could use the windowledge as a table. The only people within earshot were a group of civil servants from the Ordnance Directorate who were celebrating someone's birthday and weren't the least bit interested in what they had to say to each other.

"All right," Freeland said, "let's hear it. What's bothering you?"

"A man called John Garvey. You know him?"

"The name sounds familiar but I can't place it."

"He's in the same line of business as Roger Dent. Anyway, both of them came to see me this morning about Stefanie Ayres, because according to Garvey she is a bit iffy."

"Iffy?"

"Spent a couple of holidays in Poland, got too friendly with an oddball in that Circle she joined out at Ealing. Garvey reckons she is on a fishing trip; says he should have warned us but there was a cock-up. So sorry but these things happen."

"And the theory is that she is trying to get her hooks into you?" Freeland said.

"That's what Garvey thinks, only he doesn't seem anxious to exploit the situation."

"I don't buy his story."

"Neither do I," said Parker. "And I don't believe those jokers in the white Cortina were keeping an eye on the New Left-Wing Cooperative Bookshop either."

Freeland sought inspiration in his beer, gazed at the glass tankard as though it was a work of art. "What is it you want from me, Campbell?" he asked after a lengthy silence.

"Your advice."

"Okay, best thing you can do is keep your nose clean and stay away from Stefanie Ayres."

"I can't," Parker told him. "I like her too much."

"Then she really has got her hooks into you," Freeland said.

Sarah heard the creak of leather in the adjoining room and froze, a cucumber and tomato sandwich halfway towards her mouth. Maurice Orde was the only man she knew whose shoes announced his presence long before he or the aroma from his pipe did and she wondered what he was up to. A security check? Heads of Departments didn't go in for that sort of thing, it was beneath their dignity.

In any case, Parker never left his office for any length of time without first clearing his desk and locking the files away in the safe. His door was wide open and Maurice could see that for himself from the corridor.

As the footsteps drew nearer, Sarah looked expectantly towards the communicating door. "If you're looking for Campbell," she called, "he's gone to lunch."

"Actually, it's you I want to see," Orde told her.

"Oh yes?" Sarah put her sandwich down. "How can I help you?"

"Campbell has been looking into the background of Kurt Bender, a West German national. I believe he has obtained details of his military record of service during the last war from Bonn?"

Had it been anyone else, Sarah would have endeavoured to look perplexed but when Maurice said he believed something, he meant he knew it for a fact. She toyed with the idea of telling him that the print-out had been destroyed, then rejected it. The print-out carried a security classification of "Confidential" which meant it had been logged in, and she would look pretty silly if Maurice didn't believe her and asked to see the register.

"I think we opened a branch file on him," she said.

"May I see it please?"

Sarah left her desk, opened the three-drawer filing cabinet and took out the file. "Are you going to take it away?" she asked.

"That was the general idea."

"Then I'll need a signature."

"This is a 'Confidential' document, Miss Yendell. One only has to sign for 'Secret' and above." Orde moved towards the door. "Incidentally, since you have been with us for at least two years, I would have thought you would have known that by now."

CHAPTER 13

THE TRANSMISSION had been intercepted by 9 Signal Regiment in Cyprus and decoded by Government Communications Headquarters at Cheltenham. Originated from the office of the Commander-in-Chief of the Soviet Navy and Deputy Minister of Defence, it was addressed to the Commander of the Black Sea Fleet at Sevastopol and repeated to the Rear Admiral commanding the Mediterranean Squadron. The text stated that as soon as the United Nations Peacekeeping Force completed its withdrawal from the Sinai Peninsula, President Nasser intended to blockade the Gulf of Aqaba, Israel's sea lane to Africa and Asia. More chillingly, it stated that the Soviet Union had assured Cairo of its support in enforcing the blockade.

The originator's reference indicated that the signal had been drafted by the Chief of Main Naval Staff; what was not apparent was why the directive failed to say just what support the Black Sea Fleet and detached Mediterranean Squadron would be required to provide. The thrust was however sufficiently alarming for GCHQ to dispatch copies to the Cabinet Office, Foreign Office, the Ministry of Defence and SIS as soon as the transmission had been decoded and before the Analysts Special Intelligence had a chance to submit their interpretation of the content. Although primarily of interest to the Middle East desk officers, copies were made and immediately distributed to the Warsaw Pact and West Europe Departments. The urge to do something was too strong even for a pragmatist like Maurice Orde. Following the example set by the other two assistant directors, he decided to call a staff conference at short notice. Parker received no notice; returning late from the pub lunch at The Duke of Buckingham, he was just in time to see the rest of the Warsaw Pact team filing into the Assistant Director's office and instinctively tagged on.

There wasn't much Orde could tell them and naturally none of the assembled desk officers had anything to contribute. By common consent, it was agreed that the Admiralty were the people best qualified to say what assistance the Soviet Fleet could render. In fact, Director Naval Intelligence had already been asked for his views but in the tradition of the Silent Service, he wasn't prepared to say anything just yet. A duty roster was drawn up in case the Middle East Department needed extra watchkeepers during silent hours, but apart from this practical measure, the conference achieved very little and the meeting broke up half an hour after it had begun. Parker, however, was asked to stay behind when the others left.

"I expect you are wondering why you are not on the duty roster," Orde said when they were alone.

"I thought it a little odd," Parker admitted, "but I assumed there was a reason."

"There is – you are leaving us."

"I'm what?" Parker stared at him, unable to believe what he had heard.

"You are being posted to Amberley Lodge."

Amberley Lodge was the home of the SIS Training School a mile from Petersfield. The last time Parker had set eyes on the place was back in 1957 when he and four other Oxbridge candidates had attended the induction course.

"I don't understand . . ."

"How long have you been with us, Campbell?"

"Almost four years."

"Well, you were overdue for a change and this is definitely a leg up for you."

"What am I going to be doing at Amberley Lodge?"

"Principal Staff Officer Coord. You will be responsible for programming the various courses."

"It's kind of sudden, isn't it?"

"Well, George Chater, the chief instructor, has decided to call it a day after two heart bypass operations and the commandant is faced with a major reshuffle. You start there on Monday. You can hand over your desk to Nick Quade tomorrow and take the rest of the week off to sort out your own affairs. Nick is going to have his hands full for the next few weeks until we can find a relief suitable to run his sideshow, but that won't do him any harm. He's not been exactly overworked up to now."

Quade was responsible for the combined Albanian and Bulgarian desks which was regarded as a backwater by the other members of the Warsaw Pact team. Strictly speaking, Albania was outside the Warsaw Pact; although one of the founder members, it had been excluded from both the treaty organisation and the Mutual Economic Assistance programme in 1961 when the USSR had severed diplomatic relations following the denunciation of Albania's deviationist policy at the 22nd Congress of the Communist Party. Although the Bulgarian desk had never been recognised as a high profile job, there had been a time when the Albanian sub department had been recognised as a plum appointment. But that had been before Philby had systematically betrayed every guerrilla team the SIS had despatched to Albania by land, sea and air. The appointment had been downgraded and combined with the Bulgarian desk following the demise of the Albanian resistance movement a few weeks before Easter 1952 when twelve top agents loyal to ex-King Zog had parachuted into an ambush at Saint Gjergie near Elbasan in Northern Albania.

"Has Nick been told about this impending move?" Parker asked.

"Not yet. I felt you should be the first to know." Orde busied himself filling his pipe from a tin of Dunhill Standard Mixture, then struck a match and held it over the bowl. "I think congratulations are in order," he said between puffs.

"Thank you."

"You don't seem very enthusiastic, Campbell."

"Principal Staff Officer Coord doesn't sound much of a job."

"I think you will find it's quite a challenging one and of course the extra five hundred a year is not to be sneezed at."

"That's true," Parker agreed.

"And let's not forget a promotion is a promotion."

"Yes. Well, I suppose I'd better let my research assistant know what is happening."

"You do that," Orde told him affably.

It was, Parker thought, a funny sort of day. In the morning, Garvey and Dent had warned him that Stefanie Ayres was a security risk and had hinted he could lose his positive vetting status. Over lunch, Harry Freeland had advised him to keep his nose clean and give the American girl a wide berth, then barely an hour later he had been promoted and Orde was offering his congratulations. Still bemused, he walked into his office and began to unscramble the combination lock on his safe.

"Thank God you're back at last," Sarah said behind him. "Maurice wants to see you."

Parker completed the sequence for the third and last number, reversed the dial to zero, then moved it forward in a clockwise direction until the tumblers clicked. "I've just come from seeing him," he said and yanked the handle to open the safe.

"How did you know?"

"I happened to see the rest of the team filing into his office and thought I'd better join them."

"It's just as well you did."

"I've been promoted," Parker told her abruptly.

"You have?" Her voice rose with excitement. "Well, that's terrific, you deserve it, Campbell."

"I'm not so sure about that, but thanks anyway."

"Does this mean you will be leaving the team?"

"Yes. I hand over tomorrow."

"Who to?"

"Nick Quade."

"Oh, shit."

"Hey, come on, Nick's okay. What have you got against him?"

"I don't like men who pat me on the bottom."

"I didn't know he was a groper."

"Well, you don't happen to wear a skirt, do you? Incidentally, while I remember it, your girlfriend, Stefanie Ayres, rang while you were out to lunch. Wouldn't leave a message." Sarah retreated into her own office. "I may be wrong but I thought Miss America sounded a trifle jealous."

"Try teasing Nick Quade when I've gone," Parker told her, "and see where that gets you."

He would phone Stefanie, but not from the office. If his extension was being monitored, the exchange would know the moment he dialled 9 to obtain an outside line and he didn't want any eavesdroppers listening to that particular conversation. Lifting the receiver, he rang Benbow House and spoke to the deputy heads of Personnel and Administration. From Personnel he obtained a job description of his new post while Administration told him that his salary as Principal Staff Officer Coord at Amberley Lodge would be two thousand five hundred per annum which was what he was getting now.

"Campbell?"

"Yes, what is it now?"

Sarah wandered back into his office with the Confidential and Secret Registers. "I assume there will be a hundred per cent check of all classified documents?"

"That's the usual form." He smiled. "Don't tell me you've mislaid some of them?"

"Maurice came to see me twice during the lunch hour; the first time was shortly after you'd left when he asked for the Bender file . . ."

"So?"

"Well, he refused to sign for it."

"He didn't have to, it's only graded 'Confidential'."

"I'm aware of that." Her forehead wrinkled in a frown. "It's just that I have this funny feeling that he had deliberately waited until you were out before he asked me for it."

"You've logged it out to him on the bin card?"

"Yes."

"Then there's nothing to worry about," Parker assured her.

"I just thought you should know."

"Thanks. Tell you what, to set your mind at rest, we'll make sure none of the Secret and Top Secret documents have gone missing."

"What? Now?"

"Why not? We haven't got all that many."

They were roughly halfway through the check when the phone rang. Answering it, Parker found he had a very apologetic deputy head of Administration on the line who wanted to explain that the salary he had previously quoted was incorrect. The post had in fact been recently upgraded by the Establishment Committee and the approved remuneration was now three thousand pounds per annum. He couldn't think how the error had occurred. Neither could Parker.

As the Honorary British Consul in Seville, James Anoveros was used to dealing with stranded tourists, penniless students and the occasional burial or repatriation of a dead body. There was a recognised procedure for dealing with these contingencies, but a triple murder was not something which happened all that often and there was nothing in his instructions to cover such an incident. He therefore telephoned the British Embassy in Madrid to give a preliminary verbal report and seek advice.

The details Anoveros gave over the telephone formed the basis of two signals transmitted from the embassy's wireless room. One was addressed to the Foreign Office, the other was originated by the Resident SIS Head of Station. Both signals were classified 'Confidential' and carried an Op Immediate precedence. The content was such that central registry at Broadway wasn't sure just what department the decrypted message should go to; playing safe, the chief archivist despatched copies to the Middle East, West Europe and Rest of the World departments. Harry Freeland's copy was delivered by the last Special Despatch Service run of the day and reached Benbow House at 1645 hours. Ten minutes after it had arrived on his desk, Harry Freeland received a call from the Assistant Director Middle East.

"What do you make of it, Harry?" he asked.

"I haven't the faintest idea," Freeland said cheerfully. "I'm only too glad it's not my problem. Purely out of interest, who the hell is Hassan al Jaifi?"

"An arms broker. He's bought a lot of equipment from the US on behalf of the Iranians – the Sheridan light tank and Shillelagh missile system, M113 armoured personnel carriers, image intensification, infrared – the night vision stuff ended up with the Syrians and Egyptians. The Shah was just a middle man."

"Interesting. Who was Marcel Verlhac?"

"Damned if I know. Try West Europe."

"I will."

"So what do you reckon now, Harry?"

"I think you can put it down to Mossad."

"The Israeli Intelligence Service?"

"Why not?" said Freeland. "Who else has an axe to grind?"

Parker let himself into the flat overlooking Ravenscourt Park, picked up the circulars which had dropped through the letter box and went into the sitting room. Stefanie Ayres had told him she was usually home by six and the time was now fourteen minutes past. He pulled the L – R telephone directory from the rack below the table top, flipped it open at the Ms, moved on to the Mullinders and ran a finger down the list. A hunch that the lawyer Eastham had done some work for would not be ex-directory came good when he found a Kevin Mullinder who lived in Cheyne Walk. He dialled the number, heard a man with a faint Irish brogue say "Chelsea 1984" and promptly hung up. Lifting the phone again, he rang Stefanie and did the same thing to her when she answered.

The next step was going to be something of a gamble. Garvey

had led him to believe that the Security Service was keeping the American girl under surveillance which meant they had probably bugged her apartment. Mullinder was a trendy left-wing lawyer who was associated with any number of unpopular causes. If only half of what Eastham had told him about the kind of political activists he frequently represented was true, it was safe to assume he was persona non grata with the police, Special Branch and the Security Service. The sixty-four dollar question was whether any of these agencies had put a tap on his phone. On reflection, Parker didn't think they had. Mullinder would not be without friends and the chances were that numbered amongst them was at least one electronic whizzkid who would be only too happy to spring-clean his apartment for him. Although he had never met the lawyer, Parker was prepared to bet that nothing would give Mullinder greater pleasure than to see his protagonists with egg on their collective faces, and the Establishment knew it. Hesitating no longer, Parker lifted the receiver a third time, rang the lawyer's number and waited impatiently for him to answer.

"Mr Mullinder?" he said. "My name is Parker, Campbell Parker. We've never met but I'm a friend of Stefanie Ayres."

"Oh yes?" Mullinder sounded cautious, almost guarded.

"I hate to impose on you like this," Parker continued unruffled, "but I wonder if you could do me a favour? I've been trying to ring Stefanie but her phone appears to be out of order. Do you think you could bring her to yours if I hang on? I wouldn't normally ask but my secretary told me Stefanie had tried to get in touch while I was out of the office."

"It's no trouble," Mullinder assured him. "Don't go away, I'll be as quick as I can."

Parker wedged the receiver under his chin and hunched his right shoulder to hold it in place while he fished out a packet of Embassy and lit a cigarette. In the park below, a cricket match of sorts was in progress, umpired by a twelve-year-old whose every decision was hotly disputed.

There was a faint clatter and a breathless, inquisitive voice said, "Campbell?"

"Hi," he said. "Sarah told me you'd rung while I was out and this is the first chance I've had to call you back. What are you doing this evening?"

"Nothing much."

"You are now, we're having dinner."

"Where?" she asked.

"Somewhere quiet, somewhere off the beaten track, somewhere different."

"Sounds exciting."

"Let's hope so," he said in a neutral voice. "Now, suppose you get yourself down to South Kensington and catch a train going to Uxbridge on the Piccadilly Line. I'll meet you at Ruislip at a quarter to eight."

"How do you spell that?"

Parker told her, made sure Stefanie had understood his directions, then asked her to thank Mullinder for the use of his phone and rang off.

He pinched out his cigarette, stripped off for the quickest shower on record and dressed even more hurriedly. Exactly twelve minutes later, Parker left the flat, got into the dust-covered Austin Mini that was parked by the kerbside in all weathers and drove off.

Garvey returned to his office, walked round the desk and flopped into the swivel chair completely exhausted. The words of a Recessional hymn he used to sing in the school chapel drummed in his brain – "The tumult and the shouting dies; the Captains and the Kings depart; still stands thine ancient sacrifice, a humble and a contrite heart." Well, the Director General and the rest of the high-price help had certainly departed along with middle management, the secretaries, clerks and typists. And there was no one more humble and contrite than he was at the moment, and if tomorrow turned out as bad as today, there were no prizes for guessing who would be the sacrificial goat.

The day had started badly with Campbell Parker and had gone further downhill when Arthur Kershaw had phoned him, and had hit rock bottom after the SIS had learned about the triple shooting at the villa on the road to Mairena del Alcar. The damage limitation exercise he had been forced to set in motion had ultimately involved the Director General of Box talking to his opposite number in MI6, and you couldn't go any higher than that. And no government department had been harder to pacify than the Procurement Executive of the Ministry of Defence. Convincing them that the killers had simply been after Hassan al Jaifi and that their wretched laser sight had not been compromised had left him with an aching jaw. Now all he had to do was make one more telephone call and then he could go home to that intimate dinner party for eight which

Lynne, his wife, had arranged for the evening. With an audible sigh, Garvey lifted the phone and called the watchmen in Cheyne Walk.

"All right, let's have it," he said. "What's the little lady been up to?"

"Not a lot," the watchman told him. "Subject lunched in the office, returned home at six. Her telephone rang at six fourteen but the caller hung up as soon as she answered."

"Could have been a wrong number," Garvey said.

"Maybe. Someone came knocking on her door about ten minutes later. The caller was too far away from the mike for identification purposes but it could have been Mullinder."

"That's pure supposition."

"Perhaps, but I can't help wishing we had a tap on him."

Garvey was inclined to agree with the watchman, but the application had been turned down by the Home Secretary and it was no use bemoaning the decision. "Is that it?" he asked.

"Not quite. Subject left her apartment half an hour ago. Looked as though she was going out for the evening."

"Anyone with her?"

"Only our two shadows."

"Let's hope they don't lose her then," Garvey said sourly, and replaced the phone.

Chances were they would; it had been that sort of day and he couldn't see why it should suddenly improve.

Stefanie Ayres came in view as the last car of the Uxbridge-bound train cleared the platform. She was wearing a blazer over a blue silk dress and court shoes which emphasised her shapely legs and was one of the reasons why she drew appreciative wolf whistles from a couple of teenage youths who were waiting for a train on the up-line. Parker watched her cross the footbridge above the tracks, then waved to her as she came down the steps. Her face smiled recognition and she moved purposefully towards him to stand on tiptoe as she kissed his lips and embraced him.

"You pick the darnedest places to meet," she said. "What's the attraction about Rooslip?"

"It's pronounced Ryslip, and it's off the beaten track."

"And that's the attraction?"

"Well, there is a lido here, but we aren't going there."

"Kind of a mystery tour, huh?"

"Sort of." Parker steered her through the entrance hall to the car park outside the station where he had left the Mini.

"It's surely started out that way. Why did you phone Kevin Mullinder and ask him to fetch me to the phone?"

"Because your line was out of order." Parker saw her into the car, walked round the front and got in behind the wheel. He switched on, cranked the engine, then shifted into gear and drove out on to the main road. "I didn't see it would do any harm," he continued. "I mean, this guy Mullinder is a friend of yours, isn't he?"

"How did you know that?"

"Eastham told me. He said he had done several jobs for Mullinder and the lawyer had recommended the Sphinx Inquiry Agency when you were looking for a private investigator."

"There's nothing wrong with my phone," she said quietly, "it rang a few minutes before Kevin fetched me."

"That was me. I hung up as soon as you answered. I did the same thing to Mullinder. Of course, I had to look him up in the directory first."

"Are you crazy?" Stefanie asked in a faint voice.

"I wanted to make sure both of you were at home."

"I don't get it . . ."

"You're on a party line and I don't like interlopers eavesdropping on me."

"I don't know where you got that idea, Campbell, but I am not on a party line."

Parker glanced at her sideways. Was Stefanie really the innocent at large who hadn't the faintest idea what he was hinting at or was she being deliberately obtuse? The puzzled frown seemed authentic but it didn't prove anything.

"Why didn't you tell me you had been to Poland?"

"What is this? An inquisition?"

"The Foreign Office has been in touch with your State Department," Parker lied, "and now my superiors are not too happy about you. Matter of fact, they are using expressions like fellow traveller."

"And all because I didn't tell you that I had been to Poland?"

"Yes, that and . . ."

"My God," she said angrily, "I didn't think I had to give you people my whole life story before I asked for help." Stefanie paused as if she had run out of breath, then continued, "I've been to Poland twice because I wanted to see the country where my mother was born. Is that such a crime?"

"What about the Young People's International Friendship Society?" Parker asked, avoiding her question.

"Oh, I get it. Yeah, the International Friendship Society is run by a bunch of left-wing radicals, but when you are a student working your way through college, you take the best travel deal you can get. A bunch of us were doing Europe and we came across their office in Paris and I saw what they had on offer and decided to take advantage of it. Four years later, I went back to Warsaw with my second cousins, Martina and Gregory Ozelski."

"Who only stayed ten days."

"You are well-informed," Stefanie said coldly.

"I'm only repeating what I've been told."

They drove through Ruislip Manor and on up Eastcote Lane towards South Harrow, passing mile after mile of identical semi-detached houses. Two prominent landmarks dominated the sky-line, the church of St Mary's-on-the-Hill and a cylindrical gasometer that towered above the surrounding urban sprawl and resembled a Martian spacecraft.

"This is a fun time," Stefanie observed sourly. "What have you dragged me all the way out here for?"

"To clear the air, to get at the truth."

"Are you implying I've lied to you?"

It was a lovely spring evening, not a cloud in the sky, the sun just beginning to dip towards the horizon. The weathermen had forecast localised thunderstorms before dark; the only sign of one was inside the Mini where the atmosphere was electric.

"About Kurt Bender? Yes, I think you have been less than honest where he is concerned."

"I'm not taking any more of this. Stop the goddamned car and let me off."

"Like hell."

Parker shot past the Piccadilly Line station at South Harrow and took the first turning on the right. He didn't know the area and navigated by a sense of direction. A road sign told him he was on South Hill Avenue which he guessed would eventually lead to Harrow-on-the-Hill.

"Did you hear what I said, you limey son of a bitch?"

"Bender wrote two letters to your mother, one in '48, the other in '66. Two in eighteen years." Parker shook his head. "Why we swallowed that one I'll never know."

"Okay, there were other letters, some of them the begging kind. I guess he thought my folks were a soft touch because the first time Bender wrote, my father felt sorry for him and mailed fifty dollars to his address in Kassel."

"How many letters?" Parker asked, cutting her short.

"He wasn't a regular correspondent – once, sometimes twice a year."

"So we're talking about a minimum of twenty, maximum of forty letters?"

"I guess . . ."

"You should have been open with us."

"And what would have happened if I had laid it on the line? How much credence would you have then given Bender's story? I'll tell you in a word – zilch."

Parker thought she was probably right. He couldn't answer for Larborough and Harry Freeland but he himself would certainly have been highly sceptical.

"Why did you go to Kevin Mullinder for help?"

"Because he happened to be a neighbour, because I knew the kind of work he had been doing for the National Council for Civil Liberties and your Home Office was being particularly obstructive. I didn't give a damn about his politics."

Parker went on up the private road without having to pay a toll, reached the road junction at the top and turned left. "I didn't give a damn about his politics." Conviction, anger and defiance; all three had been present in her voice, but it didn't tell him much other than that he wasn't exactly her favourite man.

"I believe you," he said.

"Oh, that's really big of you, Campbell."

"There are others who don't."

"That's their problem."

It could be hers if the Home Office got funny and issued a deportation order. Provided he finished handing over to Quade by close of play tomorrow, he could drive up to Scarborough and have a word with Linda Norris who had taken pity on Kurt Bender in more ways than one. And while he was at it, perhaps he should stop off in Lincoln on the way back and see Tomas Rojek who had known Andrew Korwin in Warsaw when they were both in the Home Army.

"Where's the nearest subway station?" Stefanie demanded.

"A long way from here."

St Mary's Church at Harrow-on-the-Hill had existed before the Doomsday Book was compiled. The King's Head was a more recent addition and had only been around for perhaps a hundred odd years. Taking advantage of a parking space near the small green, Parker squeezed the Mini between a Bentley and a Jaguar 3.5 litre saloon.

"Why have we stopped here?"

"It looks like a nice place to have dinner."

"Yeah? Well, I hope you enjoy it, buster."

Stefanie unclipped her seat belt, got out of the car and started to walk back the way they had come. By the time Parker had scrambled out and locked the doors, she had covered a good twenty yards. He asked her where she thought she was going. Stefanie told him in no uncertain terms to get lost.

The man who got off the train at Warsaw's East Station had spent the last twenty-one years in Lublin Prison. This was the second time in eight months the Poles had brought him to their capital in the dark of the night, so he wasn't surprised when the same escorting officers led him across the marshalling yard to a closed van. Last September, a similar vehicle had conveyed them to and from police headquarters on Marcelego Nowotki, but this time, the old Jew would not be waiting to confront him with photographs, diaries, newspaper clippings and a list of questions as long as your arm. Furthermore, he wouldn't be going back to Lublin.

He had completed his sentence and kept the faith, which was more than he could say for some people. No time off for good behaviour, just twenty-one years of hard labour, breaking rocks with a sledgehammer. And then, with only eight months to go, the old Jew had had the impudence to dangle the prospect of immediate freedom in return for his cooperation. He had been tempted to spit in the kike's face but that would have been asking for trouble and there was no point in making the last two hundred and forty-three days harder to bear than the seven thousand four hundred and twenty-seven that had preceded them. So he had acted all oily and unctuous – "yes sir, no sir, I'd like to help, sir, but I do not recognise any of these faces." And the best part had been the knowledge that the Yid had known he was lying and could do nothing about it.

But all that was in the past. Tonight he would be lodged in a cell at police headquarters; tomorrow morning, the Polish Untermenschen would drive him out to the airport and the Tupolev Tu 124 Lot Airlines flight to East Berlin. It would be his first step on the road to freedom, his first step along the path of retribution. His name was Karl Werner Ulex. A former Obersturmführer, he had been born of mixed parentage at Wielun on the Polish-German border on the ninth of April 1922 and had spent part of the war with Sonderkommando Gerhardt Terboven. He had finished it in the ranks of the 184th Infantry Division defending Breslau and would have been treated like any other POW had it not been for the treachery of a Feldwebel who had betrayed him to the Polish War Crimes Commission. Among the people with whom he had a score to settle, ex-Feldwebel Kurt Bender was the one he hated most, the man he most wanted to kill.

CHAPTER 14

LINDA NORRIS was the wrong side of forty but was doing her best to disguise it. The lines above and below her eyes were buried under a layer of make-up that made her face seem like that of a Dresden figurine. She was wearing false lashes and had been a touch overgenerous with the eye shadow. Her hair was an unnatural auburn and had been cemented in a bouffant style so that the texture reminded Parker of candyfloss. She was wearing a silk blouse buttoned to a frill at the throat which hid any wrinkles in her neck, a wide patent-leather belt and a black mini skirt that left very little to the imagination.

Parker had set out from London the night before, snatched a few hours' sleep in a layby near York and arrived in Scarborough in time for breakfast. Catching Linda Norris at home had taken almost as long as the drive up. Eastham had told him she had a semi-detached near the station and it had been easy enough to get her address out of the phone book, but getting his foot inside the door had been much more difficult.

The first time he had called at the house, Linda Norris had evidently still been in bed; when he had returned an hour and a half later, one of the neighbours had told him that she'd gone shopping. Undeterred, he had tried again at lunchtime and this time had better luck. A piece of plastic with his passport-size photograph in the top right-hand corner had done the rest. The identity card was good for Queen Anne's Gate, 54 Broadway, Benbow House and Amberley Lodge; Linda Norris allowed Parker into her house because it looked impressive and she thought the card gave him some kind of statutory right of entry.

She normally received visitors in the front parlour; he got the star treatment and was shown into the sitting room at the back of the house.

"You know something," Linda said, "you're the second chap who's been to see me about Kurt in the past fortnight."

"Did the other man give you his name?" Parker asked.

"He did, but I've forgotten it. Didn't care for him at all, struck me as very shifty. Had a gammy foot, said he was a private investigator."

"Well, he certainly isn't with the Immigration Service," Parker said blandly. "That's one thing you can be sure of."

"And you are?"

"Yes, from head office in Croydon."

He could have embellished the story by telling her that he worked under Harold Nash, but that could have been dangerous. It was also unnecessary because his identity card had prepared the ground and she was ready to believe almost anything.

"That's the place where all the landing cards end up," Parker continued. "When Mr Bender completed his, he gave a false address in Scarborough and stated that he was staying with friends for an extended holiday."

"And that's why you are here?"

"Partly. The fact is, our German friend has disappeared. We know he was employed as a barman at the Bay View Hotel but he handed in his notice two months ago and didn't leave a forwarding address. However, the proprietor did say he thought Mr Bender had been lodging with you."

According to Eastham, the relationship had been a good deal closer than the usual landlady and lodger, but he would gain nothing by offending her susceptibilities.

"I don't usually take in lodgers," Linda told him, "but Kurt couldn't find any accommodation in Scarborough and I agreed to let him a room. He left on Friday the sixth of April, said he'd had enough of England, but of course that wasn't the only reason he wanted to go home."

"That's the trouble," Parker said, "he didn't return to Germany. Matter of fact, I'm here because the Federal authorities in Bonn are anxious to trace him."

"Why? What's Kurt supposed to have done?"

"He used to be a salesman for A. G. Mann in Frankfurt and it seems some of the deals he made were fraudulent."

"Christ." Linda stared at him, her jaw sagging. "Now I know why I haven't heard from him."

"Were you expecting to?"

"He said he would write as soon as he'd found somewhere to live. He'd had this windfall you see, close on a million marks; he'd won it on this sort of bingo game they have in Germany." She frowned. "Lotto Toto, or something like that. Anyway, Kurt had this friend in Cologne he used to send money to for his share of the stake in the weekly lottery."

A million Deutschmarks at the current rate of exchange was, Parker calculated, a little under ninety thousand pounds. Bender, along with vast numbers of people, would regard that as a small fortune, more than they would ever earn in a lifetime.

"I imagine he must have been very excited?"

"Happy as Larry is the expression I'd use. See, Kurt's friend had phoned the hotel to give him the news and he'd calmed down a bit by the time he came home and told me."

Bender, it seemed, had been remarkably phlegmatic about his good fortune and hadn't told any of the staff at the Bay View Hotel that he had hit the jackpot. There had been no farewell party; he had given the manager a fortnight's notice and had then quit two days later.

"Kurt was a close one all right," Linda said and laughed harshly. "Made me swear on the Bible not to say a word to the neighbours, said he didn't want them knowing he had come into money in case the charities got to hear about and wrote him begging letters."

"That doesn't make much sense," Parker said. "What chance did they get to put him on their mailing lists? I mean, he didn't stick around long enough to work out his notice."

"You've been to the Bay View?"

"Yes, I went there while you were out shopping and spoke to the proprietors. Bender told them he didn't want to leave Scarborough but his mother was getting on in years and was becoming very infirm . . ."

"His mother?" Her voice rose. "What the hell are you talking about? She was killed in the same air raid as his first wife."

"I'm only repeating what I was told," Parker said mildly. "Frau Bender is supposed to be seventy-eight years old. It seems that twenty-four hours after Kurt had given in his notice, he had a phone call from one of her neighbours to say that his mother had been taken to hospital with a fractured pelvis after falling over in her kitchen. That's the excuse he gave the hotel when he walked out on them."

"The lying bugger."

"If you say so."

"I need a drink," Linda muttered. "How about you?"

"No, I'm fine thanks."

"That's more than I am." Linda crouched in front of the nook cupboard by the chimney breast, took out a bottle of peppermint cordial, a quart of High and Dry and a tumbler and fixed herself a large gin and pep. "Sure you won't join me?"

Parker shook his head. "Thanks all the same, but I'm driving."

"Hard luck."

"Did Kurt take all his things when he left?"

"Yep, cleared out lock, stock and barrel."

"What about his laundry?"

"You mean his dirty washing?" Linda swallowed half the gin and pep, then licked her lips as though savouring the taste. "He left a pile in the linen basket which I eventually put in the dustbin. Much as I liked Kurt, I draw the line at washing his dirty socks and underpants."

Linda Norris had met Bender one afternoon in late October when she and a couple of girlfriends had lunched at the Bay View Hotel. All three had taken a fancy to the bartender but only Linda had been bold enough to ask him for a date. A fortnight later he had moved in with her, but for all their intimacy, Bender had remained a very private person.

"He was a bit of a loner, I thought. Didn't seem to have any ties with his own country, never wrote to anyone in Germany that I know of, never received any letters from home."

"What about his friend in Cologne?" Parker asked. "The joint winner of the lottery."

Linda finished the rest of the gin and pep and fixed herself another. "I don't think he exists."

"Like the crock of gold?" Parker suggested.

"Oh, I think he was expecting to come into some money all right."

"So what do you think has happened to Bender?"

"Who knows? Perhaps he had one of his funny turns and snuffed it."

"Are you saying he had a bad heart?"

"He had to watch his blood pressure."

Although aware that Bender had been medically downgraded during the war, Parker had assumed the German was physically in good shape apart from the injuries to his left leg. It was therefore something of a surprise to hear that he had a heart condition.

"Was he taking anything for it?"

"Kurt had some pills to relieve his blood pressure and of course he was supposed to watch his diet, but he never did. Mind you, he didn't look ill; matter of fact, with his colouring most people thought he lived a healthy outdoor life."

"You wouldn't have a photograph of him, would you?"

Linda Norris said she thought she had a snapshot in her handbag upstairs and left the room to fetch it. The equivalent of four large gins hadn't done a lot for her equilibrium and she bumped into the furniture on her way out. Parker wanted to go with her but she wouldn't have it and somehow she made it safely to the bedroom and back again without falling down the stairs.

The colour snapshot had been taken sometime during the winter on what had obviously been a very cold and dull-looking day. Bender was leaning against some railings, arms folded across his chest. With only the sea in the background, it wasn't easy to judge his height but Parker thought he was about five feet seven. His hair was a mousy colour and the absence of any grey in it made him seem much younger than fifty-two. A round, almost chubby face also contributed to his fairly youthful appearance.

"Where was this snapshot taken?" Parker asked.

"Redcar. Kurt hired a self-drive Anglia and we went up there one Sunday. God knows why, it was a bitterly cold day in February and everything was closed up for the winter, amusement arcades, ice-cream parlours, the lot. Anyway, we drove round the town a bit and looked at the houses on a smart estate and Kurt kept telling me how we would have a mansion with a swimming pool and a tennis court one day. Of course, I didn't believe him. Why should I when he never had two pennies to rub together?"

"Can I keep this snapshot?"

The question seemed to tax her mental faculties to the limit but she finally came to a decision. "I don't see why not; after all, the bugger walked out and left me. Why should I want to remember him?"

There were a lot of pieces missing from the jigsaw but a picture of sorts was beginning to take shape. Andrew Korwin, otherwise known as Arthur Kershaw, lived in Redcar and Parker couldn't help wondering if this was the reason why the German had visited the seaside resort in the middle of winter.

*   *   *

It was not the first time Garvey had been to Middlesbrough; it was however the first time Arthur Kershaw had taken him to the Highfield on Martin Road for lunch. He had travelled north to investigate a possible offence under Section 2 of the Official Secrets Acts and had wasted almost three precious hours eating his way through a four-course table d'hôte menu followed by coffee, brandy and cigars. By the time they returned to Kershaw's stuffy and overheated office at the Ward Tandy works, Garvey wasn't at his best and was less than razor sharp. Aware of this, he chose to use the bludgeon instead of the rapier.

"I think you know why I am here, Arthur," he began as menacingly as a man could who felt obligated to the host who had wined and dined him.

"I would be extremely worried if you didn't share my concern," Kershaw said.

Garvey stared at the older man with the blank expression of a boxer who had come storming out of his corner at the bell only to be caught by a sucker punch. It took him several moments to recover and even then he was still largely ineffective.

"There's a feeling in Whitehall that your company has not been exactly straight with us."

"I think it would be more accurate to say that Elta Industrielle has been less than honest with the Ward Tandy Group. At the risk of repeating everything I told you on Tuesday, it was Marcel Verlhac who asked to meet Victor Stevens, the head of our design team, not the other way round. We were led to believe that Elta were having technical problems with certain modifications they wished to make to the laser sight if they were to secure an order from the French Government. I told the French that Victor was going to Malaga but they insisted the meeting couldn't wait until he returned from holiday. So Victor agreed to interrupt his vacation and Marcel Verlhac arranged to meet him in Seville, ostensibly because it was only a two or three hour drive from Malaga. We had absolutely no idea that Hassan al Jaifi would be present."

The office was like a greenhouse, all glass and very little ventilation. Garvey couldn't understand how Kershaw could remain so alert in such an atmosphere when his own eyelids kept drooping. "You should have consulted us first," he said and smothered a yawn. "The Stevens Target Acquisition Laser is classified Top Secret."

"I'm fully aware of that," Kershaw told him, "but you can't expect us to answer for Elta Industrielle. The military application of Victor's work is a joint project and they don't appear to be subject to quite the same restrictions. All right, you can slap our wrists for failing to inform you before the event, but we hardly received any notice ourselves and we thought it was a technical problem." He paused, then said, "If you have a complaint, John, you should really take issue with the French Government. Meantime, I hope you will consider what physical security measures are necessary to protect this factory from sabotage."

"Sabotage?" Garvey frowned.

"Well, of course you would know better than me, but I would have said Hassan al Jaifi and Marcel Verlhac were assassinated by the Israelis. And if I'm right, I think they may try to fire-bomb the Elta Industrielle plant and perhaps this factory as well."

"Could you personally have been targeted?"

Kershaw thought about it, then shook his head. "I don't think anyone has been watching me."

Garvey wondered how much he could take on trust. Kershaw had been cleared by positive vetting at the request of the Procurement Executive in 1963 when the Ministry of Defence had expressed an interest in the prototype of the Stevens Target Acquisition Laser, popularly known as STAL. His security file had acquired several additional folios in 1966 as a result of the Bender affair. In that instance, Kershaw had shown a proper regard for security and had lost no time in reporting the incident at the Frankfurt Trade Fair to MI5. But was he being quite so open eight months later?

"No one else from the past has tried to get in touch with you, have they?" Garvey asked.

"Are you referring to my niece?"

"If Stefanie Ayres is your niece."

"I don't think there can be any doubt about that. She is too well-informed about my family to be an impostor."

"Would you like to give me an example?"

"She has a photograph of my mother in a gold locket that has been in the Korwin family for the last two hundred years. She is my sister's daughter, you can depend on it."

"Are you going to see her again?"

"Whenever Stefanie wants. Nancy and I couldn't have children and she is our kith and kin."

"What about her father? Do you have any plans to see him?"

"That's really up to Frank. He works for the State Department and I don't imagine he will find it easy to get away."

"You hope."

Kershaw reared back as if he had been struck. For a moment, Garvey thought he was going to deny vehemently the allegation until a rueful smile appeared.

"I didn't realise it was so obvious. But you are right, I don't have too high a regard for my brother-in-law. He was just a lowly consular official when I knew him in Warsaw and by all accounts he hasn't progressed very far since those days. I always felt he was a social climber and a bit of a fortune hunter, but perhaps I am being unfair . . ."

Kershaw paused as if to give him an opportunity to dismiss the suggestion. When he didn't, the former Polish officer assured him that he had no such reservations about his niece. Stefanie Ayres, it seemed, was everything he would have wanted in a daughter of his own – intelligent, charming, kind, thoughtful, amusing, compassionate.

"You don't have to worry about my niece, John. She isn't engaged in a disinformation exercise like the late, unlamented Kurt Bender."

No matter how obliquely it was put to him, Garvey did not like to be reminded of his part in the Bender affair. He had set up a meet to frighten him off and the German had dropped dead at his feet and he'd had to dispose of the body. He had done what had to be done but there would be a public outcry if it ever came to light. Fortunately, it seemed no one had missed Bender or inquired after him – except Eastham – and he had only seen him as a stepping stone to finding Andrew Korwin.

"We are straying from the point, Arthur," Garvey said curtly.

"I'm sorry, you sounded worried about Stefanie and I was merely trying to set your mind at rest."

"Your partner, Victor Stevens, must be the luckiest man alive," Garvey said, suddenly pursuing a different line.

"Yes, he had a miraculous escape."

"Do you think the killers had his name on their death list along with Hassan al Jaifi and Marcel Verlhac?"

Kershaw spread his hands in a dismissive gesture. "How could I possibly know? I'm not a professional Intelligence officer like you. But if you want me to play guessing games, I think they would have shot him for no other reason than that he happened to be there. The Israelis have no reason to regard Victor as an enemy and I'm willing to bet the Mossad have never heard of him."

"I wonder. He is a Russian Jew and he survived Treblinka. People remember things like that."

"And a lot more prefer to forget such an experience."

"Including Victor?" Garvey suggested.

"Treblinka is not his favourite topic of conversation."

Garvey felt another yawn coming on and made a determined effort to stifle it. "But he told you all about it?"

"Yes. We met after the war in the displaced persons camp at Hannover. Victor was taken prisoner in June 1941 but it was only in the following March that the death camp at Treblinka was opened."

"What did the Germans do with him during the intervening time?"

"He was held in a prisoner of war cage like hundreds of thousands of Red Army men."

"Are you telling me it took the Nazis at least eight months to discover he was a Jew?"

"I wouldn't know," Kershaw said mildly, "I wasn't there. If you are so worried about it, I can't think why you haven't asked Victor."

"We have."

Victor Stevens, previously known as Viktor Stashinsky, had been screened by an Intelligence Corps sergeant from 89 Field Security Section in 1947 when he was living in the DP camp. He had made a long and apparently full statement to the sergeant but there had been a number of curious gaps in his account. The eight months he had spent in a prisoner of war cage near Lwow had been dismissed in a few sentences and he had been almost as reticent about the time he had spent in the concentration camp. He had, however, been very forthcoming about the latter stages of the war from November '44 to May '45 when he had been a slave labourer with Krupp of Essen. Prior to that, most of his story had to be taken on trust, except of course for the number tattooed on his wrist which proved conclusively that he had been an inmate of Treblinka. Inquiries conducted sixteen years later when he was being positively vetted had failed to shed any further light on that period of his life, but this hadn't bothered the case officer. Victor had entered the UK in February 1949 and from then on there had been no

170

shortage of people who were prepared to vouch for him. There was one other factor in his favour. Back in 1947, the Intelligence Corps sergeant had observed that Viktor Stashinsky was a rabid anti-Communist and nursed an all-consuming hatred for Stalin, Beria and Molotov.

"The Israelis had no reason to go after Victor but the Russians . . ." Kershaw paused, then said, "Well, that's another matter."

Garvey sat up. Suddenly the adrenalin was flowing, the listlessness had disappeared and he was wide awake. "What exactly are you implying?" he asked.

"It could be nothing . . ."

"Suppose you let me be the judge of that."

"It was something Victor said years ago when we were in the DP camp at Hannover. We were talking about Barbarossa and the first few days of the Nazi attack on the USSR when soldiers like Victor were taken prisoner before they could join up with their units on mobilisation. He had been ordered to report to the Signals battalion supporting Major General Vlasov's infantry division in Lwow, but he never got there . . ."

"And?" Garvey prompted.

"Well, then we got on to the subject of Vlasov and the Russian Army of Liberation."

Major General A. A. Vlasov had been more fortunate than Viktor Stashinsky. He had fought his way out of Lwow and had been promoted to command the 20th Army on the Moscow Front in December 1941 where he had subsequently distinguished himself during the winter campaign. The following spring his entire army had been trapped inside the narrow salient they had driven into the German lines when Stalin had refused him permission to withdraw. In captivity, Vlasov had become thoroughly disillusioned with the Stalinist régime and had recruited a Russian Liberation Army from amongst the six hundred and fifty thousand men who had deserted from the Red Army. However, Vlasov had raised only two divisions because Himmler had been jealous and suspicious of his Russian ally and hadn't allowed him to command more than a corps. But there had been no shortage of volunteers willing to fight alongside the German Army. The Wehrmacht had been stiff with Russians and so had the SS; the 14th SS Grenadier Division had been a hundred per cent Ukrainian and the 39th SS had been pure Muscovites.

"Did Victor say he had served in the 14th SS Grenadiers?" Garvey asked.

"Not in so many words," Kershaw told him, "but at the time I remember thinking that he seemed to know an awful lot about them."

From Scarborough, Parker drove along the coast road to Bridlington and then south-west to skirt the Humber estuary via Goole before eventually picking up the A15 trunk road to Lincoln east of Scunthorpe. Two hours forty minutes and a hundred and twelve miles later, he pulled up outside the Grand Hotel in St Mary Street near the Central Station down the hill from Lincoln Cathedral. He checked into the hotel, unpacked his bag, then went down to the lobby a few minutes after six o'clock and put a trunk call through to Sarah Yendell at her flat in Bayswater. The number seemed to ring out for a very long time before she got around to answering it.

"Hi," he said, "it's me."

"Campbell?" Her voice was a mixture of surprise and delight. "Where are you calling from?"

"Lincoln," he said.

"What on earth are you doing there?"

"I'm planning to see a man called Tomas Rojek tomorrow."

"Who's he?"

"A Pole who knew Andrew Korwin in Warsaw."

"You're not still going down that path, are you?" Sarah asked a touch wearily.

"Will you do me a favour?"

"You know I will. Name it."

"I want a photocopy of Bender's military record of service."

"But Maurice has the file."

"I know." Parker hesitated. "Look, I think we had better forget it . . ."

"No, it's okay, I can get hold of the file. Where do you want me to send the photocopy?"

"To my flat in Ravenscourt Park."

"Right."

"One other thing. If you are going to mail it, don't use the post room at Broadway."

There was no need for him to explain why she would have to observe the utmost discretion.

CHAPTER 15

THE DORMER house where Tomas Rojek lived backed on to the cricket ground and enjoyed a diagonal view of Lincoln Cathedral in the background. The garden was mostly lawn with a rosebed at the bottom, beyond which was a small vegetable patch. Tall privet hedges on either flank ensured the maximum privacy from the neighbours. It was, in fact, an oasis of peace and quiet and on such a warm, sunny day, Parker couldn't think of a more pleasant way to spend a morning than lounging in a deck chair with a cup of coffee to hand.

Rojek was a short, stocky man with large capable hands ingrained with oil and grease that no amount of scrubbing with a pumice stone could remove. He was sixty-five years old and had been a lathe operator all his working life from the time he had left school in 1916. Born in the industrial suburb of Praga on the east bank of the Vistula, he had spent the war years working in a secret underground factory producing small arms for the Home Army. In the early days of the Resistance, he had manufactured copies of the Schmeisser MP38 sub-machine-gun, a few of which had been stolen from the ordnance depot near the Danzig station.

The prewar version of the Schmeisser was however a precision-made weapon that had proved both time-consuming and expensive to copy, especially as all the raw materials had to be obtained from the Germans without them realising what was going on. As far as the Occupation authorities were concerned, Rojek's factory was producing ammunition containers for the Wehrmacht using sheet metal produced in the Ruhr. To obtain the necessary materials for the Schmeissers, the Polish foreman would hide an order for high-grade steel among the requisitions for sheet metal which the German overseer signed blank after reading the top copy only. When it was delivered, the high-grade steel was then spirited away and hidden under the wooden floor of the factory.

In 1942, the RAF started to deliver the Sten gun to the Home Army. The Sten sub-machine-gun was cheap, crude, ugly and effective in that it worked. The weapon was simple, easy to copy, and except for the bolt head, could be manufactured with low-grade steel. A week after taking delivery of one, Rojek had set up a production line achieving a minimum output of thirty Stens a week.

But his experiences as an arms manufacturer wasn't the reason why Parker had gone out of his way to meet him, although he was obliged to listen to a considerable number of anecdotes before he could ask about "Talmunt", the codename Korwin was supposed to have used when he was serving in the Home Army. One of the men who had fought alongside him in the Warsaw uprising, which had begun on the first of August 1944, was Tomas Rojek. However, until Stefanie Ayres had put a name to him, "Talmunt"'s true identity had been a mystery for almost twenty-three years. Getting Rojek to talk about him wasn't difficult; like many an old soldier, an attentive audience was all the encouragement he needed to go down memory lane. He was loquacious because he also believed Parker was a freelance journalist who was hoping to do a feature on Stefanie Ayres and her long lost uncle.

"I'm glad she found him," Rojek said.

"Yes, it makes a nice story with a happy ending. All I need to do is flesh it out a bit. People like to read about heroes and by all accounts, Korwin was a hero."

"He was a very brave man and a good company commander."

"You knew him well?" Parker said.

"Not before the uprising. You have to understand that up till then, we had been organised in sections of five to six men and only the section leaders had ever met the platoon commander. Likewise, none of the section leaders knew the company commander by sight. The whole idea was to limit the number of people you could betray if you were arrested and tortured by the Gestapo. As an extra precaution, section leaders and above were known only by a codename. For instance, my section commander was known as 'Kazimir', after the Polish king, Jan Kazimir. I never learned his real name."

"So you didn't have any contact with Korwin before the uprising began on the first of August?"

"That's right. The first time our company came together was when we assembled in Targowa Street to attack the Kierbedzia Bridge."

"And Korwin had gone missing forty-eight hours before that."

"Where did you get that idea? We may have failed to take the bridge but we regrouped and captured Wilna railway station, and we held it for several days. And I might tell you there were a lot of Germans in Praga – of course, they were mostly artillerymen from the 73rd Infantry Division."

"I obviously got it wrong," Parker said genially. "Just out of interest, when was the last time you saw Mr Korwin?"

"It must have been nine or ten days after the uprising began. He was wounded by shellfire and we took him to a field dressing station."

Parker finished the rest of his coffee and placed the cup and saucer on the grass by his deck chair. Stefanie Ayres had given him two conflicting versions; here was a third. When he had interviewed her at 4 Central Buildings, she had told him that her uncle had only stopped fighting when General 'Bor' Komorowski had ordered his men to lay down their arms, which would have been on the second of October, two months after the uprising had started. But the day after she had returned from seeing him in Redcar, it seemed that Korwin had been picked up by the Gestapo two days before the insurrection had begun. Yet Arthur Kershaw was Andrew Korwin; he had Stefanie's word for it and he could think of no reason why she should lie to him. But Kershaw wasn't and never had been the Resistance leader known as "Talmunt".

"What did Captain Korwin look like when you knew him in 1944?"

"Tall, thin, studious-looking, not a bit like an army officer. I thought he might have been a university lecturer before the war."

"Did he tell you he had been a regular officer in the 9th Carpathian Lancers?"

"No."

"Or that he had been the ADC to the Garrison Commander during the first siege of Warsaw in 1939?"

"No." Rojek stirred uncomfortably in his deck chair. "Why are you wanting to know all these details, Mr Parker?"

"Because it's a fascinating story and I like to get my facts straight. You mustn't feel that you are betraying a confidence because I've already interviewed Miss Ayres." Parker reached inside his jacket. "Matter of fact, she gave me this photocopy of the letter you wrote to her."

Rojek made no attempt to take the letter from him. "Why did she do that?" he asked.

"It could have been that she wanted everyone to know how unhelpful the Civil Service had been when she was looking for her uncle. She told me why she had asked you to write a letter to her care of *The Sentinel*; now I'd like to hear it from you."

Rojek looked up, his right hand acting as a sun visor to shield his eyes from the glare. High above them, a 'V' bomber left white vapour trails in the blue sky. "Handley Page Victor," he said. "Probably from RAF Waddington."

"I'll take your word for it," Parker said.

"She came to see me one Sunday, must have been five weeks ago . . ."

Suddenly, and for no apparent reason, it seemed that Rojek had decided to confide in him. Up until then, Parker had thought the Pole had sensed he had been bluffing and had known instinctively that Stefanie hadn't admitted anything.

"Of course, she telephoned me first."

"Naturally."

"She told me her uncle was 'Talmunt' and I believed her because she certainly knew a lot about me, who I was, what I had done . . ."

Stefanie had got the information when she had gone to the offices of *The Sentinel*. People were always falling over backwards to help her and the Puzaks had been no exception. They had allowed Stefanie to go through their card index of Polish ex-servicemen and Resistance workers and she had picked on Rojek.

"She told me all about her uncle and the trouble she was having with the authorities," Rojek continued. "I couldn't see how a letter from me repeating everything she had just told me was going to help her but I was happy to do it. She's a very nice girl, Mr Parker; I couldn't refuse to help her."

"Of course you couldn't. And you've also been a great help to me."

"You're leaving?" Rojek sounded almost disappointed.

"Afraid I have to, I've got an appointment in London."

Stefanie Ayres didn't know it yet but they were going to have a heart-to-heart talk. He would grab her when she walked out of the offices of the management consultancy agency on Throgmorton Street; the problem was how to do it without being spotted by the watchmen whom Garvey had implied were keeping her under surveillance.

Harry Freeland left the Deputy Director's office overlooking Queen Anne's Gate and made his way through the maze of interconnecting passages to 54 Broadway. In a long career, he had held only two London-based appointments, the previous occasion being in 1958 when, for a little over a year, he had been the Acting Principal Staff Officer to the standing committee on Establishments and Estimates. In those far-off days, the Administrative Department had been located at 54 Broadway and he had got to know the layout of the rabbit warren pretty well. But things hadn't stood still in the last nine years and the interior of the building had been adapted to meet changing needs. Once familiar corridors were now blocked off and he had to retrace his steps a couple of times. At one point, he had even to descend to the ground floor in order to find the right staircase leading to the mezzanine. However, by trial and error, Freeland eventually arrived at the Warsaw Pact Department.

He decided as a matter of courtesy to look in on Maurice Orde but as it happened, the Assistant Director had locked his door and was elsewhere in the rabbit warren. The open door and uncluttered desk told him that, unlike his department chief, Parker wasn't even in the building. Hearing the slow and heavy click-clack of a typewriter in the adjoining room, he poked his head round the door.

"Hello," he said, "I'm Harry Freeland. We haven't met but I knew your parents when they were stationed in Washington."

Sarah Yendell looked up, her face colouring slightly. "You're in charge of the Rest of the World Department," she said as if to place him.

"Right. Where's Campbell got to?"

"He's been posted to the Training School on promotion to Principal Staff Officer Coord."

"When did this happen?"

"Nick Quade took over from him on Wednesday. Campbell reports to Amberley Lodge on Monday."

"Nick Quade?" Freeland frowned. "I don't think I know him."

"He was in charge of the combined Albanian and Bulgarian Desks. As a matter of fact, he still is; that's why he has to divide his time between the two jobs. I don't know how long that will last."

Freeland could understand now why the Deputy Director had

177

spent the last two hours endeavouring to persuade him that his own department could afford to shed yet another post. At the behest of the government, the Establishments Committee had recently spent several weeks on a cost-cutting exercise, following which the budget for the Rest of the World Department had been reduced by eight thousand pounds in the current financial year. In effect, this meant that one post had to be underimplemented and normal wastage in the typing pool could not be replaced. Every department had suffered, including the Training School, but now it was beginning to look as if some of their budgetary cuts had been restored to provide an upgraded appointment for Campbell Parker. But it hadn't ended there; although the DD hadn't said so, it had been evident that he was being invited to make good the deficiency in Maurice Orde's organisation.

"Did you want to see Campbell?" Sarah asked.

"No, I'm sure you can help me." Freeland smiled. "After all, you're the one who made my life a lot easier when you found Andrew Korwin."

"Well actually, Campbell told me where to look. All I had to do was go through the list of British exhibitors at the Frankfurt Trade Fair."

"Yes, well I don't suppose you happen to remember the name of the firm he represented, do you?"

"Yes, it was the Ward Tandy Group."

"That's the company," Freeland said and snapped his fingers.

No one had been more diligent these last few days than the head of SIS Station, Madrid. At every stage of the police investigation he had fired off another cable, a copy of which had ended up on Freeland's desk, the precedent having been established with the initial report of the triple murder. Although Victor Stevens had been mentioned in the first cable, it was only in the latest signal which had been despatched at 0900 hours Greenwich Mean Time that he had been described as the head of research and development, Ward Tandy.

"Is that what you wanted to see me about, Mr Freeland?"

Sarah Yendell might have acquired few academic qualifications but he had learned from several sources that it was a mistake to write her off as a decorative member of the upper middle class and he could see what Maurice Orde, among others, had been getting at. She was quick on the uptake and perceptive, perhaps a little too perceptive for comfort.

"No, I'm interested in Kurt Bender. His name has cropped up in another context and I'd like to see the stuff you have on him."

"I'm afraid the file has been destroyed."

"Why did you do that?"

"I didn't shred it."

"Then who did?"

"Maurice Orde's PA – on his instructions I might add."

Her voice was full of suppressed fury. Something had touched a raw nerve and Freeland doubted it was just the destruction of a file.

"Suppose you tell me what is going on," he said quietly.

"It's not something I feel very calm about, but I'll try." Sarah took a deep breath and started again. "Maurice Orde asked me for the file on Tuesday, shortly after Campbell had gone to lunch. I had this funny feeling that he had waited until Campbell had left the office before he approached me. So I asked him for a signature, which was pretty stupid of me because we'd only graded the file Confidential. The following day, we did a hundred per cent check of our classified documents for Nick Quade's benefit and Maurice confirmed that the Bender file was in his safe. Last night, Campbell rang me at home to ask if I could photocopy the papers; this morning when I asked Judy for the file, she told me it had been destroyed."

Judy was Maurice Orde's PA. Knowing her of old, Freeland could understand why there would be more than a mere generation gap between the two women. Judy had always struck him as the sort of office matriarch who would consider her appointment to be vastly superior to that of a junior research assistant.

"We had a spat," Sarah continued. "Judy got on her high horse which made me mad and I told her to get Maurice to sign the damned register if she was frightened to."

Freeland could imagine how well that must have gone down with the older woman. To say that she would have resented being told by an underling to sign an entry in the classified documents register certifying that she had shredded the Bender file would be an understatement. There would have been a lot of hissing and spitting, metaphorically speaking, the claws would have been unsheathed and the fur would have been flying in all directions.

"I knew I was being childish but she got my dander up and I wasn't prepared to back down. Anyway, I left the register on her desk and it was returned by hand of messenger – unsigned. Then, just before lunch, creepy Roger Dent dropped by the office to see me."

"Judy reported you?"

"She must have done. You should have heard Dent." Sarah pulled a face. "Would I like to explain my strange behaviour? What had made me fly off the handle? Was I having trouble with my boyfriend? Did I have money problems? Or was I feeling under the weather? I'm still not sure what it was all about."

Freeland could have told her. When people like Roger Dent pursued the line of questioning he had, they were looking for a reason to withdraw all security clearances. And once deprived of a positive vetting status, it was impossible to remain in the SIS. It seemed incredible that a former Obergefreiter could muddy the waters to such an extent but there was no escaping the feeling that Kurt Bender was in possession of information which Her Majesty's Government were determined to suppress.

"I don't know what I am going to say to Campbell . . ."

"You can tell him I've got the file and will be in touch."

Freeland could see in her eyes that the questions were forming but he had no intention of answering them. Leaving her office before she even had time to voice the first one, he made his way to the communications centre in the basement and drafted a signal to Bonn requesting Head of Station to repeat the previous transmission on Bender. He also requested that the incoming data should be addressed for his eyes only. That way, only the Deputy Director or the DG himself could have it intercepted.

Parker entered one of the pay phones outside the Underground station at Temple and placed a handful of loose change on top of the coin box. The instructions he proposed to give Stefanie Ayres were simple enough and could be put across in a few sentences; persuading her not to hang up on him was going to be the difficult thing. They hadn't exactly parted the best of friends outside the King's Head Hotel on Tuesday evening and she had refused to get in the Mini when he had tailed her down South Hill Avenue. He had kerb-crawled all the way down to the Underground station at South Harrow and would have abandoned the car and followed her up on to the platform if she hadn't gone up to the police constable who had happened to be cooling his heels in the booking hall. By the time he had produced his driving licence and convinced the officer that he had not been molesting the young lady, a westbound train had clattered over the bridge and departed again, leaving him high and dry.

He just hoped that Stefanie would hear him out and do as he asked. One look at Throgmorton Street had been enough to convince him there was no way he could grab her when she walked out of the management consultancy agency without being spotted by Garvey's people. She had to lose them all by herself and then join him in Crown Office Row by the Inner Temple garden where he had left the Mini. To do that successfully, it was essential not to break the usual pattern until the last possible moment. Every evening, she walked into the Bank station on the Central Line and used the escalator link to the Monument station where she caught either a District or Circle Line train to Sloane Square. Tonight, he wanted her to leave the train at Blackfriars a split second before the doors closed, then double back to Mansion House and take a cab to the Royal Courts of Justice in the Strand. From there, it was only a short walk to Crown Office Row.

Parker fed enough coins into the box to keep him going for several minutes and then dialled out the number. When the switchboard operator answered at the agency, he pressed button "A" and asked for extension 189. He did not recognise the voice at the other end of the line.

"My name is Campbell Parker," he told the girl. "I'm sorry but I thought Miss Ayres was on this extension?"

"She usually is, Mr Parker, but she left for Vienna this afternoon."

"Vienna?" he repeated blankly.

"Yes, she will be back on Monday. I'm her secretary, can I take a message?"

"No, it's okay," Parker told her. "I'll call again when she is in the office."

He slowly replaced the phone and then left the box. Vienna? What the hell was Stefanie doing in Vienna?

The barbed wire, the watchtowers, the minefields, the guard dogs and the killing zone that delineated the border between the German Democratic Republic and West Germany from east of Lubeck on the Baltic to the Thuringerwald was the means Walther Ulbricht, Chairman of the Council of State, had chosen to stop the westward migration of refugees. Despite the hazards, the good life on the other side of the border was however an irresistible magnet for a large number of people. Some tunnelled under the barrier, some crashed through it in armour-plated juggernauts, others floated above the obstacle in hot-air balloons. Ex-Obersturmführer Karl Werner Ulex did it the easy way courtesy of the SSD espionage section of the Ministry for State Security.

Two hours after his Lot Airline flight arrived in Berlin, Ulex had walked into the Ministry for State Security on Normannenstrasse and reported to the head of the SSD. What he had refused to do for the old Jew from Vienna he was prepared to contemplate for the German Democratic Republic. This had been made known to the East German Intelligence Service by the KGB long before he had been released from Lublin Prison.

He had spent the minimum time in Berlin; the SSD had known what they were getting and they had dispensed with the usual screening process because a transcript of his trial for war crimes was on record. So were details of his service in the Waffen SS. From Normannenstrasse, he had been passed to the main Intelligence Administration on the Gross-Berlinerdamm where he had been briefed and kitted out with clothing, identity papers and hard currency. He had also been allocated a contact in the Federal Republic before being sent on his way.

Ulex had entered West Germany through the back door reaching Munich via Prague, Linz and Salzburg. From Munich, he had travelled to Frankfurt by train to rendezvous with Herr Doktor Erwin Langbehn. Leaving his bag at the Hauptbahnhof, he had then taken the U-bahn out to Gruneburgweg and walked the rest of the way to the surgery in Aug-Siehertstrasse.

Appearances and first impressions were often deceptive but even before they met face to face, Ulex could think of several good reasons why Langbehn shouldn't be working for the East Germans. He lived in an exclusive part of town in a large house with a breathtaking view of the park. There were two cars in the drive, a BMW coupé and a cream-coloured top of the range Mercedes. Both vehicles were indicative of a lucrative practice, as were the well-dressed patients in the waiting room. He wondered what hold the SSD had on Langbehn – a close relative the wrong side of the Iron Curtain or some skeleton in the cupboard? Or did he, despite all the evidence to the contrary, subscribe to the economic philosophy expounded by Marx and Engels? Trying to solve this conundrum helped him pass the time until it was his turn to see the Herr Doktor.

Langbehn was a man who looked as though he enjoyed life's luxuries and didn't believe in stinting himself. He was tall and built like an ox but there was more fat than muscle on his frame. Nature had given him a round face and he had succeeded in inflating it still futher.

"Erica sends her regards," Ulex said, and waited for his reaction.

Langbehn removed his gold-rimmed spectacles and cleaned the lenses with a tissue for no reason other than it gave him something to do with his hands.

"And how is she keeping?" he asked without looking at Ulex.

"I wouldn't know, she has moved to Mexico City."

Langbehn replaced his glasses. "So what is it you want from me?" he asked.

"The home address of a car salesman who lives and works in Frankfurt. His name is Kurt Bender."

"Is he on the phone?"

"There are a lot of Benders in the directory and far too many of them have the letter K as an initial."

"I'm afraid that's your problem."

"What are you trying to tell me, Herr Doktor?" Ulex asked in a dangerously quiet voice.

"I can provide you with a safe house, money and papers but it is not my job to find this Kurt Bender."

"You have connections . . ."

"You can't have been listening. If you want this man you will have to find him."

Ulex stood up and leaned across the desk. He was a good head shorter than Langbehn and much lighter, but twenty-one years of breaking rocks with a sledgehammer had given him muscles of steel. When his eyes suddenly narrowed to black pinpoints of hatred and suppressed rage, he was easily the most terrifying man the Herr Doktor had ever seen.

"I want you to find Bender."

"Yes, of course." Langbehn swallowed nervously. "It may take a day or two." A sickly smile appeared on his loose mouth. "After all, tomorrow is Saturday and . . ."

"You have until Monday," Ulex said, cutting him short.

"Monday. Well, that should give me enough time, but how do I get in touch with you Herr . . . ?"

"You may call me Gustav." Ulex moved towards the door, then turned about. "I don't have a phone number but don't let that worry you. You'll be hearing from me soon enough."

"Right." Langbehn cleared his throat. "May I ask one question?"

"Depends what it is."

"How do you know Bender is in Frankfurt?"

"Because my information comes from an unimpeachable source," Ulex told him.

The unimpeachable source was the old Jew from Vienna who had interviewed him in Warsaw. Amongst the wad of newspaper clippings and photographs, there had been a grainy shot of the ex-Obergefreiter.

CHAPTER 16

ULEX LEFT the Henniger Hof on Hanauer Landstrasse where he had been staying since Friday and started walking towards the Hauptwache in the city centre. On Mondays, Herr Doktor Langbehn attended the clinic at Frankfurt University and he wanted to catch him while he was still at home. The nearest pay phone was four blocks from the hotel; when he got there, the kiosk was already occupied by a neatly dressed man in his late thirties who appeared to have taken up residence. Ulex lit a cigarette, stamped up and down the pavement, looked pointedly at his wristwatch and glowered at the younger man. By the time he condescended to leave the booth, Ulex was beginning to wish he had called Langbehn from his hotel room despite his phobia about nosey switchboard operators. Pausing only to grind the half-smoked cigarette underfoot, he shouldered his way into the kiosk, lifted the phone and fed sixty pfennigs into the meter, then dialled the surgery.

"It's Gustav," he said when Langbehn answered the phone. "What have you got for me?"

"Not a great deal," Langbehn told him in his mellifluous voice. "Your friend is no longer here; he left A. G. Mann Gesellschaft last September after giving them a week's notice."

"Any forwarding address?"

"No, he collected his severance pay in person."

"Do we know where he was living?"

"He had a rather expensive flat at 83 Münchenerstrasse near the city centre. He was six months in arrears with his rent when he walked out."

"What else?"

"The apartment house is owned by Wenke Morgen Properties."

Ulex slapped his forehead in frustration. Prising information out of Langbehn was about as easy as pulling teeth, it had to be levered out of him a bit at a time. The property company, he learned, was based in Stuttgart and was represented locally by a resident superintendent which was a somewhat overinflated title for a janitor. The only other thing Langbehn could tell him was that Bender had shared the flat with a live-in girlfriend called Jutta, surname unknown.

"Is that it?" Ulex asked.

"I don't think I care for your tone . . ."

"Just answer the damned question."

"I've nothing further to add," Langbehn told him primly.

"Right. Now all I want from you is twenty thousand Deutschmarks in cash for expenses."

"Don't be ridiculous . . ."

"In denominations of twenty, fifty and a hundred," Ulex continued relentlessly. "And make sure they are in used notes; I've got an aversion to the crispy clean variety, especially when the serial numbers run in sequence."

"What you are asking for is impossible . . ."

Langbehn was angry, his voice spluttering with indignation. Ulex could picture him sitting at his desk, the colour rising in his face, his jowls wobbling like the throat of a turkey cock.

"I haven't got that much money . . ."

"Don't give me that shit," Ulex said, his voice chilly. "My friends in Gross-Berlinerdamm told me you kept at least fifty thousand in the wall safe in your drawing room."

"You are very much mistaken if you think . . ."

"Let me tell you something, Herr Doktor. The biggest mistake you can make is to annoy me and you are beginning to do just that. Do you understand what I am saying?"

"Yes." Langbehn swallowed audibly. "When do you want the money?"

"I'll collect it tonight, eight o'clock, your place," Ulex said and put the phone down.

He left the kiosk, flagged down a cruising cab and told the driver to take him to the *Frankfurter Allgemeine* on Hellerhofstrasse. For the next hour or so, he would go through the back numbers for September 1966, reading every bit of coverage the Trade Fair had received. After that, he planned to have a quiet word with the janitor to see if he knew who Jutta was and where she was now living.

*　　*　　*

The SIS were not alone in seeking to maintain their anonymity by interviewing outsiders on someone else's turf. MI5 also had their nesting boxes around town, one of which was in Fleetbank House off the Strand where the Procurement Executive was housed. As far as Garvey was concerned, he couldn't have chosen a more appropriate place to interview Victor Stevens; the Procurement Executive were the people who had slapped a Top Secret classification on his target acquisition laser which had meant he had had to be cleared by positive vetting.

The Policia Municipal had allowed Stevens to go after questioning him on and off for thirty-six hours. However, instead of returning to England, he had continued his holiday in Malaga and had flown home on the Saturday as planned. Learning of this in advance, Garvey had phoned him at home on Saturday night and had arranged to meet him at Fleetbank House on Monday at eleven thirty.

In addition to interviewing an outsider on neutral ground, it was also standard practice to use an alias in those delicate situations where subsequently it might be necessary to deny any involvement by MI5. Although Garvey had visited the Ward Tandy factory in September '66 when he had become Kershaw's "guardian angel" and again only a few days ago, he had never met Stevens. He could therefore use an alias with impunity and in this instance had led Stevens to believe he was dealing with a Mr Campbell Parker.

To Garvey's way of thinking, Stevens was remarkably composed for someone who had seen his three companions shot to death and was fortunate to be alive. Perhaps, after his experiences in Treblinka, a triple murder was not something he could get excited about. But Garvey had seen photographs of the carnage around the swimming pool and knew that, in his shoes, he could never have returned to Malaga and spent the next two days sunning himself on the beach. It was this apparent streak of callousness that made it difficult for him to do more than congratulate Stevens on his good fortune in a most perfunctory manner.

"You were very lucky."

Stevens nodded. "I think so too, Mr Parker," he said, smiling briefly.

"And we don't want to push our luck, do we?" Garvey opened the vetting file in front of him. "I've been looking at your security papers," he said casually, "and it seems to me that there are one or two questions the case officer failed to ask when he interviewed you three years ago."

"You surprise me, I thought he was very thorough."

"Do you have any enemies, Mr Stevens – fellow prisoners who knew you in Treblinka and think they have an old score to settle?"

"What are you talking about? I have no enemies; you ask the people who know me in Middlesbrough and Redcar."

Stevens wasn't quite as calm as he had been a few minutes ago. The carefully enunciated accent he had acquired over the years had also slipped a little and the Ukrainian in him was showing through.

"Let's talk about Treblinka," Garvey went on. "How long were you in the camp?"

"Twenty-one months."

"Twenty-one months – that's incredible. How did you manage to survive? I understood most inmates went to the gas chamber in less than four months? I wonder why you were so special? Did they make you a Kapo? Did you help the SS to keep order? Plenty of Jews did."

"I don't have to sit here and listen to this," Stevens muttered, as though advising himself of his rights.

"Were you ever a member of the Russian Liberation Army?"

"No, of course I wasn't."

"I believe you," Garvey told him. "You'd have had to have been a particularly brutal member of the SS for your name to be on an Israeli hit list."

"Are you implying that I was in the SS?" Stevens asked in a voice that scarcely rose above a whisper.

"I'm not, but information to that effect has been laid by an anonymous informant. You are supposed to have been an Unter-sturmführer in the 14th SS Grenadier Division."

"I'm a Jew, Mr Parker . . ."

"I don't think so." Garvey flipped through the vetting file until he found the relevant paragraph in the subject interview. "Accord-ing to the case officer, both you and your wife, Jean, are Baptists."

"I didn't embrace the Christian faith until after the war."

"So what you are saying is that you didn't murder any Hebrews between 1941 and 1945?"

"You are a very offensive man, Mr Parker."

"Sometimes one has to be offensive to get at the truth. And unless we know the whole truth, how can we protect you?"

"Protect me? From whom?"

"Your enemies, whoever they may be. Look, let's forget what happened at Hassan al Jaifi's villa and concentrate our minds on the fact that out there someone is trying to smear you."

Garvey consulted the file again, turning the pages slowly. He didn't have a thing to go on other than Kershaw's vague innuendoes but every instinct told him that Stevens was hiding something and it was his job to drag it out into the open.

"Why didn't you go home after the war, Mr Stevens? Were you frightened to?" Bull's-eye, Garvey thought as he saw his eyes flicker. "Why don't you tell me what happened at Lwow before the SS discovered you were a Jew?" he said in his softest and most persuasive tone of voice. Stevens wanted to unburden himself but he was looking for some kind of assurance; Garvey didn't have to be a mind reader to know that. "Whatever you tell me will go no farther. You have my word."

"Can I trust you, Mr Parker?"

"Yes." An affirmative one-word answer delivered with conviction was always effective. Furthermore, experience had taught Garvey that if you were going to lie to a man, you should do it boldly.

"I may have misled the case officer who interviewed me when I was being positively vetted," Stevens admitted cautiously. "It is true I was taken prisoner at Lwow in the first few days of the war but after I had joined my unit, not before, as I had previously implied."

In fact, Stevens had reported to his Signals battalion forty-eight hours after hostilities had started. The city, which had been repeatedly bombed by the Luftwaffe, had been in a complete state of chaos with fires burning out of control, the mains water supply reduced to a trickle and every power station out of action. Major General Vlasov had received nothing but conflicting orders from the Front commander – Lwow was to be held to the last man and the last round – the garrison was to withdraw immediately to new defensive positions. The only people who hadn't been confused were the NKVD.

"There were a hundred and eighty Ukrainian nationalists in the local prison," Stevens continued. "They weren't criminals, they hadn't stolen anything or harmed anyone. They had been locked up for their political beliefs because they didn't want to be governed by Moscow. The NKVD couldn't be bothered to evacuate them and they didn't want to present the Germans with a potential Fifth Column. So they marched the prisoners to a field on the outskirts of town and shot them five at a time through the back of the head. I was there, I saw it happen."

"It must have been very distressing for you."

"Distressing?" Stevens laughed harshly. "You English," he spluttered, "you have no idea what the war was really like. How many of you died of starvation? How many of you went to the gas chamber or were hung in the street from a lamp post?" His voice dropped suddenly to a low monotone void of any expression, symptomatic of a man going through an emotional trauma. "Two days later I was taken prisoner."

The Germans had herded twenty thousand Red Army men into a field, surrounded the area with knee-high coils of barbed wire and called it a POW cage. There had been no latrines, no washing facilities, no barrack huts. They had slept on the ground under the stars and every now and again, the guards had thrown scraps of food over the wire and they had fought each other for it like dogs snarling over a bone that had already been picked clean. The only water they had had to drink had come from a stagnant ditch so that within days, dysentery had been rife and men had started to die of cholera.

"There was excrement everywhere and the stench was terrible." Stevens gagged and hastily clapped a hand over his mouth. "I'm sorry," he mumbled, "but sometimes I can still smell the foul air."

"How long were you in the cage?" Garvey asked.

"It took the Germans about three weeks to screen everyone, then they separated us by nationalities, Communists and non-Communists. A lot of Ukrainians welcomed the Germans as liberators."

"Including you?"

Stevens nodded. "I joined the Ukrainian Self-Defence Brigade; we policed the rear areas and hunted down the partisans who were operating behind the German lines. You may not believe this, Mr Parker, but the local population hated the partisans more than they did the Fascists."

"They supported you?"

"We wouldn't have been able to pacify the Ukraine without their help."

"If you were that successful, why did you end up in Treblinka?"

"I fell victim to a takeover bid."

In May 1943, Himmler had decided to recruit a Ukrainian army for the war against Bolshevism and recruiting had begun in Lwow for a new SS formation, the 14th SS Grenadier Division Galicia. The Self-Defence Brigade had been conscripted en masse and then screened for racial impurities.

"I'd been circumcised," Stevens told him. "That's how they discovered I was a Jew."

He had spent eight months in Treblinka and for a large part of the time had been employed in the crematorium. Those who worked there were not exempted from the gas chamber; at best, their fate was merely postponed for a few pitiful weeks. Stevens had not been liquidated with his co-workers because the SS overseer of the crematorium had taken a liking to him and had arranged his transfer to the staff mess as a waiter. Subsequently, the camp commandant had learned of his work on the military application of lasers and had written to Albert Speer, Minister of Armaments and War Production suggesting that better use could be made of his talents.

"I joined Krupp's in January 1944 . . . ."

"Which is not what you told us the last time you were interviewed."

"I lied to the case officer to protect myself." In his nervousness, Stevens tugged at the index finger of his right hand and made the knuckle crack. "What will happen to me, Mr Parker?"

It was not a question Garvey could answer. He could only recommend what they should do about Stevens; the actual decision would have to be made by the Director General. Obviously, his security clearance would be withdrawn, though what good that would do when the target acquisition laser was his own brainchild was highly problematical.

"What is going to happen to me?" Stevens repeated.

"Well, obviously I shall have to make a full report."

"To the Foreign Office?"

"I expect they will be informed."

"Please don't let them send me back to the Soviet Union." Stevens leaned across the desk and seized his wrists in a grip of iron. "I'll be dead within twenty-four hours, tried and executed for war crimes."

"Nonsense." Garvey tried to free his wrists and found himself involved in something of a wrestling match.

"You don't understand. In August 1942, my company captured

191

six partisans near a village called Morostok on the edge of the Pripet Marshes. Two of them were women . . ."

"I think you have given me all the information we need." There were things Garvey didn't want to hear because they would only exacerbate an already difficult problem.

"The Germans decided to make an example of them and ordered us to build a scaffold which resembled the swings you see in a children's playground . . ."

"That's enough, Mr Stevens," Garvey said. But there was no stopping him.

"Instead of a trap door, we had this long plank supported by a couple of trestles. The partisans had to climb up on to the plank and stand there while an NCO put a noose around their necks and the officer in command passed the death sentence on them . . ."

"It's not necessary to tell me all this," Garvey said desperately.

"But I was the man who kicked the trestles over."

Shit, shit, shit. Garvey closed his eyes briefly while pondering what he could say to Stevens which would put his mind at rest. "It's going to be all right," he said lamely and knew immediately that Stevens didn't believe him.

It took Parker less than an hour to discover that his new job was a non-event appointment. The next long induction course started on the first of September; there were a couple of week-long survival courses plus an escape and evasion exercise between October and the end of January 1968 with a forty-eight hour resistance to interrogation ordeal for selected officers to round off the financial year. The programmes had been run off and all the necessary staff work had been done with the result that there was nothing left to coordinate.

There were no Special Forces to train because the SIS had abandoned the idea of establishing Resistance networks in Latvia, Estonia, Lithuania and the Ukraine. There were two very sound reasons for this. First and foremost was the fact that by 1955 all the wartime Resistance groups which the Wehrmacht had left behind had either been penetrated or liquidated by the KGB. The other contributory cause had been the inability of the SIS to mount a successful operation against the USSR. Of the scores of agents put ashore in the Baltic or dropped by parachute into the Ukraine, not a single one had survived for more than a few days. There was of course nothing like a series of disasters to discourage would-be volunteers and the numbers coming forward had slowed to a trickle before drying up altogether.

The only extraneous commitment which now remained was the occasional lecture to other government departments. Going through the diary of forthcoming events, Parker saw he was down to give a lecture to Ministry of Defence Branch Security Officers in four days' time. Between then and the induction course beginning on the first of September, there was just one other lecture. Long before lunchtime, he had completed the takeover from his predecessor, unpacked his personal belongings and settled in. When Freeland arrived shortly after three o'clock, he had adjourned to the rose garden with a paperback.

"So how do you think you are going to like the Training School?" Freeland asked, joining him on the rustic bench seat.

"It's a great place for a rest cure," Parker said dryly.

Amberley Lodge was a large Georgian residence with twelve main bedrooms, an oak-panelled dining room, ballroom, drawing room, library and a games room large enough to accommodate two full-size billiard tables. There was also a conservatory, as well as stables which were now used as an indoor pistol range. It was a touch less grand than Chequers, the Tudor country residence of the Prime Minister in the Chilterns, because the estate only ran to fifteen acres instead of seven hundred, but it did have a large ornamental lake designed by Capability Brown and a couple of grass tennis courts.

"What about the job?"

"There isn't one, Harry. When George Chater was chief instructor here, he didn't have a principal staff officer coord. The poor guy retired prematurely because of a heart condition and his successor, who is a good ten years younger and as fit as a flea, gets an assistant. And to cap it all, there was no need to upgrade my appointment; if the Establishment Committee is looking for ways and means of economising, they could cut the post out and no one would be any the wiser."

"I think someone was trying to find you a sinecure, Campbell."

"Seems like it. If I were a gambling man, I would bet my shirt that Dent and Garvey were behind it."

"Because of your association with Stefanie Ayres which you have me to thank for."

"Well, there is also my involvement with Kurt Bender."

"Quite." Freeland stood up. "Why don't we stroll over to the stable block. I've got something in my car which will interest you."

"Could it be Bender's record of military service?"

"It certainly could."

Parker got to his feet and started after the older man. "Sarah phoned me at home on Friday to say that you had the file and would be in touch."

"Did Sarah also tell you that it had been shredded and that she had collected a rap over the knuckles for making a fuss about it?"

"No, she didn't." Parker stopped in his tracks. "Who's been on at her?"

"Well, Dent for one. He dropped the odd hint about her security clearance, but nothing will come of it."

"Can you guarantee that?"

"Put it this way; I can always get Larborough to ask an awkward question in the House."

"Thanks. I wouldn't want anything to happen to Sarah on my account."

"She's a nice girl," Freeland agreed. "Thinks a lot of you, Campbell."

"Along with the Brigade of Guards," Parker said with a laugh.

Freeland had signed out a self-drive Ford Zephyr from the motor pool. Unlocking the front offside door, he leaned across the seat, opened the glove compartment and took out a sheaf of papers.

"Bender's record of service. I signalled Bonn on Friday asking them to repeat the original facsimile. Lucky I did; if I'd left it one more day, their Communications Centre would have automatically destroyed the file copy."

"What do you make of it, Harry?"

"I found myself wondering who Terboven was, what he had done and why Bender had never been called as a witness, assuming he was brought to trial."

"Is there any way we can find out?"

"We could start by asking the Israelis if they have anything on Terboven. No doubt Bender could tell us but he seems to be a pretty elusive guy."

"I think he is dead," Parker said.

"What?"

"I talked to his girlfriend up in Scarborough, a woman called Linda Norris. She said he had a bad heart and wouldn't be surprised if he had snuffed it. All right, I know it's not much to go on but he does seem to have dropped off the edge of the world. As far as I can make out, no one has seen him since the sixth of April when he walked out on Linda after telling her he was going home. Anyway, I'm wondering how many unidentified bodies there are in mortuaries up and down the country?"

"You are not seriously suggesting that we take this Linda Norris on a Cook's Tour of every charnel house in the UK, are you?"

"No, I figured we could take a few short cuts. First of all, there are the injuries Bender received to his back and legs during the war. These are fully documented in the medical history sheet attached to his record of service. Then there is this . . ." Parker went through his wallet and took out the snapshot Linda Norris had given him. "I got this picture from his girlfriend," he continued; "it was taken up at Redcar one Sunday in February. A few weeks later, Bender told her he had won a million Deutschmarks on Lotto Toto."

"Really?"

"Something else you should know – Andrew Korwin lives in Redcar."

"So does his partner, Victor Stevens, and he's a man who obviously has enemies."

"Bad ones?"

"The kind who don't draw the line at killing people," Freeland said, and then told him about the triple murder at Hassan al Jaifi's villa in Spain.

"Are you saying Bender had something to do with it?"

"I don't know. We both fastened on to Korwin because Bender claimed he had seen him at the Trade Fair, but what if Stevens had also been there representing the Ward Tandy Group? What if he was the man our missing German was hoping to part from a million D marks?"

"We're talking about blackmail?"

"That's the usual name for extortion," Freeland said.

"What's his guilty secret?"

"Search me, Campbell. All I know is that he was born Viktor Stashinsky at Zhitomir in the Ukraine and came out of the same DP camp as Korwin."

Parker rested both arms on the roof of the Ford Zephyr. Bender was beginning to look like a bounty hunter; he had stumbled across Korwin and had written to the Ayres hoping they would reward him. If Harry was right, it seemed fate had also dealt him a bonus in the person of Victor Stevens. Two acquaintances from the past who were going to make him rich, one out of gratitude, the other out of fear. Parker wondered what the mathematical odds were against all three men coming together at the same time in the same place.

"I think we should concentrate on finding our German friend, Harry."

"So do I," said Freeland. "I'll talk to Iain Wirral and see what we can turn up through Missing Persons."

CHAPTER 17

GARVEY REMOVED the fifth and last sheet of foolscap from the carriage and then returned the Underwood typewriter to the clerk's office next door before checking the report for errors. Although he hadn't made any notes during the interview with Victor Stevens, his recollection was so vivid that even now, approximately six hours later, he still had total recall and could repeat what had been said almost word for word. He read the text line for line, corrected the typing errors in ink, then signed and dated the last page. The document would never have got past the supervisor of the typing pool but he had decided that the material was far too sensitive for her girls to work from his draft. With this in mind, he had, in fact, deliberately waited until everyone had gone home before starting to produce the fair copy two-finger style on a borrowed typewriter. It was perhaps stretching it a bit to claim that the improper disclosure of the material would cause exceptionally grave damage to the nation, but it could do serious harm, and Garvey had no hesitation in grading it Secret.

He pinned the document to the front of the existing PV file on Stevens and locked it away in his safe. First thing tomorrow he would walk the file into the Deputy Director and dump the problem in his lap. Meantime, he had only one more phone call to make before packing it in for the day. Returning to his desk, he lifted the receiver and rang the watchmen in Cheyne Walk.

"This is Garvey," he said. "What's our girl been doing with herself today?"

"Keeping a low profile," the watchman told him. "She returned from Vienna on the nine thirty flight and went straight to the office from Heathrow, worked all through the lunch hour and got home about five minutes ago. Nothing secretive about that."

Maybe so, thought Garvey, but her departure for Vienna certainly had been and they had all been caught napping. The watchmen had guessed that Stefanie Ayres was going away for the weekend when she had taken a suitcase into the office but it hadn't occurred to them that she was going abroad.

"I suppose there's no chance of finding out what she was up to in Vienna?"

"You suppose correctly," Garvey said. "I wouldn't know where to begin and we can hardly ask her to tell us without letting the cat out of the bag."

They had recovered the counterfoil she had surrendered to the British European Airways desk at Heathrow and as a result, had managed to trace the travel agent who had sold her the ticket. They had also learned that Stefanie Ayres had made the booking from her office seventy-two hours before the departure date and had arranged for her secretary to collect and pay for the ticket. But that was as far as they had been able to go.

"I'm not happy with this set-up, we need more resources if we are to do the job properly."

It was a favourite complaint with the watchmen, one Garvey had heard many times before. "You'll have to manage with what you've got," he said.

Stefanie Ayres was not the only person in London MI5 were required to keep under surveillance and there was a limit to the number of man hours that could be allocated to her case. In any event, reinforcing the team with extra personnel wouldn't have made a scrap of difference on Friday. With Vienna less than two hours by BAC One-eleven jet, Garvey would still have decided there was insufficient time to brief the SIS and invite them to put a tail on her when she arrived at Schwechat airport. The fact remained that without forewarning of her intentions, there was no way they could have followed her once she had left the departure lounge to board the plane.

"Would it help if I had a word with our chief, Mr Garvey?"

The watchmen were controlled by 'A' Branch. Garvey supposed the Assistant Director in charge might be more inclined to listen to one of his own men than to him. "It might be an idea," he conceded.

"I'll see what I can do then."

"Okay. Talk to you tomorrow."

Garvey put the phone down, checked to make sure he hadn't left anything out which should be locked away overnight, and was about to leave the office when the phone rang. With considerable reluctance, he lifted the receiver and discovered the caller was Dent.

"Yes, Roger," he said wearily, "what can I do for you?"

"It's the other way round," Dent told him. "I've just had a phone call from Campbell Parker."

"Really? What did he want?"

"Your phone number," Dent said and allowed himself a brief, dismissive snigger before clearing his throat. "Naturally I wouldn't let him have it."

"Good."

"So he asked me to give you a message. He said he had arranged to meet Stefanie Ayres at his flat in Ravenscourt Park this evening and wanted you to know."

"What on earth's he playing at, Roger?"

"Search me, old boy. I thought you had made it pretty clear that he should give that young woman a very wide berth if he wanted to retain his vetting status."

Garvey picked up on the way Dent was now dissociating himself from the thinly veiled warning they had given Parker. Last Tuesday, he had been all for taking a firm line with the SIS man and had been instrumental in getting him posted to the quiet backwater of the Training School, but now it was a different story. Dent sensed trouble in the offing and was anxious to distance himself from the fallout.

"Can you remember his actual words, Roger?"

"I've more or less quoted them verbatim. The only other thing Parker told me was that he had some unfinished business to attend to . . ." Dent chuckled ". . . whatever that may mean."

"No doubt we shall know soon enough," Garvey said, remembering belatedly to thank him for calling before hanging up.

The watchmen hadn't fallen down on the job; they weren't aware that Parker was planning to see the Ayres girl because he had phoned her at the office. He had wanted to put a phone tap on the agency where she worked but the barrister 'A' Branch retained as their legal adviser had counselled against it and his own assistant director had declined to support him. It had been a lousy decision, the antics of both Parker and Stefanie Ayres had demonstrated that. The workplace was their Achilles heel and to plug it he would now have to go private and hire someone to effect an illegal entry with a view to bugging the premises. It was not, however, the sort of decision that should be taken on the spur of the moment.

*　　*　　*

Jutta Hossbach had been a voluptuous-looking blonde when she had been living with Kurt Bender. Now she had shorn her long tresses to become an equally voluptuous-looking brunette with an urchin cut and a beauty spot on the left cheekbone. She had also moved down a peg or two and was now living in a three-room flat above a Chinese takeaway near the Hauptbahnhof. Back in September '66, Jutta Hossbach was supposed to have been a floorwalker in one of Frankfurt's large department stores; eight months later, her tarty appearance suggested she was a street-walker.

Ulex had got her surname, a description of her former appearance and her new address from the janitor of the apartment building on Münchenerstrasse. When he arrived at her flat a few minutes before seven, Jutta had just finished applying her war paint and was ready to start work. She was wearing a black satin blouse, a red velvet, thigh-length skirt and high-heeled shoes of the same colour. Butterflies adorned her nylon stockings which had jet black seams and she sported a thin gold chain around her right ankle. There were enough copper bracelets on Jutta's wrists to ward off any danger of her falling victim to rheumatism. The way she greeted him at the door bore all the hallmarks of the true professional.

"Have you been to see me before?" she asked in a throaty voice that was meant to be sexy.

"This is my first visit," Ulex told her.

"So how did you get hold of my address?"

"From a friend; he said you would show me a good time."

"Oh, I will." Jutta stepped aside so that he could enter the room, then closed the door behind him before walking over to the window to draw the curtains. "After you have given me a present," she added.

"Is that what Kurt Bender used to do?"

Jutta turned about, her face contorted with anger. "Where did you meet that fucking pig? Are you a friend of his?"

"I'm his worst enemy," Ulex said calmly.

"Not while I'm alive. The bastard walked out on me, said he knew a man who would give us a lot of money."

He could not recall seeing anyone who looked so feline; Jutta was hissing and spitting like a cat, eyes narrowed to slits. The sight of his wallet calmed her down a bit, especially when he took out thirty Deutschmarks in tens and then added a twenty. A slow smile spread across her face; unbuttoning the satin blouse, she tucked the money into her bra, then reached behind her, unzipped the velvet mini skirt and stepped out of it.

"You ever hear from Bender?"

Jutta backed him towards the divan bed while at the same time deftly undoing his slacks. "You don't want to talk about Kurt," she said, reverting to her throaty voice as she began to massage him.

"If I'm paying the piper, I call the tune."

"What's that supposed to mean?"

"It means I would like an answer to my question."

Jutta withdrew her hand, walked over to the dressing table and returned with a condom she had taken from the centre drawer. "He phoned me just the once, a few days after he had arrived in England. That's the last I heard of him."

"Did he say where he was phoning from?"

"Not Kurt. He was frightened Wenge Morgen Properties would learn where he was and come after him for the six months arrears on his rent."

The whore hadn't lied to him; Bender was in England, everything he had read in the back numbers of the *Frankfurt Allgemeine* pointed to it.

"They sold all our furniture . . ."

"Who did?"

"Wenge Morgen, the property company that owns the apartment building on Münchenerstrasse. They said Kurt owed them seven thousand; I had to sell all my jewellery."

"Tough," Ulex murmured and closed his eyes, savouring a pleasure he hadn't known for twenty-one years as Jutta went to work with both hands.

"If you catch up with Kurt, be sure you give him a good hiding from me."

Ulex planned to do more than that. Bender was slime, always had been from the day he had joined Terboven's Ukrainian Sonderkommando as a replacement. He had no stomach for guerrilla warfare and had been squeamish about the methods that were needed to extract information from captured partisans and suspected couriers. There was, for instance, the case of the villager they had caught wandering in the forest near Yavorov. He had been about seventy years old, a stooped, wizened little man with a bald head. He had claimed he had been looking for mushrooms but they had found six live rounds of 7.62 mm ammunition in the pockets of his jacket. He had ordered Bender to execute the old man hoping it would put some backbone into him, but the gutless Obergefreiter had contrived to trip over a tree root and dig the barrel of his Schmeisser into the ground, plugging it with earth. Bender had deliberately rendered his sub-machine-gun unsafe to fire, but he hadn't let him get away with that old dodge. He had given him his own 9mm Walther P38 semi-automatic and had forced him to ram the four and a quarter inch barrel into the Ukrainian's mouth before he squeezed the trigger and blew his skull apart. And afterwards, the spineless arsehole had thrown up and had then got blind drunk on the home-made brandy they had found when they searched the old man's house. And to think that some fool had actually promoted the creep to Feldwebel.

That had been twenty-three years ago. When he caught up with him in England tomorrow, the day after, a week from now, or whenever, it would be Bender who would be biting on the bullet. The thought appealed to Ulex.

"I knew I could put a smile on your face." Jutta's hand was working overtime to arouse him, the bracelets clinking on her wrist. "You've not been very active, have you?" she said archly.

"No," said Ulex, "I've been saving myself for you."

A clock chimed the half hour and reminded him that he had arranged to collect twenty thousand Deutschmarks from Langbehn at eight. But it wouldn't hurt the Herr Doktor to cool his heels for a bit.

The last time they had met on a railway platform, Stefanie Ayres had been wearing a blazer over a blue silk dress. This time when she stepped off the District Line train at Ravenscourt Park she was in jeans and a sweater under a reefer jacket. There were other differences too; there was no welcoming smile and she didn't stand on tiptoe to kiss him either.

"Hi, Campbell," she said in a matter of fact voice. "Mind telling me what I am doing here?"

"You're coming to have a bite to eat with me. Okay?"

"I don't know how you talked me into it. I'd made a resolution not to see you again."

"So you told me on the telephone." Parker took possession of a slim hand and led her down to the entrance hall below. "But of course I already knew you were trying to avoid me."

"Yeah?"

"I tried to phone you on Friday and your secretary told me you had gone to Vienna for the weekend."

"I needed a break, things were getting on top of me at the office."

"Spur of the moment thing, was it?"

"Definitely. I just rang the travel agents and asked them what they could offer."

"You were lucky, Vienna is pretty popular at this time of the year." Parker walked her under the railway bridge into Ravenscourt Road. "Where did you stay?"

"The Bristol. You know it?"

"I've walked past it a few times, never dared to go inside. I always had a feeling that dining there wouldn't leave much change from a month's salary."

"What are you trying to do, Campbell?" she asked with a faint smile. "Make me feel guilty?"

"Heaven forbid. Indeed, I wouldn't have minded going to Vienna myself, but three's a crowd."

"There was no travelling companion. That's what you wanted to know, wasn't it, Campbell?"

"Yes."

She laughed. "That's honest."

"I try to be." He showed Stefanie into the flat, then poured her a dry Martini.

"You remembered – I'm impressed."

"The wine's being chilled in the fridge and supper is on the table."

"I'm even more impressed."

"It's a cold collation, all I had to do was put it on a plate. I went to our local deli soon as I got here."

Parker drank some of his whisky, wondered how he was going to question Stefanie without starting another fight. He had had it all figured out on the way up to town, but now that they were face to face he was no longer in control – she was. There was a charisma about her and she had this certain effect on him which he couldn't explain.

"So what did you do on your own in Vienna?" he asked lamely.

"The usual tourist scene. The whole of the Ringstrasse, the Natural History Museum, the Palace, St Stephen's Church, the Opera House, the Riding School, Mayerling, the Vienna Woods and the giant wheel in the Prater. They have a plaque telling you this is where they made *The Third Man* movie with Joseph Cotten and Orson Welles . . .''

Stefanie Ayres had arrived in Vienna on Friday evening and departed early this morning. It seemed to Parker that she had crammed an awful lot into those forty-eight hours and the cynic in him suspected she might have prepared the itinerary for his benefit.

"I took a couple of days off too. Went up to Scarborough to meet Linda Norris.''

"Yeah?" Her forehead creased in a puzzled frown. "Should I know her?''

"Oh, didn't I tell you?" Parker removed her glass and topped it up from the pitcher. "She was Bender's girlfriend.''

"So what did this Linda Norris have to say for herself?" Stefanie asked him calmly.

"She told me Bender had a bad heart and could snuff it at any time.''

"Good God.''

"According to her, Kurt reckoned he had come into a lot of money.''

"You mean he'd struck it rich?''

"Yes.''

"I doubt if Andrew was his benefactor.''

"Right.'' Parker was conscious of walking on eggshells. The last time he had broached the tricky subject of her family, Stefanie had blown a fuse and walked out on him. "Did your uncle mention his partner, Victor Stevens, when you went to see him?''

"No. What's so special about him, Campbell?''

The continued use of his first name was misleading. Stefanie might sound casual and unconcerned about the way their conversation was going but there was a definite undercurrent and he could read the danger signals.

"He's a Russian, changed his name by deed poll from Viktor Stashinsky, came out of the same DP camp as your uncle.''

"And?''

"I think maybe Kurt Bender was looking to him for a hand-out.''

"Well, I wouldn't know about that. Did you discover anything else?''

Here we go, Parker thought. This is where we light the blue touchpaper and wait for the inevitable explosion. "I dropped in to see Tomas Rojek on the way back to London,'' he said carefully.

"You really are kind of sneaky, aren't you?''

"We had an interesting conversation . . ."

"And he told you that I had asked him to write to me care of *The Sentinel*?"

"Yes."

"And now you would like an explanation." She finished the Martini and put the glass down. "I guess you're entitled to one."

Suddenly, the heart-to-heart talk he had promised himself last Friday was no longer important. "Look, you don't have to . . ."

"Your Home Office was giving me the run around," Stefanie said, cutting him short. "Kevin Mullinder advised me to go to Larborough; he said the MP could make himself a real pain in the ass for the government and I needed to have some sort of evidence to prove that my uncle was still alive. So he became 'Talmunt' – okay?"

"Yes."

"Good. I'm glad we've got that straightened out. Now, if you are through cross-questioning me, I've got better things to do."

She was halfway across the room when he grabbed a wrist and pulled her to him. A clenched fist punched him in the chest a couple of times until he managed to pinion the other arm.

"I don't want you to leave," he said fiercely. "Not now, not ever."

It was crazy. To all intents and purposes, his career had been wrecked by this girl and she would probably end up destroying what little future he had left, but he was hooked and didn't want to face the rest of his life without her. And that too was ridiculous because he had only known her for a few short days. Furthermore, after his marriage to Sheila and the pain of her death, he had gone out of his way to avoid any kind of emotional involvement. Yet suddenly, here he was behaving like some moonstruck adolescent. But he didn't want to question his feelings, nor did he want to delve too deeply into the reasons why this young, beautiful and well-connected Polish American girl was apparently so attracted to him.

"Do you understand what I am saying?"

Her eyes grew wider and she searched his face as though looking for a catch. Then, accepting that he had meant every word, she stopped struggling and raised herself on tiptoe to kiss him on the lips.

*   *   *

Even before she was captured, the woman was dead on three counts; she was a partisan, a Jewess and a political commissar. Her name was Vera Ivanovina Bolshakov. In June 1941, she had been a Starshii Leitenant, a senior lieutenant, with a motor transport battalion of the 5th Soviet Army operating on the southern boundary of the Pripet Marshes. Had she been captured in the giant encirclement battle for Kiev, the telltale red stars on her sleeve would have automatically singled her out for special treatment.

In a speech to his assembled generals on the thirtieth of March 1941, Hitler had announced that the Red Army political commissars were the propagandists of ideologies directly opposed to National Socialism and were to be liquidated. Stevens had only learned of that decree after the war but he had seen it carried out when he was being held in the POW cage near Lwow. The commissar of his Signals battalion had anticipated the sort of treatment he could expect to receive and had removed the insignia from his uniform, but it hadn't done him any good. The interrogators had spotted the tiny holes in the sleeve of his tunic where the stars had been and the guards had made him kneel down by the ditch which had been their only source of water and had shot him in the back.

But Starshii Leitenant Vera Ivanovina Bolshakov had not been captured in the battle for Kiev. She and a small number of survivors from her unit had slipped into the Pripet Marshes where they had operated as partisans behind the German lines, waging war against the invader and Ukrainian collaborators alike with a ferocity not seen since the Middle Ages. Lenin had said that the purpose of terror was to terrify and Vera Ivanovina Bolshakov and her followers had certainly adhered to that maxim to the letter. It had been their excesses against the indigenous population, which had included the decapitation of a village headman and his wife for collaborating with the Fascists, that had eventually led to their betrayal and capture.

Stevens remembered Vera Bolshakov as a slender young woman in her early thirties with close-cropped black hair and lean ascetic features. She had been wearing a uniform of sorts, baggy whipcord trousers, Cossack-type blouse under a leather jerkin and a flat peaked cap. She had also been armed with a Makarov 9mm automatic pistol which she had not attempted to use when the hut where she and the other five partisans were holed up had been surrounded by a platoon from the Ukrainian Self-Defence Brigade. Thirteen months of living rough had burned off every spare ounce of flesh on her body and no one had suspected there was a second woman in the band until the Feldwebel in charge of the platoon had ordered Stevens to strip search all six for concealed weapons.

He hadn't discovered that Vera Bolshakov was a Jewess until the moment of her execution. The partisans had been marched to the village whose headman they had murdered and had been paraded in front of the whole population. The subsequent drumhead court martial had been staged to demonstrate the Wehrmacht's determination to protect the villagers from roving guerrilla bands. At the same time, it had also served to show them what would happen to anyone who was tempted to join the partisans in the Marshes. The scaffold had been erected before the trial had started in order that the sentence could be executed in the shortest possible time after the inevitable verdict had been returned.

All six convicted partisans had been forced to stand shoulder to shoulder on the platform while an NCO had put a noose around each neck, and the president of the court martial had sentenced them to death. In those last few moments, he had been close enough to Vera Bolshakov to hear her murmuring the words of a Hebrew prayer to herself and he had inadvertently echoed them. Vera Bolshakov had heard him and he had known from the expression in her eyes that she intended to denounce him. It had been all the encouragement Stevens had needed to kick the trestles over. In his anxiety to silence her, he had anticipated the executive word of command and had damn nearly botched the multiple hanging. The drop should have broken their necks instantaneously but thanks to him, all six had been slowly strangled. And he had stood there watching her dancing at the end of a rope, praying that the German Oberleutnant commanding their company couldn't understand what she was gurgling as she choked to death.

It had taken him fifteen long years to erase the memory of that terrible day from his mind; a man called Parker had reawakened it in a matter of an hour. In sixty brief minutes he had destroyed his world and had brought him to this prefabricated hut in the factory yard where he had finalised his ideas for a target acquisition laser. Somehow, there was no more fitting place in which to put the record straight and complete the melancholy task he had set himself. With a heavy heart, he folded the letter, tucked it into an envelope and addressed it to The Editor, The *Evening Gazette*, The Gazette Building, Burough Road, Middlesbrough. There were two other letters of explanation, one to Jean, the other to his friend and business partner, Arthur Kershaw. He tore three stamps from the book he had purchased from a machine on the way to the factory and stuck them on the envelopes.

It was over, finished, done with. Picking up the letters, Stevens walked over to the door, switched off the lights and left the office. He heard the telephone ring as he got into the Rover and knew it was Jean again. She had phoned him once before, anxious to know when he was coming home and he had told her to expect him around nine thirty. The clock in the dashboard was showing five minutes to ten and she was probably getting a little irate with him. He started the car, reversed out of the parking slot reserved for the head of Research and Development, and drove off towards the main entrance. There was no need to sound the horn; the nightwatchman heard the car coming and left the hut to open the factory gates.

"All finished, Mr Stevens?" he asked cheerily.

"Yes, Bert, I've got it all sorted out at last."

"Ted."

"What?"

'My name's Ted, sir.'

"Oh, of course. I'm sorry, my mind was on something else."

"That's all right, Mr Stevens, the wife is always telling me how absentminded I am."

"Well, I shan't forget again," Stevens said and wished him good night.

He drove through the factory gates and turned right on the road. He mailed the letters at the first post box he came to, then headed out of town to pick up the A19 and drive south. There wasn't a lot of traffic about and he put his foot down, using the powerful 3.5 litre engine to eat up the miles. At Thirsk, he switched to the A61 and travelled west for eight miles before taking the minor road to Masham. The man-made lakes were only a few minutes beyond the village.

No one saw him leave the road and bump across the moor, no other vehicle passed along the road while he sat there in the Rover smoking one last cigarette. It would, he thought, have been better if he had died with Ingrid, Hassan al Jaifi and Marcel Verlhac; then at least Jean would have been spared the pain of knowing what he had been. When he had finished the cigarette, he lowered the window on his side a few inches, then started the engine again, shifted the automatic gear into drive and flattened the accelerator. The Rover was doing approximately forty miles an hour when it plunged into the lake and disappeared beneath the surface.

CHAPTER 18

THE NIGHTMARE began for Garvey a few minutes after three o'clock in the morning with a persistent summons from the telephone which Lynne, his wife, insisted should remain out in the hall of their mews flat. Still half-asleep, he crawled out of bed, felt his way to the door and opened it quietly, then tiptoed past the children's bedroom and the au pair's. By the time he got within reaching distance of the phone, the imperious ringing tone and the possibility that some drunk had dialled the wrong number had put him in a foul temper.

"Yes?" he said liverishly. "What do you want?"

"Is that you, Mr Garvey?"

"Yes – who's this?"

"It's me, of course, Arthur Kershaw."

Garvey clutched the phone tighter, a dozen alarm bells ringing in his head. Nobody contacted him at this hour of the morning unless there was a crisis and suddenly he knew, even before Kershaw told him, that it had everything to do with Victor Stevens.

"All right, Arthur," he said quietly, "keep calm, start from the beginning and tell me what's wrong."

"Keep calm? How very English!" Kershaw's guttural accent always came through when he was excited or angry, and he was close to losing his composure right now. "Yesterday he had an interview in London with one of your people – a Mr Campbell Parker – or weren't you aware of this?"

"I don't think we have a Mr Campbell Parker, but that's beside the point."

"I disagree. I don't know what this man Parker said to Victor but he was very quiet and depressed when he arrived back here early yesterday evening."

Stevens had left the factory at the usual time of six o'clock and had gone home to Redcar. Just over an hour later, he had returned to the factory to work on some technical refinement to the target acquisition laser system, or so he had told his wife, Jean.

"Jean rang his office and spoke to him at nine," Kershaw went on, "and Victor told her he had almost finished and would be home at nine thirty by the latest. When he didn't return, Jean phoned his office again but couldn't get an answer. In the end, she got through to the nightwatchman and learned he had left the factory a few minutes after ten."

Garvey listened in silence, content to let the other man rattle on for a little longer while he assessed the implications. It seemed Stevens hadn't told anyone what had happened at the interview in London, not even his wife. That was the one good thing to have emerged so far and it made him feel slightly less vulnerable.

"Who else knows Victor is missing?" he asked.

"I rang the police, gave them the number of his Rover."

"When was this?"

"Just before I rang you," Kershaw told him.

The North Riding constabulary would circulate the registration number of the car to their mobiles but they were unlikely to raise a hue and cry until they had something more definite to go on. Garvey reckoned he could therefore count on a breathing space in which to tidy things up at his end. But first of all it was necessary to carry out the usual security checks.

"Have you been down to the factory, Arthur?"

Kershaw didn't answer him. In the background, Garvey could hear a woman's voice and was immediately on his guard.

"Where are you calling from?" he asked.

"I'm with Jean," Kershaw told him.

"Is there anyone else who can keep her company?"

"Well, Nancy's here."

"In that case, I'd like you to get down to the factory as soon as you can. I'm not saying something is wrong but my superiors will want to know if anything is missing."

"I understand."

"Good. Perhaps you would phone me back after you've had a look."

Garvey replaced the phone and went into the living room. He hoped Stevens hadn't done anything stupid but remembering his distraught behaviour yesterday, it was difficult to be sanguine about it. If Stevens was convinced that the British Government intended to send him back to the USSR, there was no telling what he might do. But it was his job to anticipate the worst; that was why a grateful public paid him a handsome salary. Suddenly feeling in need of a cigarette, Garvey helped himself to a filter tip from the silver box on the coffee table which had been a wedding present from his colleagues.

If Stevens had killed himself, he was likely to have left a note explaining why he had done so. Most suicides did and it was too much to hope that he would have been an exception. How much damage he could do to MI5 from the grave was problematical, but Garvey was under few illusions about his own position. The Director General wasn't going to thank him for dragging that confession out of Stevens, nor would the politicians when they heard about it. On the other hand, was there any reason why the DG or anyone else should know what Stevens had told him?

Garvey left his cigarette burning in the ashtray while he pulled out the old Empire Aristocrat portable which he kept on the floor under the writing bureau where it was out of sight. He blew the dust off, found half a dozen sheets of foolscap in one of the drawers and set the machine up on the coffee table. All he had to do was edit the report he had typed yesterday evening, deleting all references to the execution of the six partisans at Morostok. He would also need to doctor the bit about the Ukrainian Self-Defence Brigade, making it seem that Stevens had declined to join them, but the rest of the interview could stand. In passing, he toyed with the idea of explaining why he had used Parker's name as a pseudonym when conducting the interview but, on reflection, Garvey decided there was no point in disclosing more than he had to at this stage.

Parker measured a heaped teaspoon of instant coffee into each cup, added boiling water from the electric kettle, then carried the tray into the bedroom. Stefanie hadn't moved since he had slipped out of bed and was still fast asleep curled up on her right side. He put the tray on the bedside table and leaning across, gently squeezed her shoulder until she opened her eyes.

"Hi." A sleepy smile appeared on her mouth. "What time is it?"

"Six thirty."

"My God, it's the middle of the night."

"Yes. I'm sorry, it's this new job of mine down at Petersfield; my boss is likely to send out a search party if I'm not in the office by eight thirty."

"Sounds grim. What's it like?"

"My new appointment? It's okay, I guess." Parker sat down on the edge of the bed. "How do you like your coffee?" he asked. "I have to tell you I've no milk, only cream and sugar."

"I'll take it black," Stefanie told him and sat up. She was wearing one of his pyjama tops which was several sizes too large for her so that her hands had disappeared inside the sleeves. "You don't talk about yourself much, do you, Campbell?"

"I told you about my life with Sheila," he said quietly.

"But nothing at all about your family. Are your parents still alive?"

"My mother is. My father was a wartime officer in the Duke of Wellington's and was killed in action in Normandy in July 1944 on my twelfth birthday. My mother married again in 1947, a solicitor she met when she got a job as a legal secretary. A half-sister arrived a year later, the half-brother in 1950 was definitely an afterthought. Malcolm is still at Oundle, Lois is in her first year at Keele University reading History, the family home is now in Shrewsbury. End of story."

"What did your father do before he joined the army?"

"He was an architect."

"So what made you choose the Foreign Service as a career?"

"I suppose it seemed a good idea at the time," Parker said.

"But now you're not so sure?"

"Everyone goes through a bad patch when the grass looks greener on the other side."

"Right." Stefanie nodded emphatically. "But if you should start looking, let me know first."

Parker gazed at her thoughtfully. "Are you serious?"

"I'm in the business of recruiting and placing executives and you're the sort of high-flyer we are looking for."

"Me?"

"You're a linguist, aren't you?"

"Polish and German."

"Well, there you are then," Stefanie said triumphantly, "you have something to offer."

"Maybe you could persuade your uncle to give me a job with the Ward Tandy Group?"

There was a tense silence and it became a bit of a strain to hold the smile on his lips.

"You could do better."

"It was meant to be a joke," Parker told her.

"I know that, but I was talking about the job."

Just over a week ago, Stefanie had returned from Redcar overjoyed at having met her long lost uncle at last. Now it seemed she had reservations about his business affairs. He wondered if she had found out what had happened at Hassan al Jaifi's villa in Spain.

"What have you got against the Ward Tandy Group?" he asked.

"Part of the company is involved in the arms trade."

At first, Parker thought her objections were based on moral grounds but it transpired Stefanie was convinced that Defence was way down the list of priorities for the Labour Government and believed the Group could suffer if there were any further cutbacks in Defence expenditure.

"Much as I like Andrew, I wouldn't allow you to join his company. Apart from an uncertain future, you would also be sacrificing a great deal of personal freedom. The firm is engaged on secret work and there would be restrictions on where you could travel."

"Who told you that?"

"Nancy did. I was hoping they would come to Poland with me in the summer and at first she was all for it. But then Andrew said he would have to ask permission to go behind the Iron Curtain and doubted if the Ministry of Defence would agree."

"He's probably right," Parker told her.

"Yeah? Well, I don't think Andrew was all that keen on the idea anyway."

There was, he thought, a hint of contempt in Stefanie's voice which was hard to comprehend. By all accounts, there was nothing in Poland for Korwin except a lot of unhappy memories and pain. With the exception of his sister, he had lost his entire family in the war and had suffered the most ghastly tortures at the hands of the Gestapo. How he had survived was nothing short of a miracle, but there was more to it than that. Korwin had served in the Home Army, the Armja Krajowa, and that made him a reactionary Fascist as far as the Communist government was concerned. Although a naturalised British subject, it could be that he feared this would not afford him complete protection once behind the Iron Curtain. At best, he would not be the first victim of a smear campaign; at worst, he would not be the first man to be arrested and thrown into jail on spurious charges.

"What time did you say you wanted to be in the office?" Stefanie asked.

"Eight thirty."

"We'd better get a move on then. Give me five minutes and I'll be with you. Okay?"

"Sure."

Parker carried the tray out into the kitchen, emptied what was left of the cream down the sink, then washed and dried the crockery. He wondered when Stefanie had first mooted the idea of going to Poland and why she had been so keen for Korwin to accompany her.

Every day of every week of the year, upwards of fifty unhappy or disturbed men, women and children leave home for one reason or another and disappear without trace. Apart from traffic convictions, Department B14 at New Scotland Yard also maintained indexes on Juveniles and Missing Persons. In round numbers, B14 invariably had the equivalent of a small town on their books but all the senior executive officer in charge of records had been able to tell Detective Chief Superintendent Wirral was that Kurt Bender was not one of the twenty thousand plus names currently on the list.

The German had left Linda Norris on Friday the sixth of April but since then, neither she nor anyone else had been concerned enough to contact the police and report him missing. Wirral had never expected more than a negative feedback from B14 and wasn't disappointed. The more promising line of inquiry had always been the Forensic Science Service and the six laboratories dotted around England and Wales. In addition to a complement of principal scientific officers, each lab had a staff of police liaison officers under a detective chief inspector. On the assumption that Bender was dead and a local pathologist had been unable to establish the actual cause of death, Wirral had circulated details of his age, physical characteristics and medical history to each liaison cell. At eleven thirty, barely eighteen hours after Wirral had raised the query, the Home Office forensic science laboratory at Wetherby in Yorkshire came up with a match. A few minutes later, he rang Harry Freeland at Benbow House to give him the news.

"The body was found on Monday the fifteenth of May," Wirral told him. "It was netted ten miles offshore by a fishing smack from Whitby. The pathologist who carried out the initial postmortem reckoned the corpse had been in the water for about six weeks."

"It can't be Bender then," Freeland said. "Not if the body has been floating around since the beginning of April."

"Yes, well, as it happens, the pathologist isn't prepared to be hard and fast about that, especially as he wasn't able to establish the cause of death. What the North Riding constabulary have in the mortuary at Northallerton is the body of a man weighing approximately eleven stone, some five feet seven inches tall and aged between forty-five and sixty."

"Anything else? Colour of hair? Eyes?"

"Dark hair, some evidence that he was in the habit of dyeing the grey bits. The eyes are missing."

"It's not a lot to go on."

"There's more," Wirral said. "At some time in the past, the deceased had lost most of the calf from the left leg. Although the body was in an advanced state of decomposition, the pathologist found traces of other injuries to the back and legs. His description tallies with the war wounds Bender received during the Polish campaign in 1939."

"Parker was right then," Freeland said thoughtfully.

"It would seem so. Of course, officially we won't be a hundred per cent sure until Linda Norris identifies the body, which won't be easy for her no matter how well she might have known Bender. According to the pathologist, the face and hands had largely been destroyed by sulphuric acid administered after death."

"Looks as though someone was anxious to ensure the body couldn't be identified."

"That's not all, Harry. That same someone also shackled the corpse to a concrete block before dumping it in the sea. You put those two facts together and you can understand why the local police are reluctant to rule out foul play."

"What's their thinking now?"

Wirral laughed. "Give us a chance, Harry. I got all this from the DCI at Wetherby laboratory. I haven't spoken to the detective chief superintendent in charge of the North Riding CID yet. When I do, I'll tell him there is reason to believe that Bender had a heart condition and may have died from natural causes."

"How are you going to satisfy his curiosity?"

Freeland had unerringly put his finger on the problem. Whatever thanks he received from the detective chief superintendent would be accompanied by an avalanche of questions, and explaining how Bender had come to the notice of Special Branch was going to be one of the hardest to answer.

"I was hoping you were going to tell me," Wirral said.

"You could say the West German authorities had been asking after him."

"I could, but it wouldn't stand up for long. While the police in Scarborough are trying to run down the doctor who prescribed those heart kickers for Bender, he will want to liaise with Frankfurt and get all the background information he can."

"I suppose we shall have to brief him about Kershaw," Freeland said reluctantly.

"I don't see how we can withhold the information, Harry."

"Maybe not," said Freeland, "but you'll have to stall him as long as you can. I can't even authorise you to give him Kershaw's name."

Wirral could appreciate why Freeland would have to go cap in hand to the Deputy Director of the SIS. He could also understand why the Director General would undoubtedly have to consult his opposite number in MI5, but it didn't make life any the easier for him.

Ulex flew into Heathrow on a Lufthansa Boeing 727 flight from Frankfurt which arrived at Terminal 2 at 1040 hours, five minutes behind schedule. The West German passport supplied by the main Intelligence Administration of the State Security Department on the Gross-Berlinerdamm was accepted without a questioning glance by Immigration. So was the landing card he had completed during the final approach to the airport. His only item of cabin baggage was an executive briefcase, but no customs officer asked him to open it when he passed through the Nothing to Declare channel after collecting his suitcase from the baggage carousel. Turning right in the concourse, he went over to the Bureau de Change and cashed six thousand Deutschmarks into sterling. He then left the terminal building, crossed the road to the taxi rank and told the cab driver to take him to the Hyde Park Hotel where the Reisebüro in Frankfurt had reserved a single room on his behalf.

After checking into the hotel, Ulex went up to his room on the third floor and unpacked his few belongings. He then unlocked the executive briefcase, tipped the money out on to the bed and removed the false bottom. Tucked underneath were the necessary props to sustain the legend he had created for himself. They included a very dog-eared snapshot of a young woman, a wartime identity card issued by the German Occupation Authorities in Warsaw, and a seaman's paybook from the Polish Mercantile Marine dating back to 1961. He tucked the papers into the breastpocket of his jacket, repacked the money and then went down to the lobby and asked the desk clerk if he could have a safe-deposit box. It was one thing to walk around with five hundred and thirty pounds in his wallet, but there was no way he was prepared to leave over fourteen thousand Deutschmarks in a hotel bedroom or carry it around London in a briefcase.

Shortly before noon, Ulex left the hotel and walked down the Brompton Road. From a small bookshop and stationer's opposite Harrods he bought a copy of the *London Streetfinder* which included a diagram of the Underground. From the SSD in East Berlin he had learned that the offices of *The Sentinel* were in Varley Mall; they had also furnished him with the name and telephone number of the proprietor. After leaving the shop, he continued on down the Brompton Road until he came across a public phone box from which he rang Mrs Irena Puzak and introduced himself as Marc Jankowski.

Amberley Lodge was ex-directory, the pay phone outside the mess ante room was not. It was there for the benefit of students on residential courses and members of the permanent staff. Humorists maintained it was bugged, cynics regularly unscrewed the mouthpiece to make sure no foreign bodies had been implanted, and on one notable occasion, a drunken student had virtually demolished the booth in a desire to satisfy himself that a wire mike had not been drilled into the wooden frame. Rumour had it that all security clearances had subsequently been withdrawn from him on the grounds that he was both mentally unstable and an obvious alcoholic. One thing was however beyond dispute; lodged in the mess rules was a written assurance from the commandant of the Training School to the effect that the pay phone was clean.

A fortnight ago, Parker would have taken this assurance on trust; now however he was one of the confirmed cynics and had thought it prudent to ring Stefanie Ayres from a pay phone in Petersfield before driving up to London yesterday. On the pretext of filling up the Mini, he had again driven into the market town, this time to call Sarah Yendell and ask her if she still had Kershaw's office number.

"I wrote it down on a piece of paper which I left on your desk," Sarah told him.

"Are you saying you didn't make a note of it?"

"I'm afraid I am. But if you give me your phone number, I'll go down to the library and look it up in *Kelly's Trade Directory* and call you back."

"Well, if you could do that, I'd be very grateful. I'm on Petersfield 1291."

Parker waited for Sarah to repeat the number, then thanked her again and hung up. The phone box was just down the road from the level crossing outside the station. As he waited for Sarah to call back, the gates closed across the road, halting the traffic. A horn blared in the distance, then blared again a few seconds before a fast down train to Portsmouth thundered across the road and hurtled through the station. Presently, the gates opened and the traffic started moving again; the phone however remained obstinately silent. An elderly woman approached the box and began to circle it, trying to catch his eye when he did his best to ignore her. It got harder to do so when she started tapping on the glass, and he heaved a sigh of relief when the phone rang at last just as she was about to open the door.

"Campbell?"

"That's me," he said.

"The number you want is Middlesbrough 21149," Sarah told him.

"Thanks."

"I didn't bother to get his ex-directory number but if you should want it, I can use the Merlin codeword on the Enquiries supervisor and call you back again."

"I don't think I am going to need it."

"Okay." Sarah paused, then said, "Can I ask a question?"

"Sure."

"Why do you want to ring Mr Kershaw again?"

"Because I'm curious to know how he feels about Poland now," Parker said.

"That's all right then – as long as it doesn't have anything to do with the late Kurt Bender."

Parker reared back as if he'd been struck. "What did you say?"

"Bender is dead. Didn't Harry Freeland tell you? There's a hell of a flap going on here; Maurice Orde has been in and out of the Director General's office ever since the news broke."

"What does he have to do with it?"

"Of course, you wouldn't know. The Deputy Director left for Washington yesterday and Maurice is standing in for him."

Parker heard Sarah say something about Nick Quade wanting her, then found himself listening to a burring noise and realised she had hung up. He replaced the phone and backed out of the kiosk.

"About time," the elderly woman said as she squeezed past him.

Bender: he wondered why he found it so hard to grasp the fact that the German was dead when he had mooted the possibility of a fatal heart attack. But had Bender died from natural causes? What if he had been murdered? Where had his body been found? The questions multiplied in his mind but all of them would have to wait until he could get hold of Freeland.

The gates of the level crossing closed for the second time and a slow up-line train to London pulled out of the station. He lit a cigarette and paced up and down the street casting frustrated glances at the elderly woman in the phone box. He sent a score of telepathic messages urging her to hurry up but she was resistant to auto-suggestion and carried on blissfully until finally she ran out of small change and was forced to terminate the call.

"About time," Parker said as he changed places with her.

He dialled Trunks, asked the operator to connect him with Middlesbrough 21149 and fed the coin box with enough loose change to keep him going for at least three minutes. The vagaries of the telephone system were such that sometimes a long-distance call was made inaudible by interference on the line, but on this occasion, there was no static induction and Kershaw sounded as if he were in an adjoining room.

"My name is Humphries," Parker told him. "I'm with the Foreign Office. You may remember that I rang you just over a fortnight ago about your niece, Stefanie Ayres . . ."

"I recognise your voice," Kershaw said, interrupting him. "Your name is Parker, not Humphries."

It was pointless to deny it. What puzzled him was how Kershaw knew when he had been very careful to use an alias on the phone. You could use your real name when meeting an outsider face to face on neutral territory; when at home, you masqueraded under an assumed one. That was the rule and he was damned sure he had observed it to the letter. Stefanie must have told her uncle, it was the only explanation he could think of.

"Then you know who I am, Mr Kershaw," he said. "I'm calling to . . ."

"You're a bastard, that's what you are."

"What?"

"Are you deaf or merely an imbecile?" Kershaw shouted.

"Who do you think you're talking to?" Parker demanded angrily.

"The swine who has driven Victor to commit suicide."

The stream of invective which followed barely registered with Parker. Nothing Kershaw said made any sense. "What exactly am I supposed to have done?" he asked.

"Are you trying to tell me you don't know? Oh, that's very clever . . ."

The pips suddenly intruded, momentarily silencing the tirade. Knowing he would be cut off at any moment, Parker fed three shillings into the coin box and punched Button 'A' to hold the connection open.

"Do you mind repeating all that?" he said when Kershaw came back on the line.

"Yesterday you interviewed Victor in London. He comes back very depressed, goes into the office last night and writes me a letter. It's delivered to my house second post. You want to hear what he says? I tell you. 'Dear Arthur,' he writes, 'I have had a terrible time with Mr Campbell Parker today. Someone told him I had joined the SS in the war and committed many crimes against the Jews. This is not true but I was forced to join the Ukrainian Self-Defence Brigade, and now I know the British Foreign Office will send me back to Russia. Mr Parker promised me this wouldn't happen but I do not trust him, nor do I believe a word he says. I am sorry it has to end like this . . .'"

"Jesus," Parker murmured and closed his eyes.

"You do well to pray," Kershaw told him and slammed down the phone.

CHAPTER 19

ULEX LEFT the Underground station at Archway and walked to the offices of *The Sentinel* in Varley Mall. In Berlin he had been told that the newspaper was on its last legs and one look at the premises was enough to convince him it could fold any time in the not too distant future. The paper was run at a loss, crippled by a diminishing circulation which the SSD in Normanenstrasse maintained would ultimately prove terminal. Although it was kept afloat financially by the owner, no one was immortal, least of all Mrs Irena Puzak, though on meeting her, Ulex found it hard to believe she was in her mid-seventies. Within a matter of minutes, he also discovered she was far too alert for his liking and a lot sharper than he had bargained for. She began by talking to him in Polish, then switched to English in mid-sentence before asking him if he would prefer to converse in German. He guessed that Irena Puzak was testing him, as if she doubted his nationality.

"I prefer my native tongue," he told her in fluent Polish.

"Good." A faint smile led him to think he had done the right thing. "I believe you left Poland in April 1962 . . . ?"

"Correction," he said, interrupting her. "I jumped ship in 1964."

"Yes, of course. You must forgive me, Mr Jankowski, I'm getting very forgetful in my old age."

Not you, Ulex thought. The mistake had been intentional, a ruse to wrong foot him. The disarming smile was intended to make him lower his guard.

"There is something I don't quite understand," she continued almost apologetically. "If life under the Communists was so bad, why did you wait nineteen years before escaping?"

"It wasn't easy for someone like me to get taken on as a deckhand."

"Why you in particular?"

"I was born at Wielun on the old Polish-German border of mixed parentage. My mother was German, my father Polish; the authorities didn't trust me because of the German connection."

Everything he had told Irena Puzak was true except that he had reversed the facts; it was his father who had been German.

"Anyway, I managed to get a job as a dock labourer at Gdansk and gradually made a name for myself with the local branch of the Communist Party." Ulex took out his seaman's paybook and showed it to Irena Puzak. "That's how I managed to join the Polish Mercantile Marine. It took me another two years to completely win their trust. For the first twelve months I was kept on the Gdansk, Riga, Tallinn, Leningrad run. After that, I did a few trips to Stockholm and even came to Tilbury a couple of times, but I had to wait until January 1963 before they would let me go ashore and then only in company. I jumped ship in Hamburg."

"Why there, Mr Jankowski?"

Ulex smiled. This was going to be one of the easier questions to answer. "Because I thought the West Germans would grant me political asylum more readily than any other country on account of my mother. Naturally, I didn't let on that I had killed a number of their fellow countrymen when I was serving in the Home Army."

In truth, it had been the other way round. He had served with Sonderkommando Gerhardt Terboven and the men he had killed had all been in the Polish Resistance. The best cover stories were based on fact; incidents which he had personally observed formed the basis of his, and all he had done was turn them around to the opposite viewpoint.

"That's when I met Andrew Korwin; he was my company commander in the Home Army."

"Ah, yes, so you said on the phone this morning." Irena Puzak pressed a buzzer on her desk. "I think my husband should come in on this. I'd like him to hear your story if you've no objection?"

"Please. I'll be happy to answer any questions he may have," Ulex told her.

He assumed her husband was the elderly clerk he had noticed in the outer office and was confident he could deal with him. When Puzak shambled into the room clutching a wad of name cards, he found it hard not to smile.

"What can you tell us about Andrew Korwin?" he asked, after his wife had introduced them and they had shaken hands.

"Amongst other things, he was the ADC to the Garrison Commander of Warsaw in 1939, was taken prisoner when the city surrendered and ended up in Colditz after an unsuccessful attempt to escape from Stalag XXa at Thorn on the Vistula. In November 1941 he went down with pneumonia and was admitted to Leipzig General Hospital from where he escaped six weeks later."

Both the Puzaks were doing their best to appear indifferent but he could tell they were excited. They had obviously heard the same story from someone else and he fancied he knew who had told them.

"He made his way to Warsaw and joined the Underground by forming his own Resistance cell. I met him in February '43 when individual cells were being bonded together and organised into companies and platoons. First operation we did was the abduction, trial and execution of a police informer."

Ulex told them about the six freight cars of small arms ammunition Korwin's group had set on fire in the marshalling yards near the Central Station and of the foot patrol they had ambushed and shot down in the Wola district. The information was palpably true and there was no way the Puzaks could refute it because he had been present when the Gestapo had interrogated Korwin at police headquarters in Nowy Swiat after he had been arrested forty-eight hours before the Warsaw uprising had begun.

"What does 'Talmunt' mean to you?" Puzak asked when he paused for breath.

"Nothing," Ulex said. "Why should it?"

"'Talmunt' was the codename used by Korwin."

Ulex stared at each of the Puzaks in turn. If they were trying to trap him, they were making a bad job of it. "Rubbish," he said harshly. "Whoever told you that certainly didn't know Andrew Korwin."

"It was his niece, Stefanie Ayres."

"Sounds English."

"She's American," Irena Puzak told him.

"And she is over here?"

"Yes."

It was likely the American girl had seen Korwin and knew where he was living. If so, she could save him a lot of time and trouble, but the Puzaks weren't the sort of people to disclose her address lightly and he didn't want to arouse their suspicion by asking for it. Her address was probably on a card like the ones Puzak had been examining while he had been talking. If it came to it, he could always burgle the house and who knows, he might even obtain Korwin's address at the same time.

"You've gone very quiet, Mr Jankowski," Puzak said.

"You're surprised? You shouldn't be. Who wouldn't be overcome to learn that a friend he has presumed dead all these years is still alive? I had no such expectation when I came here."

"Quite so."

Ulex wiped the smile from his face and looked concerned. "At the same time, I am alarmed. When I knew my friend, he was called 'Wola'."

"'Wola'?" Puzak repeated and glanced at his wife.

"Yes, it's the name of the district where he recruited most of his men. Now I ask myself why should his niece think he was 'Talmunt'?" It was the last thing the Puzaks had expected from him and it was obvious they didn't know what to make of it. "I think perhaps you should ask her that question yourselves," he said and stood up.

"No, I have a better idea." Puzak moved to the desk and wrote something down on scrap of paper and gave it to Ulex. "This is her telephone number, Mr Jankowski – why don't you ask her?"

Garvey massaged both temples with his fingertips in an effort to relieve a splitting headache that four codeines had failed to shift. It had been a bad morning and the afternoon was giving every sign of being a damn sight worse. The edited version of his interview with Stevens had only begun to look suspect after he had smuggled it into the office and compared it with the original in his safe. Any typist could have told him the office machines were pica typeface whereas the Empire Aristocrat portable was élite, but Garvey had only become aware of the difference when the two reports were lying side by side on his desk.

He had solved one problem only to create another. If he had submitted the edited version, he would have had to explain that he had typed it at home and the Assistant Director would then have lit a fire under him for committing a gross breach of security. He had looked at the original again with a view to submitting it, but knowing Stevens had disappeared leaving what amounted to a suicide note behind, the content had struck him as even more highly dangerous than before. If Stevens had killed himself and allegations were subsequently made that MI5 had in some way been responsible for his act of self-destruction, the hunt would be on for a scapegoat and he would be the number one contender.

After an agonising debate with himself, Garvey had shredded the original and decided to have the edited version retyped, this time on the office Underwood. Of all the choices open to him, this had seemed the safest. Getting one of his clerks to do it had also seemed a lot safer than sending it down to the typing pool where the supervisor would have noticed that the so-called draft had been done on a portable and would have reported the irregularity to the Branch security officer.

There had however been one snag to the preferred solution. Although safer, it had been a lot slower, which had made life fraught because the Assistant Director had specifically wanted the interview report on his desk at start of business. When it hadn't arrived by mid-morning, he had started to get highly aerated; by the time the finished copy had been completed, the Assistant Director had worked himself into a thoroughly unpleasant temper. In a mood to find fault with everything, he had fastened on to the pseudonym and had demanded to know why Garvey had led Stevens to believe he was being interviewed by a Mr Campbell Parker.

The mind-numbing headache had started with that question and had got progressively worse as the morning had worn on and they had learned that Stevens had written more than one suicide note. The fact that no classified papers had been removed from the factory had been regarded as small consolation by his superiors; their primary concern had been, and always would be, to make sure they had a leakproof umbrella over their heads.

The phone rang and set his head throbbing even more painfully. Eyes closed as though in prayer, he lifted the receiver from the cradle and held it to his ear. "Garvey," he croaked; then a cool voice told him he was talking to the watchman and a feeling that the afternoon would go from bad to worse was confirmed.

"We've been rumbled," the watchman told him bluntly.

"Would you like to be a little more specific?" Garvey said acidly.

"There's not a lot to it. Some guy from Pansonic TV and Radio Repairs arrived in a small Ford van just after two thirty and fifteen minutes later our monitor died on us."

"Maybe something is wrong with your receiver?" Garvey suggested hopefully.

"No, he found the transmitter all right. We heard him undo every screw before the sound went phut."

Shit. Shit. Shit. Garvey ran a hand through his hair but it did nothing to soothe his headache. "Was Miss Ayres at home when this happened?" he asked.

"No, but Mullinder was. We heard him in the flat telling the repair man how she had been having trouble with the vertical hold before the tube burned out."

"Clever."

"It gets cleverer," the watchman told him. "When the repair man found the bug, neither he nor Mullinder said a word. There was an interval of at least five minutes between the time we saw the repair man enter the apartments and when we heard him inside her flat. I reckon our lawyer friend must have told him what to expect."

"What did you say the name of the firm was?"

"Pansonic TV and Radio Repairs. They're completely legit."

"Any idea who arranged for the repair man to call?" Garvey asked.

"Not really. Miss Ayres arrived home at seven twenty-five this morning after spending the night with Parker. She changed and left for the office an hour later. She didn't use the phone during that time, but of course it could be she got Mullinder to do it when she left the keys to her flat with him. Then again, she may have rung the firm from the office."

Garvey could think of several other possibilities but all of them were immaterial. One thing and one thing alone stood out a mile; Parker had warned her she was under electronic surveillance and one way or another, he would get him for that.

"What do you want us to do now, Mr Garvey?"

The bug inside the TV set had relayed every phone call the Ayres woman had made from her sitting room; now they were stone deaf and would have to rely on their eyes. "Just observe and follow," Garvey told him.

But that was strictly for the time being. After the stunt she had just pulled, he couldn't see how the legal adviser to 'A' Branch could possibly object to a phone tap on her office number. Furthermore, the Assistant Director could damn well take his jacket off and get him one of those new-fangled shotgun microphones you aimed at a window which the Home Office was busy developing.

And after he had heard what had happened at Cheyne Walk, perhaps he wouldn't think that using Parker's name at the interview had been such a bad idea after all.

Parker rarely visited Benbow House; consequently, his face wasn't known to the receptionist on duty in the entrance hall. There was, however, nothing wrong with his identity card and the passport-size photograph in the top right-hand corner was a better than average likeness, but even so, it didn't appear to meet with the approval of the security guard. He stared at the ID for what seemed an excessively long time before ducking inside his booth to check it against some information he had on a millboard. A few moments later, he reappeared looking embarrassed.

"I'm afraid it's no longer valid for Benbow House, sir," he said apologetically.

"What on earth are you talking about?"

"Your right of access has been withdrawn, sir."

"You mean I can't come in?" Parker asked incredulously.

"It won't get you in to Queen Anne's Gate or 54 Broadway either."

He had left the Mini in the station yard at Petersfield and caught a semi-fast train to Waterloo because he needed to see Harry Freeland, and now this mournful cretin was telling him he was persona non grata.

"When the hell was I blackballed?" he demanded.

"Sir?"

"That information you were looking at on your millboard, when is it dated?"

"The twenty-fifth of May."

The day after he had handed over to Nick Quade. They might not have withdrawn his security clearances but they had done the next best thing, shunting him off to Amberley Lodge and denying him access to the nerve centres in London.

"I might have guessed," Parker muttered.

"Yes, sir."

"I assume I'm not banned from using the phone?"

Parker didn't wait for permission but went straight to the reception booth towards the back of the hall and asked one of the girls to ring extension 0911. When Freeland answered, he grabbed the phone from her.

"Hello, Harry," he said, "it's me, Campbell. I'm downstairs in the hall but I'm not allowed to come up. Can you do something about it?"

After expressing considerable surprise, Freeland said he most certainly could, then asked to speak to one of the girls on the reception desk, followed by the security guard. Parker couldn't hear what was said but the security guard turned brick red and it was evident from the venomous way he told the receptionist to make out a visitor's pass for "this gentleman" that he wasn't exactly best pleased.

The girl handed Parker a ballpoint and invited him to complete the blank pass. In the box headed "Purpose of visit" he wrote "Liaison" and put "Self" in answer to the question which asked him to state who he was representing. He then signed the form and returned it to the girl for time and date stamping. The piece of paper did not however permit him to wander around the building unaccompanied and the girl escorted him up to Freeland's office on the sixth floor.

"It's a funny old world, Harry," he said when they were alone.

"That's putting it mildly. What exactly have you been up to, Campbell?"

"I think Messrs Dent, Garvey and the rest don't like the company I've been keeping." Parker slumped into a chair. "Remember what you told me when I first got into this thing? You said that any time I ran into something that seemed like an official brick wall, either to back off or come to you before I went barging on."

"And now you've crunched into the wall and it's too late to back off?"

"Something like that."

"You want to tell me about it?"

"Someone interviewed Victor Stevens in London yesterday. I don't know what passed between them, but after returning to Middlesbrough, he promptly sat down and wrote a suicide note, then disappeared."

"Who told you this?"

"His partner, Arthur Kershaw. I rang him this afternoon on another matter. He had a letter from Victor saying it was all my fault."

"Because whoever interviewed him yesterday had used your name. Right?"

Parker nodded, helped himself to a cigarette from the packet

Freeland was offering, then leaned forward to catch a light. "I'm betting it was Garvey," he added.

"You can't be sure of that."

"I can't think of a better candidate; he's undoubtedly the nurse-maid MI5 appointed to look after Kershaw and you know how he tried to warn me off Stefanie Ayres."

"Do you trust that girl, Campbell?"

Parker hesitated. "I know I love her," he said eventually.

"With respect, that isn't what I asked you."

Although Freeland's smile took the sting out of his words, he still resented the inference, especially as it happened to be true. There wasn't anything he wouldn't do for Stefanie Ayres but every now and again, a doubt that was difficult to ignore niggled at his mind.

"We're straying from the point, Harry. If Stevens could find the time to write a suicide note to Kershaw as well as to his wife, who else did he send one to? The editor of some newspaper perhaps?"

"You're being a little premature, aren't you, Campbell? We don't know he is dead . . ."

"Bender is though," Parker said, cutting him short.

"You've heard the news then?"

"Yes, Sarah Yendell told me."

"I phoned Amberley Lodge a couple of times to tell you but they said you had gone into Petersfield."

"You don't have to explain anything to me, Harry."

Freeland laughed, genuinely amused. "When you put it like that, I obviously need to," he said.

"I'm sorry." Parker shook his head. "I'm getting jumpy, seeing conspiracies where none exist. But humour me for a minute; let's suppose that he did write to a newspaper editor. Okay, the guy can't use it before the inquest has been held, but what happens after the coroner's jury has returned a verdict?"

"We might be able to slap a 'D' notice on the editor . . ."

"I can just see the Cabinet Office instructing the chief press secretary to do that on my behalf. I think this government will try to remain aloof and ignore the whole damned business until it's too late. Kershaw has my name and the press can find me."

The Diplomatic List contained the names of all SIS officers and like the Army List, it was not a classified document. Every major library had a copy and any enterprising journalist could find him because there was only one Campbell amongst the Parkers. From there, it was only a short step to putting a face to a name and then he could start looking for another job because he would be no damn use to the Service after his picture had appeared in the newspapers.

"Will you do something for me?" Freeland asked.

"Depends what it is," Parker said cautiously.

"I want you to write down everything that has happened to you from the moment I briefed you to meet Stefanie Ayres. I want a complete diary of events, and I do mean complete and unexpurgated. Hold nothing back; if you've been sleeping with her, say so and don't be coy about whose idea it was or who made most of the running."

"What good will that do?"

"When you've finished the diary of events, we will get it notarised by a commissioner for oaths, then I'll walk the document straight into the DG and tell him he's got to shelter you from the fallout."

"You're chancing your arm a bit, aren't you, Harry? I mean, I don't expect you to go out on a limb for me."

"I already have," Freeland said. "I did that when I overruled the security guard and told him I was damn well going to see you whether he liked it or not."

"Hey, I don't want you to get into trouble on my behalf."

"Trouble is second nature to me," Freeland told him cheerfully. "You don't think I'd still only be an assistant director if I'd kept my nose clean, do you?"

The tyre tracks were first noticed shortly after a quarter to four by a group of schoolchildren from Masham who were playing near the lakes but it didn't occur to them to report it straight away. That would have meant returning to the village and they weren't ready to do that until it was time to go home. The first adults to come across them were a couple of anglers. Although they arrived on the scene a few minutes after five, they didn't see the tyre marks until almost an hour later when they decided to try another spot because the fish weren't biting where they were.

The tyre marks clearly indicated that the vehicle had not halted on the lip and must have gone straight in. They had no doubts about this; had the driver stopped and reversed back the way he had come, there should have been an overlap somewhere between the lake and the road. In their opinion, no driver, man or woman, was skilled enough to back a vehicle the best part of three hundred yards without deviating so much as a tyre's width from the original track. Both anglers had cycled out to the lakes and it took them just twenty minutes to ride some five miles into Masham; running the village constable to ground however took somewhat longer.

The village lay within the Ripon subdivision of the North Riding constabulary but as far as the police constable was concerned, his immediate superior was the inspector at Thirsk. Much as he knew and trusted the anglers, he was not prepared to report the incident until he had seen the tyre tracks for himself. By the time he had ridden out to the scene and back again, it was close on seven thirty.

The vehicle was thought to be lying in at least thirty, possibly forty feet of water. The North Riding constabulary was a comparatively small force policing a large area of real estate; consequently, specialists like frogmen were either provided by the Regional Crime Squad or borrowed from the appropriate military establishment. In this particular instance, the nearest source was the army's 38th Corps Engineer Regiment at Ripon which was only twelve miles from the lakes. An hour after the Chief Constable had asked for assistance, a team of four sappers under the command of a sergeant was on the scene. Although it wasn't difficult to calculate the approximate position of the vehicle, the water was extremely murky and there was a great deal of silt. They were therefore somewhat lucky to find the car at the first attempt. The Rover was tipped over on to its near side. With the aid of his underwater flashlight, the sergeant could see there was a body lying on the floor behind the two front seats. The driver's window had been lowered approximately three inches and the interior was flooded. However, the pressure was such that he was unable to open either door on the nearside and he was obliged to leave the body where it was for the time being.

A Leyland heavy recovery vehicle and a Coles Crane with lifting gear were summoned from the barracks; with night closing in, lighting at the site was to be provided by a towed generator. By the time the convoy arrived, the frogmen had already succeeded in righting the vehicle. They had also carried out a detailed underwater reconnaissance and were ready to anchor two pulleys to the lake bed while the Leyland was being manoeuvred into position on the bank. The winch gear was then strung out and the steel-wire hawser passed through the pulleys before being shackled to the rear axle of the Rover. Once this had been completed, the car was dragged along the bed towards the bank and the shallower water where the Coles Crane was standing by to complete the rest of the recovery operation. Although the plan was simple enough, it was time-consuming since it was necessary to unshackle the hawser and reconnect it again when the rear axle was almost level with the first pulley. Consequently, it was after midnight before the Rover was finally lifted out of the lake and set down on the bank.

Although the vehicle registration number had led the police to believe that the dead man was Victor Stevens, formal identification was necessary, which was why an ambulance was on site to take the body to the mortuary at the Middlesbrough City Hospital. Their supposition was subsequently confirmed by Mrs Jean Stevens who was accompanied by Mr and Mrs Arthur Kershaw. The police officer who was present during the identification reported that the grief-stricken widow had told him she knew the name of the man who had been responsible for her husband's death and was going to make sure he paid for it.

CHAPTER 20

"THE STAR Chamber" was not a new experience for Parker. Eight days ago, Maurice Orde, Roger Dent and John Garvey had invaded his office at 54 Broadway to grill him about his relationship with Stefanie Ayres. Today Garvey was missing, the venue was the library at Amberley Lodge and this time it seemed Orde was going to be present throughout the interview instead of withdrawing before it began.

"Stevens is dead," Orde told him without any kind of preamble, then busied himself with his pipe. "His body was recovered from the bottom of a lake near Masham," he added, pretty much as an afterthought.

Parker could not remember mentioning Stevens to either man, yet they were obviously aware that he had heard of him. That had to mean they had seen a copy of the deposition he had prepared at Freeland's request.

"I'm sorry to hear it," Parker said quietly.

"Both the widow and his business partner appear to hold you responsible for his death." Orde clamped the pipe between his teeth and lit it, then put the tobacco pouch away. "Why do you think that is, Campbell?"

"Because whoever interviewed him in London the day before yesterday used my name."

"Oh, I don't doubt it; what intrigues me is how Mr Kershaw knows you are with the Foreign Office?"

"I think Stefanie Ayres must have told him."

"I might have guessed that young woman would have had a hand in it," Dent said irritably. "I presume you didn't see fit to remain incognito when you interviewed her?"

"Oh, come on, 4 Central Buildings belongs to the Foreign Office. Do I have to say more?" It seemed he did if Dent's puzzled expression was anything to go by. "Look," Parker said, trying not to sound exasperated, "Harry Freeland had warned me that she was a highly intelligent young woman and I wasn't going to take any chances. Stefanie Ayres came to Matthew Dalton Street expecting to meet an official from the Foreign Office. What do you suppose would have happened if she hadn't been able to find my name in the Diplomatic List afterwards? She would have gone straight back to Larborough and we would have ended up with egg on our faces."

"And what makes you think we won't?" Dent asked belligerently.

Orde inspected his pipe, discovered it had gone out and took his time about relighting it. "I think Roger may have a point," he said between puffs. "The inquest is to be held on Wednesday the fourteenth of June."

"That's pretty quick."

"Well, as you should know, the folks up north don't believe in letting the grass grow under their feet. The thing is, the widow is after your blood, Campbell, and she means to have her day in court. We can't muzzle the coroner, the suicide note will be produced in evidence and your name is bound to be mentioned, which means the press will be looking for you as soon as a verdict is returned."

"That would make me highly visible."

Orde didn't contradict him which Parker thought was ominous. He waited, hoping Orde would eventually tell him what the DG had in mind but it seemed his former boss had suddenly lost his voice.

"Well, don't keep me in suspense, Maurice," he said quietly.

"Harry Freeland recommended that we should post you to one of our embassies but I am not sure the Foreign Office will be willing to accommodate us."

In Parker's experience, career diplomats tended to regard the SIS officers in their midst with disdain but their reluctance to shelter him was not founded on mere antipathy. If the press started a witch hunt, there could well come a time when they would have to disclose where he was supposed to have been serving when Stevens was being questioned. And perhaps for a while that might satisfy the press, but there was always the risk that sooner or later some journalist would start digging away and discover he hadn't been posted to Timbuktu or wherever until after Stevens had topped himself.

"So what do we do, Maurice? Brazen it out?"

"We'd like to . . ."

"But there's a problem," Dent said, chipping in, "and her name is Stefanie Ayres."

"You're not going to give me that old, old story again, are you? The one where she is working for the Polish Intelligence Service?"

"And despite what you were told, you are still seeing her. Right, Campbell?"

"A couple of times."

"Did you warn Miss Ayres that her flat had been bugged?"

"Are you telling me she is under surveillance, Roger?"

"Don't come all innocent with me. Who was playing cloak and dagger only hours after we had politely warned you off? Who contacted Stefanie Ayres through a third party and arranged to meet her at Ruislip? I've got to hand it to you, Campbell, you made Garvey's people look pretty silly. They followed her on to the Piccadilly Line train at South Kensington not knowing where she was going and three quarters of an hour later found themselves stranded out in the sticks. You're waiting to meet her with a car and they've no way of following you because Ruislip is outer suburbia and there is no such thing as a taxi rank in the station yard."

"I was just being careful," Parker told him.

"If you will forgive me, I think you behaved rather foolishly, Campbell," Orde said mildly, "especially as John Garvey had told you he suspected Miss Ayres had been recruited by the Opposition."

Stefanie had visited Poland twice, once with a group of students sponsored by the Young People's International Friendship Society. To Garvey's way of thinking, this apparently made her a hostile Intelligence agent.

"Maybe, in retrospect, I should have backed off, but Garvey wasn't exactly candid with me, Maurice. All I got from him was a veiled threat that I could lose my security status if I didn't watch my step. Hell, if she was that much of a security risk, why haven't we deported her?"

"Because Box are still gathering evidence which has now become vastly more difficult thanks to you," Dent snapped.

"What am I supposed to have done?"

Dent enjoyed telling him. According to MI5, Stefanie Ayres had arranged to have her flat spring-cleaned after he had warned her to be careful what she said in the privacy of her home.

"Result? No eavesdropping facility and the effectiveness of the surveillance operation is severely reduced. And who supervised the spring-cleaning? Why, none other than Kevin Mullinder, that well-known guardian of civil liberties."

It looked bad, very bad. What was it Stefanie had said when he had hinted she was on a party line? "I don't know where you got that idea, Campbell." He had wondered then if she really was the innocent abroad; now he knew she wasn't. But the Security Service had had their hooks into her long before he had appeared on the scene.

"Did Garvey tell you why MI5 were keeping her under surveillance? I mean, they surely didn't have my interest at heart when they set it up. Hell, they didn't even know I existed."

The question was addressed to Dent but it was Orde who answered it. "They had reason to believe Miss Ayres was engaged on a disinformation exercise."

"Was?" Parker queried.

"With Stevens dead, it is beginning to look as though she may have accomplished her task."

UK PROVIDES SAFE HAVEN FOR WAR CRIMINAL. NAZI HENCHMAN DESIGNS TANK SIGHT FOR BRITISH ARMY. The headlines suggested themselves and even the most uninformed layman could appreciate the embarrassment they would cause the government. Stevens had pioneered a target acquisition system that could revolutionise armoured warfare but to date no Defence contract had been placed with the Ward Tandy Group. Attacking Stevens was one way of ensuring the government continued to vacillate.

"Is that the line MI5 are taking, Maurice?"

"Yes."

"But if we accept that, we have to believe that Stefanie Ayres wasn't bothered about the harm she would be doing to her uncle."

It was also a fact that the Security Service was tacitly admitting that they knew Victor Stevens had had something to hide and had been doing their best to protect him at the behest of the Ministry of Defence.

"That's past history, Campbell. What we have to decide is how best to handle your involvement." Orde reached for the heavy brass ashtray on the low table in front of him and drew it nearer, then tapped out his pipe. "Quite frankly, all we can do is sit tight and hope for the best."

"And if some reporter should run me to ground?"

"Well, I don't think you would have much of a future with us, do you?"

Maurice Orde was only stating the obvious but it still came as a blow. "When do I start looking for another job?" Parker asked with a wry smile.

"Oh, we hope it won't come to that, but if it should, you won't find us ungenerous. Regrettably, you haven't been with us long enough to earn even a modified pension but you will receive a gratuity commensurate with your length of service. By way of a resettlement grant, we will also pay you the equivalent of your present salary for three years."

"Tax free," Dent added.

"What's the catch, Roger?"

"No catch. Of course, we wouldn't like you to give any interviews, but that's already taken care of under the Official Secrets Acts. Right?"

"Absolutely."

"I'm glad we understand one another," Dent said smoothly.

They were asking him to put his head on the block for Garvey. Asking? Parker frowned; they were ordering him to do it. In Service terms, it was a damage limitation exercise, a way of reducing the number of inevitable casualties from two to one.

"I'm sorry it has to be this way," Orde said quietly.

"It's not your fault, Maurice." It wasn't entirely his either but he wasn't looking for sympathy.

"Of course, as I've already said, it may not come to anything, in which case you've nothing to worry about. Meanwhile, I recommend you keep your head below the parapet."

"I'm supposed to be giving a lecture to Ministry of Defence Branch security officers on Friday."

"The commandant will arrange for one of the instructors to handle it," Dent said and got to his feet.

It looked as if Orde was going to ignore a none too subtle hint that it was time they were leaving but after some hesitation he followed Dent's example. They had travelled down from London by car and their departure was delayed while Parker despatched one of the security guards to dig their driver out of the staff canteen. Orde felt obliged to make small talk while they were waiting but no one else shared his passion for cricket and his efforts fell on stony ground. Less than five minutes after their car had disappeared down the drive, Parker was on the phone to Detective

Chief Superintendent Wirral asking for the address of Mullinder's law practice.

Few solicitors enjoyed a better location than Temple, Meade and Woodthorpe Associates in Bell Yard. Their offices were less than a stone's throw from the Royal Courts of Justice and were exactly midway between the chambers in Middle Temple and Lincoln's Inn Fields whose barristers they regularly briefed. They were also within easy walking distance of Fleet Street which was perhaps why the practice had tended to specialise in libel actions. Although civil litigation was their bread and butter, they were involved in a certain amount of criminal work. This fag end of the business, as the managing clerk haughtily described it, was handled almost entirely by Kevin Mullinder.

Mullinder was in his late thirties, had carried away a First from Birmingham University, made a clean sweep of all the prizes at Law College and had had absolutely no difficulty in securing a position as an articled clerk. In his particular year, he had been the first graduate to be offered a full partnership which, in view of his peripheral activities with the National Council for Civil Liberties and his espousal of unpopular causes, had surprised many of his contemporaries from university days. Around Chancery Lane, it was said of Temple, Meade and Woodthorpe Associates that Mullinder was their social conscience on view. He was tall, well-built and was said to have a keen sense of humour; he was not at all like the trendy left-winger Parker had imagined.

"It's good of you to see me without an appointment," Parker said. "We haven't actually met before but we have spoken on the telephone. I'm a friend of Stefanie's."

"That's right. I thought your voice sounded familiar. You asked me to bring Stefanie to the phone."

"Yes, her's was out of order."

"So you said at the time." Mullinder waved him to a chair, then sat down again himself. "Now, what can I do for you, Mr Parker? My secretary said it was a personal matter?"

"You could say it was very personal."

"Oh." Mullinder's smile faded a little. "Well, perhaps I should point out that I don't handle divorce cases."

"I'm about to lose my job," Parker said abruptly, "and if I do, it will be largely your fault."

Mullinder stared at him as if he had taken leave of his senses. "Is this some sort of a joke?" he asked softly.

"Not to me. Yesterday afternoon you were present when a service operator from Pansonic TV and Radio Repairs checked Stefanie Ayres's flat in Cheyne Walk and removed a small electronic monitor."

"I think you had better leave, Mr Parker."

If he didn't, Mullinder proposed to evict him; that was the unspoken threat and he looked strong enough to do it.

"I'm the man who warned Stefanie that her apartment had probably been bugged."

"You?" Mullinder sounded highly sceptical.

"I work for the government, that's how I knew."

"I don't see how I can possibly help you . . ."

"Some of my colleagues think Stefanie is a spy," Parker continued.

"That's absurd."

"I'd like to agree with you but the fact is she does invite suspicion. I mean, look at it from their point of view. Would you expect an American girl who has only been in London since January to know how to get hold of a specialist in electronic countermeasures? And then we have Dennis Eastham of the Sphinx Inquiry Agency; he's hardly one of the names a management consultant would have on their need-to-know list. But I think they are the sort of experts who would be found in your address book."

"What are you implying?"

"I'm not implying anything. I happen to know you put Stefanie on to the Sphinx Inquiry Agency when she came to you for help. That's why I'm pretty sure you arranged for Pansonic to give her flat the once-over."

"Are you going to leave of your own accord or do you want me to summon a policeman and have you evicted?"

Parker smiled. "Do you suppose there would be any response?"

For a moment, it looked as though he had just struck a match over a powder keg, but then Mullinder saw the irony and grinned. "Probably not," he agreed.

"Well, I'll tell you something, I don't think they would be in a mad rush to come to my assistance either."

Mullinder's smile became even broader. "Seems we have something in common after all."

"Perhaps more than you realise," Parker said quietly. "You have a reputation for championing the underdog; you should recognise one when you see him. Whatever harassment Stefanie Ayres may have suffered is nothing compared to the amount of flak I am receiving."

"You are on our side, is that what you are saying?"

"Like you, I've done Stefanie more than the odd favour."

"Pansonic didn't sweep the flat."

The barriers were down and the rest of the explanation followed in a rush. Mullinder had his own specialist in electronic surveillance. He had arranged for the repair man to call simply to hoodwink the Security Service whom he assumed were watching the building.

"Pansonic are a highly reputable firm as MI5 will have discovered when they checked them out. To maintain the illusion, we deliberately jiggered my set up before their man arrived so that if anyone questioned him afterwards he could truthfully say that he had had to replace the tube. Anyway, while he was attempting to rectify the fault, we went upstairs to Stefanie's apartment and did it over."

"I think they overheard you."

"So what if they did? They're not likely to do anything about it; chances are MI5 entered Stefanie's flat illegally."

Parker shook his head. "From what I hear, it was all above board."

"You mean they actually asked the Home Secretary for permission before they bugged the flat?" Mullinder laughed. "That's a turn-up for the book. It doesn't make any difference though; MI5 won't come after me because they wouldn't like the attendant publicity."

"You're probably right. Just out of interest, when did Stefanie come to you with her problem?"

"Last Wednesday," Mullinder said promptly. "She said a friend had hinted she was on a party line and did I know anyone who could do something about it? Took me almost a week to get hold of my friendly technician and arrange a date to suit everybody. But Stefanie was wrong about her phone being tapped; the bug was inside the TV. Even when it is dormant, a transmitter gives off a signal. My technician picked it up as soon as he activated the sweeper. The sweeper works a bit like a mine detector and it ran the source to ground in no time . . ."

Parker wasn't listening. Wednesday: Stefanie had met him in

Ruislip on the Tuesday evening and the very next day she had gone to Mullinder. He had given her the benefit of the doubt which only went to show how stupid he was. Stefanie wasn't naïve, she had known all along what he had meant by a party line. A trained Intelligence agent could not have handled the situation more deftly.

"What made Stefanie come to you for help, Mr Mullinder? You don't advertise in the newspapers and there isn't a sign outside your door which says – 'Experienced lawyer happy to embrace unpopular causes'."

"Stefanie's predecessor at the management recruiting agency threw a house-warming party for her shortly after she arrived in London. We were invited."

"We?" Parker asked.

"I'm married," Mullinder told him patiently. "You don't think I would have left a repair man alone in my flat while we were busy looking at Stefanie's, do you?"

"This party would have been in January?" Parker said, ignoring the question.

"Yes. We subsequently invited Stefanie to dinner a couple of times and she repaid our hospitality on each occasion. No man could ask for a better publicity agent than my wife, Brenda, and since the two girls became good friends I suppose that was how Stefanie knew I was the sort of lawyer who frequently tangled with the authorities. Anyway, as you undoubtedly know already, she had this bee in her bonnet about a missing relative whom she believed was living in England under an assumed name. So, after the Home Office had been less than helpful, she sought my advice and I put her on to Dennis Eastham."

"When was this?"

"I can't remember the exact date but it was sometime towards the end of March."

And shortly after that she had gone to Larborough and involved the MP. As far as Parker could tell, the timescale was not at variance with the story she had given him.

"Funny thing," Mullinder continued, "I've never seen anyone so excited as Stefanie was when she returned from Middlesbrough. You would have thought she'd come into a small fortune. Then she spends a long weekend in Vienna and suddenly all the fizz has gone from the champagne, and all those plans she had for seeing her uncle again seem to have gone by the board."

"Well, who knows, maybe her uncle didn't share her enthusiasm for another reunion and she was slow to catch on?"

"You're probably right."

Parker got the impression that Mullinder now wanted to see the back of him and consequently was ready to agree with everything he said.

"That weekend in Vienna was certainly arranged on the spur of the moment," Mullinder said reflectively. "It could be that Stefanie felt rejected and was trying to get over the disappointment."

Stefanie hadn't felt rejected, nor did Parker believe that things had been getting on top of her at the office as she had claimed. Vienna hadn't been something in the way of a consolation trip; it had arisen because of what had happened up in Middlesbrough. It was the one overriding impression that remained with him long after he had left Mullinder and was on his way back to Petersfield.

Stefanie walked into the bedroom, undressing as she went. Sloane Square was nine stops down the line from Monument, but it was a sultry evening and the journey had taken four times as long as usual because of a train failure between St James's Park and Victoria. It had been standing room only in her car and getting stuck in a tunnel hemmed in on all sides by a mass of sweating humanity for almost an hour had been no fun whatever. Naked by the time she reached the bathroom, she stepped under the shower, drew the plastic curtain and turned the regulator to the left. A spray of ice-cold water struck her in the face, cascaded over her shoulders, raised the nipples on her breasts and made her gasp. After a couple of minutes, she moved the regulator to tepid and soaped her body all over, then washed down with a sponge. The phone began to ring while she was still towelling herself dry.

Much as Stefanie hoped otherwise, she knew it couldn't be Campbell. He would be unaware that she had had her apartment disinfested and wouldn't ring her at home. In her experience, most people gave up if they didn't get a quick response but this particular caller seemed determined to keep trying. The constant jangle finally got to her and slipping on a bathrobe, she went into the living room to answer the phone. A harsh voice told her she was talking to Marc Jankowski.

"Do I know you, Mr Jankowski?" she asked, frowning.

"No. We've never met, but I knew your uncle in Warsaw and

Mrs Puzak suggested I got in touch with you. I tried to do so yesterday evening but you were out."

His plaintive tone of voice annoyed her more than somewhat but that wasn't the only thing that took her breath away. "Mrs Puzak gave you my phone number?" Stefanie said incredulously.

"Mr Puzak did. Is that such a crime?"

"No, I just think he should have asked me first."

"It is of little consequence . . ."

"You've got a nerve."

"You remind me so much of Andrew Korwin. Such arrogance, it must run in the family. I am looking forward to meeting you."

"Did the Puzaks give you my address?"

"Regrettably they did not."

"Well, you won't get it from me, you can count on that, Mr Jankowski."

"That would be a great pity, Miss Ayres. I feel we have so much in common." The harsh voice had now become silky, almost like the purring of a cat.

"You are very much mistaken," Stefanie told him.

"No, I think not, especially when I tell you we have a mutual acquaintance in Vienna."

"We have a mutual acquaintance in Vienna." A mundane enough statement but so full of menace it sent a shiver down her spine. Heart pumping, mouth dry with fear, she slammed the phone down, then stood there unable to move.

1967

Wednesday, 14 June
TO
Monday, 19 June

CHAPTER 21

STEFANIE AYRES walked out of the Underground station at Sloane Square and started looking for a taxi. On fine evenings she usually walked down the King's Road as far as Oakley Street, then turned left for Cheyne Walk. When it was raining, she caught either a Number 11, 19 or 22 bus from the square and alighted at Chelsea Town Hall. A phone call from a stranger fifteen days ago had prompted a change of routine. Although she had not heard from Marc Jankowski since then, she knew he had not gone away but was still out there waiting for an opportunity to strike. A taxi was therefore the safest way of travelling that last mile home from the Underground station to her apartment in Cheyne Walk.

Jankowski knew where to find her. He had been to the offices of *The Sentinel* in Varley Mall and while the Puzaks might not have disclosed her address, he was undoubtedly aware of their card index on Polish exiles. *The Sentinel* was run from two rooms on the ground floor of a terraced house in a side street. There was no burglar alarm and no security locks on the large sashcord window in the editorial office at the back which looked out on to an overgrown garden that was screened from the neighbouring properties by an equally overgrown privet hedge. Stephanie was sure that even the most ham-fisted amateur could burgle the place and get clean away, safe in the knowledge that no one was on the premises after dark to raise the alarm.

If there had been a break-in, she was convinced that Mrs Puzak wouldn't have admitted it. She had, in fact, telephoned the newspaper proprietor a couple of days ago to find out what, if anything, she knew about Mr Jankowski and had got some very cagey answers. There had been no need to tell Mrs Puzak that her husband shouldn't have given her phone number to a stranger. From the apologetic tone, it had been evident that she was pretty unhappy about the disclosure and had been all too anxious to assure Stefanie that nothing else had gone wrong. Vandals had occasionally smashed the odd pane of glass round the back but nothing had ever been stolen, Stefanie had her word for that. But that wasn't worth a whole lot and it was therefore only prudent to assume that Jankowski knew where she worked and where she lived.

Vigilance by itself was not enough to combat the threat; to stay out of harm's way, she had decided to vary her routine as much as possible. A few minutes after leaving the station, she picked up a cab from outside the Royal Court theatre and was dropped off outside the entrance to the apartment building in Cheyne Walk.

Stefanie checked her mailbox in the hall hoping there would be a postcard from Vienna, but the only letter was a circular from an insurance company touting for business. There were no messages on the answering machine in her flat either, but that could have been her fault because she had obviously forgotten to switch it on before she left for the office. Except that she could have sworn she remembered seeing the tiny red indicator light glowing. Someone had been in the flat while she was at work; it wasn't her imagination, she could actually smell their presence. Stefanie wrinkled her nose; correction, she could smell the cigarette the intruder had been smoking. Turkish; she would know that aroma anywhere, Brenda Mullinder was always smoking them. Of course – Brenda. What the hell was the matter with her? The Mullinders had been to dinner yesterday evening; it had been her way of saying thank you to Kevin.

Stefanie opened a window, then fixed herself a very strong, very dry Martini. The alcohol was supposed to help her unwind but even after two in a row, she still felt tense and on edge. Her eyes drifted towards the phone. And where was Campbell Parker when she needed him? – silent as a Trappist monk. No, that was unfair; he was in deep trouble because he had gone out of his way to help her. She couldn't blame him for keeping his head down while that inquest was going on up in Middlesbrough.

The inquest; that ought to be over by now. Leaving her drink on the low table by the armchair, she went over to the phone and rang the Kershaws' home number in Redcar. The pleasure she evinced at hearing Nancy's voice on the line was entirely genuine.

"Hi," she said, "it's me, Stefanie. I just wanted to know how you are both faring after what happened today. It can't have been very pleasant for either of you."

"It wasn't," Nancy said quietly, "but it was far worse for Jean. The press were there in force but fortunately Arthur was able to fend them off. He's had quite a time of it these last few days what with the Ministry of Defence wanting to make sure that nothing was missing at the factory."

"But the inquest is over?"

"Oh yes – the jury returned the usual verdict of suicide while the balance of the mind was disturbed. I daresay the reporters will be looking for that Mr Parker now because he's certainly got some explaining to do. Hopefully, it will all have blown over by the time we get back."

"You're going away?" Stefanie asked, surprised.

"Yes. We haven't had a break so far this year and Arthur feels we need a holiday, so we are off to Switzerland this coming Saturday."

Listening to Nancy, it seemed her husband also wanted time to himself to consider what he was going to about the business. A year ago, Hispano Suisse of Zürich had launched a takeover bid and although it had failed, the Swiss company were still interested in acquiring shares in the Ward Tandy Group.

"I think that's probably one of the reasons why we are going to Engelberg," Nancy continued.

Stefanie could hear Arthur muttering something in the background and caught the word "nonsense" before he came on the phone. "You don't want to pay any attention to Nancy," he said briskly. "Business has nothing to do with it, I happen to like the mountains."

"So do I."

"Well, why don't you come with us, Stefanie?"

"I'd like to but I'm not sure I can get away from the office."

"Yes, I expect it must be difficult at this time of the year."

Stefanie frowned. The invitation had sounded spontaneous – did she now detect a note of relief that she had declined to join them in Engelberg?

"Nancy wants to know what you have been doing with yourself since we saw you?"

"Oh, making friends. A Mr Jankowski phoned me the other day, said he knew you and wanted to get in touch."

"Jankowski? I knew a Marc Jankowski in Warsaw, we fought in the Home Army together. How on earth did he get in touch with you, Stefanie?"

"Through Mrs Puzak."

It was the only question she could answer but not surprisingly, Andrew, as she sometimes called him, had many others. He hadn't seen or heard from Marc Jankowski since the day the Gestapo had arrested him and had believed he was dead. But the one thing he didn't ask her was how Jankowski knew he was living in England.

"What do I say if he calls me again?" Stefanie asked.

"You can give Marc my phone number and home address and say I would be happy to hear from him."

Stefanie undertook to do that, promised to keep in touch and sent her love to Nancy, then put the phone down. There had been no mention of Kurt Bender from first to last and it was inconceivable that he wasn't aware that the former German NCO was dead. If she had spotted the small paragraph on page three of the *Daily Telegraph* before Campbell had told her, why hadn't he? And if not, why hadn't the British Foreign Office seen fit to inform him? She finished the rest of her drink, went into the bedroom and started to change out of her office clothes. As was lately becoming a repetitive occurrence, the phone started ringing when she was half-undressed. She returned to the living room and lifted the receiver.

"Miss Ayres?"

The voice was guttural and vaguely familiar. "Yes. Who am I speaking to?"

"My name is Doctor Jakobson. I'm calling from my surgery in Kennington Park Road. I understand a Mr Parker is a friend of yours?"

Campbell. Her stomach lurched; doctors were invariably the bearers of bad news, especially ones she had never heard of. "What's happened?" she asked, her voice high with anxiety. "Has he been injured? Is he all right?"

"He's had an accident right outside my surgery," Jakobson told her. "Nothing too serious, but your friend has been taken to Lambeth General Hospital with a fractured ankle and suspected concussion."

"You say he's at the Lambeth General?"

"Yes, in Brook Drive by Harmsworth Park. The nearest Underground station is the Oval . . ."

"It's okay, Doctor Jakobson," Stefanie told him, "I'll get a minicab."

She put the phone down, thanking him as she did so, then ran into the bedroom, rummaged through her handbag and returned with a pocket diary. She looked up the number of the hire firm she had used before and told the despatcher of Fleetways of Chelsea she wanted a minicab as soon as possible. She did not stop to ask herself what Campbell had been doing in Lambeth; he was hurt and needed her. That was the only thought on her mind as she whipped off her white satin slip and changed into jeans and a sweater.

Across the road, the watchman rang Garvey at Leconfield House. The shotgun mike had not been an unqualified success and he had only captured intermittent snatches of the various conversations Stefanie Ayres had had with her uncle, a Doctor Jakobson and the despatcher at Fleetways. Garvey had never heard of Jankowski, wasn't interested to know who she was planning to visit in hospital and didn't want her followed when she left the flat. The Stevens suicide was about to become the newspaper story of the week and Management wanted everyone to keep their heads well down. It made the watchman wonder what the hell he and the rest of the surveillance team were doing in Cheyne Walk.

The bedroom was at the front of the house looking out on to Ravenscourt Road. From the window, Parker could see the whole of the street from the railway bridge on the right to the junction with Dorville Crescent on the left. Although less than two hours had elapsed since Maurice Orde had phoned to warn him that the coroner's jury had delivered their verdict, the press reporters were already gathering in strength. How they had managed to run him down quite so soon was a bit of a mystery but he could understand now why the DG had sent him on indefinite leave forty-eight hours before the inquest opened. The last thing he had wanted to see was Fleet Street camping on the doorstep of Amberley Lodge.

The SIS hadn't entirely abandoned him. Yesterday, Roger Dent had turned up with a written brief detailing precisely what he could and could not say to the press, and that only in extremis. Everybody hoped he would be able to remain incommunicado, which sounded fine, but short of doing a bunk, leaving the phone off the hook after Maurice had called was about the only practical measure he could take. He had also disconnected the buzzer and intercom to his flat, but this wouldn't stop the reporters making a nuisance of themselves with the other residents.

As Dent had observed with some feeling, it was a great pity the inquest had not been held on the sixth or seventh of June; for six days, the Arab-Israeli War had grabbed all the headlines and dominated the television newscasts. The destruction of Nasser's Air Force on Day One, the rout of the Egyptian armour in the Sinai, the capture of Jerusalem and the storming of the Golan Heights; there had been no shortage of news from the fourth to the tenth of June and practically the whole nation had derived considerable satisfaction from the knowledge that the Israelis were doing to Nasser what Eden and Mollet had failed to do in 1956. A few days ago, the inquest at Middlesbrough would have been ignored by Fleet Street, but peace had broken out since then and column inches were going begging.

Parker crossed from the bedroom to the living room only to discover that a contingent of press photographers had taken root in the park. He backed away from the window before they saw him, went into the kitchen and made himself a cup of coffee. The envelope containing some notes on Gerhardt Terboven which Harry Freeland had sent to him while he was still at Amberley Lodge was on the dresser and for want of something better to do, he started to read them again.

Standartenführer Gerhardt Terboven was dead, that was official. He had been killed in action in January 1945 at Bobrek, a small village approximatley twelve miles north of Auschwitz concentration camp. His command vehicle, a Hannomag half-track, had been hit by a 120mm mortar bomb which had blown the six-man crew to pieces. Terboven had survived the initial explosion because he had dismounted and had been moving up on foot towards the left forward platoon when the vehicle had been struck. Debris from the half-track had severed his right forearm and had left the right leg below the knee hanging by a tendon. The nearest aid post had been two miles back down the road and one of his Unterscharführers had rushed Terboven there in a Kübelwagen, but he had died before the medics could get him on the operating table.

Stormtroopers from the Sonderkommando had buried his body by the roadside. It had subsequently been exhumed in March 1949 by the Polish authorities acting on information supplied by Obersturmführer Karl Werner Ulex who had been sentenced to twenty-one years hard labour for war crimes. The corpse had been in an advanced state of decomposition and had resembled a log. The combat fatigues had completely rotted away leaving only the buttons, but a metal identity disc bearing Terboven's name, initials and serial number had been found on a chain around the neck.

Parker could understand now why Kurt Bender had never been called as a witness after he had made a statement to the Allied War Crimes Commission following his release from a Soviet POW camp in 1948. The Russians, the Poles and the Israelis had all indicted Terboven for war crimes but although the Russians had sentenced him to death in absentia, there had never been a trial as such. The grisly remains found in the shallow grave near Bobrek nine months after Bender had made a sworn affidavit had been accepted as Gerhardt Terboven and the case against him had been closed.

Parker tucked the notes back inside the envelope, then had another look at the brief Dent had given him. It was all very well for Maurice Orde and the DG to hope he wouldn't have to deal with the press but they weren't camped on their doorsteps. Nor would they have to cope with the neighbours who were likely to get more and more incensed the longer the siege continued. One thing was self-evident to Parker. The reporters weren't going to leave Ravenscourt Road without a story of some kind and it was preferable they heard the sanitised version from his lips before they hacked one that was largely based on innuendo and speculation. Convinced of this, he gulped down the dregs of his coffee, then braced himself to go downstairs and meet the press.

The rush started as soon as he opened the front door. Surrounded by a crowd of reporters, TV cameramen and photographers, the impromptu press conference rapidly degenerated into a shouting match. At his suggestion, it was eventually agreed that he would talk to a dozen journalists whose copy would subsequently be pooled amongst the other newsmen. In the end, however, he also found himself playing host to the London correspondents of *Newsweek*, the *Chicago Herald Tribune*, *Le Monde*, *Le Figaro* and *Der Spiegel* as well as staff men from the Tass news agency, Reuters and AP. When they left an hour later, a dense fog of stale cigarette smoke permeated the living room and he was out of beer, whisky, gin and sherry. That was the debit side of the ledger; on the credit side, a kind of peace descended on Ravenscourt Road and the phone didn't immediately ring when he replaced the receiver.

The minicab driver hugged the Thames from Cheyne Walk along the Chelsea Embankment into Grosvenor Road and on to Millbank. There was a thirty mile an hour speed limit all the way to Lambeth Bridge but at times he was touching sixty, weaving in and out of the traffic like a whippet after a hare. Unfortunately, the lights were invariably against them so that the frenetic bursts of speed merely got them from one traffic jam to the next in double-quick time. Things weren't much better south of the river and the one-way circuit which led them up Lambeth Palace Road before they could get on to the A23 seemed interminably long. Thirty-five minutes after leaving her apartment, Stefanie Ayres paid off the minicab outside Lambeth General Hospital, then sought out the porter manning the Inquiries desk in the entrance hall to ask what ward Campbell Parker was in.

"Parker," the porter repeated and ran a finger down the list of names under P in the indexed admissions register. "Got a Parkinson and a Partington, but no Parker. When was he admitted?"

"I'm not sure, an hour and a half, perhaps two hours ago. There was a traffic accident somewhere on Kennington Park Road . . ."

"Ah, well, that explains it; he won't have been officially admitted yet. You want Casualty – outside, turn left, then left again. You can't miss it."

Stefanie had heard that one before but this time the assurance turned out to be accurate. Finding the Casualty department was easy enough, finding someone who could answer her questions proved far more difficult. Finally, she managed to corner a staff nurse who had been on duty since two o'clock that afternoon.

"We haven't had a Mr Parker in here," the nurse told her.

"But you must have done," Stefanie protested. "He was injured in a traffic accident not far from this hospital – broken ankle, minor head injuries, suspected concussion."

"No."

"How can you be so sure without checking the register?"

"Because I don't need to look at the admissions. I know the injuries we have had to deal with."

"A Doctor Jakobson phoned me," Stefanie said, trying to contain her anger. "He said the accident had occurred right outside his surgery in Kennington Park Road and implied he had sent for an ambulance."

"How does he spell his name?" the staff nurse asked. "With a c or a k?"

"With a k, I think." Stefanie frowned. "Anyway, it sounded like Jakobson."

The staff nurse produced the appropriate telephone directory and went through the listings. "I think you must have been the victim of a cruel hoax. No matter how you spell the name, there is no Doctor Jakobson in this neighbourhood."

Stefanie felt the blood drain from her face as the realisation hit her. "You're right," she said shakily, "it must have been someone's idea of a practical joke."

It hadn't been a hoax but it was easier to accept that explanation than to say why she thought it was something far more sinister. The man who called himself Jakobson had deliberately lured her to this hospital. "Come into my parlour, said the spider to the fly." To ensure she was a sitting target, he had urged her to use the Underground and get out at the Oval, but who was going to believe that? Not the staff nurse, not the porter.

Stefanie returned to the main entrance and used one of the pay phones in the entrance hall to ring for a minicab. Fleetways of Chelsea couldn't help her and suggested she rang back in half an hour when they might have something. She tried two local hire firms; one was already taking bookings for nine o'clock onwards, the other wasn't interested in a fare to Cheyne Walk. Frustrated, she put the phone down and sought advice from the porter.

"What do you have to do to get a cab round here?" she asked.

"You don't find too many taxis cruising the streets in this part of town. Your best bet is Waterloo Station."

"How far is that?"

"A mile." He shrugged. "Maybe a mile and a bit. Go down Brook Drive into Kennington Road and you can pick up a bus to Westminster Bridge Road. Waterloo's no distance from there."

Stefanie thanked him, left the hospital and walked out through the gates into Brook Drive. Eight fifteen on a fine June evening, the street practically empty, the world an oasis of peace and quiet save for the distant hum from the traffic on Kennington Road. She turned right and set off at a brisk pace towards the old lunatic asylum of Bedlam in Harmsworth Park which was now the home of the Imperial War Museum.

She looked for signs of danger and saw none in the approaching grey-coloured van, or the girl on a motor scooter or in the elderly man walking his dog in the park on her right. Danger came from behind in the shape of a Ford Cortina that suddenly shot across the road and mounted the pavement.

Physical agility, quick reflexes and the absence of iron railings combined to save her. Breaking to her right, Stefanie dived over the hip-high brick wall bordering the park, turned a complete somersault and landed heavily on her back. The Cortina continued along the pavement for a good twenty yards, then bounced back on to the road and cut across to the left side. Less than a minute later, it had disappeared into Kennington Road.

The old man ran towards her, his voice raised in anger, the Yorkshire terrier snapping at his heels. By the time he reached her, he was red in the face, gasping for breath and ready for a heart attack. The dog went on barking until his nose scented an interesting smell near the brick wall and he went over to investigate the source.

"Are you all right?" his owner gasped.

"I don't think any bones are broken," Stefanie told him with a brittle laugh.

"Who was the bloody lunatic who tried to run you down?"

"I don't know, some drunk driver probably."

"Bastard should be locked up. Did you get his number?"

"No." Stefanie got gingerly to her feet. "My mind was on other things."

"Pity."

"Yeah, I know, it's too bad."

"You ought to see a doctor," the old man told her.

"Don't worry, I'm going to."

"I'll come with you."

He was quite adamant about that and nothing she could say would make him change his mind. In the end, they reached a compromise and agreed he could escort her as far as the hospital where she then kissed him on the cheek and walked inside.

Reaction set in after she tried to ring the Mullinders from one of the pay phones and found they were out. Suddenly, her legs felt as if they were made of cottonwool and she couldn't stop shivering. As far as she knew, Campbell was somewhere in Petersfield but out of sheer desperation, she tried his number in Ravenscourt Park and couldn't believe her luck when he answered.

"It's me," she said in a tight voice. "I'm in terrible trouble . . ."

"Where are you calling from?"

"Lambeth General Hospital. Someone tried to kill me . . ."

"Stay there," Parker told her. "I'll be right over."

"Make it as quick as you can," she pleaded, then hung up and sank down on her haunches, hugging herself as the tears streamed down her cheeks.

Chapter 22

Parker had seen her when she was happy, amused, sexually aroused, overjoyed, excited and angry but until now he had never seen Stefanie looking thoroughly frightened. He found her waiting for him in the entrance hall of Lambeth General, her face the colour of paste, her body rigid, her hands ice cold to the touch. It was as if she had turned to stone and when he gently told her they were going home, there was very little reaction other than a brief nod to show that she had understood. One arm around her waist for support, he walked Stefanie to the Mini and helped her into the car, then got in behind the wheel and drove through the gates, heading for the Albert Embankment on the south side of the river.

"What happened exactly?" he asked her presently.

"Someone drove a car straight at me just after I left the hospital." Her voice was detached, almost wooden.

"I meant from the beginning."

"Oh. Well, this doctor phoned, said his name was Jakobson, and told me that you'd had an accident right outside his surgery and had been taken to hospital."

"He mentioned me by name?"

"Yes. He said, 'I understand Mr Parker is a friend of yours.'" Stefanie opened her handbag, took out a crumpled packet of Chesterfields and found it was empty. "I don't suppose you've got a cigarette?"

Parker dug a packet of Embassy out of his jacket pocket and gave it to her. "Perhaps you could light one for me while you're at it?" he said.

"Sure."

"This Doctor Jacobson . . ."

"Jakobson," Stefanie said, correcting him.

"Do you know him?"

"No. I'd never heard of the man before tonight." Stefanie lit two cigarettes with a book of matches and passed one to Parker. "I wouldn't have stirred out of the apartment if he hadn't mentioned your name."

It wasn't just the fact that a total stranger had linked him to Stefanie Ayres which bothered Parker. He was also concerned that Jakobson must know her by sight.

"He's seen you somewhere before?"

"Who? Jakobson?" She pursed her lips. "Not necessarily. He wanted me to come by Underground and get out at the Oval."

"And did you?"

"No. I told Jakobson I intended to hire a minicab." She laughed sourly. "I should never have paid off the driver, then none of this would have happened."

"Who did you see at the hospital?" Parker asked.

"The hall porter and the staff nurse in Casualty."

"Did you give your name to either of them?"

"No, I just asked for you."

Jakobson could have been loitering in the hall near the information desk and had identified her when she inquired after him. "Who else was present when you spoke to the porter?"

"No one." Stefanie leaned forward and stubbed out her cigarette in the ashtray under the shelf. "Sure, there were people coming and going because it was visiting hour but I didn't have to wait in line to speak to the porter."

Parker figured that had to mean Jakobson knew her by sight. He had been parked somewhere near the hospital, had watched her leave and had waited for the right opportunity before he had tried to run her down.

"Were there any witnesses around when this Jakobson attempted to kill you?"

"Only an old man walking his dog in the park. I'm afraid I didn't get his name."

It seemed that in any event he had been too far away to see the registration number of the car or describe the driver. All he had been able to tell her was the make and colour of the vehicle.

"Knowing it was a dark blue Ford Cortina doesn't help much, does it, Campbell?"

Parker lowered the window on his side and flicked his cigarette stub into the road. "Not a lot," he agreed.

"Funny thing is, I thought his voice sounded vaguely familiar."

"What are you saying?"

259

"Just over two weeks ago, I had a phone call from a man who claimed he was Marc Jankowski . . ."

Parker drove on down Nine Elms Lane into Battersea Park Road and continued on towards Clapham Junction. Jankowski, she told him, had served in the Home Army and had known Andrew Korwin in Warsaw, an assertion that had been confirmed by her uncle. Jankowski had surfaced again after twenty-three years of silence and was hoping to meet his old comrade-in-arms, a prospect which her uncle had apparently welcomed.

"Andrew said to give him his phone number and home address next time he called."

"When did Andrew tell you this?"

"This evening when I rang him about the inquest."

"Was this before or after Doctor Jakobson phoned?"

"Before."

"And when you said his voice sounded vaguely familiar, are you saying he reminded you of Jankowski?"

"Yes."

Jankowski had been to see the Puzaks and had telephoned Stefanie that same night after they had given him her phone number. More than a fortnight had then passed without any further word from him until tonight when he had called himself Jakobson. Parker wondered what he had been doing with himself during the past fifteen days and why he should want to kill Korwin's niece.

"I'm sorry your name was dragged into the inquest, Campbell," Stefanie said in a low voice. "I hope it won't jeopardise your career?"

"No chance," he lied.

Stefanie looked as though she was about to help herself to another cigarette from the packet on the shelf but then changed her mind and leaned back in the seat, her eyes half-closed. Parker drove on through Wandsworth towards Barnes.

"This isn't the way to Cheyne Walk," Stefanie murmured.

"We're going to my place."

"What for?"

"Because if this Jankowski knows you by sight, it's possible he may have followed you home from work. He obviously knows we are acquainted but as we haven't seen each other since he rang you up, there's a pretty good chance he has no idea where I live."

"That makes sense to me."

"I'm glad it does."

Parker went on through Barnes, crossed the river by Hammersmith Bridge and made his way to Ravenscourt Park via Bridge View Avenue and King Street. There were no reporters loitering outside the house. The story he had given them about Victor Stevens who had once been Viktor Stashinski, renegade Ukrainian Jew and member of the Nazi-led Self-Defence Brigade, had provided all the copy they had needed for tomorrow's headlines. The press would, however, be back; he had no illusions on that score. Before the Sundays were due to hit the newsstands, some investigative journalist would be looking for a new angle and would zero in on him.

"We're home," he said, "you can open your eyes now."

Stefanie sat up, got stiffly out of the car and waited for him to join her on the pavement. "Sorry about that," she said, "I don't even remember dropping off."

"You've had a bad shock, it takes it out of you."

Parker locked the car, then led her up to his flat on the second floor and switched on the lights.

"What would you like to drink? Tea? Coffee?"

"Coffee will be fine."

"I wish I could offer you something stronger but the press were here earlier this evening and all I'm left with is some tomato juice."

"I don't think I could face any of the hard stuff anyway."

"There's plenty of food. What can I get you to eat?"

"Nothing, thanks. I'm not at all hungry." Stefanie followed him into the kitchen and sat down at the table. "It isn't even ten o'clock yet and I'm completely bushed."

"As I said, it's nervous as well as physical exhaustion, a natural reaction."

"You think so?"

"I know so."

In Korea, after the third battle of The Hook, he had fallen asleep for fifteen solid hours and had subsequently woken up feeling dog tired.

"You go and get into bed, I'll bring the coffee along as soon as it has percolated. Tomorrow, we'll call your office and tell them you're sick, then you stay here while I have a word with Mrs Puzak."

Too weary to argue with him, Stefanie got up from the table and went into the bedroom. When Parker brought her a cup of coffee a few minutes later, she was lying on her stomach dead to the world, head over to the left, her dark hair spread out like a fan on the pillow. She had kicked off her shoes as soon as she entered the room and had started undressing while she moved towards the bed. Leaving the coffee on the chest of drawers, he picked up her discarded clothes, put them on a chair and quietly left the room.

Some men returning from the wars burdened themselves with lethal souvenirs; Parker had been one of the law-abiding majority and had brought nothing back from Korea. The only weapon to hand was a bread knife with a serrated cutting edge, but it was better than nothing. He took it with him into the living room and made himself comfortable in an armchair. Although he had no reason to suppose Jankowski knew where he lived, it was not in his nature to leave anything to chance. It was his intention to stay awake all night; however, by the early hours of the morning he found it impossible to keep his eyes open any longer.

Parker woke up shortly before seven with a stiff neck, a dry mouth and a tongue that felt as if it had been coated with paste. The rest of his anatomy seemed to be in an equally deplorable condition, but it improved dramatically after a few deep-breathing exercises and a bit of bending and stretching. He washed and shaved, tiptoed into the bedroom to get a change of clothing and came back out again without disturbing Stefanie. When dressed, he reconnected the buzzer and intercom, then cooked breakfast. At eight o'clock, he roused Stefanie with orange juice, scrambled eggs, toast and a pot of fresh coffee on a tray.

"You spoil me," she told him, "but I love it."

"Better make the most of it then; after this, you'll have to fend for yourself until I return."

"I can't stay here . . ."

"Let's not get into an argument. There's a man out there walking the streets who is set on killing you. The number one suspect is Marc Jankowski but the police can't do anything unless we can give them his description. Right?"

"I guess so. How long do you think I'll have to stay here?"

"I don't know." Parker shrugged. "Several days, perhaps longer."

"In that case, I'm going to need some clothes, underwear and so on."

"If you ring the Mullinders and tell them what you want, I'll deliver the key to your apartment and arrange a time and place to collect your things. The rest I'll get from Marks and Spencer." Parker eyed her. "I reckon you are about the same size as Sheila was – medium, thirty-six?"

"Thirty-four bust, English size," Stefanie said, "and nothing too sexy."

Parker laughed. "I'll see if I can get you something with elastic round the legs," he said.

He left the flat at a quarter to nine and walked down the road to the Underground station, stopping off on the way to get the *Daily Telegraph* and *Daily Express* from the newsagent on the corner. Although he hadn't made the front page of either newspaper, he had rated two columns on page three of the *Telegraph* and an even bigger splash on the inside page of the *Express*. In one picture he looked startled, while in the other the photographer had managed to make him look pop-eyed. From the surreptitious glances of the other passengers in his car, it was evident that he was still all too recognisable. But worse still, the newspapers had given his home address.

At the Embankment station, he changed on to the Northern Line and went on up to Archway from where it was only a five minute walk to the offices of *The Sentinel* in Varley Mall. If Mrs Puzak was surprised to see him again, her face certainly didn't show it, nor did she give him any reason to assume that she had read the newspapers that morning.

"This is an unexpected pleasure, Mr Parker," she said with exaggerated courtesy. "What can I do for you?"

"First of all, could I use your phone to make a local call?"

Her eyebrows rose marginally. "But of course," she said and waved an inviting hand towards the instrument.

Parker dialled the number of his flat, spoke to Stefanie and told her not to open the door to anyone unless she knew who they were. "My address is in today's papers," he added and let it go at that.

Most people overhearing his conversation with Stefanie would have been moved to pass some remark, but not Irena Puzak.

"Miss Ayres is staying with me," Parker explained.

"Indeed?" The eyebrows rose again, perhaps registering disapproval although it was difficult to tell.

"Someone tried to kill her last night. We think it might have been Marc Jankowski."

"Jankowski." The name came out in a sort of strangled gasp as though she had been winded. "Why would he want to kill her?"

"Search me. Your husband didn't give him Stefanie's address as well as her phone number, did he?"

"No, he did not make that mistake."

"But you have her address on record?"

"Yes."

"Does Jankowski know about your card index system?"

"I'm afraid so."

"I see." Parker looked round the office. "Have you had a window broken or any other signs of a forced entry since he came to see you?"

"No." Irena Puzak shook her head to emphasise the point.

"Well, I suppose that's something to be thankful for. Trouble is, we don't know what Mr Jankowski looks like, whereas you most certainly do."

"You would like me to describe him?"

"That is the general idea," Parker said.

Irena Puzak did not have to rely on words to describe Jankowski. As a young woman, she had longed to be a successful artist and had trained in Paris. Although she had not realised her ambition, she had shown considerable promise as a portrait painter and her talent had not diminished with the passage of time. On a sheet of blank foolscap, a face began to take shape – deep-set eyes, a narrow sharply defined nose, prominent cheekbones, a cleft chin, small earlobes, scar tissue on the right side of the neck. The hair was grey, cut short and parted on the left side. Beneath the portrait she wrote – height five nine, weight eleven stone, then added two question marks.

"I'm afraid that's the best I can do, Mr Parker."

"I think it looks good enough to hang in the National Portrait Gallery."

"What will you do with my picture?"

"I'll give it to the police and let them make as many photocopies as they need."

Parker folded the sheet and tucked it into the breast pocket of his jacket, then shook hands with Irena Puzak, thanking her for being so helpful. He walked back to the station, found an empty phone booth and rang the exchange at Queen Anne's Gate and 54 Broadway. When the operator came up, he placed a handkerchief over the mouthpiece to muffle his voice and asked for Sarah Yendell on extension 2615. When she answered, he identified himself and told her not to use his name.

"I know when to be discreet," Sarah told him.

"Can Nick Quade hear what you are saying?" Parker asked.

"No, the door's closed, he has someone with him."

"I'm in trouble, Sarah . . ."

"I know, it's in all the newspapers. How can I help?"

"Stefanie and I need somewhere to hide."

"Stefanie." Her voice was full of disapproval and he could picture her expression, the slight wrinkling of the nose as if there was a bad smell in the vicinity.

"Someone tried to kill her last night."

"Really?" Disapproval was replaced by scepticism. "Were you there when it happened?"

"No."

"Ah, well, as my old nanny used to say, seeing is believing."

"Okay, so you don't like Stefanie, but are you prepared to help me?"

"You know I am."

Parker heard the pips go, fed a shilling into the box and pressed button 'A'. "That cottage your parents own in the Test Valley," he continued. "Is anyone down there at the moment?"

"I don't know, I'd have to check with Mother."

"Would you do that? I'll call you back this afternoon."

"How long do you want it for?"

"As long as it takes the police to find Jankowski."

"Who's he?"

"The man who tried to kill Stefanie."

"It's serious then?"

"You bet it is. Listen, if the cottage is free, can you get the key to me this evening?"

Sarah told him she had her own key, then asked if there was anything else she could do. Parker said there was; for reasons he was reluctant to disclose, he wanted the names of the principal shareholders in the Ward Tandy Group.

"There's no great hurry," he told her, "tomorrow will do."

"That's what I like about you," Sarah said, "you're so undemanding."

Parker replaced the phone, backed out of the kiosk and went over to the newsagents to buy a packet of cigarettes. Armed with the loose change from a pound, he returned to the kiosk and made two further phone calls, one to Harry Freeland, the other to Kevin Mullinder.

*   *   *

265

Stephanie hoped it would be a case of third time lucky. She had telephoned Brenda Mullinder at ten fifteen and had failed to get an answer. At eleven o'clock, she had rung her again and had got an engaged tone; now, barely ten minutes later, it was beginning to look as though she had gone out again. After deciding to give it a few more seconds, she was about to hang up when the ringing tone stopped and a voice with a muted Irish accent said "hello"

"Hi, Brenda," she said, "it's me, Stefanie."

That much was easy, explaining what had happened to her last night, where she was now, and what she was planning to do was quite another matter. With her constant interruptions, Brenda wasn't exactly helpful either.

"Have you been to the police?" she asked.

"No. What can I tell them? A man I've never met, never seen, tried to run me down. How much notice do you think they would take of that?"

"Not a lot."

"Damn right."

"So what are you going to do?"

"Lie low for a bit. I've told the office that I've picked up some bug and will be off for the rest of the week, but I'm going to need some clothes."

"Where did you say you were?"

"I'm staying with Campbell Parker."

"Not the same Campbell Parker I've been reading about?"

Stefanie gritted her teeth. She liked Brenda Mullinder but the Irish girl had a mind like a grasshopper and an irritating habit of changing the subject of any conversation in mid-sentence.

"Please listen to me," she said tersely. "Campbell has got the key to my apartment and will be giving it to Kevin. Could you pack a couple of skirts, sweaters, blouses, a nightdress, my make-up and anything else you think I might need?"

"Of course."

"Thanks. I don't know how I'm going to collect the suitcase yet but I'll call you again after I have discussed the problem with Campbell." Stefanie hesitated, uncertain for a moment how she was going to explain what she wanted Brenda to do with her mail, then said, "If there are any letters for me in my pigeon hole, you can pack them as well. Except, I'd like you to hang on to anything from Vienna."

"But you're not going to tell me why?"

"I will eventually."

"Okay. Well, you look after yourself, Stefanie. You hear?"

Stefanie said she would, told Brenda to do the same and hung up. She looked at the phone, wondered if she dared use it to call Vienna. It certainly wouldn't be bugged and it would be months before Campbell found out, if ever. The hesitation lasted all of half a minute, then she lifted the receiver and dialled the twelve digits of the international code, the area code and subscriber's number.

Ulex folded the *Daily Sketch* in half and left it on the adjoining seat with the picture of the man in the armchair uppermost. The letterpress below described him as "Foreign Office man Campbell Parker photographed at home in Ravenscourt Park." To make it even easier for him, the reporter had disclosed his full address in the opening paragraph. Ulex thought there was something to be said for the freedom of the press after all. If it hadn't been for the newspapers he wouldn't have known where to look for Stefanie Ayres, if it hadn't been for the *Daily Sketch* he wouldn't have caught this westbound train on the District Line.

The American girl had enjoyed a large slice of luck last night but it would be a different story the next time he went after her. Nothing would be left to chance; he would stalk her as he would a deer and would hold off until he was certain of a kill. There was also another consideration; the longer he took, the more money he would receive. State Security in East Berlin wouldn't like it, but what could they do? Great Britain, in common with other Western countries, did not recognise the German Democratic Republic and therefore there was no embassy in London, just a small unaccredited trade mission in Cheapside.

Albrecht Heiness, the deputy head of the trade mission and covert SSD officer, could huff and puff about the delay and lack of results until he was blue in the face but there was nothing he could do about it. Heiness didn't have the resources to assign a full-time case officer to monitor his every move. An embassy would have enabled State Security to establish a proper Intelligence-gathering organisation in the UK; as it was, they were obliged to operate on a shoestring. Heiness had to content himself with whatever few crumbs he put his way and he had given the SSD Chief a small handful when he had contacted him after seeing the Puzaks. Two days later, he had checked out of the Hyde Park Hotel and had started looking for his quarry in earnest.

Bender had cheated him. He would never have spotted the small paragraph, but Heiness had an assistant whose job it was to read every newspaper from cover to cover and he had told him the Obergefreiter was dead. Although an old score had gone unsettled, Bender had in fact done him a good turn by dying when he had. The Obergefreiter had pointed him in the right direction, had been instrumental in putting a small fortune his way and had provided a ready-made excuse for proceeding cautiously which grudgingly, Heiness had been forced to accept. It was enough to make a man smile with inner happiness.

Hammersmith: Ulex glanced at the route map displayed in a panel above the opposite window and saw that the next stop would be Ravenscourt Park. He took out the copy of the *London Street-finder* he'd bought in Knightsbridge and looked up Ravenscourt Road. Out of the station, turn right; nothing could be simpler. He tucked the street index back into his jacket pocket, got to his feet and moved up to the doors ready to alight when the train drew into the platform.

Between the end of the morning rush hour and the start of the evening peak, most trains ran half-empty. His was no exception and only four other passengers got off at Ravenscourt Park. Without making it obvious, Ulex ensured he was the last to pass through the barrier in the entrance hall below and was gratified to see that no one was going his way. He checked the number of the first Edwardian semi-detached outside the station and reckoned the converted house where Parker lived was on the left side of the road beyond the railway bridge.

One thirty-five and the street was deserted. Seek, locate, destroy; good tactical principles to observe on a battlefield but not entirely applicable in this instance. He pushed the gate open, walked up the front path and checked the panel in the porch, then pressed the button opposite Parker's name. The American girl had to be here because she certainly wasn't at the flat in Cheyne Walk. All he had got when he'd phoned her last night and again this morning was an invitation from an answering machine to leave his name, number and message after the tone.

He pressed the button a second time and a metallic voice said, "Yes? Who's that?"

"Wolfe Siebert, UP," Ulex told her, raising his voice a tone. "I was hoping to interview Mr Parker."

"I'm afraid he's not at home."

"Could I ask when you expect him to return?"

"You could try again at three o'clock."

Ulex thanked her, said he would probably do that, and walked away. The intercom had distorted her voice and made it virtually unrecognisable but the American accent had come through loud and clear. He had found his quarry again; keeping track of her was going to be another matter. Albrecht Heiness might jib at the idea but he would have to lend him a helping hand if he wanted a result.

CHAPTER 23

IT WAS the second time Parker had met Harry Freeland at the Duke of Buckingham in Villiers Street. A little over three weeks ago, the pub had been crowded with civil servants, including a group from the army's Ordnance Directorate. Today things were different; with only twenty minutes to go before closing time, all the office workers were back at their desks, the lounge bar was three parts empty and corner tables were going begging. Freeland had chosen one farthest from the bar.

"It's good of you to meet me, Harry," Parker told him. "Most people in your position wouldn't."

"I think that's a bit of an exaggeration."

"Oh, come on, right now I'm about as popular as a dose of clap."

"Well, I wouldn't know about that." Freeland laughed, then pointed to the spare glass of whisky on the table. "I ordered you a double, thought you might need it."

"You're right, I do." Parker sat down, picked up his glass and raised it. "Cheers."

"Prosit," Freeland responded automatically, then said, "Now, suppose you tell me what's going on? I mean, why the hell did you allow those people on the top floor to put you up front to carry the can for Garvey?"

"I was already overexposed; too many outsiders knew who I was, what I really did. Maurice Orde and Roger Dent made it very clear that I would be finished with the SIS if the press succeeded in running me to ground, and I knew Arthur Kershaw was thirsting for my blood. Garvey is not exactly my best friend but there is no point in both of us getting the chop. Of course, I wouldn't like you to think I was being entirely altruistic," he added dryly. "There were attractive financial inducements."

"So what are you going to do now?"

"Stefanie and I are going into hiding." Parker took out the pencil likeness Irena Puzak had drawn for him and passed it across the table. "On account of this man."

"Does he have a name?"

"He calls himself Marc Jankowski." There wasn't much else Parker could tell him except why Stefanie believed he was the mysterious Doctor Jakobson who had lured her to Lambeth Hospital and had then tried to kill her. "I know it's not a lot to go on, Harry."

"That's putting it mildly," Freeland said.

"But I thought you might like to show it to Wirral."

"And what do you expect Iain to do with it?" He held up both hands to silence Parker before he trotted out a whole list of suggestions. "All right, Special Branch can check this Jankowski against their records – maybe he's a subversive or one of the undesirable aliens they have on their list. They can also compare notes with MI5, but what if both agencies have nothing on him? Are you hoping he can persuade the Commissioner of Police and the Home Office to circulate copies of this drawing to every chief constable in the land?"

"Something like that."

"You want to tell me what crime this Jankowski has committed? And don't trot out that sorry tale about how he tried to kill Stefanie Ayres because I'm willing to bet the Commander of L Division doesn't know a damned thing about it."

Parker assumed that L Division of the Metropolitan Police was responsible for the London Borough of Lambeth and unfortunately, Harry was right. Stefanie hadn't reported the attempt on her life. She hadn't even asked for the name and address of the one witness who could have supported her story. No one was going to take her allegations seriously if the first the police heard about the incident was almost twenty-four hours after it had occurred. There was, however, another angle which might induce them to sit up and take notice.

"Enlighten me, Harry," he said. "What does a man have to do to become an undesirable alien?"

"At the turn of the century he would have been an anarchist who came here from Russia or the Baltic States, in the thirties he would have been someone like Julius Streicher, the arch anti-Semite of the Third Reich. Today, he could be a political agitator like Danny Cohn Benedict or someone with links to organised crime."

"How about a former criminal?"

"Are you saying Jankowski is?" Freeland asked.

"No, but the man who calls himself Jankowski could be. The real Jankowski served alongside Andrew Korwin in the Home Army but Stefanie's uncle hasn't seen or heard from him since 1944. Then suddenly, twenty-three years later, he surfaces and gets in touch with the Puzaks, hoping they can tell him where he can find his old comrade-in-arms. Naturally, they wanted to know what he had been doing with himself since 1945 and apparently he was able to satisfy their curiosity. But supposing he is an impostor and everything he told the Puzaks was a pack of lies? Where else might he have spent all those missing years?"

"In prison," Freeland said flatly, "possibly for war crimes."

"That's my thinking." Parker finished the rest of his whisky. "Can we find out if anyone convicted of war crimes has been released from prison within the last month or so?"

"I don't see why not. Leave it with me and I'll make some inquiries."

"The sooner we can get an answer . . ." Parker began, then left the rest unsaid. A sense of urgency was one thing Harry Freeland had never lacked and he didn't need any gingering up from him.

"Can I hang on to this drawing, Campbell?"

"It's yours, I have one of my own." He had stopped off at an office suppliers on the way to meet Freeland and had persuaded the salesman to Xerox a copy, having led him to believe he was thinking of buying a photocopier.

Freeland got to his feet. "So how do we keep in touch if you are going into hiding?" he said.

"You're leaving?"

"'Fraid so, I've got a staff meeting at four."

Parker nodded. "Okay," he said, "best thing I can do is call you from time to time."

"You do that." Freeland started towards the door. "And ask for extension 008. The exchange supervisor has given me a new number – don't ask me why."

They parted company in Villiers Street, Freeland to return to Benbow House in Southwark, Parker to make his way to Marks and Spencer in Oxford Street.

Kershaw waited until the assistant manager had left the room before he unlocked the deed box and removed the share certificates.

One hundred and fifty thousand preference shares in the Ward Tandy Group. When the issue had been floated, they had been worth one pound each, in today's *Financial Times* they were quoted at eighty-nine shillings and threepence. Three weeks ago they had stood at a hundred and five shillings but had fallen sharply after Victor had commmitted suicide. Between the announcement of his death and the inquest they had staged a modest recovery; unfortunately, the coroner's jury had returned their verdict before the close of trading yesterday and they had fallen back.

They had drifted downward again today and there was no telling when the fall would bottom out but even so, Kershaw wasn't too perturbed by the vagaries of the market. The shares had reached an all-time high when Hassan al Jaifi and Marcel Verlhac had been killed, presumably because a number of investors had thought that if Israeli Intelligence were worried enough to eliminate the Arab arms dealer, the laser tank sight had to be a winner. Victor had come within an inch of death on that occasion and the demand for Ward Tandy shares had risen; barely a month later, they had plummeted in the light of his wartime involvement with the Ukrainian Self-Defence Brigade. Last night, he had been worth just under six hundred and seventy thousand pounds; by eleven o'clock on Monday morning he would be a rich man no matter what happened on the floor of the Stock Exchange in the meantime. Two and a half million tax free and all of it safely deposited in a numbered account in a Zürich bank.

The hundred and fifty thousand shares wouldn't give Hispano Suisse control of the group but they would provide the Swiss company with a platform from which to launch a successful takeover bid. Furthermore, they could go into the market through a nominee and quietly acquire a lot more shares before they rocketed back up.

Kershaw placed the share certificates in an envelope which he then tucked into the inside pocket of his jacket. The strongbox also contained the deeds to his house in Redcar, two life insurance policies, various investment bonds, National Savings certificates to the value of five thousand pounds and a quantity of jewellery, including a valuable pair of diamond and sapphire earrings. He pressed a bell to summon the assistant manager, informed him that he wished to remove the earrings and amended the inventory accordingly. No mention was made of the shares he had taken from the box.

Back at the factory, Kershaw locked the envelope in the office safe and then carried on as though nothing had happened. His secretary was under the impression that he would be spending a fortnight in Switzerland on holiday, but tomorrow would be the last day he would ever drive through the gates to spend anything up to ten hours in this stuffy, badly ventilated office high above the shop floor. After the money had been paid into his account at the Union Bank of Switzerland in Zürich, he and Nancy would leave Engelberg and travel the world before settling in Brazil or some other country in South America which did not have an extradition treaty with the UK. He had not yet discussed the matter with Nancy but both her parents were dead and she had no family ties which would make her want to stay in England. In any event, he was determined that no one, least of all Harold Wilson, was going to rob him of his hard-earned fortune.

Bender had been the man who was responsible for his decision to sell up and get out. Last September, he had successfully fought off a takeover bid by Hispano Suisse, but that had been before the Trade Fair. After Frankfurt, nothing had been the same. Bender had spotted his photograph in the newspaper and had gone to the Ward Tandy stand in the exhibition hall and despite being rebuffed in no uncertain terms, had eventually traced him to Middlesbrough. He had telephoned the factory pretending to be the UK representative of A. G. Mann Gesellschaft of Frankfurt and his secretary had put him through. Although Bender had not made any threatening demands, the sly reference to events long ago in Warsaw had left him in no doubt that the former Obergefreiter expected to be suitably rewarded.

He had, of course, immediately conveyed the gist of their conversation to Garvey, just as he had previously reported their encounter at the Trade Fair. From then on, Garvey had taken charge and had told him what to do, what to say in his dealings with Bender. It had taken the car salesman from Frankfurt some time to make his expectations known, but he had finally got round to it. A quarter of a million in used five and ten pound notes; it had been a preposterous demand even allowing for the face value of his shares in Ward Tandy and he had made that very point before meekly submitting, as Garvey had instructed him to do.

He had arranged to meet Bender at seven thirty in the evening in the lounge bar of the Wheatsheaf on the outskirts of Whitby on Friday the sixth of April. Garvey had provided the quarter of a million evenly split between fives and tens in three hundred and seventy-five bundles. Only the top and bottom banknote of each packet had been genuine, the remainder had been sheets of blank paper of similar quality and thickness cut to size. The money had been packed in two large suitcases which he had conveyed to the pub in the boot of his Jaguar.

The date, the time and the place for the rendezvous had all been chosen by Garvey who had obviously done his homework and had known the Wheatsheaf would be more crowded on a Friday than on any other evening during the week. He had got there ten minutes ahead of Bender and had passed the time chatting to a stooge provided by MI5 whose job it was to make sure he didn't stick out like a sore thumb amongst all the locals. The money had attracted the former German NCO like a bee to a honeypot and he had arrived bang on time though they had not acknowledged each other's presence by so much as a glance. Shortly before eight o'clock, he had said good night to the stooge and walked out into the car park where Bender had joined him a few minutes later.

He had unlocked the trunk of the Jaguar and stood by while Bender had opened both suitcases and drooled over the money. The idiot hadn't even bothered to check the currency; it had been enough for him to pull out three or four cellophane packets and stroke them as he might caress a woman. Bender had, however, been surprised to find that a quarter of a million in used banknotes weighed considerably more than he did. Consequently, he had been forced to carry the suitcases one at a time when transferring them to the self-drive Vauxhall he'd hired from Avis.

They had parted company in the car park, Bender to head south across the moors to Pickering, while he returned to Redcar. Garvey and two men posing as police officers had intercepted Bender and forced him to stop some miles from the nearest habitation. They had simply intended to put the fear of God into the former NCO before getting him a seat on the first available flight to Frankfurt. Unfortunately, one of Garvey's people had been a little too enthusiastic in his role as a hard-nosed officer with a penchant for using his fists and Bender had succumbed to a fatal heart attack. Although they had disposed of the body and returned the Vauxhall to Avis without drawing attention to themselves, it had been their bad luck and his that six weeks later a fishing smack from Whitby had hauled Bender out of the sea.

The telephone intruded on his thoughts and he answered it

irritably. What he heard from Nancy made him feel even more ill-humoured, though he managed to conceal it from her.

"You say Stefanie is thinking of joining us after all?" he repeated blankly.

"Yes, won't that be nice?"

Nice for whom, he wondered. Yesterday, when he'd half-heartedly suggested to Stefanie that she might care to come with them, it seemed the office couldn't spare her. Now she had tele-phoned Nancy to say they could.

"She will be company for you when I'm in Zürich on Monday," he said lamely.

"You don't sound very enthusiastic, Arthur."

He wasn't. He didn't want any interlopers on the scene when he talked Nancy into going round the world. "You're wrong," Ker-shaw told her. "I'm just a little surprised, that's all. Is she going to be with us for the whole fortnight?"

"Just the first week."

"Good."

"That's not a very nice thing to say, Arthur."

"I meant I'm glad we shall have some time to ourselves," he said with feeling.

Parker didn't like the rendezvous Sarah had chosen. Victoria station on the Underground was the next stop down the line from St James's Park and he knew a number of the clerks and typists at Broadway used the District and Circle Lines to and from work. But Sarah Yendell had argued that homeward-bound commuters never looked at the passengers waiting on the platform because they were either strap-hanging, dozing or had their noses buried in a newspaper. "Expect me ten minutes either side of five fifteen," she had told him on the phone, and it was now a quarter to six. Nick Quade had never been noted for staying at the office but tonight of all nights he had chosen this one to put in some overtime.

Another train to Richmond pulled into the station and glided to a halt. The doors opened and the commuters waiting on the plat-form made way for those passengers who wanted to get out. Maurice Orde: Parker spotted the Assistant Director before he stepped out of the car and hastily turned about as if to consult the Underground route map on the wall behind him. What the hell was Maurice doing at Victoria? Where was it he lived? Some village near Gatwick? Yes, of course, he would have to get off here for the

276

main line station. He had been in the third car from the front because he had bumped into Sarah Yendell on the platform at St James's Park and had passed the time chatting to her while they waited for the next train.

Parker heard the doors close and turned about again in time to catch a glimpse of Sarah before the train disappeared into the tunnel. Lip-reading had never been one of his skills and her frantic mouthing behind the glass window was incomprehensible. What had she been trying to tell him? To stay where he was or get on the next train and join her at Sloane Square? When in doubt, stay put; that was one maxim he had learned from the hard-bitten veteran he had been lucky enough to have as his platoon sergeant in Korea. Sooner or later, Sarah would realise he hadn't understood her message and would double back to find him. He was on his second cigarette before the supposition became a fact and she appeared on the platform, threading a path through the crowd to join him.

"Hi, Campbell," she said brightly and kissed him on the cheek. "That was a bit of a giggle, wasn't it? I nearly died when old Maurice latched on to me."

Parker wouldn't have described it as a bit of a giggle but he let it pass. There was nothing Maurice Orde or anyone else at Queen Anne's Gate could do to him but Management could make life difficult for Sarah if she had been seen in his company.

"Is that for me?" Her eyes were on the green carrier bag from Marks and Spencer he was holding and her smile was teasing. "Oh, you shouldn't have bothered, Campbell."

"Some underclothes for Stefanie," he mumbled.

"Really?"

Parker had never met anyone like Sarah who could convey such arch innuendo in one simple word but he refused to be side-tracked. "About the cottage?" he reminded her.

"Yes, of course." Sarah opened her handbag and took out a brass key. "This is the only one I have, so you and Stefanie will have to come to some arrangement. To find the cottage you go through Stockbridge on the road to Salisbury and take the last turning on the right before you start climbing the hill out of the village. Roughly four hundred yards along this side road, you'll come to a narrow lane on your right which leads straight to the cottage."

A train to Ealing Broadway drew into the station and she steered him into the third car as if he were an invalid in need of assistance. Between Victoria and South Kensington where Sarah got off, she told him all he could possibly need to know about the cottage in the Test Valley. So far as the principal shareholders of Ward Tandy were concerned, Daddy had been in touch with some of his friends in the City and they were making inquiries on his behalf. With any luck, she hoped to have a list of the more important names before end of trading tomorrow.

"Take care, Campbell," she said and kissed him again, this time on the mouth. Then she was gone, a trim, happy-go-lucky brunette in high heels and a mini dress, soon to be lost in the crowd on the platform at South Kensington.

Garvey was halfway to the door when the telephone rang and for a moment he was tempted to ignore it and go on home, but circumspection got the better of him and he reluctantly returned to his desk to answer it. After the splash Parker had been given in the newspapers, he supposed it was almost inevitable that the watchmen in Cheyne Walk should be getting restless.

"You're not going to like this, Mr Garvey," the watchman told him, "but I am damned sure we're looking at an empty flat. Miss Ayres didn't come home last night and there's been no sign of her all day."

"She probably went straight into the office from wherever she was staying."

"I don't think so. One of her colleagues rang her flat at half past nine and left a message on the answering machine to say he was sorry to hear she had gone down with some bug and hoped she would soon be better."

"Well, there's your answer," Garvey said impatiently, "you haven't seen her because she's in bed with the 'flu."

"Yes? So who rang the office to tell him she wouldn't be in?"

"One of her neighbours?" Garvey suggested.

"No one has been near her flat, Mr Garvey. This shotgun mike might not be up to much but believe me, we would have picked up something if she'd had a visitor – a door opening – the sound of footsteps – a murmur of voices. But except for that one phone call, the place has been like a tomb. No, I tell a lie, the phone did ring a second time but the caller declined to leave a message on the answering machine."

Stefanie Ayres had spent the night elsewhere. She might or might not be feeling unwell, but what did it matter whether she was lying or not? Before very much longer she was going to find herself back in New York. No one was going to serve a deportation order on her but the DG knew someone who knew the MD of the management agency she worked for. A few words in the right ear and Stefanie Ayres would be on her way. Meanwhile, what was the point of keeping her under surveillance? Not a lot, but it wasn't up to him.

"Tell you what I'm going to do . . ." Garvey broke off to clear a tickle in his throat before continuing. "First thing tomorrow I'll have a word with my Assistant Director and suggest we close the operation down."

"That's the best news I've heard all day," the watchman told him.

"I thought you might say that," Garvey said and hung up.

Parker surrendered his ticket to the collector at the barrier and walked out of the station into Ravenscourt Road. Twenty-five minutes past six; Stefanie would be wondering what had happened to him. Instinctively, he quickened his pace as if by hurrying he could save that extra minute which would make all the difference. He pushed the gate open, dug out his keys as he walked up the front path and unlocked the street door. He took the stairs two at a time, used the other Yale key to unlock the door to his flat and called out to Stefanie as he pushed it open. The door swung back exactly two inches before the security chain held it fast.

"Stefanie?" He put his mouth to the gap and raised his voice. "It's me, Stefanie, I'm home."

"Coming, Campbell."

He heard her footsteps in the hall and wondered what she had been doing in the bedroom, then her face appeared in the crack.

"Are you okay?" he asked.

"I'm fine." Stefanie partially closed the door and released the security chain to let him in. "I didn't mean to lock you out of your own apartment but I thought it was better to be safe than sorry."

"Hey, it's me who should be apologising to you. I didn't intend being this late, everything took much longer than I'd expected." He held out the Marks and Spencer shopping bag. "This is yours by the way. Nothing too sexy, royal blue with an inch of lace."

"You're a terrific guy, Campbell. Tell me what I owe you . . ."

"Nothing," Parker said, cutting her short.

"I can't have that."

"Look, the subject's closed; if you feel bad about it, you can buy me a box of cigarettes or something."

"Okay, it's a deal."

"I'm glad that's settled." Parker went on through to the kitchen, filled the electric kettle under the tap and plugged it in, then looked out two mugs and measured a heaped teaspoonful of instant coffee into each. "Incidentally, I gave your key to Mullinder and arranged to collect your things from his office tomorrow."

"Thanks."

Her flat, almost apathetic voice set the alarm bells ringing for Parker. "What happened while I was out?" he asked.

"Nothing – well, I spoke to a Mr Wolfe Siebert on the intercom when he called. He said he was from UP and wanted to interview you. I told him you were out and suggested he came back at three o'clock, which he didn't." A worried frown creased her forehead. "He had a funny voice, unnaturally high-pitched, even allowing for the distortion on the intercom. I thought afterwards that perhaps he was trying to disguise it."

"Did you see him?"

Stefanie nodded. "I went through to the bedroom and watched him walk off towards the station. About an hour later, a small green van drove past the house and parked up the street. It's still there."

"What about the driver?"

"He just locked the van and walked away."

Parker wasn't inclined to attach too much significance to the van. Motorists were always using the street as a convenient parking space, much to the annoyance of the residents. On the other hand, he didn't like the sound of the UP reporter. Reaching inside his jacket, he took out the drawing and showed it to Stefanie.

"Is this the UP man?" He saw the answer in her eyes; before she could say a word, he said, "Mrs Puzak sketched this likeness of Marc Jankowski. Thank God Mrs Izzard didn't forget to close the street door."

"Who's she?"

"An absentminded old lady on the ground floor. She lets the postman in when he calls so that he can deliver the mail to each flat."

"Oh."

"I think maybe I'd better take a look at this van."

From the bedroom, Parker could just see the small green van

which was parked on the same side of the road a good twenty yards away. He thought about telephoning the police to report that it had been stolen but the registration number was obscured by the Volkswagen parked directly behind it.

"Did you get a good look at the driver,?" he asked.

"It wasn't Jankowski, if that's what you mean," Stefanie told him.

"That settles it, we're moving on. You'll find a shopping bag in the kitchen; empty the fridge and pack whatever tinned food from the store cupboard you think we'll need while I throw a few things into a suitcase."

Stefanie didn't question his decision, nor did she ask why they should want to take a load of food with them. Unnerved by her second encounter with Jankowski, she was prepared to do anything Parker asked of her without thinking twice about it. Exactly ten minutes later, they left the flat and drove off in the direction of Brentford to follow the Great West Road to Staines and the A30 trunk route to Stockbridge.

Parker didn't think they were being followed but he didn't know the opposition were fielding a three-car team and the small green van was hanging well back.

CHAPTER 24

THE VALLEY stretched before Ulex, a broad, flat water meadow between gentle rolling uplands crowned with woods of birch, oak, chestnut and beech. Stockbridge lay to his right, a neat village bisected by a broad highway that ran arrow straight like a Roman road to Salisbury. A church with a spire, Georgian houses with slate roofs, a garage with old-fashioned manually operated pumps on the forecourt, the Grosvenor Hotel, a few shops, an art gallery and a solitary police house; he did not think he had much to fear from the law or the eleven hundred inhabitants of Stockbridge. His only problem was locating the bolt hole where Parker and the American girl were hiding.

Albrecht Heiness and the surveillance team had lost them at the last moment. It had been relatively easy to track the Mini through the commuter belt but once in the open country beyond Basingstoke it had been a very different story. To avoid being spotted, the driver of the lead vehicle had had to drop farther and farther back. By the time they reached the outskirts of Stockbridge, the Mini had been a good half-mile ahead of Heiness. He had seen it turn off to the right on the far side of the village and had sought to close the gap. Unfortunately for him, the side road had been all twists and turns and Heiness had put his foot down and had covered at least four miles before it had dawned on him that the Mini was no longer in front.

Between the point where Heiness had decided to double back and the junction with the A30 trunk route, there were no fewer than three lanes branching off in an equal number of directions. Had it been darker, they would have seen the glare from Parker's headlights and known which track he had taken; at nine o'clock on a June night however there had been no need for him to use even the sidelights.

Parker had disappeared somewhere along one of the narrow

lanes; that was all Heiness had been able to tell him before they had parted company. The hours Ulex had spent in Ravenscourt Road cooped up in the small, dark green van with the sun blazing down on the roof had all been for nothing. Shortly after ten o'clock last night, Heiness had decided he didn't have the resources to maintain the operation at the same intensity for more than a few more hours and had withdrawn his team.

The truth was that Heiness was frightened of being arrested by the British Special Branch since this would inevitably lead to his expulsion. His fear was prompted by the knowledge that members of the East German Trade Delegation needed special permission to travel beyond a twenty-mile radius from the centre of London, and Stockbridge was sixty-eight miles from Marble Arch. Although the same restriction applied to the whole of the Eastern Bloc, the Russians and the other member states of the Warsaw Pact were allowed to maintain large diplomatic staffs in the UK which made the task of the British Special Branch extremely difficult. It was, in fact, virtually impossible to identify all the KGB and GRU officers in the Soviet Embassy but the East German Trade Delegation was a much smaller organisation and it was therefore easier for the British to sort the wheat from the chaff.

Heiness was prepared to keep an eye on the converted Edwardian house in Ravenscourt Road for the next twenty-four hours in case Parker returned to his flat with the American girl, but that was all. Berlin, he claimed, had made it clear that he was not to endanger the State Security cell in England in pursuit of a short-term objective. Left to his own devices, Ulex had passed the night in a wood on the hillside two hundred yards from the junction with the A30 trunk route. He had opened a farm gate, driven the van into the adjoining field and continued on down the side of the wood until he had found a clearing well back from the side road below. The vehicle was now in a hollow deep inside the wood where it wouldn't be seen unless someone actually blundered into it.

From the forward edge of the wood, Ulex had a commanding view of the valley and the village to his right. If Parker went into Stockbridge, he would see him, but he couldn't play the waiting game for ever; sooner or later, he would have to come out into the open and start looking for the two of them on his flat feet.

Ulex heard the car before he saw it. The tinny noise from the exhaust suggested there was a loose baffle in the silencer and the sound seemed to come from his left. A few moments later, a familiar, dirt-stained white Mini emerged from the sunken lane on the other side of the road roughly two hundred yards from his position and went on up to the junction. Parker was driving and it looked as if he was alone. But even if Korwin's niece was with him, they would be back. Ulex was quite sure of that, just as he now knew where to look for their hiding place.

Stefanie waited until the Mini was no longer in sight, then went back inside the cottage. Although Campbell had told her not to expect him before five, he was inclined to be unpredictable and she didn't propose to hang around. The cottage epitomised rural England – thatched roof, Virginia creeper and honeysuckle clinging to the stone walls, roses over the oak door. The telephone was equally rustic and looked as if it had been installed around the turn of the century. The subscriber trunk dial system had not yet reached this corner of Hampshire and she had to get the operator to connect her with Chelsea 1984.

Brenda Mullinder was not an early riser and the Irish girl sounded half-asleep when she answered the phone.

"I've packed a suitcase for you," Brenda told her between yawns and apologies. "Kevin has taken it into the office."

"Could you pack another one?"

"What did you say?"

"Campbell is on his way up to town, I don't intend to be here when he returns."

"Have you two had a quarrel or something?"

"Nothing like that. The fact is, I have to go to Switzerland on business and I'd rather Campbell didn't tag along."

"I understand – at least, I think I do." Brenda tried to suppress a yawn and failed. "How am I going to get this suitcase to you?"

"Could you meet me in front of the information board at Victoria Station?"

"What time?"

The simple questions were invariably the hardest to answer. Campbell had told her he was going to catch a train from Winchester but she didn't know how far that was from Stockbridge or how she was going to get there yet. She would also need to draw some money from her account with the Chase National Bank in the City. It was difficult to calculate how long all that would take but she made a stab at it, then glanced at her wristwatch.

"Shall we say two o'clock?"

"That'll be fine with me. Is there anything else you'll be wanting besides clothes?"

"I don't think so."

"What about your passport?"

"I've got it with me."

"Right. I'll see you at two then," Brenda said and hung up.

Stefanie replaced the receiver and went upstairs to collect her handbag. The main bedroom faced south and looked out on to the narrow sunken lane which eventually merged with the road above. The man walking towards the cottage was still a good hundred yards away and although his features weren't recognisable at that distance, there was no mistaking the clothes he was wearing. Stefanie had seen the same Lovat-green jacket and pants in Ravenscourt Road yesterday morning and knew it was Jankowski. She didn't understand how he had managed to track her to this isolated cottage, but that was beside the point. He was here, she was alone, and he meant to kill her. She drew back from the window, her throat suddenly tight with fear, her limbs trembling. Terror combined with indecision to paralyse all further movement and precious seconds were lost before she recovered her wits and ran downstairs.

The front door opened on to a lawn which sloped down to the lane and beyond that there was nothing but open water meadow, totally devoid of cover. The back door on the north side of the cottage offered the only concealed line of escape through the walled kitchen garden and on past the dilapidated barn that served as a garage. She closed the back door behind her, sprinted along the cinder path between the cordon apple trees and opened the gate in the wall, then struck out across the field towards the road on the hillside above. A long, unbroken hedge to her front marked the line of the road; her immediate aim was to reach the ditch in front of it before Jankowski saw her. To this end, she rang on, lungs bursting, a stitch lancing into her side.

The ditch was nearly three feet deep and bone dry; it was also full of stinging nettles which did her hands and face no good at all when she tumbled into them. Keeping her head below the lip, Stefanie crept along the ditch until she found a spot that was relatively clear. Then, kneeling down, she leaned forward against the bank and slowly raised her head above the lip to peer through a fringe of cow parsley at the cottage below.

Jankowski appeared from behind the barn and walked towards

the gate in the wall. He tried the latch tentatively, found the gate wasn't bolted on the inside and pushed it open. He stood there looking into the kitchen garden, apparently unable to make up his mind; then, as if sensing that someone was watching him, he turned slowly about.

Stefanie inched back from the crest and crouched down in the bottom of the ditch, praying as she had never prayed before that Jankowski wouldn't take it into his head to search the area before he broke into the cottage. Her face and hands felt as though they were on fire where the nettles had stung her; sweat trickled into the corners of her eyes and made them smart. She would have preferred to cower there like an ostrich with its head in the sand, but commonsense told her there was only one way to find out what Jankowski was up to. "Here goes," she murmured to herself and cautiously raised her head again.

Jankowski hadn't moved. He was still watching the road as if he knew she was somewhere up there on the hillside. A bee landed a few inches in front of her nose to pollinate a patch of buttercups before moving on to some clover. Away in the distance she could hear a truck grinding along in low gear. Jankowski heard it too and pointed like a gun dog. "Do something," Stefanie implored him silently, "hide, run away, turn your back, just don't stand there."

The truck came on, steadily drawing nearer. At the last moment, the grating whine from the propshaft finally galvanised Jankowski into action and he disappeared into the kitchen garden, closing the gate behind him. As he did so, Stefanie got to her feet and ran up and down the ditch looking for a way through the hedge that nature had made almost impregnable with brambles. Up on the road, a gravel truck thundered past heading towards the junction with the A30 trunk route. She had perhaps only a few more seconds before Jankowski felt safe enough to show himself again and the only hole in the hedgerow she could find looked nowhere big enough. In sheer desperation, she got down on all fours and wriggled through the gap, pushing her handbag ahead of her to leave both arms and shoulders free to enlarge the hole. Hair ravaged and hands scratched and dirty, she emerged on the other side and started running.

Safety lay in reaching the main road on the outskirts of Stockbridge without Jankowski seeing her and if this meant running until she dropped, then so be it. Ignoring the knifing pain in her side, she jogged on past the Y-junction with the narrow sunken lane that led to the cottage. Less than a quarter of a mile to go now – two more bends and the road junction would be in sight. She heard a car behind her and ran even faster, too frightened to look over her shoulder to see who it was. Moments later, a woman driving a pale blue Vauxhall overtook her.

The longest quarter of a mile finally came to an end and turning left at the junction, Stefanie ran on down the hill into Stockbridge. She did not stop running until she reached the phone box near the Grosvenor Hotel. She had only to lift the receiver and dial 999 for the operator to connect her with the police, except that she didn't know the name of the cottage or the damned lane it was in. She could guide the police to the cottage but that meant staying where she was and answering hundreds of questions afterwards, and she had a job to do in Switzerland.

But if she didn't inform the police, how was she going to warn Campbell not to go near the cottage? Think. Think. Think. He would have left the Mini in the car park at Winchester station, wouldn't he? Well then, all she had to do was leave a message for him on a slip of paper under the windshield wipers.

Stefanie opened her handbag, took out a mirror and comb and did something about her hair, then she left the phone box and walked over to the garage cum taxi office on the other side of the road.

Ulex opened the back door and stepped inside the kitchen. He hadn't expected to find the place wide open and Parker couldn't have made things easier for him if he'd tried. Stefanie Ayres was alone in the house, his for the taking. One good backhand chop; that was all it would take to break her pretty neck. Ulex slipped off his shoes and began to check out the cottage room by room – study, hall, downstairs cloakroom, main living and dining room. No sign of the bitch. He went up the staircase, testing each step to see if it creaked before putting his full weight on it.

There were four rooms off the landing and he could see into all three bedrooms from the top of the stairs. The bathroom had to be behind the closed door at the far end of the landing to his right. Maybe she was soaking herself in the tub and had fallen asleep? And with Parker out of the house, there was no reason for her to lock the door. All he had to do was tiptoe in, grab both ankles and raise her legs until the bath water closed over her head and she drowned. What could be easier? He turned the handle, opened the door stealthily and found the bathroom was empty.

Maybe he'd got the wrong house? No, he didn't think so; there was a fresh patch of sump oil on the floor of the barn and his nose had detected the presence of exhaust fumes. He checked all three bedrooms in turn and found some items of men's clothing in the large room at the opposite end of the landing to the bathroom. There was also a pair of pyjamas and a nightdress under the pillows.

Ulex went downstairs and checked the kitchen. A few rashers of bacon, four eggs, a slab of butter on a saucer in the fridge, a packet of frozen peas in the freezer compartment – tinned fruit, Heinz soups and a tin of ham in the store cupboard. They had been here and they would be back. And when they returned, he would be waiting for them. Parker, of course, would not be aware of his presence until he stabbed him in the kidneys with the carving knife.

A month ago when Parker had last visited the Sphinx Inquiry Agency in the Caledonian Road, Melanie, the blonde secretary-receptionist had been wearing a black leather mini skirt and a blouse. Today, the latest fashion was a pair of skin-tight toreador pants in shocking pink with a matching short-sleeved angora sweater. One thing remained constant however; discreet dabs of perfume behind each ear was not Melanie's style and the smell of her cheap scent pervaded the air.

"Well, well," she said, "fancy seeing you again. How does it feel to be famous?"

"Lucrative. According to my agent, half the publishers in London want my signature on a contract."

"Nice for some." A bright smile lit up her face and disappeared again like a neon sign. "Dennis the Menace isn't in," she informed him, then added, "just for a change."

"It's Maxi I want to see."

"The Malteser?" Melanie got up and teetered round the desk on four-inch heels. "I doubt if he will want to see you, but we can always ask."

Parker moved swiftly to intercept her before she reached the door. "Let's surprise him."

"Why don't you do that," she said, squeezing his arm.

Zanti had the *Mirror* open at the racing page and was studying the form. Completely immersed, he did not look up when Parker entered his office.

"I'm busy, Melanie," he growled. "Come back in five minutes."

"What do you fancy for the two thirty at Sandown?" Parker asked and got his immediate attention.

"You, you," Zanti spluttered, then grabbed a paperknife and pointed it at him. "You'd better get out of my office while you can still walk."

"Put it down," Parker told him mildly, "otherwise I'll take the paperknife off you and shove it somewhere that will make your eyes water. And if you've read the newspapers, you'll know there are plenty of other ways I can make life intolerable for you."

"What do you want?" Zanti did his best to sound truculent but was sensible enough to put the knife down first.

"A little information about the occupants of a white Cortina, registration number EGY 996C."

"I don't know what the fuck you're talking about."

"Let me refresh your memory then. The last time I was here, you went walkabout after I left. First, you stood in line for a bus, then you changed your mind and crossed the road to walk up and down the pavement like a superannuated tart. Not satisfied with that, you make a beeline for St Pancras Station, pick up a cab and disappear up the Euston Road, heading towards Marylebone at a rate of knots."

"So what?"

"After I'd left the agency, you asked Melanie where I had gone and she told you I was in the Ace Café up the street. You then phoned your friendly security man who gave you precise instructions. You waited half an hour to give him time to get a surveillance team into the area before you marked my card for them."

"You've got a vivid imagination," Zanti said and laughed.

"And you haven't got any. That's why you can't see that you're neck deep in the shit." A supercilious smile under the Clark Gable moustache told him he wasn't getting through to Zanti. "If you don't believe me, talk to Iain Wirral."

"Who's he when he's at home?"

Parker walked round the desk and removed a buff-coloured paperback that was sandwiched between an out of date *Who's Who* and the twenty-eighth edition of Archbold *Criminal Pleading, Evidence and Practice* in the bookrest on the windowledge. The paperback was the *Police and Constabulary Almanac Official Register* for 1967;

checking the index, Parker looked up the section dealing with the Metropolitan Police and placed the listing in front of Zanti, open at the appropriate page.

"Detective Chief Superintendent Wirral," he said. "You'll find him halfway down the page under the list of Special Branch officers."

"What about him?"

"A few weeks ago, your partner, Dennis Eastham, returned home to find that his house had been burgled. Nothing had been stolen but the intruder had left a packet of cocaine in the lavatory cistern as a warning of what could happen to him if he didn't back off. The man who did that was acting unlawfully, so was the superior officer who told him to do it. It will be your turn next and this time it won't stop at just a warning. Wirral will tell you that no one is safe while they are in business."

"Yeah?" Zanti chewed his bottom lip. "Maybe what you say is true, but what can I do about it?"

"You can help me make them redundant," Parker told him.

"Okay, I'm listening."

"Soon after the cocaine incident, a security officer visited you at the agency. He told you to forget all about Kurt Bender and said he expected to be informed should anyone inquire after the where-abouts of Andrew Korwin. Right?"

"Yes."

"And he gave you a phone number?"

"Right again."

"So what's the number?"

Zanti hesitated, gripped by indecision. A worried frown creased his forehead and was still there when he wrote the number on a slip of paper and pushed it across the desk.

"Thanks. You've made a wise decision."

"Is that it then?"

"If I could just borrow your phone, then I'll get out of your hair."

Parker didn't wait for his permission; lifting the receiver, he dialled 499-6000. Although Garvey only said hello, he recognised his voice immediately. "Have a nice day," Parker told him, "and be sure to enjoy your job while it lasts."

CHAPTER 25

FOR THE umpteenth time since she had arrived at Victoria Station, Stefanie glanced at her wristwatch, then checked the time by the clock above the information board. Twenty-one minutes past two and no sign of Brenda Mullinder, and the train to Dover left at two thirty. She had seventy-five pounds, two hundred and forty US dollars and a boat and train ticket to Engelberg in her purse but nothing to wear other than the clothes she stood up in.

Seven minutes to go: there was another train to Dover in an hour but that would mean changing the time of her appointment in Zürich and she had already done that once today. If she rang them again, they might conclude she wasn't serious.

Six minutes in hand: what on earth was Brenda playing at? In her shoes, she would have rung for a minicab but Brenda was somewhat quixotic and preferred to use public transport even if it took for ever. All the same, the buses hadn't gone on strike and Victoria was the next stop from Sloane Square on the Underground for God's sake. She would give the Irish girl one more minute; then, if there was still no sign of her, she would board the train.

"I bet you'd almost given me up for lost."

Stefanie put a hand to her chest and swung round. "Good grief, Brenda," she said breathlessly, "where did you spring from?"

"I had to take a taxi," Brenda said, dumping a suitcase at her feet. "Some man threw himself under a train at South Kensington and nothing was coming through. Of course, they waited until we were six deep on the platform before they told us what had caused the delay. Anyway, here I am at last."

"And am I glad to see you," Stefanie said and hugged her.

"You said you were going to Switzerland on business so I packed a suit along with your other things. Okay?"

"Couldn't be better."

"So what do I tell Mr Parker when he asks me where you are?"

"Tell him you don't know."

"Oh, come on, Steffie, he isn't going to believe that."

"I guess it wouldn't hurt to say I'd gone to Switzerland, but don't volunteer the information."

"What's he done to you? Don't you care about him?"

"I like him."

"You've got a funny way of showing it."

"Listen, this is something I have to do for my family. When it's over, I'll be as nice as pie to Campbell, if he'll let me."

Brenda shook her head. "I hope you know what you're doing."

"Trust me." Stefanie hugged her again, then picked up the suitcase. "Now I have to go."

"Sure. Take care of yourself."

"You too."

Twenty-seven minutes past two: Stefanie started running, flashed her ticket at the collector on the gate and disappeared from view.

Parker held the door open with his shoulder, lifted the suitcase into the phone booth, then followed it inside. He didn't know what Brenda Mullinder had packed for Stefanie but if the weight was anything to go by, there were enough clothes in the suitcase to keep her going for a month. He took the phone off the hook, fed tuppence into the box, then rang the number for Benbow House and asked the switchboard operator for extension oo8. He had tried to contact Harry Freeland before going to see Mullinder and had been told he had been called to Queen Anne's Gate. This time around, he had better luck.

"It's you know who," he said. "Have you got anything for me, Harry?"

"Yes. A former Obersturmführer called Karl Werner Ulex was released from Lublin Prison on the twenty-third of May. He had been sentenced to twenty-one years' hard labour for war crimes committed in Poland and the Ukraine . . ."

Parker recalled the dossier Freeland had sent him on Gerhardt Terboven. Ulex was the man who had identified the body the Poles had exhumed from a roadside grave near the village of Bobrek as that of his former commanding officer. It was on the basis of his testimony that Terboven had been declared officially dead.

"What's also interesting," Freeland continued, then the pips cut

292

in and Parker hastily fed sixpence into the box before they were cut off.

"You were saying?" he prompted.

"Kurt Bender was the man who put Ulex away. If it hadn't been for him, he would have been repatriated with the other POWs. Apparently, Bender recognised him when he was transferred to a labour camp outside Kharkov. Ulex had been there for roughly eight months helping to rebuild the city and was hiding out in the camp under an assumed name. He had gone to considerable trouble to conceal his SS background after the Terboven Sonderkommando had been disbanded towards the end of January 1945. During the siege of Breslau he'd even found a tattooist who had removed his blood group."

"Where did you get all this information, Harry?"

"From Simon Wiesenthal in Vienna."

Simon Wiesenthal, the Nazi hunter and former Jewish architect from Lwow who had been arrested by a Ukrainian auxiliary policeman shortly after the Germans had attacked the USSR on the twenty-second of June 1941 and had driven the Red Army out of the former Polish city. Wiesenthal had survived almost four years in a dozen different concentration camps. After the war, he had become what he was because he had felt it was something he had to do. Wiesenthal was the man who had done more than anyone else to track down Obersturmbannführer Adolf Eichmann and bring him to justice. It was said that currently he still had over twenty-two thousand names on his list of wanted men.

"Are we getting a photograph of Ulex?" Parker asked. In his own mind he was convinced that the former SS officer and Jankowski were the same man but the police would ask for proof before they acted on the information.

"One's on the way," Freeland told him. "It should be with us on Saturday, Monday at the latest."

Parker grunted. Monday was three days away and a lot could happen in seventy-two hours.

"Incidentally, Bender also filed a report on Gerhardt Terboven soon after he had been repatriated from the Soviet Union. He submitted it to the Hesse Länder Office for the Prosecution of National Socialist Crimes of Violence and was informed by the State Prosecutor that Terboven was dead. Bender refused to believe it and years later a copy of his sworn statement found its way to Simon Wiesenthal's documentation office in Vienna."

Vienna: the penny suddenly dropped. Stefanie had gone to Vienna full of high spirits a week after meeting her uncle for the first time and had returned looking more than somewhat deflated.

"Do you have the number of Wiesenthal's office in Vienna?" he asked.

"Are you thinking what I'm thinking, Campbell?"

"I'd be very surprised if I wasn't," Parker told him.

"The number is 42 37 85. If he isn't in the office, one of his helpers will know where to find him."

The pips broke in again, leaving Parker just enough time to thank him before they were cut off. He put the phone down briefly, then lifting the receiver again, he dialled Trunks and asked the operator to connect him with Stockbridge 523. The number rang out and went on ringing but Stefanie didn't answer. Parker broke the connection, picked up the phone a third time and called Sarah Yendell.

"You're too early, Campbell," she said before he had a chance to say more than hello. "I don't have the list of names you want yet."

"That isn't the reason why I rang you," Parker told her, "but I am asking for another favour."

"I'd have been surprised if you were just passing the time of day."

"Would you look up the Merlin codeword for the week and get on to the GPO exchange supervisor. Tell her you want to know what international calls were made from 01-995-23671 in the last forty-eight hours."

"But that's your number."

"Exactly. You'd better do the same for Stockbridge 523."

"One thing I won't have to ask is who made them," Sarah said tartly.

"No, that's obvious," Parker agreed.

"Where are you now?"

"In London – outside Mullinder's office in Bell Yard. Phone me at the cottage as soon as you've got an answer." There was a fast train to Bournemouth at forty minutes past the hour which stopped at Winchester. With any luck, he could catch the 1440 from Waterloo and be in Winchester an hour later. From there it was only nine miles to Stockbridge. "Any time after four will do," he added.

Sarah chuckled. "I'm glad you're not in a hurry for the information," she said, and put the phone down.

Parker reached for the suitcase, backed out of the kiosk and walked down Bell Yard past the Royal Courts of Justice into the Strand. He waited for a break in the traffic, then crossed the road and flagged down a cab. Arriving at Waterloo with time in hand before the Bournemouth train departed, he rang the cottage again, but there was still no answer.

Ulex eyed the phone, wondered if it would ring a third time. Once could be a wrong number, twice within the space of fifteen minutes had to be someone who was determined to get in touch. Yet everything he had seen in the cottage indicated that it was not occupied on a regular basis by the owners. He knew this because there were a couple of photographs of a general in army uniform on the desk in the study and he'd also found an old rates demand plus a receipted copy of an electricity bill addressed to Lieutenant General Sir Michael Yendell when he'd forced the centre drawer. If that wasn't proof enough that the general was the owner, he was also listed under his title in the local telephone directory.

Friends and acquaintances of the general would obviously phone him at his regular address before they tried the cottage. But maybe they had and been told he was spending the weekend in Stockbridge. When Parker and the American girl were already there? It didn't seem likely. Someone for Parker then? Ulex looked at the photograph of the general in full dress uniform and in a moment of animosity and frustration, swept it off the desk and stamped on it. What the hell did it matter who had been on the phone? He had been paid to take care of Stefanie Ayres, and that meant Parker too since he seemed determined to get in his way.

But where in God's name were they? Parker had left the cottage shortly after eight o'clock and it was now ten minutes after three. The Ayres girl must have gone with him because she certainly wasn't in the house or the grounds. So what had they been doing for the past seven hours? Where had they gone? When would they be back? Supposing someone had found the green van he'd left in the woods? How much longer could he afford to stay here? The questions multiplied in his mind and made him even more agitated. He craved a cigarette and there was a packet in his jacket, but the aroma would still be there hours after he had smoked it and Parker might detect it when he opened the door.

That was how one of the Rottenführers in his company had found the terrorist, Andrew Korwin, two days before the Warsaw uprising had begun. An informer had told one of the Polish auxiliary policemen attached to the Terboven Sonderkommando that the Resistance leader known as "Wola" was hiding in an apartment at Gorczewska Avenue 79 in the same district which had inspired his codename. There had been no sign of the Polish terrorist when the arresting party had arrived at the address. The only occupants of the one-bedroom apartment had been a thirty-five-year-old widow with her nine-year-old son and younger sister aged fifteen. The woman of the house had sworn on the crucifix she had been wearing on a chain round her neck that there were only the three of them living in the flat. Whoever had told the Herr Rottenführer that she had a lover was a filthy liar, and a preliminary search had seemed to bear her out. The Rottenführer had been on the point of leaving when it had suddenly dawned on him that the cabbage boiling on the stove was not the aroma he could smell.

He had inspected the woman's hands and those of her young sister but had found no trace of nicotine. But someone who smoked cigarettes had been in the flat and not so long ago either. The Rottenführer hadn't bothered to waste any further time on searching the apartment again. Instead, he had grabbed the nine-year-old boy by the heels and dangled him out of the window overlooking the courtyard four storeys below. The woman hadn't needed to be told by the Polish auxiliary policeman what would happen to her son if she continued to be uncooperative. In her eagerness to appease the Herr Rottenführer, she had shown him the secret hiding place under the floorboards in the bedroom where Korwin had taken refuge when he had seen the arresting party arrive in a Kübelwagen.

Ulex had learned the hard way that you benefited from other people's mistakes and he had no intention of repeating the error Korwin had made. A distant rumble interrupted his thoughts. Artillery fire? Nonsense, the war had ended twenty-two years ago. A thunderstorm then, one that had been threatening since early afternoon. Ulex went to the back door and looked up at the lowering sky in the west in time to see the jagged flash of forked lightning. The thunderclap followed some fifteen seconds later and, after allowing for a force 4 to 5 south-westerly breeze, he calculated the storm was unlikely to reach Stockbridge for at least another hour. The elements however proved him wrong. Barely twenty minutes later the storm was right overhead, then the clouds broke and the rain lashed against the windows in a near tropical downpour.

Parker wiped the condensation from the window and watched the countryside flashing past. The train was somewhere south of Basingstoke and was if anything, several minutes ahead of schedule but in his anxiety it seemed to him they were crawling along. He actually found himself hoping that Stefanie had run out on him because that was infinitely preferable to the possibility that somehow Ulex had managed to find her again.

Ulex, Bender and Terboven: he couldn't put them out of his mind. Of the three, only Bender had been a hundred per cent Ayran. Ulex had been born in Wielun of a Polish mother, while Gerhardt Terboven had been a second generation Transylvanian Saxon whose grandparents had settled in Romania in 1868. It was all there in the dossier Freeland had sent him, how the family had always remained spiritually and politically in touch with the Heimat, how Gerhardt Terboven himself had returned to the homeland in 1932 to join the SS at the age of twenty-three. Some of the most fanatical Nazis had come from the Auslanddeutschen, foremost of whom had been Standartenführer Gerhardt Terboven. He had given his name to a Sonderkommando composed of a motley collection of Latvians, Lithuanians, Russians, Poles and Ukrainians who had operated in the rear area murdering thousands of Jews before the more efficient extermination camps at Treblinka and Auschwitz had made them redundant. Thereafter, they had been employed on antipartisan duties, collecting and shedding other disparate organisations like the band of Ukrainian separatists Bender had been attached to in January 1944 after he had been medically upgraded and declared fit for combat again.

Serving under the umbrella of the Terboven Sonderkommando had evidently been too much for Bender. He had witnessed things which had turned his stomach and had kindled a desire to see that Obersturmführer Karl Werner Ulex and others of a like ilk were brought to justice. Bender had started out as a fundamentally decent man; if in later years his image had become a little tarnished, it could be because he had seen too many former SS men emerging as high-ranking officials in the postwar world and had wanted a share of the honeypot for himself.

Parker moved out into the corridor as the train began to slow down a quarter of a mile from Winchester station. He was in the seventh carriage from the front which placed him almost exactly opposite the entrance hall when the Bournemouth express drew up alongside the platform and came to a halt. Parker lowered the window, opened the door from the outside and got out; surrendering his ticket at the gate, he passed through the entrance hall and ran across the yard to the car park. Although the thunderstorm had moved away, rain was still falling heavily from a leaden sky. Someone, probably another driver, had left a message for him under the wipers of the Mini but the paper was sodden and the ink had run, making it impossible to decipher the writing. If someone had bumped him, it wasn't terribly obvious and he was in too much of a hurry to make a detailed inspection of the vehicle. His only concern was to find out what had happened at the cottage; unlocking the door, he got in behind the wheel and started the engine.

He drove out of the car park, picked up the Stockbridge Road and headed out of town, chafing at the thirty-mile-an-hour speed restriction. Once clear of the city, he put his foot down and pushed the Mini to the limit. The loose baffles in the silencer produced a deep-throated snarl which created a false impression of power. Tyres hissing on the smooth wet surface of the road, he took the car slip-sliding around each bend. A couple of times he found himself aquaplaning with the back end fishtailing, but somehow he managed to retain control. Nine minutes after leaving the station, he came down the hill into Stockbridge, joined the A30 trunk route and went on past the Grosvenor Hotel and the squat granite-faced church before turning off to the right.

Still doing nearly fifty, he swung off the side road into the narrow lane leading to Rose Cottage and unerringly found a waterlogged pothole with the nearside wheel hard enough to make him think the shock absorber had gone. He dropped down into third and instinctively eased his foot on the accelerator, then sounded the horn as he went past the cottage and turned into the barn beyond the kitchen garden.

Parker switched off the ignition, undid the seat belt and got out of the Mini. The horn hadn't drawn Stefanie to the window, but that didn't necessarily mean that Rose Cottage was empty. He searched the barn looking for some kind of implement which would serve as a weapon and eventually found an old billhook. Part of the wooden handle had rotted away, the tapered blade was pitted with rust and the cutting edge was blunt; it was however about the same size as a tyre lever and slightly heavier. It was also more intimidating than the wheelbrace, box spanner and Tommy bar in the Mini's tool kit.

If Ulex was inside the cottage, he would probably expect him to come through the kitchen garden. As always, the trick was to do the unexpected, if only he could be sure exactly what that was. Concealing the billhook under his jacket, Parker left the barn and keeping to the lane, trotted back to the cottage. He took out the Yale key, opened the front door and stepped cautiously inside the hall.

"I'm home, Stefanie," he called out, taking a firm grasp on the billhook.

Study to the right, cloakroom to the left, kitchen right and forward, staircase, lounge and dining room directly opposite. Every door was ajar which meant there would be no telltale click to warn him if he happened to be looking in the wrong direction when Ulex made his move. Although there was no sign of an intruder, Parker could feel his malevolent presence and tried to draw him out into the open.

"Where are you, Stefanie?" he asked in a louder voice and started towards the staircase.

Nothing happened. He put one foot on the bottom step and went slowly on up towards the landing. One, two, three, four steps; the inside wall restricted his view now and he could no longer see the kitchen and study. He heard a faint whisper of stockinged feet and whirled about, using the billhook like a tennis racket to deliver a backhand that flailed the air and missed the target by a good foot.

Ulex was below him, a compact, fit-looking man with deep-set eyes, a narrow sharply defined nose, prominent cheekbones and a cleft chin. He had kicked off his shoes and there was a carving knife in his right hand which he handled like a rapier. He advanced up the staircase, feinting with the knife in the hope that Parker would take another swing at him and miss so that he could slip in under his guard and drive the blade into his chest.

Parker retreated before him, reached the top step of the first flight of steps and turned the corner. Ulex came on, a confident smile on his mouth as he continued to make threatening lunges at him with the knife. It was then that Parker did the unexpected. Instead of slashing at the SS man, he hurled the billhook at his face and caught him above the left eye. Ulex staggered back, blood pouring from a deep gash, then lost his balance and tumbled down the staircase. He was still on his hands and knees in the hall when Parker cannoned into him, made a grab for the knife and held on to his wrist with both hands.

There was nothing scientific about the way they fought, kicking, biting, head-butting. One moment they were on the floor, the next they were both on their feet trying to knee each other in the groin. Then Parker suddenly grabbed a handful of hair with his left hand and smashed Ulex against the door frame using his head as a battering ram while maintaining a lock on the knife hand. Kick, scrape, stamp; Parker used his feet as a weapon and caught Ulex with the heel of his shoe and crushed his toes. Ulex screamed, the carving knife slipped from his grasp and clattered on to the floor; fending him off with a hand, Parker swooped on it and stuck the blade into the left side of the German's chest. Ulex stared at him, his mouth open, his eyes mirroring disbelief; then he slid down the wall to sit on his rump with his legs splayed apart. Unable to support himself any longer, he slowly toppled over and lay still. Blood seeped through his shirt front to form a puddle that gradually spread across the parquet floor.

It was a good five minutes before Parker stopped shaking and regained his breath. Commonsense told him that Ulex wouldn't have hung around had Stefanie been in the cottage but before he did anything else, he had to make sure. He went from room to room calling her name and searching every nook and cranny where a body could have been hidden and was relieved and thankful to discover his assumption had been correct.

His wristwatch had been smashed in the fight but according to the grandfather clock in the hall, it was twenty-five minutes past four. Ordinarily, he could have counted on finding Harry Freeland in his office but he usually left early on a Friday to spend the weekend in Lichfield with his wife, Jenny. He went into the study, called the Trunks operator and gave her the number of Benbow House. Considering he had also to go through the local switchboard and Freeland's PA, he was connected in a remarkably short time.

"Thank God I caught you, Harry."

"That sounds ominous."

"Well, put it this way," Parker said, "We don't have to wait for a photograph from Vienna and there's no need to go cap in hand to Iain Wirral. Ulex is dead."

"Where are you?"

"At a place called Rose Cottage outside Stockbridge. It belongs to Sarah Yendell's parents."

"Christ. The things that girl will do for you . . ."

"Yes. Listen, I'm afraid the hall's in a bit of a mess. Is there any chance the Training School can provide a removal van and a couple of cleaners to help tidy things up?"

"Consider it done."

"Thanks, Harry."

"Never mind that, just tell me how to find Rose Cottage."

"Are you coming too?"

"I think I'd better," Freeland said. "I've been in the garbage disposal business longer than you. Now, let's have those directions."

As briefly and clearly as he could, Parker described the turning Freeland should look out for as he came through Stockbridge and how far he should travel along the side road before branching off into the narrow, sunken lane.

"Any idea when I can expect to see you?" he asked, winding up.

"After dark," Freeland said and then hung up.

Parker returned to the hall and stood there for some moments looking down at Ulex; then crouching beside the dead man, he went through the contents of his pockets. Amongst the effects was a leather wallet containing thirty-seven pounds ten shillings and a photograph of Stefanie Ayres which explained a lot of things. Deep in thought, the sudden discordant jangle caught him unprepared and set his pulse racing. Answering the phone in the study, he was relieved to hear Sarah's voice on the line.

"You are going to have a larger bill than usual this quarter, Campbell," she said.

"How come?"

"Stefanie made two calls to Vienna yesterday on your phone. The first lasted five minutes, the second went on for almost half an hour. The exchange supervisor couldn't tell me what number she was calling."

"It doesn't matter, I think I know who she spoke to."

"Stefanie also used the phone in the cottage this morning to make a trunk call to Chelsea 1984."

"I know who that is too," Parker said.

"What does your crystal ball tell you about the main shareholders of the Ward Tandy Group?"

"Nothing. I'm relying on you for that."

Sarah began to reel off a list of names she had got from her father. None of them meant anything to Parker but he could well believe they were influential people. So it seemed were most of the friends and acquaintances Kershaw had made since he had been living in the north of England. Parker sensed there was a lot more Sarah could have told him if he had let her. Time however was running on and gently but firmly he managed to get her off the phone. As soon as she had cleared the line, he raised the international operator and booked a call to Vienna 42 37 85. Ten minutes later the operator called back and put him through.

"Mr Wiesenthal?" he said. "My name is Campbell Parker. You don't know me but we have a mutual friend called Stefanie Ayres who rang you twice yesterday."

"I do not know what you are talking about, Mr Parker."

"You want me to tell you what she said?"

"No, I'm not interested. Furthermore, I don't propose to continue this conversation."

"I'm looking at a dead man," Parker told him. "Ex-Obersturmführer Karl Werner Ulex of the Terboven Sonderkommando; last time you saw him in Warsaw he was wearing a prison uniform."

Although Wiesenthal didn't say anything, Parker could tell he had his undivided attention. And once he had that, the rest was comparatively easy. By the time he had finished, Wiesenthal had agreed to put him in touch with the people Stefanie Ayres had been dealing with. All Parker had to do then was think up a convincing argument which would persuade Harry Freeland to see things from his point of view and put everything back as he had found it with the exception of a bloodstained snapshot.

CHAPTER 26

THE BLACK Rover limousine carried a Zürich licence number and displayed CD plates. It came complete with an English-speaking driver in a dark grey double-breasted suit and a peaked cap, a uniform which was considered appropriate for the chauffeur of Her Britannic Majesty's Consul General. He had met Parker by prior arrangement at 0855 hours near Obermatt Bahnhof approximately six miles from Engelberg.

From Obermatt they continued on Route 374 through the pine- and larch-covered lower slopes of the Rigidalstock. Some ten minutes later they crossed the Luzern–Stans–Engelberg railway a quarter of a mile below the restaurant at Grünenwald. Occasionally, Parker caught a glimpse of the Engelberger Aa in the deep gorge to his right but for the most part he could see little more than the next bend in the road as it snaked through the wooded foothills. Then suddenly they were out of the treeline and running parallel with the railway past a man-made lake and the cable car station to Gerschnialp. The mountain resort stretched before them and rising above the far outskirts of the village, Parker could see the onion-shaped dome of the Benedictine abbey.

"Do you know where the Hotel Hess is, Martin?" he asked the driver.

"Yes, first left, then left again."

A hundred yards farther on, Martin tripped the indicator and turned into a narrow road that led past the Bahnhof. A small park on the left before the railway station, a café, a sports shop, two boutiques and a picture gallery on the opposite side of the road. And farther up the street, a greengrocer's, a bakery, a photographer's with the latest Nikon cameras on show in the window, and more souvenir shops selling cuckoo clocks, hand-carved Alpine walking sticks, cowbells, wooden calendars and fancy leather belts.

They turned left again at the T-junction and went on to the Hotel

Hess, a hundred yards or so beyond the Europa. One member of the backup team had gone on ahead and was already in place watching the front of the hotel from the small public garden across the way. Leaving Martin to make a U-turn before parking the Rover on the grass verge, Parker got out of the car, crossed the road and entered the lobby. From the girl on the reception desk, he learned that Kershaw was waiting for him in a private room next to the à la carte restaurant.

Although they had never met before, no introductions were necessary because there was no mistaking the man whose jaw had been rebuilt by a plastic surgeon. The only thing that surprised Parker about him was the limpness of his handshake. Somehow he had fancied Kershaw would have a grip of iron.

"I assume you know why I am here?" Parker said.

Kershaw nodded. "Mr Freeland telephoned the hotel late yesterday evening and spoke to me. What I don't understand is why he should have sent you, Mr Parker?"

"That's easy to explain. My picture has been in all the newspapers and he thought you were more likely to trust a familiar face."

"He could have sent Mr Garvey."

"John Garvey works for a different firm in a different field and they don't operate abroad. We do, and the tip-off came from our Austrian station. Now you don't know any of our people in Vienna and Garvey isn't equipped to deal with this situation."

"And you are?"

"Yes."

"After what happened to Victor?"

"I didn't destroy him, your niece did that. Except that Stefanie Ayres is not your niece, is she, Mr Kershaw?"

"I began to have certain reservations about her," Kershaw said cautiously.

"Well, I'm here to tell you that she has been using Simon Wiesenthal's documentation centre in Vienna to pass information to Tel Aviv. She's even got Mossad, the Israeli Intelligence Service, dancing to her tune."

"I see."

"And Stefanie is here in Engelberg, isn't she?"

"Yes. She and Nancy have gone for a walk." Kershaw cleared his throat. "I had some business to attend to in Zürich . . ."

"I know, so do the Israelis, thanks to Stefanie Ayres. I think Mrs

Kershaw must have told her about your business appointment. Anyway, there's a Mossad snatch team waiting for you in Zürich; if things had gone to plan, they would have lifted you when you left the Union Bank of Switzerland."

"So what are we going to do?"

"Get you out of Switzerland before they come looking for you. First thing we'll do is move you to a safe house in Luzern." Parker stood up. "Let's go," he said, "I've got a car from the Consular Service outside."

"What about Nancy? I just can't walk out and leave her without a word."

"One of my men will stay behind and explain what's happened when she returns to the hotel. The police will arrest Miss Ayres; no charges will be preferred but they will detain her for six hours. Mrs Kershaw will have joined you in Luzern before she is released."

"Good."

Parker waited for him to make a move but Kershaw seemed in no hurry to leave. "We ought to be going," he said politely but firmly.

"The hotel bill?"

"That's all taken care of."

"What about my clothes?"

"I'll have them packed and sent on to you."

"You seem to have thought of everything, Mr Parker," Kershaw said and got to his feet.

"Let's hope so." Parker followed him out of the room and along the corridor past the reception desk in the corner of the lobby. "Our car is the Rover on your right," he said as they came down the front steps.

Martin had opened the rear nearside door and was standing by to close it again once their passenger was inside the limousine. Leaving Martin to it, Parker walked over to the public gardens and exchanged a few words with the backup man. No last minute instructions were necessary; the backup man knew exactly what he had to do and the whole charade was entirely for Kershaw's benefit.

"No worries," Parker said as he joined him in the back of the Rover. "Everything's going to be all right." He leaned forward and tapped the chauffeur on the shoulder. "Whenever you're ready, Martin," he added.

Martin didn't need any urging; shifting into gear, he pulled away from the verge and drove off towards the Europa, then turned right at the T-junction. Engelberg was essentially a winter resort; tourists still came to the village in summer but in nothing like the same numbers and there were relatively few pedestrians about on the streets.

"Nice place," Parker said casually.

"We like it."

"Yes? How long have you been coming here?"

"Since 1959, but we've skipped the odd year here and there." Kershaw cleared his throat twice in rapid succession as if he had some sort of nervous tickle. "What will happen to the girl?" he asked.

"Stefanie?" Parker shrugged. "Well, as I said, the Swiss have no reason to prefer charges."

"No – you misunderstood me. I meant, what will happen to her if she returns to England?"

"I haven't the faintest idea. Depends on whether the Home Office thinks there is any substance to the allegations she has been making about you."

"It's all lies what she is saying. You mark my words, the KGB are behind it."

"You're wrong, it was Kurt Bender. He recognised you from a photograph which appeared in the *Frankfurter Allgemeine* when you attended the Trade Fair. I don't know why Bender wrote to Stefanie's mother last September claiming he had seen her brother, but my guess is he was hoping she would confront you face to face and then the world would know who you really were. When he didn't hear from the family, I think he became disillusioned and tried his hand at a little blackmail."

"I tell you again, that young woman is a pathological liar."

"The Israelis don't think she is lying; they despatched a snatch team to the El Al Airline office in Vienna soon after she fingered you. Then sometime last Thursday they changed their base of operations to Zürich, using the same cover when she told them you were going to spend a fortnight in Engelberg."

"The Jews." His lip curled. "They have this obsession about the Holocaust so they're prepared to believe any smear, any slander. They think they are the only people who suffered at the hands of the Nazis but I tell you, no one suffered more than we Poles."

They were out of the village now and starting the climb up to the Grünenwald. After that, it was downhill all the way to Luzern.

"Tell me something, Gerhardt," Parker said quietly, "When did you murder Andrew Korwin? As soon as he told you exactly where to find the jewellery he had buried in the grounds of the family home on Ujazdowskie Boulevard?"

"What are you saying?"

"Or did you keep him alive until January 1945? Was he the man you buried at Bobrek?"

"You don't actually believe all this nonsense, do you?" Kershaw said and searched his face looking for a sign that would confirm his assertion, and saw none.

"You're smarter than Eichmann was," Parker continued. "No one has ever been able to find a single photograph of Gerhardt Terboven anywhere, and that was your trump card. By July 1944 you knew the war was as good as lost and you were looking at a possible death sentence if you were tried for war crimes. So officially you had to die and take someone else's place, and Korwin filled the bill. There were grounds for believing he was the only surviving member of his family and I suspect he bore more than a passing resemblance. To be on the safe side, you got a friendly SS surgeon to carve up your face. A little disfigurement was infinitely preferable to a hangman's noose. Right?"

"This is not the first time I have been accused of being Gerhardt Terboven, Mr Parker. The smears started back in 1961 when it became known that my company was developing a laser gun sight that was light years ahead of our competitors at home and abroad. Needless to say, these allegations were refuted by MI5 and the Home Office time and time again."

Parker knew different. The Home Office hadn't actually refuted the allegations, they had simply maintained there wasn't sufficient evidence to prove beyond doubt that Kershaw was Gerhardt Terboven. The KGB and their satellites had conducted so many character assassinations against members of the Polish expatriate community in England that they tended to regard any application for extradition based on alleged war crimes with the deepest suspicion. Stefanie had gone to Vienna with her head in the clouds because she had found the man who had murdered her uncle. Simon Wiesenthal had brought her down to earth with a bump when he had told her that her sworn affadavit was not enough to secure his extradition. It was then that she had begun to think about obtaining justice by other means.

"It is a great pity that your superiors at the Foreign Office did not see fit to check the facts with the Home Secretary when Miss Ayres came to see you. But no, you took her word on trust and she twisted you round her little finger. Well, believe me, everything she told you is a pack of lies."

"Is that why you decided she had to die?" Parker took out the bloodstained snapshot and showed it to him. "I imagine this was taken when Stefanie Ayres spent the weekend with you in Redcar. It has been cut in two with a pair of scissors and I reckon you were on the missing half. I found the snapshot on the body of your loyal subordinate, ex-Obersturmführer Karl Werner Ulex. Without it, he wouldn't have known who to look for."

They were running parallel with the railway again and were approaching the restaurant opposite Grünenwald station. In a little over five minutes from now they would reach the clearing where Parker had left the Volkswagen he had rented on arrival at Zürich airport.

"Ulex was the man who pronounced you dead and he figured you owed him a slice of your good fortune. That's why he kept silent when Simon Wiesenthal interviewed him in Warsaw while he was still in prison. As soon as Ulex was released, he made his way to England and ran you to ground."

"You are going to find yourself in very serious trouble when I report this conversation to your superiors."

"You won't get the chance. Martin is an Israeli Intelligence officer and he is taking you to Tel Aviv. And don't worry about what my superiors will say. Harry Freeland is a very unusual and very interesting man. The little finger of his left hand is missing; it was amputated a joint at a time in the spring of '44. The operation was performed without the benefit of an anaesthetic by an SS butcher who used a pair of pincers from a carpenter's tool chest to extract information about the French Resistance in the Chartres area. Naturally he's inclined to be a bit hostile towards people of your ilk."

Some of the bends in the road were so tight that Martin had to change down into second gear to negotiate them. He was doing roughly fifteen miles an hour around a particularly sharp curve when Terboven seized his chance and attempted to leave the car.

"Childproof locks," Parker told him laconically. "The door can only be opened from the outside."

Terboven appeared to shrink before his eyes, drawing in on himself as if attempting to crawl back inside the womb. "You are sending an innocent man to his death," he muttered hoarsely and repeated the accusation over and over again until they reached the rendezvous near Obermatt Bahnhof where the other members of the Israeli snatch squad were waiting with a transit van. All the fire had gone out of his belly and when they opened the door, Terboven simply got out of the Rover and meekly accompanied them to the transit van and just as meekly allowed the doctor to put him out with a shot of Pentathol.

All the fire had gone out of Parker too. Long after the Israelis had departed with their prisoner, he was still sitting there in the rented Volkswagen. A small voice inside his head urged him to go to Stefanie, another reminded him of what Terboven had said. Maybe he hadn't taken her every word on trust but she had certainly twisted him round her little finger in her crusade to bring Terboven to justice. No, he did not have to go to her; if Stefanie really wanted him, she knew where he lived.

Parker started the engine, drove out of the clearing and turned right to go on down to Luzern. He hoped Stefanie would make the first move but somehow he doubted if she would.